Great Stories
from the
German Romantics

GREAT STORIES FROM THE GERMAN ROMANTICS

DOVER THRIFT EDITIONS

Ludwig Tieck
Jean Paul Richter

Translated from the 1827 German edition
by Thomas Carlyle

DOVER PUBLICATIONS, INC.
MINEOLA, NEW YORK

DOVER THRIFT EDITIONS

GENERAL EDITOR: SUSAN L. RATTINER
EDITOR OF THIS VOLUME: TERRI ANN GEUS

Bibliographical Note

This Dover edition, first published in 2020, is a reprint of five stories by Ludwig Tieck and two stories by Jean Paul Richter, translated from the German by Thomas Carlyle in *Tales by Musaeus, Tieck, Richter,* Chapman and Hall, Limited, London, 1827 edition. A Note has been specially prepared for this edition.

Library of Congress Cataloging-in-Publication Data

Names: Tieck, Ludwig, 1773–1853, author. | Jean Paul, 1763–1825, author. |
    Carlyle, Thomas, 1795–1881, translator.
Title: Great stories from the German romantics / Ludwig Tieck, Jean Paul
    Richter; translated from the 1827 German edition by Thomas Carlyle.
Other titles: Tales by Musaeus, Tieck, Richter. Selections
Description: Mineola, New York: Dover Publications, Inc., 2020. | Series:
    Dover thrift editions | This Dover edition, first published in 2020, is
    a reprint of five stories by Ludwig Tieck and two stories by Jean Paul
    Richter translated from the German by Thomas Carlyle in *Tales by
    Musaeus, Tieck, Richter,* Chapman and Hall, Limited, London, 1827
    edition.
Identifiers: LCCN 2020002175 | ISBN 9780486844794 (paperback) | ISBN
    048684479X (paperback)
Subjects: LCSH: German fiction—19th century—Translations into English. |
    Short stories, German—Translations into English.
Classification: LCC PT1327 .T35 2020 | DDC 833/.609145—dc23
LC record available at https://lccn.loc.gov/2020002175

Manufactured in the United States by LSC Communications
84479X01
www.doverpublications.com

2 4 6 8 10 9 7 5 3 1

2020

Note

LUDWIG TIECK (1773–1853) WAS born in Berlin and learned Greek, Latin, and Italian during his early school years. His later studies included Shakespeare and Elizabethan drama. In his early twenties, he attempted to make his living by writing short stories. He married and settled in Jena, Germany, in 1798, where his writing won the praise of August and Friedrich Schlegel, leading critics of the early Romantic school. Credited as a founding father of the Romantic movement, Tieck is best known for his fantastic stories and novellas. From 1812 to 1817, Tieck combined his earlier stories and dramas in three volumes under the title *Phantasus*. This collection featured the stories that appear in this edition. In later life, Tieck served as a literary adviser and art critic at the Court Theater in Dresden and edited the translation of Shakespeare by August Schlegel. In 1842 he was invited to Berlin by Friedrich Wilhelm IV, King of Prussia, where he received a pension and would remain until he died as court author in residence. Tieck became the greatest literary authority in Germany after Johann Wolfgang von Goethe.

Johann Paul Friedrich Richter (1763–1825), better known as Jean Paul, was born in Bavaria, and, after a short course of study in theology, devoted himself to the study of literature. Best known for his witty, humorous, and satirical novels and stories, along with his writings on aesthetics, he was one of the first German Romantic writers. Though his influence was great in the early 1800s, he is the least translated into English. It was around the time of Richter's move to Berlin in 1800 that he met and became friends with August and Friedrich Schlegel, as well as Ludwig Tieck. At this time, Richter had already written *Life of Quintus Fixlein* (1796) and a considerable number of other works. His work is characterized by wild metaphors and complex plots, causing some literary critics to hold him in highest regard while others view his work with indifference. Among his admirers was the English writer Thomas Carlyle, who has translated the stories in this edition.

Contents

Contents

LUDWIG TIECK

THE FAIR-HAIRED ECKBERT[1]

IN A DISTRICT of the Harz dwelt a Knight, whose common designation in that quarter was the Fair-haired Eckbert. He was about forty years of age, scarcely of middle stature, and short light-coloured locks lay close and sleek round his pale and sunken countenance. He led a retired life, had never interfered in the feuds of his neighbours; indeed, beyond the outer wall of his castle he was seldom to be seen. His wife loved solitude as much as he; both seemed heartily attached to one another; only now and then they would lament that Heaven had not blessed their marriage with children.

Few came to visit Eckbert; and when guests did happen to be with him, their presence made but little alteration in his customary way of life. Temperance abode in his household, and Frugality herself appeared to be the mistress of the entertainment. On these occasions Eckbert was always cheerful and lively; but when he was alone, you might observe in him a certain mild reserve, a still, retiring melancholy.

His most frequent guest was Philip Walther; a man to whom he had attached himself, from having found in him a way of thinking like his own. Walther's residence was in Franconia; but he would often stay for half a year in Eckbert's neighbourhood, gathering plants and minerals, and then sorting and arranging them. He lived on a small independency, and was connected with no one. Eckbert frequently attended him in his sequestered walks; year after year a closer friendship grew betwixt them.

There are hours in which a man feels grieved that he should have a secret from his friend, which, till then, he may have kept with niggard anxiety; some irresistible desire lays hold of our heart to open itself wholly, to disclose its inmost recesses to our friend, that

---

[1] Prefatory Introduction to Tieck, *suprà*, at p. 330, Vol. VI. of *Works* (Vol. I. of *Miscellanies*).

so he may become our friend still more. It is in such moments that tender souls unveil themselves, and stand face to face; and at times it will happen, that the one recoils affrighted from the countenance of the other.

It was late in Autumn, when Eckbert, one cloudy evening, was sitting, with his friend and his wife Bertha, by the parlour fire. The flame cast a red glimmer through the room, and sported on the ceiling; the night looked sullenly in through the windows, and the trees without rustled in wet coldness. Walther complained of the long road he had to travel; and Eckbert proposed to him to stay where he was, to while away half of the night in friendly talk, and then to take a bed in the house till morning. Walther agreed, and the whole was speedily arranged: by and by wine and supper were brought in; fresh wood was laid upon the fire; the talk grew livelier and more confidential.

The cloth being removed, and the servants gone, Eckbert took his friend's hand, and said to him: "Now you must let my wife tell you the history of her youth; it is curious enough, and you should know it." "With all my heart," said Walther; and the party again drew round the hearth.

It was now midnight; the moon looked fitfully through the breaks of the driving clouds. "You must not reckon me a babbler," began the lady. "My husband says you have so generous a mind, that it is not right in us to hide aught from you. Only do not take my narrative for a fable, however strangely it may sound.

"I was born in a little village; my father was a poor herdsman. Our circumstances were not of the best; often we knew not where to find our daily bread. But what grieved me far more than this, were the quarrels which my father and mother often had about their poverty, and the bitter reproaches they cast on one another. Of myself too, I heard nothing said but ill; they were forever telling me that I was a silly stupid child, that I could not do the simplest turn of work; and in truth I was extremely inexpert and helpless; I let things fall; I neither learned to sew nor spin; I could be of no use to my parents; only their straits I understood too well. Often I would sit in a corner, and fill my little heart with dreams, how I would help them, if I should all at once grow rich; how I would overflow them with silver and gold, and feast myself on their amazement; and then spirits came hovering up, and showed me buried treasures, or gave me little pebbles which changed into precious stones; in short, the strangest fancies occupied me, and when I had to rise and help with anything, my inexpertness was still greater, as my head was giddy with these motley visions.

"My father in particular was always very cross to me; he scolded me for being such a burden to the house; indeed he often used me rather cruelly, and it was very seldom that I got a friendly word from him. In this way I had struggled on to near the end of my eighth year; and now it was seriously fixed that I should begin to do or learn something. My father still maintained that it was nothing but caprice in me, or a lazy wish to pass my days in idleness: accordingly he set upon me with furious threats; and as these made no improvement, he one day gave me a most cruel chastisement, and added that the same should be repeated day after day, since I was nothing but a useless sluggard.

"That whole night I wept abundantly; I felt myself so utterly forsaken, I had such a sympathy with myself that I even longed to die. I dreaded the break of day; I knew not on earth what I was to do or try. I wished from my very heart to be clever, and could not understand how I should be worse than the other children of the place. I was on the borders of despair.

"At the dawn of day I arose, and scarcely knowing what I did, unfastened the door of our little hut. I stept upon the open field; next minute I was in a wood, where the light of the morning had yet hardly penetrated. I ran along, not looking round; for I felt no fatigue, and I still thought my father would catch me, and in his anger at my flight would beat me worse than ever.

"I had reached the other side of the forest, and the sun was risen a considerable way; I saw something dim lying before me, and a thick fog resting over it. Ere long my path began to mount, at one time I was climbing hills, at another winding among rocks; and I now guessed that I must be among the neighbouring Mountains; a thought that made me shudder in my loneliness. For, living in the plain country, I had never seen a hill; and the very word Mountains, when I heard talk of them, had been a sound of terror to my young ear. I had not the heart to go back, my fear itself drove me on; often I looked round affrighted when the breezes rustled over me among the trees, or the stroke of some distant woodman sounded far through the still morning. And when I began to meet with charcoal-men and miners, and heard their foreign way of speech, I had nearly fainted for terror.

"I passed through several villages; begging now and then, for I felt hungry and thirsty; and fashioning my answers as I best could when questions were put to me. In this manner I had wandered on some four days, when I came upon a little footpath, which led me farther and farther from the highway. The rocks about me now assumed a different and far stranger form. They were cliffs so piled on one another, that it looked as if the first gust of wind would hurl them all this way and that. I knew not whether to go on or stop. Till now I had slept by night in the woods, for it was the finest season of the year, or in some remote shepherd's hut; but here I saw no human dwelling at all, and could not hope to find one in this wilderness; the crags grew more and more frightful; I had many a time to glide along by the very edge of dreadful abysses; by degrees my footpath became fainter, and at last all traces of it vanished from beneath me. I was utterly comfortless; I wept and screamed; and my voice came echoing back from the rocky valleys with a sound that terrified me. The night now came on, and I sought out a mossy nook to lie down in. I could not sleep; in the darkness I heard the strangest noises; sometimes I took them to proceed from wild-beasts, sometimes from wind moaning through the rocks, sometimes from unknown birds. I prayed; and did not sleep till towards morning.

"When the light came upon my face, I awoke. Before me was a steep rock; I clomb up, in the hope of discovering some outlet from the waste, perhaps of seeing houses or men. But when I reached the top, there was nothing still, so far as my eye could reach, but a wilderness of crags and precipices; all was covered with a dim haze; the day was gray and troubled, and no tree, no meadow, not even a bush could I find, only a few shrubs shooting up stunted and solitary in the narrow clefts of the rocks. I cannot utter what a longing I felt but to see one human creature, any living mortal, even though I had been afraid of hurt from him. At the same time I was tortured by a gnawing hunger; I sat down, and made up my mind to die. After a while, however, the desire of living gained the mastery; I roused myself, and wandered forward amid tears and broken sobs all day; in the end, I hardly knew what I was doing; I was tired and spent; I scarcely wished to live, and yet I feared to die.

"Towards night the country seemed to grow a little kindlier; my thoughts, my desires revived, the wish for life awoke in all my veins. I thought I heard the rushing of a mill afar off; I redoubled my steps; and how glad, how light of heart was I, when at last I actually gained the limits of the barren rocks, and saw woods and meadows lying before me, with soft green hills in the distance! I felt as if I had stept out of hell into a paradise; my loneliness and helplessness no longer frightened me.

"Instead of the hoped-for mill, I came upon a waterfall, which, in truth, considerably damped my joy. I was lifting a drink from it in the hollow of my hand, when all at once I thought I heard a slight cough some little way from me. Never in my life was I so joyfully surprised as at this moment: I went near, and at the border of the wood I saw an old woman sitting resting on the ground. She was dressed almost wholly in black; a black hood covered her head, and the greater part of her face; in her hand she held a crutch.

"I came up to her, and begged for help; she made me sit by her, and gave me bread, and a little wine. While I ate, she sang in a screeching tone some kind of spiritual song. When she had done, she told me I might follow her.

"The offer charmed me, strange as the old woman's voice and look appeared. With her crutch she limped away pretty fast, and at every step she twisted her face so oddly, that at first I was like to laugh. The wild rocks retired behind us more and more: I never shall forget the aspect and the feeling of that evening. All things were as molten into the softest golden red; the trees were standing with their tops in the glow of the sunset; on the fields lay a mild brightness; the woods and the leaves of the trees were standing motionless; the pure sky looked out like an opened paradise, and the gushing of the brooks, and, from time to time, the rustling of the trees, resounded through the serene stillness, as in pensive joy. My young soul was here first taken with a forethought of the world and its vicissitudes. I forgot myself and my conductress; my spirit and my eyes were wandering among the shining clouds.

"We now mounted an eminence planted with birch-trees; from the top we looked into a green valley, likewise full of birches; and down below, in the middle of them, was a little hut. A glad barking reached us, and immediately a little nimble dog came springing round the old woman, fawned on her, and wagged its tail; it next came to me, viewed me on all sides, and then turned back with a friendly look to its old mistress.

"On reaching the bottom of the hill, I heard the strangest song, as if coming from the hut, and sung by some bird. It ran thus:

> Alone in wood so gay
> 'Tis good to stay,
> Morrow like today,
> Forever and aye:
> O, I do love to stay
> Alone in wood so gay.

"These few words were continually repeated, and to describe the sound, it was as if you heard forest-horns and shalms sounded together from a far distance.

"My curiosity was wonderfully on the stretch; without waiting for the old woman's orders, I stept into the hut. It was already dusk; here all was neatly swept and trimmed; some bowls were standing in a cupboard, some strange-looking casks or pots on a table; in a glittering cage, hanging by the window, was a bird, and this in fact proved to be the singer. The old woman coughed and panted: it seemed as if she never would get over her fatigue: she patted the little dog, she talked with the bird, which only answered her with its accustomed song; and for me, she did not seem to recollect that I was there at all. Looking at her so, many qualms and fears came over me; for her face was in perpetual motion; and, besides, her head shook from old age, so that, for my life, I could not understand what sort of countenance she had.

"Having gathered strength again, she lit a candle, covered a very small table, and brought out supper. She now looked round for me, and bade me take a little cane-chair. I was thus sitting close fronting her, with the light between us. She folded her bony hands, and prayed aloud, still twisting her countenance, so that I was once more on the point of laughing; but I took strict care that I might not make her angry.

"After supper she again prayed, then showed me a bed in a low narrow closet; she herself slept in the room. I did not watch long, for I was half stupefied; but in the night I now and then awoke, and heard the old woman coughing, and between whiles talking with her dog and her bird, which last seemed dreaming, and replied with only one or two words of its rhyme. This, with the birches rustling before the window, and the song of a distant nightingale, made such a wondrous combination, that I never fairly thought I was awake, but only falling out of one dream into another still stranger.

"The old woman awoke me in the morning, and soon after gave me work. I was put to spin, which I now learned very easily; I had likewise to take charge of the dog and the bird. I soon learned my business in the house: I now felt as if it all must be so; I never once remembered that the old woman had so many singularities, that her dwelling was mysterious, and lay apart from all men, and that the bird must be a very strange creature. Its beauty, indeed, always struck me, for its feathers glittered with all possible colours; the fairest deep blue, and the most burning red, alternated about his neck and body; and when singing, he blew himself proudly out, so that his feathers looked still finer.

"My old mistress often went abroad, and did not come again till night; on these occasions I went out to meet her with the dog, and she used to call me child and daughter. In the end I grew to like her heartily; as our mind, especially in childhood, will become accustomed and attached to anything. In the evenings, she taught me to read; and this was afterwards a source of boundless satisfaction to me in my solitude, for she had several ancient-written books, that contained the strangest stories.

"The recollection of the life I then led is still singular to me: Visited by no human creature, secluded in the circle of so small a family; for the dog and the bird made the same impression on me which in other cases long-known friends produce. I am surprised that I have never since been able to recall the dog's name, a very odd one, often as I then pronounced it.

"Four years I had passed in this way (I must now have been nearly twelve), when my old dame began to put more trust in me, and at length told me a secret. The bird, I found, laid every day an egg, in which there was a pearl or a jewel. I had already noticed that she often went to fettle privately about the cage, but I had never troubled myself farther on the subject. She now gave me charge of gathering these eggs in her absence, and carefully storing them up in the strange-looking pots. She would leave me food, and sometimes stay away longer, for weeks, for months. My little wheel kept humming round, the dog barked, the bird sang; and withal there was such a stillness in the neighbourhood, that I do not recollect of any storm or foul weather all the time I stayed there. No one wandered thither; no wild-beast came near our dwelling: I was satisfied, and worked along in peace from day to day. One would perhaps be very happy, could he pass his life so undisturbedly to the end.

"From the little that I read, I formed quite marvellous notions of the world and its people; all taken from myself and my society. When I read of witty persons, I could not figure them but like the little shock; great ladies, I conceived, were like the bird; all old women like my mistress. I had read somewhat of love, too; and often, in fancy, I would sport strange stories with myself. I figured out the fairest knight on Earth; adorned him with all perfections, without knowing rightly, after all my labour, how he looked: but I could feel a hearty pity for myself when he ceased to love me; I would then, in thought, make long melting speeches, or perhaps aloud, to try if I could win him back. You smile! These young days are, in truth, far away from us all.

"I now liked better to be left alone, for I was then sole mistress of the house. The dog loved me, and did all I wanted; the bird replied to all my questions with his rhyme; my wheel kept briskly turning, and at bottom I had never any wish for change. When my dame returned from her long wanderings, she would praise my diligence; she said her house, since I belonged to it, was managed far more perfectly; she took a pleasure in my growth and healthy looks; in short, she treated me in all points like her daughter.

"'Thou art a good girl, child,' said she once to me, in her creaking tone; 'if thou continuest so, it will be well with thee: but none ever prospers when he leaves the straight path; punishment will overtake him, though it may be late.' I gave little heed to this remark of hers at the time, for in all my temper and movements I was very lively; but by night it occurred to me again, and I could not understand what she meant by it. I considered all the words attentively; I had read of riches, and at last it struck me that her pearls and jewels might perhaps be something precious. Ere long this thought grew clearer to me. But the straight path, and leaving it? What could she mean by this?

"I was now fourteen; it is the misery of man that he arrives at understanding through the loss of innocence. I now saw well enough that it lay with me to take the jewels and the bird in the old woman's absence, and go forth with them and see the world which I had read of. Perhaps, too, it would then be possible that I might meet that fairest of all knights, who forever dwelt in my memory.

"At first this thought was nothing more than any other·thought; but when I used to be sitting at my wheel, it still returned to me, against my will; and I sometimes followed it so far, that I already saw myself adorned in splendid attire, with princes and knights around me. On awakening from these dreams, I would feel a sadness when I looked up, and found myself still in the little cottage. For the rest, if I went through my duties, the old woman troubled herself little about what I thought or felt.

"One day she went out again, telling me that she should be away on this occasion longer than usual; that I must take strict charge of everything, and not let the time hang·heavy on my hands. I had a sort of fear on taking leave of her, for I felt as if I should not see her any more. I looked long after her, and knew not why I felt so sad;

it was almost as if my purpose had already stood before me, without myself being conscious of it.

"Never did I tend the dog and the bird with such diligence as now; they were nearer to my heart than formerly. The old woman had been gone some days, when I rose one morning in the firm mind to leave the cottage, and set out with the bird to see this world they talked so much of. I felt pressed and hampered in my heart; I wished to stay where I was, and yet the thought of that afflicted me; there was a strange contention in my soul, as if between two discordant spirits. One moment my peaceful solitude would seem to me so beautiful; the next the image of a new world, with its many wonders, would again enchant me.

"I knew not what to make of it; the dog leaped up continually about me; the sunshine spread abroad over the fields; the green birch-trees glittered; I always felt as if I had something I must do in haste; so I caught the little dog, tied him up in the room, and took the cage with the bird under my arm. The dog writhed and whined at this unusual treatment; he looked at me with begging eyes, but I feared to have him with me. I also took one pot of jewels, and concealed it by me; the rest I left.

"The bird turned its head very strangely when I crossed the threshold; the dog tugged at his cord to follow me, but he was forced to stay.

"I did not take the road to the wild rocks, but went in the opposite direction. The dog still whined and barked, and it touched me to the heart to hear him; the bird tried once or twice to sing; but as I was carrying him, the shaking put him out.

"The farther I went, the fainter grew the barking, and at last it altogether ceased. I wept, and had almost turned back, but the longing to see something new still hindered me.

"I had got across the hills, and through some forests, when the night came on, and I was forced to turn aside into a village. I blushed exceedingly on entering the inn; they showed me to a room and bed; I slept pretty quietly, only that I dreamed of the old woman, and her threatening me.

"My journey had not much variety; the farther I went, the more was I afflicted by the recollection of my old mistress and the little dog; I considered that in all likelihood the poor shock would die of hunger, and often in the woods I thought my dame would suddenly meet me. Thus amid tears and sobs I went along; when I stopped to rest, and put the cage on the ground, the bird struck up his song, and brought but too keenly to my mind the fair habitation I had left. As human nature is forgetful, I imagined that my former journey, in my childhood, had not been so sad and woful as the present; I wished to be as I was then.

"I had sold some jewels; and now, after wandering on for several days, I reached a village. At the very entrance I was struck with something strange; I felt terrified and knew not why; but I soon bethought myself, for it was the village where I was born! How amazed was I! How the tears ran down my cheeks for gladness, for a thousand singular remembrances! Many things were changed: new houses had been built, some just raised when I went away, were now fallen, and had marks of fire on them; everything was far smaller and more confined than I had fancied. It rejoiced my very heart that I should see my parents once more after such an absence. I found their little cottage, the well-known threshold; the door-latch was standing as of old; it seemed to me as if I had shut it only yesternight. My heart beat violently, I hastily lifted that latch; but faces I had never seen before looked up and gazed at me. I asked for the shepherd Martin; they told me that his wife and he were dead three years ago. I drew back quickly, and left the village weeping aloud.

"I had figured out so beautifully how I would surprise them with my riches: by the strangest chance, what I had only dreamed in childhood was become reality; and now it was all in vain, they could not rejoice with me, and that which had been my first hope in life was lost forever.

"In a pleasant town I hired a small house and garden, and took to myself a maid. The world, in truth, proved not so wonderful as I had painted it: but I forgot the old woman and my former way of life rather more, and, on the whole, I was contented.

"For a long while the bird had ceased to sing; I was therefore not a little frightened, when one night he suddenly began again, and with a different rhyme. He sang:

> Alone in wood so gay,
> Ah, far away!
> But thou wilt say
> Some other day,
> 'Twere best to stay
> Alone in wood so gay.

"Throughout the night I could not close an eye; all things again occurred to my remembrance; and I felt, more than ever, that I had not acted rightly. When I rose, the aspect of the bird distressed me greatly; he looked at me continually, and his presence did me ill. There was now no end to his song; he sang it louder and more shrilly than he had been wont. The more I looked at him, the more he pained and frightened me; at last I opened the cage, put in my hand, and grasped his neck; I squeezed my fingers hard together, he looked at me, I slackened them; but he was dead. I buried him in the garden.

"After this, there often came a fear over me for my maid; I looked back upon myself, and fancied she might rob me or murder me. For a long while I had been acquainted with a young knight, whom I altogether liked: I bestowed on him my hand; and with this, Sir Walther, ends my story."

"Ay, you should have seen her then," said Eckbert warmly; "seen her youth, her loveliness, and what a charm her lonely way of life had given her. I had no fortune; it was through her love these riches came to me; we moved hither, and our marriage has at no time brought us anything but good."

"But with our tattling," added Bertha, "it is growing very late; we must go to sleep."

She rose, and proceeded to her chamber; Walther, with a kiss of her hand, wished her good-night, saying: "Many thanks, noble lady; I can well figure you beside your singing bird, and how you fed poor little *Strohmian*."

Walther likewise went to sleep; Eckbert alone still walked in a restless humour up and down the room. "Are not men fools?" said he at last: "I myself occasioned this recital of my wife's history, and now such confidence appears to me improper! Will he not abuse it? Will he not communicate the secret to others? Will he not, for such is human nature, cast unblessed thoughts on our jewels, and form pretexts and lay plans to get possession of them?"

It now occurred to his mind that Walther had not taken leave of him so cordially as might have been expected after such a mark of trust: the soul once set upon suspicion finds in every trifle something to confirm it. Eckbert, on the other hand, reproached himself for such ignoble feelings to his worthy friend; yet still he could not cast them out. All night he plagued himself with such uneasy thoughts, and got very little sleep.

Bertha was unwell next day, and could not come to breakfast; Walther did not seem to trouble himself much about her illness, but left her husband also rather coolly. Eckbert could not comprehend such conduct; he went to see his wife, and found her in a feverish state; she said her last night's story must have agitated her.

From that day, Walther visited the castle of his friend but seldom; and when he did appear, it was but to say a few unmeaning words and then depart. Eckbert was exceedingly distressed by this demeanour: to Bertha or Walther he indeed said nothing of it; but to any person his internal disquietude was visible enough.

Bertha's sickness wore an aspect more and more serious; the Doctor grew alarmed; the red had vanished from his patient's cheeks, and her eyes were becoming more and more inflamed. One morning she sent for her husband to her bedside; the nurses were ordered to withdraw.

"Dear Eckbert," she began, "I must disclose a secret to thee, which has almost taken away my senses, which is ruining my health, unimportant trifle as it may appear. Thou mayest remember, often as I talked of my childhood, I could never call to mind the name of the dog that was so long beside me: now, that night on taking leave, Walther all at once said to me: 'I can well figure you, and how you fed poor little *Strohmian*.' Is it chance? Did he guess the name; did he know it, and speak it on purpose? If so, how stands this man connected with my destiny? At times I struggle with myself, as if I but imagined this mysterious business; but, alas! it is certain, too certain. I felt a shudder that a stranger should help me to recall the memory of my secrets. What sayest thou, Eckbert?"

Eckbert looked at his sick and agitated wife with deep emotion; he stood silent and thoughtful; then spoke some words of comfort to her, and went out. In a distant chamber, he walked to and fro in indescribable disquiet. Walther, for many years, had been his sole companion; and now this person was the only mortal in the world whose existence pained and oppressed him. It seemed as if he should be gay and light of heart, were that one thing but removed. He took his bow, to dissipate these thoughts; and went to hunt.

It was a rough stormy winter-day; the snow was lying deep on the hills, and bending down the branches of the trees. He roved about; the sweat was standing on his brow; he found no game, and this embittered his ill-humour. All at once he saw an object moving in the distance; it was Walther gathering moss from the trunks of trees. Scarce knowing what he did, he bent his bow; Walther looked round, and gave a threatening gesture, but the arrow was already flying, and he sank transfixed by it.

Eckbert felt relieved and calmed, yet a certain horror drove him home to his castle. It was a good way distant; he had wandered far into the woods. On arriving, he found Bertha dead: before her death, she had spoken much of Walther and the old woman.

For a great while after this occurrence, Eckbert lived in the deepest solitude: he had all along been melancholy, for the strange history of his wife disturbed him, and he dreaded some unlucky incident or other; but at present he was utterly at variance with himself. The murder of his friend arose incessantly before his mind; he lived in the anguish of continual remorse.

To dissipate his feelings, he occasionally moved to the neighbouring town, where he mingled in society and its amusements. He longed for a friend to fill the void in his soul; and yet, when he remembered Walther, he would shudder at the thought of meeting with a friend; for he felt convinced that, with any friend, he must be unhappy. He had lived so long with his Bertha in lovely calmness; the friendship of Walther had cheered him through so many years; and now both of them were suddenly swept away. As he thought of these things, there were many moments when his life appeared to him some fabulous tale, rather than the actual history of a living man.

A young knight, named Hugo, made advances to the silent melancholy Eckbert, and appeared to have a true affection for him. Eckbert felt himself exceedingly surprised; he met the knight's friendship with the greater readiness, the less he had anticipated it. The two were now frequently together; Hugo showed his friend all possible attentions; one scarcely ever went to ride without the other; in all companies they got together. In a word, they seemed inseparable.

Eckbert was never happy longer than a few transitory moments: for he felt too clearly that Hugo loved him only by mistake; that he knew him not, was unacquainted with his history; and he was seized again with the same old longing to unbosom himself wholly, that he might be sure whether Hugo was his friend or not. But again his apprehensions, and the fear of being hated and abhorred, withheld him. There were many hours in which he felt so much impressed with his entire worthlessness, that he believed no mortal not a stranger to his history, could entertain regard for him. Yet still he was unable to withstand himself: on a solitary ride, he disclosed his whole history to Hugo, and asked if he could love a murderer. Hugo seemed touched, and tried to comfort him. Eckbert returned to town with a lighter heart.

But it seemed to be his doom that, in the very hour of confidence, he should always find materials for suspicion. Scarcely had they entered the public hall, when, in the glitter of the many lights, Hugo's looks had ceased to satisfy him. He thought he noticed a malicious smile; he remarked that Hugo did not speak to him as usual; that he talked with the rest, and seemed to pay no heed to him. In the party was an old knight, who had always shown himself the enemy of Eckbert, had often asked about his riches and his wife in a peculiar style. With this man Hugo was conversing; they were speaking privately, and casting looks at Eckbert. The suspicions of the latter seemed confirmed; he thought himself betrayed, and a tremendous rage took hold of him. As he continued gazing, on a sudden he discerned the countenance of Walther, all his features, all the form so well known to him; he gazed, and looked, and felt convinced that it was none but Walther who was talking to the knight. His horror cannot be described; in a state of frenzy he rushed out of the hall, left the town overnight, and after many wanderings, returned to his castle.

Here, like an unquiet spirit, he hurried to and fro from room to room; no thought would stay with him; out of one frightful idea he fell into another still more frightful, and sleep never visited his eyes. Often he believed that he was mad, that a disturbed imagination was the origin of all this terror; then, again, he recollected Walther's features, and the whole grew more and more a riddle to him. He resolved to take a journey, that he might reduce his thoughts to order; the hope of friendship, the desire of social intercourse, he had now forever given up.

He set out, without prescribing to himself any certain route; indeed, he took small heed of the country he was passing through. Having hastened on some days at the quickest pace of his horse, he, on a sudden, found himself entangled in a labyrinth of rocks, from which he could discover no outlet. At length he met an old peasant, who took him by a path leading past a waterfall: he offered him some coins for his guidance, but the peasant would not have them. "What use is it?" said Eckbert. "I could believe that this man, too, was none but Walther." He looked round once more, and it was none but Walther. Eckbert spurred his horse as fast as it could gallop, over meads and forests, till it sank exhausted to the earth. Regardless of this, he hastened forward on foot.

In a dreamy mood he mounted a hill: he fancied he caught the sound of lively barking at a little distance; the birch-trees whispered in the intervals, and in the strangest notes he heard this song:

> Alone in wood so gay,
> Once more I stay;
> None dare me slay,
> The evil far away:
> Ah, here I stay,
> Alone in wood so gay.

The sense, the consciousness of Eckbert had departed; it was a riddle which he could not solve, whether he was dreaming now, or had before dreamed of a wife and friend. The marvellous was mingled with the common: the world around him seemed enchanted, and he himself was incapable of thought or recollection.

A crooked, bent old woman, crawled coughing up the hill with a crutch. "Art thou bringing me my bird, my pearls, my dog?" cried she to him. "See how injustice punishes itself! No one but I was Walther, was Hugo."

"God of Heaven!" said Eckbert, muttering to himself; "in what frightful solitude have I passed my life?"

"And Bertha was thy sister."

Eckbert sank to the ground.

"Why did she leave me deceitfully? All would have been fair and well; her time of trial was already finished. She was the daughter of a knight, who had her nursed in a shepherd's house; the daughter of thy father."

"Why have I always had a forecast of this dreadful thought?" cried Eckbert.

"Because in early youth thy father told thee: he could not keep this daughter by him for his second wife, her stepmother."

Eckbert lay distracted and dying on the ground. Faint and bewildered, he heard the old woman speaking, the dog barking, and the bird repeating its song.

THE TRUSTY ECKART

BRAVE BURGUNDY NO longer
   Could fight for fatherland;
The foe they were the stronger,
   Upon the bloody sand.

He said: "The foe prevaileth,
   My friends and followers fly,
My striving naught availeth,
   My spirits sink and die.

No more can I exert me,
   Or sword and lance can wield;
O, why did he desert me,
   Eckart, our trusty shield!

In fight he used to guide me,
   In danger was my stay;
Alas, he's not beside me,
   But stays at home today!

The crowds are gathering faster,
   Took captive shall I be?
I may not run like dastard,
   I'll die like soldier free."

Thus Burgundy so bitter,
   Has at his breast his sword;
When, see, breaks-in the Ritter
   Eckart, to save his lord!

With cap and armour glancing,
 Bold on the foe he rides,
His troop behind him prancing,
 And his two sons besides.

Burgundy sees their token,
 And cries: "Now, God be praised!
Not yet we're beat or broken,
 Since Eckart's flag is raised."

Then like a true knight, Eckart
 Dash'd gaily through the foe:
But with his red blood flecker'd,
 His little son lay low.

And when the fight was ended,
 Then Burgundy he speaks:
"Thou hast me well befriended,
 Yet so as wets my cheeks.

The foe is smote and flying;
 Thou'st saved my land and life;
But here thy boy is lying,
 Returns not from the strife."

Then Eckart wept almost,
 The tear stood in his eye;
He clasp'd the son he'd lost,
 Close to his breast the boy.

"Why diedst thou, Heinz, so early,
 And scarce wast yet a man?
Thou'rt fallen in battle fairly;
 For thee I'll not complain.

Thee, Prince, we have deliver'd;
 From danger thou art free:
The boy and I are sever'd;
 I give my son to thee."

Then Burgundy our chief,
   His eyes grew moist and dim;
He felt such joy and grief,
   So great that love to him.

His heart was melting, flaming,
   He fell on Eckart's breast,
With sobbing voice exclaiming:
   "Eckart, my champion best,

Thou stoodst when every other
   Had fled from me away;
Therefore thou art my brother
   Forever from this day.

The people shall regard thee
   As wert thou of my line;
And could I more reward thee,
   How gladly were it thine!"

And when we heard the same,
   We joy'd as did our prince;
And Trusty Eckart is the name
   We've call'd him ever since.

The voice of an old peasant sounded over the rocks, as he sang this ballad; and the Trusty Eckart sat in his grief, on the declivity of the hill, and wept aloud. His youngest boy was standing by him: "Why weepest thou aloud, my father Eckart?" said he: "Art thou not great and strong, taller and braver than any other man? Whom, then, art thou afraid of?"

Meanwhile the Duke of Burgundy was moving homewards to his Tower. Burgundy was mounted on a stately horse, with splendid trappings; and the gold and jewels of the princely Duke were glittering in the evening sun; so that little Conrad could not sate himself with viewing and admiring the magnificent procession. The Trusty Eckart rose, and looked gloomily over it; and young Conrad, when the hunting train had disappeared, struck up this stave:

> On good steed,
> Sword and shield
> Wouldst thou wield,
> With spear and arrow;
> Then had need
> That the marrow
> In thy arm,
> That thy heart and blood,
> Be good,
> To save thy head from harm.

The old man clasped his son to his bosom, looking with wistful tenderness on his clear blue eyes. "Didst thou hear that good man's song?" said he.

"Ay, why not?" answered Conrad: "he sang it loud enough, and thou art the Trusty Eckart thyself, so I liked to listen."

"That same Duke is now my enemy," said Eckart; "he keeps my other son in prison, nay has already put him to death, if I may credit what the people say."

"Take down thy broad-sword, and do not suffer it," cried Conrad; "they will tremble to see thee, and all the people in the whole land will stand by thee, for thou art their greatest hero in the land."

"Not so, my son," said the other; "I were then the man my enemies have called me; I dare not be unfaithful to my liege; no, I dare not break the peace which I have pledged to him, and promised on his hand."

"But what wants he with us, then?" said Conrad, impatiently.

Eckart sat down again, and said: "My son, the entire story of it would be long, and thou wouldst scarcely understand it. The great have always their worst enemy in their own hearts, and they fear it day and night; so Burgundy has now come to think that he has trusted me too far; that he has nursed in me a serpent in his bosom. People call me the stoutest warrior in our country; they say openly that he owes me land and life; I am named the Trusty Eckart; and thus oppressed and suffering persons turn to me, that I may get them help. All this he cannot suffer. So he has taken up a grudge against me; and every one that wants to rise in favour with him increases his distrust; so that at last he has quite turned away his heart from me."

Hereupon the hero Eckart told, in smooth words, how Burgundy had banished him from his sight, how they had become entire strangers to each other, as the Duke suspected that he even meant to rob him of his dukedom. In trouble and sorrow, he proceeded to relate how the Duke had cast his son into confinement, and was threatening the life of Eckart himself, as of a traitor to the land.

But Conrad said to his father: "Wilt thou let me go, my old father, and speak with the Duke, to make him reasonable and kind to thee? If he has killed my brother, then he is a wicked man, and thou must punish him; but that cannot be, for he could not so falsely forget the great service thou hast done him."

"Dost thou know the old proverb?" said Eckart:

> "Doth the king require thy aid,
> Thou'rt a friend can ne'er be paid;
> Hast thou help'd him through his trouble
> Friendship's grown an empty bubble.

Yes; my whole life has been wasted in vain. Why did he make me great, to cast me down the deeper? The friendship of princes is like a deadly poison, which can only be employed against our enemies, and with which at last we unwarily kill ourselves."

"I will to the Duke," cried Conrad: "I will call back into his soul all that thou hast done, that thou hast suffered for him; and he will again be as of old."

"Thou hast forgot," said Eckart, "that they look on us as traitors. Therefore let us fly together to some foreign country, where a better fortune may betide us."

"At thy age," said Conrad, "wilt thou turn away thy face from thy kind home? I will to Burgundy; I will quiet him, and reconcile him to thee. What can he do to me, even though he still hate and fear thee?"

"I let thee go unwillingly," said Eckart; "for my soul forebodes no good; and yet I would fain be reconciled to him, for he is my old friend; and fain save thy brother, who is pining in the dungeon beside him."

The sun threw his last mild rays on the green Earth: Eckart sat pensively leaning back against a tree; he looked long at Conrad, then said: "If thou wilt go, my little boy, go now, before the night grow altogether dark. The windows in the Duke's Castle are already glittering with lights, and I hear afar off the sound of trumpets from the feast; perhaps his son's bride may have arrived, and his mind may be friendlier to us."

Unwillingly he let him go, for he no longer trusted to his fortune: but Conrad's heart was light; for he thought it would be an easy task to turn the mind of Burgundy, who had played with him so kindly but a short while before. "Wilt thou come back to me, my little boy?" sobbed Eckart: "if I lose thee, no other of my race remains." The boy consoled him; flattered him with caresses: at last they parted.

Conrad knocked at the gate of the Castle, and was let in; old Eckart stayed without in the night alone. "Him too have I lost," moaned he in his solitude; "I shall never see his face again."

Whilst he so lamented, there came tottering towards him a gray-haired man; endeavouring to get down the rocks; and seeming, at every step, to fear that he should stumble into the abyss. Seeing the old man's feebleness, Eckart held out his hand to him, and helped him to descend in safety.

"Which way come ye?" inquired Eckart.

The old man sat down, and began to weep, so that the tears came running over his cheeks. Eckart tried to soothe him and console him with reasonable words; but the sorrowful old man seemed not at all to heed these well-meant speeches, but to yield himself the more immoderately to his sorrows.

"What grief can it be that lies so heavy on you as to overpower you utterly?" said Eckart.

"Ah, my children!" moaned the old man.

Then Eckart thought of Conrad, Heinz and Dietrich, and was himself altogether comfortless. "Yes," said he, "if your children are dead, your misery in truth is very great."

"Worse than dead," replied the old man, with his mournful voice; "for they are not dead, but lost forever to me. O, would to Heaven that they were but dead!"

These strange words astonished Eckart, and he asked the old man to explain the riddle; whereupon the latter answered: "The age we live in is indeed a marvellous age, and surely the last days are at hand; for the most dreadful signs are sent into the world, to threaten it. Every sort of wickedness is casting off its old fetters, and stalking bold and free about the Earth; the fear of God is drying up and dispersing, and can find no channel to unite in; and the Powers of Evil are rising audaciously from their dark nooks, and celebrating their triumph. Ah, my dear sir! we are old, but not old enough for such prodigious things. You have doubtless seen the Comet, that wondrous light in the sky, that shines so prophetically down upon us? All men predict evil; and no one thinks of beginning the reform with himself, and so essaying to turn off the rod. Nor is this enough; but portents are also issuing from the Earth, and breaking mysteriously from the depths below, even as the light shines frightfully on us from above. Have you never heard of the Hill, which people call the Hill of Venus?"

"Never," said Eckart, "far as I have travelled."

"I am surprised at that," replied the old man; "for the matter is now grown as notorious as it is true. To this Mountain have the Devils fled, and sought shelter in the desert centre of the Earth, according as the growth of our Holy Faith has cast down the idolatrous worship of the Heathen. Here, they say, before all others, Lady Venus keeps her court, and all her hellish hosts of worldly Lusts and forbidden Wishes gather round her, so that the Hill has been accursed since time immemorial."

"But in what country lies the Hill?" inquired Eckart.

"There is the secret," said the old man, "that no one can tell this, except he have first given himself up to be Satan's servant; and, indeed, no guiltless person ever thinks of seeking it out. A wonderful Musician on a sudden issues from below, whom the Powers of Hell have sent as their ambassador; he roams through the world, and plays, and makes music on a pipe, so that his tones sound far and wide. And whoever hears these sounds is seized by him with visible yet inexplicable force, and drawn on, on, into the wilderness; he sees not the road he travels; he wanders, and wanders, and is not weary; his strength and his speed go on increasing; no power can restrain him; but he runs frantic into the Mountain, from which he can nevermore return. This power has, in our day, been restored to Hell; and in this inverse direction, the ill-starred, perverted pilgrims are travelling to a Shrine where no deliverance awaits them, or can reach them any more. For a long while, my two sons had given me no contentment; they were dissolute and immoral; they despised their parents, as they did religion; but now the Sound has caught and carried them off, they are gone into unseen kingdoms; the world was too narrow for them, they are seeking room in Hell."

"And what do you intend to do in such a mystery?" said Eckart.

"With this crutch I set out," replied the old man, "to wander through the world, to find them again, or die of weariness and woe."

So saying, he tore himself from his rest with a strong effort; and hastened forth with his utmost speed, as if he had found himself neglecting his most precious earthly hope; and Eckart looked with compassion on his vain toil, and rated him in his thoughts as mad.

It had been night, and was now day, and Conrad came not back. Eckart wandered to and fro among the rocks, and turned his longing eyes on the Castle; still he did not see him. A crowd came issuing through the gate; and Eckart no longer heeded to conceal himself; but mounted his horse, which was grazing in freedom; and rode into the middle of the troop, who were now proceeding merrily and carelessly across the plain. On his reaching them, they recognised him; but no one laid a hand on him, or said a hard word to him; they stood mute for reverence, surrounded him in admiration, and then went their way. One of the squires he called back, and asked him: "Where is my Conrad?"

"O! ask me not," replied the squire; "it would but cause you sorrow and lamenting."

"And Dietrich!" cried the father.

"Name not their names any more," said the aged squire, "for they are gone; the wrath of our master was kindled against them, and he meant to punish you in them."

A hot rage mounted up in Eckart's soul; and, for sorrow and fury, he was no longer master of himself. He dashed the spurs into his horse, and rode through the Castle-gate. All drew back, with timid reverence, from his way; and thus he rode on to the front of the Palace. He sprang from horseback, and mounted the great steps with wavering pace. "Am I here in the dwelling of the man," said he, within himself, "who was once my friend?" He endeavoured to collect his thoughts; but wilder and wilder images kept moving in his eye, and thus he stept into the Prince's chamber.

Burgundy's presence of mind forsook him, and he trembled as Eckart stood in his presence. "Art thou the Duke of Burgundy?" said Eckart to him. To which the Duke answered, "Yes."

"And thou hast killed my son Dietrich?" The Duke said, "Yes."

"And my little Conrad too," cried Eckart, in his grief, "was not too good for thee, and thou hast killed him also?" To which the Duke again answered, "Yes."

Here Eckart was unmanned, and said, in tears: "O! answer me not so, Burgundy; for I cannot bear these speeches. Tell me but that thou art sorry, that thou wishest it were yet undone, and I will try to comfort myself; but thus thou art utterly offensive to my heart."

The Duke said: "Depart from my sight, false traitor; for thou art the worst enemy I have on Earth."

Eckart said: "Thou hast of old called me thy friend; but these thoughts are now far from thee. Never did I act against thee; still have I honoured and loved thee as my prince; and God forbid that

I should now, as I well might, lay my hand upon my sword, and seek revenge of thee. No, I will depart from thy sight, and die in solitude."

So saying, he went out; and Burgundy was moved in his mind; but at his call, the guards appeared with their lances, who encircled him on all sides, and motioned to drive Eckart from the chamber with their weapons.

> To horse the hero springs,
>   Wild through the hills he rideth:
> "Of hope in earthly things,
>   Now none with me abideth.
>
> My sons are slain in youth,
>   I have no child or wife;
> The Prince suspects my truth,
>   Has sworn to take my life."
>
> Then to the wood he turns him,
>   There gallops on and on;
> The smart of sorrow burns him,
>   He cries: "They're gone, they're gone
>
> All living men from me are fled,
>   New friends I must provide me,
> To the oaks and firs beside me,
>   Complain in desert dead.
>
> There is no child to cheer me,
>   By cruel wolves they're slain;
> Once three of them were near me,
>   I see them not again."
>
> As Eckart cried thus sadly,
>   His sense it pass'd away;
> He rides in fury madly
>   Till dawning of the day.
>
> His horse in frantic speed
>   Sinks down at last exhausted;
> And naught does Eckart heed,
>   Or think or know what caused it;

> But on the cold ground lie,
>   Not fearing, loving longer;
> Despair grows strong and stronger,
>   He wishes but to die.

No one about the Castle knew whither Eckart had gone; for he had lost himself in the waste forests, and let no man see him. The Duke dreaded his intentions; and he now repented that he had let him go, and not laid hold of him. So, one morning, he set forth with a great train of hunters and attendants, to search the woods, and find out Eckart; for he thought, that till Eckart were destroyed, there could be no security. All were unwearied, and regardless of toil; but the sun set without their having found a trace of Eckart.

A storm came on, and great clouds flew blustering over the forest; the thunder rolled, and lightning struck the tall oaks: all present were seized with an unquiet terror, and they gradually dispersed among the bushes, or the open spaces of the wood. The Duke's horse plunged into the thicket; his squires could not follow him: the gallant horse rushed to the ground; and Burgundy in vain called through the tempest to his servants; for there was no one that could hear him.

Like a wild man had Eckart roamed about the woods, unconscious of himself or his misfortunes; he had lost all thought, and in blank stupefaction satisfied his hunger with roots and herbs: the hero could not now be recognised by any one, so sore had the days of his despair defaced him. As the storm came on, he awoke from his stupefaction, and again felt his existence and his woes, and saw the misery that had befallen him. He raised a loud cry of lamentation for his children; he tore his white hair; and called out, in the bellowing of the storm: "Whither, whither are ye gone, ye parts of my heart? And how is all strength departed from me, that I could not even avenge your death? Why did I hold back my arm, and did not send to death him who had given my heart these deadly stabs? Ha, fool, thou deservest that the tyrant should mock thee, since thy powerless arm and thy silly heart withstood not the murderer. Now, O now were he with me! But it is in vain to wish for vengeance, when the moment is gone by."

Thus came on the night, and Eckart wandered to and fro in his sorrow. From a distance he heard as it were a voice calling for help. Directing his steps by the sound, he came up to a man in the darkness, who was leaning on the stem of a tree, and mournfully entreating to be guided to his road. Eckart started at the voice, for it seemed familiar to him; but he soon recovered, and perceived that the lost wayfarer was the Duke of Burgundy. Then he raised his hand to his sword, to cut down the man who had been the murderer of his children; his fury came on him with new force, and he was upon the point of finishing his bloody task, when all at once he stopped, for his oath and the word he had pledged came into his mind. He took his enemy's hand, and led him to the quarter where he thought the road must be.

> The Duke foredone and weary
> Sank in the wilder'd breaks;
> Him in the tempest dreary
> He on his shoulders takes.

> Said Burgundy: "I'm giving
> Much toil to thee, I fear."
> Eckart replied: "The living
> On Earth have much to bear."

> "Yet," said the Duke, "believe me,
> Were we out of the wood,
> Since now thou dost relieve me,
> Thy sorrows I'll make good."

> The hero at this promise
> Felt on his cheek the tear;
> Said he: "Indeed I nowise
> Do look for payment here."

> "Harder our plight is growing,"
> The Duke cries, dreading scath,
> "Now whither are we going?
> Who art thou? Art thou Death?"

> "Not Death," said he, still weeping,
> "Or any fiend am I;
> Thy life is in God's keeping,
> Thy ways are in his eye."

> "Ah," said the Duke, repenting,
> "My breast is foul within;
> I tremble, while lamenting,
> Lest God requite my sin.

My truest friend I've banish'd,
  His children have I slain,
In wrath from me he vanish'd,
  As foe he comes again.

To me he was devoted,
  Through good report and bad;
My rights he still promoted,
  The truest man I had.

Me he can never pardon,
  I kill'd his children dear;
This night, to pay my guerdon,
  I' th' wood he lurks, I fear.

This does my conscience teach me,
  A threat'ning voice within;
If here to-night he reach me,
  I die a child of sin."

Said Eckart: "The beginning
  Of our woes is guilt;
My grief is for thy sinning,
  And for the blood thou'st spilt.

And that the man will meet thee
  Is likewise surely true;
Yet fear not, I entreat thee,
  He'll harm no hair of you."

Thus were they going forward talking, when another person in the forest met them; it was Wolfram, the Duke's Squire, who had long been looking for his master. The dark night was still lying over them, and no star twinkled from between the wet black clouds. The Duke felt weaker, and longed to reach some lodging, where he might sleep till day; besides, he was afraid that he might meet with Eckart, who stood like a spectre before his soul. He imagined he should never see the morning; and shuddered anew when the wind again rustled through the high trees, and the storm came down from the hollows of the mountains, and went rushing over his head. "Wolfram," cried the Duke, in his anguish, "climb one of these tall pines, and look about if thou canst spy no light, no house or cottage, whither we may turn."

The Squire, at the hazard of his life, clomb up a lofty pine, which the storm was waving from the one side to the other, and ever and anon bending down the top of it to the very ground; so that the Squire wavered to and fro upon it like a little squirrel. At last he reached the top, and cried: "Down there, in the valley, I see the glimmer of a candle; thither must we turn." So he descended and showed the way; and in a while, they all perceived the cheerful light; at which the Duke once more took heart. Eckart still continued mute, and occupied within himself; he spoke no word, and looked at his inward thoughts. On arriving at the hut, they knocked; and a little old housewife let them in: as they entered, the stout Eckart set the Duke down from his shoulders, who threw himself immediately upon his knees, and in a fervent prayer thanked God for his deliverance. Eckart took his seat in a dark corner; and there he found fast asleep the poor old man, who had lately told him of his great misery about his sons, and the search he was making for them.

When the Duke had done praying, he said: "Very strange have my thoughts been this night, and the goodness of God and his almighty power never showed themselves so openly before to my obdurate heart: my mind also tells me that I have not long to live; and I desire nothing save that God would pardon me my manifold and heavy sins. You two, also, who have led me hither, I could wish to recompense, so far as in my power, before my end arrive. To thee, Wolfram, I give both the castles that are on these hills beside us; and in future, in remembrance of this awful night, thou shalt call them the Tannenhäuser, or Pine-houses. But who art thou, strange man," continued he, "that hast placed thyself there in the nook, apart? Come forth, that I may also pay thee for thy toil."

> Then rose the hero from his place,
> And stept into the light before them;
> Deep lines of woe were on his face,
> But with a patient mind he bore them.

> And Burgundy, his heart forsook him,
> To see that mild old gray-hair'd man;
> His face grew pale, a trembling took him,
> He swoon'd and sank to earth again.

"O, saints of heaven," he wakes and cries,
"Is't thou that art before my eyes?
  How shall I fly? Where shall I hide me?
  Was't thou that in the wood didst guide me?
  I kill'd thy children young and fair,
  Me in thy arms how couldst thou bear?"

  Thus Burgundy goes on to wail,
And feels the heart within him fail;
Death is at hand, remorse pursues him,
With streaming eyes he sinks on Eckart's bosom;
And Eckart whispers to him low:
"Henceforth I have forgot the slight,
  So thou and all the world may know,
  Eckart was still thy trusty knight."

Thus passed the hours till morning, when some other servants of the Duke arrived, and found their dying master. They laid him on a mule, and took him back to his castle. Eckart he could not suffer from his side; he would often take his hand and press it to his breast, and look at him with an imploring look. Then Eckart would embrace him, and speak a few kind words to him, and so the Prince would feel composed. At last he summoned all his Council, and declared to them that he appointed Eckart, the trusty man, to be guardian of his sons, seeing he had proved himself the noblest of all. And thus he died.

Thenceforward Eckart took on him the government with all zeal; and every person in the land admired his high manly spirit. Not long afterwards a rumour spread abroad in all quarters, of a strange Musician, who had come from Venus-Hill, who was travelling through the whole land, and seducing men with his playing, so that they disappeared, and no one could find any traces of them. Many credited the story, others not; Eckart recollected the unhappy old man.

"I have taken you for my sons," said he to the young Princes, as he once stood with them on the hill before the Castle; "your happiness must now be my posterity; when dead, I shall still live in your joy." They lay down on the slope, from which the fair country was visible for many a league; and here Eckart had to guard himself from speaking of his children; for they seemed as if coming towards him from the distant mountains, while he heard afar off a lovely sound.

"Comes it not like dreams
　　Stealing o'er the vales and streams?
　　Out of regions far from this,
　　Like the song of souls in bliss?"

This to the youths did Eckart say,
And caught the sound from far away;
And as the magic tones came nigher,
A wicked strange desire
Awakens in the breasts of these pure boys,
That drives them forth to seek for unknown joys.

"Come, let's to the fields, to the meadows and mountains,
The forests invite us, the streams and the fountains;
Soft voices in secret for loitering chide us,
Away to the Garden of Pleasure they'll guide us."

The Player comes in foreign guise,
Appears before their wondering eyes;
And higher swells the music's sound,
And brighter glows the emerald ground;
The flowers appear as drunk,
Twilight red has on them sunk;
And through the green grass play, with airy lightness,
Soft, fitful, blue and golden streaks of brightness.
Like a shadow, melts and flits away
All that bound men to this world of clay;
In Earth all toil and tumult cease,
Like one bright flower it blooms in peace;
The mountains rock in purple light,
The valleys shout as with delight;
All rush and whirl in the music's noise,
And long to share of these offer'd joys;
The soul of man is allured to gladness,
And lies entranced in that blissful madness.

The Trusty Eckart felt it,
　　But wist not of the cause;
His heart the music melted,
　　He wondered what it was.

The world seems new and fairer,
  All blooming like the rose;
Can Eckart be a sharer
  In raptures such as those?

"Ha! Are those tones restoring
  My wife and bonny sons?
All that I was deploring,
  My lost beloved ones?"

Yet soon his sense collected
  Brought doubt within his breast;
These hellish arts detected,
  A horror him possessed.

And now he sees the raging
  Of his young princes dear;
Themselves to Hell engaging,
  His voice no more they hear.

And forth, in wild commotion,
  They rush, not knowing where;
In tumult like the ocean,
  When mad his billows are.

Then, as these things assail'd him,
  He wist not what to do;
His knighthood almost fail'd him
  Amid that hellish crew.

Then to his soul appeareth
  The hour the Duke did die;
His friend's faint prayer he heareth,
  He sees his fading eye.

And so his mind's in armour,
  And hope is conquering fear;
When see, the fiendish Charmer
  Himself comes piping near!

His sword to draw he essayeth,
 And smite the caitiff dead;
But as the music playeth,
 His strength is from him fled.

And from the mountains issue
 Crowds of distorted forms,
Of Dwarfs a boundless tissue
 Come simmering round in swarms.

The youths, possess'd, are running
 As frantic in the crowd:
In vain is force or cunning;
 In vain to call aloud.

And hurries on by castle,
 By tower and town, the rout;
Like imps in hellish wassail,
 With cackling laugh and shout.

He too is in the rabble;
 May not resist their force,
Must hear their deafening babble,
 Attend their frantic course.

But now the Hill appeareth,
 And music comes thereout;
And as the Phantoms hear it,
 They halt, and raise a shout.

The Mountain starts asunder,
 A motley crowd is seen;
This way and that they wander,
 In red unearthly sheen.

Then his broad-sword he drew it,
 And says: "Still true, though lost!"
And with mad force he heweth
 Through that Infernal host.

His youths he sees (how gladly!)
  Escaping through the vale;
The Fiends are fighting madly,
  And threatening to prevail.

The Dwarfs, when hurt, fly downward,
  And rise up cured again;
And other crowds rush onward,
  And fight with might and main.

Then saw he from a distance
  The children safe, and cried:
"They need not my assistance,
  I care not what betide."

His good broad-sword doth glitter
  And flash i' th' noontide ray;
The Dwarfs, with wailing bitter,
  And howls, depart away.

Safe at the valley's ending,
  The youths far off he spies;
Then faint and wounded, bending,
  The hero falls and dies.

So his last hour o'ertook him,
  Fighting like lion brave;
His truth, it ne'er forsook him,
  He was faithful to the grave.

Now Eckart having perish'd,
  The eldest son bore sway;
His memory still he cherish'd,
  With grateful heart would say:

"From foes and wreck to save me,
  Like lion grim he fought;
My throne, my life, he gave me,
  And with his heart's blood bought."

And soon a wondrous rumour
  The country round did fill,
That when a desp'rate humour
  Doth send one to the Hill,

There straight a Shape will meet him
  The Trusty Eckart's ghost,
And wistfully entreat him
  To turn, and not be lost.

There he, though dead, yet ever
  True watch and ward doth hold;
Upon the Earth shall never
  Be man so true and bold.

PART II

More than four centuries had elapsed since the Trusty Eckart's death, when a noble Tannenhäuser, in the station of Imperial Counsellor, was living at Court in the highest estimation. The son of this knight surpassed in beauty all the other nobles of the land, and on this account was loved and prized by every one. Suddenly, however, after some mysterious incidents had been observed to happen to him, the young man disappeared; and no one knew or guessed what was become of him. Since the times of the Trusty Eckart, there had always been a story current in the land about the Venus-Hill; and many said that he had wandered thither, and was lost forever.

One of those that most lamented him was his young friend Friedrich von Wolfsburg. They had grown up together, and their mutual attachment seemed to each of them to have become a necessary of life. Tannenhäuser's old father died: Friedrich married some years afterwards; already was a ring of merry children round him, and still he heard no tidings of his youthful friend; so that, in the end, he was forced to conclude him dead.

He was standing one evening under the gate of his Castle, when he perceived afar off a pilgrim travelling towards the mansion. The wayfaring man was clad in a strange garb; and his gait and gestures the Knight thought extremely singular. On his approaching nearer, Wolfsburg thought that he knew him; and at last he became convinced that the stranger was no other than his long-lost friend, the Tannenhäuser. He felt amazed, and a secret horror took possession of him, as he recognised distinctly these much-altered features.

The two friends embraced; then started back next moment; and gazed astonished at each other as at unknown beings. Of questions, of perplexed replies, were many. Friedrich often shuddered at the wild look of his friend, which seemed to burn as with unearthly light. The Tannenhäuser had reposed himself a day or two, when Friedrich learned that he was on a pilgrimage to Rome.

The two friends by and by renewed their former intimacy; took up their old topics, and told stories to each other of their youth; but the Tannenhäuser always carefully concealed where he had been since then. Friedrich, however, pressed him to disclose it, now that they were once more on their ancient confidential footing: the other long endeavoured to ward off the friendly prayer; but at last he exclaimed: "Well, be it so; thy will be done! Thou shalt know all; but cast no reproaches on me after, should the story fill thee with inquietude and horror."

They went into the open air, and walked a little in a green wood of the pleasure-grounds, where at last they sat down; and now the Tannenhäuser hid his face among the grass, and, with loud sobs, held back his right hand to his friend, who pressed it tenderly in his. The woe-worn pilgrim raised himself, and began his story in the following words:

"Believe me, Wolfsburg, many a man has, at his birth, an Evil Spirit linked to him, that vexes him through life, and never lets him rest, till he has reached his black destination. So has it been with me; my whole existence has been but a continuing birth-pain, and my awakening will be in Hell. For this have I already wandered so many weary steps, and have so many yet before me on the pilgrimage which I am making to the Holy Father, that I may endeavour to obtain forgiveness at Rome. In his presence will I lay down the heavy burden of my sins; or fall beneath it, and die despairing."

Friedrich attempted to console him, but the Tannenhäuser seemed to pay little heed to what he said; and, after a short while, he proceeded in the following words: "There is an old legend of a Knight who is said to have lived many centuries ago, under the name of the Trusty Eckart. They tell how, in those days, a Musician issued from some marvellous Hill; and, by his magic tones, awoke in the hearts of all that heard him so deep a longing, such wild wishes, that he led them irresistibly along with his music, and forced them to rush in with him to the Hill. Hell had then opened wide her gates to poor mortals, and enticed them in with seductive music. In boyhood I often heard this story, and at first without particularly minding it; yet ere long it so took hold of me, that all Nature, every sound, every flower, recalled to me the story of these heart-subduing tones. I cannot tell thee what a sadness, what an unutterable longing used to seize me, when I looked on the driving of the clouds, and saw the light lordly blue peering out between them; or what remembrances the meadows and the woods would awaken in my deepest heart. Oftentimes the loveliness and fulness of royal Nature so affected me, that I stretched out my arms, as if to fly away with wings; that I might pour myself out like the Spirit of Nature over mountain and valley; that I might brood over grass and forest, and inhale the riches of her blessedness. And if by day the free landscape charmed me, by night dark dreaming fantasies tormented me; and set themselves in louring grimness before me, as if to shut up my path of life forever. Above all, there was one dream that left an ineffaceable impression on my feelings, though I never could distinctly call the forms of it to memory. Methought there was a vast tumult in the streets; I heard confused unintelligible speaking; it was dark night; I went to my parents' house; none but my father was there, and he sick. Next morning I clasped my parents in my arms, and pressed them with melting tenderness to my breast, as if some hostile power had been about to tear them from me. 'Am I to lose thee?' said I to my father. 'O! how wretched and lonely were I without thee in this world!' They tried to comfort me, but could not wipe away the dim image from my remembrance.

"I grew older, still keeping myself apart from other boys of my age. I often roamed solitary through the fields: and it happened one morning, in my rambles, that I had lost my way; and so was wandering to and fro in a thick wood, not knowing whither to turn. After long seeking vainly for a road, I at last on a sudden came upon an iron-grated fence, within which lay a garden. Through the bars, I saw fair shady walks before me; fruit-trees and flowers; and close by me were rose-bushes glittering in the sun. A nameless longing for these roses seized me; I could not help rushing on; I pressed myself by force through between the bars, and was now standing in the garden. Immediately I sank on my knees; clasped the bushes in my arms; kissed the roses on their red lips, and melted into tears. I had knelt a while, absorbed in a sort of rapture, when there came two maidens through the alleys; the one of my own years, the other elder. I awoke from my trance, to fall into a higher ecstasy. My eye lighted on the younger, and I felt at this moment as if all my unknown woe was healed. They took me to the house; their parents, having learned my name, sent notice to my father, who, in the evening, came himself, and brought me back.

"From this day, the uncertain current of my life had got a fixed direction; my thoughts forever hastened back to the castle and the maiden; for here, it seemed to me, was the home of all my wishes. I forgot my customary pleasures, I forsook my playmates, and often visited the garden, the castle and Emma. Here I had, in a little time, grown, as it were, an inmate of the house, so that they no longer thought it strange to see me; and Emma was becoming dearer to me every day. Thus passed my hours; and a tenderness had taken my heart captive, though I myself was not aware of it. My whole destination seemed to me fulfilled; I had no wish but still to come again; and when I went away, to have the same prospect for the morrow.

"Matters were in this state, when a young knight became acquainted in the family; he was a friend of my parents; and he soon, like me, attached himself to Emma. I hated him, from that moment, as my deadly enemy; but nothing can describe my feelings, when I fancied I perceived that Emma liked him more than me. From this hour, it was as if the music, which had hitherto accompanied me, went silent in my bosom. I meditated but on death and hatred; wild thoughts now awoke in my breast, when Emma sang her well-known songs to her lute. Nor did I hide the aversion which I felt; and when my parents tried to reason and remonstrate with me, I grew fierce and contradictory.

"I now roved about the woods and rocky wastes, infuriated against myself. The death of my rival was a thing I had determined on. The young knight, after some few months, made a formal offer of himself to the parents of my mistress, and she was betrothed to him. All that was rare and beautiful in Nature, all that had charmed me in her magnificence, had been united in my soul with Emma's image; I fancied, knew or wished for no other happiness but Emma; nay I had wilfully determined that the day, which brought the loss of her, should also bring my own destruction.

"My parents sorrowed in heart at such perversion; my mother had fallen sick, but I paid no heed to this; her situation gave me little trouble, and I saw her seldom. The wedding-day of my enemy was coming on; and with its approach increased the agony of mind which drove me over woods and mountains. I execrated Emma and myself with the most horrid curses. At this time I had no friend; no man would take any charge of me, for all had given me up for lost.

"The fearful marriage-eve came on. I had wandered deep among the cliffs, I heard the rushing of the forest-streams below; I often shuddered at myself. When the morning came, I saw my enemy proceeding down the mountains: I assailed him with injurious speeches; he replied; we drew our swords, and he soon fell beneath my furious strokes.

"I hastened on, not looking after him, but his attendants took the corpse away. At night, I hovered round the dwelling which enclosed my Emma; and a few days afterwards, I heard in the neighbouring cloister the sound of the funeral-bell, and the grave-song of the nuns. I inquired; and was told that Fräulein Emma, out of sorrow for her bridegroom's death, was dead.

"I could stay no longer; I doubted whether I was living, whether it was all truth or not. I hastened back to my parents; and came next night, at a late hour, to the town where they lived. Here all was in confusion; horses and military wagons filled the streets, soldiers were jostling one another this way and that, and speaking in disordered haste: the Emperor was on the point of undertaking a campaign against his enemies. A solitary light was burning in my father's house when I entered; a strangling oppression lay upon my breast. As I knocked, my father himself, with slow, thoughtful steps, advanced to meet me; and immediately I recollected the old dream of my childhood; and felt, with cutting emotion, that now it was receiving its fulfilment. In perplexity, I asked: 'Why are you up so late, Father?' He led me in, and said: 'I may well be up, for thy mother is even now dead.'

"His words struck through my soul like thunderbolts. He took a seat with a meditative air; I sat down beside him. The corpse was lying in a bed, and strangely wound in linen. My heart was like to burst. 'I wake here,' said the old man, 'for my wife is still sitting by me.' My senses failed; I fixed my eyes upon a corner; and, after a little while, there rose, as it were, a vapour; it mounted and wavered; and the well-known figure of my mother gathered itself visibly together from the midst of it, and looked at me with an earnest mien. I wished to go, but I could not; for the form of my mother beckoned to me, and my father held me in his arms, and whispered to me, in a low voice: 'She died of grief for thee.' I embraced him with a childlike transport of affection; I poured burning tears on his breast. He kissed me; and I shuddered; for his lips, as they touched me, were cold, like the lips of one dead. 'How art thou, Father?' cried I, in horror. He writhed painfully together, and made no reply. In a few moments, I felt him growing colder; I laid my hand on his heart, but it was still; and; in wailing delirium, I held the body fast clasped in my embrace.

"As it were a gleam, like the first streak of dawn, went through the dark room; and behold, the spirit of my father sat beside my mother's form; and both looked at me compassionately, as I held the dear corpse in my arms. After this my consciousness was over: exhausted and delirious, the servants found me next morning in the chamber of the dead."

So far the Tannenhäuser had proceeded with his narrative: Friedrich was listening to him with the deepest astonishment, when all on a sudden he broke off, and paused with an expression of the keenest pain. Friedrich felt embarrassed and immersed in thought; they both returned in company to the Castle, but stayed in the same room apart from others.

The Tannenhäuser had kept silence for a while, then he again began: "The remembrance of those hours still agitates me deeply; I understand not how I have survived them. The world, and its life, now appeared to me as if dead and utterly desolate; without thoughts or wishes I lived on from day to day. I then became acquainted with a set of wild young people; and endeavoured, in the whirl of pleasure and intoxication, to lay the tumultuous Evil Spirit that was in me. My ancient burning impatience again awoke; and I could no longer understand myself or my wishes. A debauchee, named Rudolf, had become my confidant; he, however, always laughed to scorn my longings and complaints. About a year had passed in this way, when my misery of spirit rose to desperation; there was something drove me onwards, onwards, into unknown space; I could have dashed myself down from the high mountains into the glowing green of the meadows, into the cool rushing of the waters, to slake the burning thirst, to stay the insatiability of my soul: I longed for annihilation; and again, like golden morning clouds, did hope and love of life arise before me, and entice me on. The thought then struck me, that Hell was hungering for me, and was sending me my sorrows as well as my pleasures to destroy me; that some malignant Spirit was directing all the powers of my soul to the Infernal Abode; and leading me, as with a bridle, to my doom. And I surrendered to him; that so these torments, these alternating raptures and agonies, might leave me. In the darkest night, I mounted a lofty hill; and called on the Enemy of God and man, with all the energies of my heart, so that I felt he would be forced to hear me. My words brought him: he stood suddenly before me, and I felt no horror. Then in talking with him, the belief in that strange Hill again rose within me; and he taught me a Song, which of itself would lead me by the straight road thither. He disappeared, and for the first time since I had begun to live, I was alone with myself; for I now understood my wandering thoughts, which rushed as from a centre to find out another world. I set forth on my journey; and the Song, which I sang with a loud voice, led me over strange deserts; but all other things besides myself I had forgotten. There was something carrying me, as on the strong wings of desire, to my home: I wished to escape the shadow which, amid the sunshine, threatens us; the wild tones which, amid the softest music, chide us. So travelling on, I reached the Mountain, one night when the moon was shining faintly from behind dim clouds. I proceeded with my Song; and a giant form stood by me, and beckoned me back with his staff. I went nearer: 'I am the Trusty Eckart,' said the superhuman figure; 'by God's goodness, I am placed here as watchman, to warn men back from their sinful rashness.'—I pressed through.

"My path was now as in a subterraneous mine. The passage was so narrow, that I had to press myself along; I caught the gurgling of hidden waters; I heard spirits forming ore, and gold and silver, to entice the soul of man; I found here concealed and separate the deep sounds and tones from which earthly music springs: the farther I went, the more did there fall, as it were, a veil from my sight.

"I rested, and saw other forms of men come gliding towards me; my friend Rudolf was among the number. I could not understand how they were to pass me, so narrow was the way; but they went along, through the middle of the rock, without perceiving me.

"Anon I heard the sound of music; but music altogether different from any that had ever struck my ear before. My thoughts within me strove towards the notes: I came into an open space; and strange radiant colours glittered on me from every side. This it was that I had always been in search of. Close to my heart I felt the presence of the long-sought, now-discovered glory; and its ravishments thrilled into me with all their power. And then the whole crowd of jocund Pagan gods came forth to meet me, Lady Venus at their head, and all saluted me. They have been banished thither by the power of the Almighty; their worship is abolished from the Earth; and now they work upon us from their concealment.

"All pleasures that Earth affords I here possessed and partook of in their fullest bloom; insatiable was my heart, and endless my enjoyment. The famed Beauties of the ancient world were present; what my thought coveted was mine; one delirium of rapture was followed by another; and day after day, the world appeared to burn round me in more glorious hues. Streams of the richest wine allayed my fierce thirst; and beauteous forms sported in the air, and soft eyes invited me; vapours rose enchanting around my head: as if from the inmost heart of blissful Nature, came a music and cooled with its fresh waves the wild tumult of desire; and a horror, that glided faint and secret over the rose-fields, heightened the delicious revel. How many years passed over me in this abode I know not: for here there was no time and no distinctions; the flowers here glowed with the charms of women; and in the forms of the women bloomed the magic of flowers; colours here had another language; the whole world of sense was bound together into one blossom, and the spirits within it forever held their rejoicing.

"Now, how it happened, I can neither say nor comprehend; but so it was, that in all this pomp of sin, a love of rest, a longing for the old innocent Earth, with her scanty joys, took hold of me here, as keenly as of old the impulse which had driven me hither. I was again drawn on to live that life which men, in their unconsciousness, go on leading: I was sated with this splendour, and gladly sought my former home once more. An unspeakable grace of the Almighty permitted my return; I found myself suddenly again in the world; and now it is my intention to pour out my guilty breast before the chair of our Holy Father in Rome; that so he may forgive me, and I may again be reckoned among men."

The Tannenhäuser ceased; and Friedrich long viewed him with an investigating look, then took his hand, and said: "I cannot yet recover from my wonder, nor can I understand thy narrative; for it is impossible that all thou hast told me can be aught but an imagination. Emma still lives, she is my wife; thou and I never quarrelled, or hated one another, as thou thinkest: yet before our marriage, thou wert gone on a sudden from the neighbourhood; nor didst thou ever tell me, by a single hint, that Emma was dear to thee."

Hereupon he took the bewildered Tannenhäuser by the hand, and led him into another room to his wife, who had just then returned from a visit to her sister, which had kept her for the last few days from home. The Tannenhäuser spoke not, and seemed immersed in thought; he viewed in silence the form and face of the lady, then shook his head, and said: "By Heaven, that is the strangest incident of all!"

Friedrich, with precision and connectedness, related all that had befallen him since that time; and tried to make his friend perceive that it had been some singular madness which had, in the mean while, harassed him. "I know very well how it stands," exclaimed the Tannenhäuser. "It is now that I am crazy; and Hell has cast this juggling show before me, that I may not go to Rome, and seek the pardon of my sins."

Emma tried to bring his childhood to his recollection; but the Tannenhäuser would not be persuaded. He speedily set out on his journey; that he might the sooner get his absolution from the Pope.

Friedrich and Emma often spoke of the mysterious pilgrim. Some months had gone by, when the Tannenhäuser, pale and wasted, in a tattered pilgrim's dress, and barefoot, one morning entered Friedrich's chamber, while the latter was in bed asleep. He kissed his lips, and then said, in breathless haste: "The Holy Father cannot, and will not, forgive me; I must back to my old dwelling." And with this he went hurriedly away.

Friedrich roused himself; but the ill-fated pilgrim was already gone. He went to his lady's room; and her maids rushed out to meet him, crying that the Tannenhäuser had pressed into the apartment early in the morning, with the words: "She shall not obstruct me in my course!"—Emma was lying murdered.

Friedrich had not yet recalled his thoughts, when a horror came over him: he could not rest; he ran into the open air. They wished to keep him back; but he told them that the pilgrim had kissed his lips, and that the kiss was burning him till he found the man again. And so, with inconceivable rapidity, he ran away to seek the Tannenhäuser, and the mysterious Hill; and, since that day, he was never seen any more. People say, that whoever gets a kiss from any emissary of the Hill, is thenceforth unable to withstand the lure that draws him with magic force into the subterraneous chasm.

THE RUNENBERG

A YOUNG HUNTER was sitting in the heart of the Mountains, in a thoughtful mood, beside his fowling-floor, while the noise of the waters and the woods was sounding through the solitude. He was musing on his destiny; how he was so young, and had forsaken his father and mother, and accustomed home, and all his comrades in his native village, to seek out new acquaintances, to escape from the circle of returning habitude; and he looked up with a sort of surprise that he was here, that he found himself in this valley, in this employment. Great clouds were passing over him, and sinking behind the mountains; birds were singing from the bushes, and an echo was replying to them. He slowly descended the hill; and seated himself on the margin of a brook, that was gushing down among the rocks with foamy murmur. He listened to the fitful melody of the water; and it seemed to him as if the waves were saying to him, in unintelligible words, a thousand things that concerned him nearly; and he felt an inward trouble that he could not understand their speeches. Then again he looked aloft, and thought that he was glad and happy; so he took new heart, and sang aloud this hunting-song:

> Blithe and cheery through the mountains
>   Goes the huntsman to the chase,
> By the lonesome shady fountains,
>   Till he finds the red-deer's trace.
>
> Hark! his trusty dogs are baying
>   Through the bright-green solitude;
> Through the groves the horns are playing:
>   O, thou merry gay green wood!

In some dell, when luck hath blest him,
    And his shot hath stretch'd the deer,
Lies he down, content, to rest him,
    While the brooks are murmuring clear.

Leave the husbandman his sowing,
    Let the shipman sail the sea;
None, when bright the morn is glowing,
    Sees its red so fair as he,

Wood and wold and game that prizes,
    While Diana loves his art;
And, at last, some bright face rises:
    Happy huntsman that thou art!

Whilst he sung, the sun had sunk deeper, and broad shadows fell across the narrow glen. A cooling twilight glided over the ground; and now only the tops of the trees, and the round summits of the mountains, were gilded by the glow of evening. Christian's heart grew sadder and sadder: he could not think of going back to his birdfold, and yet he could not stay; he felt himself alone, and longed to meet with men. He now remembered with regret those old books, which he used to see at home, and would never read, often as his father had advised him to it: the habitation of his childhood came before him, his sports with the youth of the village, his acquaintances among the children, the school that had afflicted him so much; and he wished he were again amid these scenes, which he had wilfully forsaken, to seek his fortune in unknown regions, in the mountains, among strange people, in a new employment. Meanwhile it grew darker; and the brook rushed louder; and the birds of night began to shoot, with fitful wing, along their mazy courses. Christian still sat disconsolate, and immersed in sad reflection; he was like to weep, and altogether undecided what to do or purpose. Unthinkingly, he pulled a straggling root from the earth; and on the instant, heard, with affright, a stifled moan underground, which winded downwards in doleful tones, and died plaintively away in the deep distance. The sound went through his inmost heart; it seized him as if he had unwittingly touched the wound, of which the dying frame of Nature was expiring in its agony. He started up to fly; for he had already heard of the mysterious mandrake-root, which, when torn, yields such heart-rending moans, that the person who has hurt it runs distracted by its wailing. As he turned to go, a stranger man was standing at his back, who looked at him with a friendly countenance, and asked him whither he was going. Christian had been longing for society, and yet he started in alarm at this friendly presence.

"Whither so fast?" said the stranger again.

The young hunter made an effort to collect himself, and told how all at once the solitude had seemed so frightful to him, he had meant to get away; the evening was so dark, the green shades of the wood so dreary, the brook seemed uttering lamentations, and his longing drew him over to the other side of the hills.

"You are but young," said the stranger, "and cannot yet endure the rigour of solitude: I will accompany you, for you will find no house or hamlet within a league of this; and in the way we may talk, and tell each other tales, and so your sad thoughts will leave you: in an hour the moon will rise behind the hills; its light also will help to chase away the darkness of your mind."

They went along, and the stranger soon appeared to Christian as if he had been an old acquaintance. "Who are you?" said the man; "by your speech I hear that you belong not to this part."

"Ah!" replied the other, "upon this I could say much, and yet it is not worth the telling you, or talking of. There was something dragged me, with a foreign force, from the circle of my parents and relations; my spirit was not master of itself: like a bird which is taken in a net, and struggles to no purpose, so my soul was meshed in strange imaginations and desires. We dwelt far hence, in a plain, where all round you could see no hill, scarce even a height: few trees adorned the green level; but meadows, fertile corn-fields, gardens stretched away as far as the eye could reach; and a broad river glittered like a potent spirit through the midst of them. My father was gardener to a nobleman, and meant to breed me to the same employment. He delighted in plants and flowers beyond aught else, and could unweariedly pass day by day in watching them and tending them. Nay he went so far as to maintain, that he could almost speak with them; that he got knowledge from their growth and spreading, as well as from the varied form and colour of their leaves. To me, however, gardening was a tiresome occupation; and the more so as my father kept persuading me to take it up, or even attempted to compel me to it with threats. I wished to be a fisherman, and tried that business for a time; but a life on the waters would not suit me: I was then apprenticed to a tradesman in the town; but soon came home from this employment also. My father happened

to be talking of the Mountains, which he had travelled over in his
youth; of the subterranean mines and their workmen; of hunters
and their occupation; and that instant there arose in me the most
decided wish, the feeling that at last I had found out the way of life
which would entirely fit me. Day and night I meditated on the
matter; representing to myself high mountains, chasms and pine-
forests; my imagination shaped wild rocks; I heard the tumult of the
chase, the horns, the cry of the hounds and the game; all my dreams
were filled with these things, and they left me neither peace nor rest
any more. The plain, our patron's castle, and my father's little
hampered garden, with its trimmed flower-beds; our narrow dwelling;
the wide sky which stretched above us in its dreary vastness, embracing
no hill, no lofty mountain, all became more dull and odious to me.
It seemed as if the people about me were living in most lamentable
ignorance; that every one of them would think and long as I did,
should the feeling of their wretchedness but once arise within their
souls. Thus did I bait my heart with restless fancies; till one morning
I resolved on leaving my father's house directly and forever. In a
book I had found some notice of the nearest mountains, some charts
of the neighbouring districts, and by them I shaped my course. It
was early in spring, and I felt myself cheerful, and altogether light
of heart. I hastened on, to get away the faster from the level country;
and one evening, in the distance, I descried the dim outline of the
Mountains, lying on the sky before me. I could scarcely sleep in my
inn, so impatient did I feel to have my foot upon the region which
I regarded as my home: with the earliest dawn I was awake, and
again in motion. By the afternoon, I had got among my beloved
hills; and here, as if intoxicated, I went on, then stopped a while,
looked back; and drank, as in inspiring draughts, the aspect of these
foreign yet well-known objects. Ere long, the plain was out of sight;
the forest-streams were rushing down to meet me; the oaks and
beeches sounded to me from their steep precipices with wavering
boughs; my path led me by the edge of dizzy abysses; blue hills were
standing vast and solemn in the distance. A new world was opened
to me; I was never weary. Thus, after some days, having roamed
over great part of the Mountains, I reached the dwelling of an
old forester, who consented, at my urgent request, to take me in,
and instruct me in the business of the chase. It is now three months
since I entered his service. I took possession of the district where I
was to live, as of my kingdom. I got acquainted with every cliff and
dell among the mountains; in my occupation, when at dawn of day

we moved to the forest, when felling trees in the wood, when practising my fowling-piece, or training my trusty attendants, our dogs, to do their feats, I felt completely happy. But for the last eight days I have stayed up here at the fowling-floor, in the loneliest quarter of the hills; and tonight I grew so sad as I never was in my life before; I seemed so lost, so utterly unhappy; and even yet I cannot shake aside that melancholy humour."

The stranger had listened with attention, while they both wandered on through a dark alley of the wood. They now came out into the open country, and the light of the moon, which was standing with its horns over the summit of the hill, saluted them like a friend. In undistinguishable forms, and many separated masses, which the pale gleam again perplexingly combined, lay the cleft mountain-range before them; in the background a steep hill, on the top of which an antique weathered ruin rose ghastly in the white light. "Our roads part here," said the stranger; "I am going down into this hollow; there, by that old mine-shaft, is my dwelling: the metal ores are my neighbours; the mine-streams tell me wonders in the night; thither thou canst not follow me. But look, there stands the Runenberg, with its wild ragged walls; how beautiful and alluring the grim old rock looks down on us! Wert thou never there?"

"Never," said the hunter. "Once I heard my old forester relating strange stories of that hill, which I, like a fool, have forgotten; only I remember that my mind that night was full of dread and unearthly notions. I could like to mount the hill some time; for the colours there are of the fairest, the grass must be very green, the world around one very strange; who knows, too, but one might chance to find some curious relic of the ancient time up there?"

"You could scarcely fail," replied the stranger; "whoever knows how to seek, whoever feels his heart drawn towards it with a right inward longing, will find friends of former ages there, and glorious things, and all that he wishes most." With these words the stranger rapidly descended to a side, without bidding his companion farewell; he soon vanished in the tangles of the thicket, and after some few instants, the sound of his footsteps also died away. The young hunter did not feel surprised, he but went on with quicker speed towards the Runenberg: thither all things seemed to beckon him; the stars were shining towards it; the moon pointed out as it were a bright road to the ruins; light clouds rose up to them; and from the depths, the waters and sounding woods spoke new courage into him. His steps were as if winged; his heart throbbed; he felt so great a joy within him, that it rose to pain. He came into places he had never seen before; the rocks grew steeper; the green disappeared; the bald cliffs called to him, as with angry voices, and a lone moaning wind drove him on before it. Thus he hurried forward without pause; and late after midnight he came upon a narrow footpath, which ran along by the brink of an abyss. He heeded not the depth which yawned beneath, and threatened to swallow him forever; so keenly was he driven along by wild imaginations and vague wishes. At last his perilous track led him close by a high wall, which seemed to lose itself in the clouds; the path grew narrower every step; and Christian had to cling by projecting stones to keep himself from rushing down into the gulf. Ere long, he could get no farther; his path ended underneath a window: he was obliged to pause, and knew not whether he should turn or stay. Suddenly he saw a light, which seemed to move within the ruined edifice. He looked towards the gleam; and found that he could see into an ancient spacious hall, strangely decorated, and glittering in manifold splendour, with multitudes of precious stones and crystals, the hues of which played through each other in mysterious changes, as the light moved to and fro; and this was in the hand of a stately female, who kept walking with a thoughtful aspect up and down the apartment. She seemed of a different race from mortals; so large, so strong was her form, so earnest her look; yet the enraptured huntsman thought he had never seen or fancied such surpassing beauty. He trembled, yet secretly wished she might come near the window and observe him. At last she stopped, set down the light on a crystal table, looked aloft, and sang with a piercing voice:

> What can the Ancient keep
> That they come not at my call?
> The crystal pillars weep,
> From the diamonds on the wall
> The trickling tear-drops fall;
> And within is heard a moan,
> A chiding fitful tone:
> In these waves of brightness,
> Lovely changeful lightness,
> Has the Shape been form'd,
> By which the soul is charm'd,
> And the longing heart is warm'd.
> Come, ye Spirits, at my call,

Haste ye to the Golden Hall;
Raise, from your abysses gloomy,
Heads that sparkle; faster
Come, ye Ancient Ones, come to me!
Let your power be master
Of the longing hearts and souls,
Where the flood of passion rolls,
Let your power be master!

On finishing the song, she began undressing; laying her apparel in a costly press. First, she took a golden veil from her head; and her long black hair streamed down in curling fulness over her loins: then she loosed her bosom-dress; and the youth forgot himself and all the world in gazing at that more than earthly beauty. He scarcely dared to breathe, as by degrees she laid aside her other garments: at last she walked about the chamber naked; and her heavy waving locks formed round her, as it were, a dark billowy sea, out of which, like marble, the glancing limbs of her form beamed forth, in alternating splendour. After a while, she went forward to another golden press; and took from it a tablet, glittering with many inlaid stones, rubies, diamonds and all kinds of jewels; and viewed it long with an investigating look. The tablet seemed to form a strange inexplicable figure, from its individual lines and colours; sometimes, when the glance of it came towards the hunter, he was painfully dazzled by it; then, again, soft green and blue playing over it, refreshed his eye: he stood, however, devouring the objects with his looks, and at the same time sunk in deep thought. Within his soul, an abyss of forms and harmony, of longing and voluptuousness, was opened: hosts of winged tones, and sad and joyful melodies flew through his spirit, which was moved to its foundations: he saw a world of Pain and Hope arise within him; strong towering crags of Trust and defiant Confidence, and deep rivers of Sadness flowing by. He no longer knew himself: and he started as the fair woman opened the window; handed him the magic tablet of stones, and spoke these words: "Take this in memory of me!" He caught the tablet; and felt the figure, which, unseen, at once went through his inmost heart; and the light, and the fair woman, and the wondrous hall, had disappeared. As it were, a dark night, with curtains of cloud, fell down over his soul: he searched for his former feelings, for that inspiration and unutterable love; he looked at the precious tablet, and the sinking moon was imaged in it faint and bluish.

He had still the tablet firmly grasped in his hands when the morning dawned; and he, exhausted, giddy and half-asleep, fell headlong down the precipice.——

The sun shone bright on the face of the stupefied sleeper; and, awakening, he found himself upon a pleasant hill. He looked round, and saw far behind him, and scarce discernible at the extreme horizon, the ruins of the Runenberg; he searched for his tablet, and could find it nowhere. Astonished and perplexed, he tried to gather his thoughts, and connect together his remembrances; but his memory was as if filled with a waste haze, in which vague irrecognisable shapes were wildly jostling to and fro. His whole previous life lay behind him, as in a far distance; the strangest and the commonest were so mingled, that all his efforts could not separate them. After long struggling with himself, he at last concluded that a dream, or sudden madness, had come over him that night; only he could never understand how he had strayed so far into a strange and remote quarter.

Still scarcely waking, he went down the hill; and came upon a beaten way, which led him out from the mountains into the plain country. All was strange to him: he at first thought that he would find his old home; but the country which he saw was quite unknown to him; and at length he concluded that he must be upon the south side of the Mountains, which, in spring, he had entered from the north. Towards noon, he perceived a little town below him: from its cottages a peaceful smoke was mounting up; children, dressed as for a holiday, were sporting on the green; and from a small church came the sound of the organ, and the singing of the congregation. All this laid hold of him with a sweet, inexpressible sadness; it so moved him, that he was forced to weep. The narrow gardens, the little huts with their smoking chimneys, the accurately-parted corn-fields, reminded him of the necessities of poor human nature; of man's dependence on the friendly Earth, to whose benignity he must commit himself; while the singing, and the music of the organ, filled the stranger's heart with a devoutness it had never felt before. The desires and emotions of the bygone night seemed reckless and wicked; he wished once more, in childlike meekness, helplessly and humbly to unite himself to men as to his brethren, and fly from his ungodly purposes and feelings. The plain, with its little river, which, in manifold windings, clasped itself about the gardens and meadows, seemed to him inviting and delightful: he thought with fear of his abode among the lonely mountains amid waste rocks; he wished that he could be allowed to live in this peaceful village; and so feeling, he went into its crowded church.

The psalm was just over, and the preacher had begun his sermon. It was on the kindness of God in regard to Harvest; how His goodness feeds and satisfies all things that live; how marvellously He has, in the fruits of the Earth, provided support for men; how the love of God incessantly displays itself in the bread He sends us; and how the humble Christian may therefore, with a thankful spirit, perpetually celebrate a Holy Supper. The congregation were affected; the eyes of the hunter rested on the pious priest, and observed, close by the pulpit, a young maiden, who appeared beyond all others reverent and attentive. She was slim and fair; her blue eye gleamed with the most piercing softness; her face was as if transparent, and blooming in the tenderest colours. The stranger youth had never been as he now was; so full of charity, so calm, so abandoned to the stillest, most refreshing feelings. He bowed himself in tears, when the clergyman pronounced his blessing; he felt these holy words thrill through him like an unseen power; and the vision of the night drew back before them to the deepest distance, as a spectre at the dawn. He issued from the church; stopped beneath a large lime-tree; and thanked God, in a heartfelt prayer, that He had saved him, sinful and undeserving, from the nets of the Wicked Spirit.

The people were engaged in holding harvest-home that day, and every one was in a cheerful mood; the children, with their gay dresses, were rejoicing in the prospect of the sweetmeats and the dance; in the village square, a space encircled with young trees, the youths were arranging the preparations for their harvest sport; the players were seated, and essaying their instruments. Christian went into the fields again, to collect his thoughts and pursue his meditations; and on his returning to the village, all had joined in mirth, and actual celebration of their festival. The fair-haired Elizabeth was there, too, with her parents; and the stranger mingled in the jocund throng. Elizabeth was dancing; and Christian, in the mean time, had entered into conversation with her father, a farmer, and one of the richest people in the village. The man seemed pleased with his youth and way of speech; so, in a short time, both of them agreed that Christian should remain with him as gardener. This office Christian could engage with; for he hoped that now the knowledge and employments, which he had so much despised at home, would stand him in good stead.

From this period a new life began for him. He went to live with the farmer, and was numbered among his family. With his trade, he likewise changed his garb. He was so good, so helpful and kindly; he stood to his task so honestly, that ere long every member of the house, especially the daughter, had a friendly feeling to him. Every Sunday, when he saw her going to church, he was standing with a fair nosegay ready for Elizabeth; and then she used to thank him with blushing kindliness: he felt her absence, on days when he did not chance to see her; and at night, she would tell him tales and pleasant histories. Day by day they grew more necessary to each other; and the parents, who observed it, did not seem to think it wrong; for Christian was the most industrious and handsomest youth in the village. They themselves had, at first sight, felt a touch of love and friendship for him. After half a year, Elizabeth became his wife. Spring was come back; the swallows and the singing-birds had revisited the land; the garden was standing in its fairest trim; the marriage was celebrated with abundant mirth; bride and bridegroom seemed intoxicated with their happiness. Late at night, when they retired to their chamber, the husband whispered to his wife: "No, thou art not that form which once charmed me in a dream, and which I never can entirely forget; but I am happy beside thee, and blessed that thou art mine."

How delighted was the family, when, within a year, it became augmented by a little daughter, who was baptised Leonora. Christian's looks, indeed, would sometimes take a rather grave expression as he gazed on the child; but his youthful cheeriness continually returned. He scarcely ever thought of his former way of life, for he felt himself entirely domesticated and contented. Yet, some months afterwards, his parents came into his mind; and he thought how much his father, in particular, would be rejoiced to see his peaceful happiness, his station as husbandman and gardener; it grieved him that he should have utterly forgotten his father and mother for so long a time; his own only child made known to him the joy which children afford to parents; so at last he took the resolution to set out, and again revisit home.

Unwillingly he left his wife; all wished him speed; and the season being fine, he went off on foot. Already at the distance of a few miles, he felt how much the parting grieved him; for the first time in his life, he experienced the pains of separation; the foreign objects seemed to him almost savage; he felt as if he had been lost in some unfriendly solitude. Then the thought came on him, that his youth was over; that he had found a home to which he now belonged, in which his heart had taken root; he was almost ready to lament the lost levity of younger years; and his mind was in the saddest mood, when he turned aside into a village inn to pass the night. He could not understand how he had come to leave his kind wife, and the parents she had given him; and he felt dispirited and discontented, when he rose next morning to pursue his journey.

His pain increased as he approached the hills: the distant ruins were already visible, and by degrees grew more distinguishable; many summits rose defined and clear amid the blue vapour. His step grew timid; frequently he paused, astonished at his fear; at the horror which, with every step, fell closer on him. "Madness!" cried he, "I know thee well, and thy perilous seductions; but I will withstand thee manfully. Elizabeth is no vain dream; I know that even now she thinks of me, that she waits for me, and fondly counts the hours of my absence. Do I not already see forests like black hair before me? Do not the glancing eyes look to me from the brook? Does not the stately form step towards me from the mountains?" So saying, he was about to lay himself beneath a tree, and take some rest; when he perceived an old man seated in the shade of it, examining a flower with extreme attention; now holding it to the sun, now shading it with his hands, now counting its leaves; as if striving in every way to stamp it accurately in his memory. On approaching nearer, he thought he knew the form; and soon no doubt remained that the old man with the flower was his father. With an exclamation of the liveliest joy, he rushed into his arms; the old man seemed delighted, but not much surprised, at meeting him so suddenly.

"Art thou with me already, my son?" said he: "I knew that I should find thee soon, but I did not think such joy had been in store for me this very day."

"How did you know, father, that you would meet me?"

"By this flower," replied the old gardener; "all my days I have had a wish to see it; but never had I the fortune; for it is very scarce, and grows only among the mountains. I set out to seek thee, for thy mother is dead, and the loneliness at home made me sad and heavy. I knew not whither I should turn my steps; at last I came among the mountains, dreary as the journey through them had appeared to me. By the road, I sought for this flower, but could find it nowhere; and now, quite unexpectedly, I see it here, where the fair plain is lying stretched before me. From this I knew that I should meet thee soon; and, lo, how true the fair flower's prophecy has proved!"

They embraced again, and Christian wept for his mother; but the old man grasped his hand, and said: "Let us go, that the shadows of the mountains may be soon out of view; it always makes me sorrowful in the heart to see these wild steep shapes, these horrid chasms, these torrents gurgling down into their caverns. Let us get upon the good, kind, guileless level ground again."

They went back, and Christian recovered his cheerfulness. He told his father of his new fortune, of his child and home: his speech made himself as if intoxicated; and he now, in talking of it, for the first time truly felt that nothing more was wanting to his happiness. Thus, amid narrations sad and cheerful, they returned into the village. All were delighted at the speedy ending of the journey; most of all, Elizabeth. The old father stayed with them, and joined his little fortune to their stock; they formed the most contented and united circle in the world. Their crops were good, their cattle throve; and in a few years Christian's house was among the wealthiest in the quarter. Elizabeth had also given him several other children.

Five years had passed away in this manner, when a stranger halted from his journey in their village; and took up his lodging in Christian's house, as being the most respectable the place contained. He was a friendly, talking man; he told them many stories of his travels; sported with the children, and made presents to them: in a short time, all were growing fond of him. He liked the neighbourhood so well, that he proposed remaining in it for a day or two; but the days grew weeks, and the weeks months. No one seemed to wonder at his loitering; for all of them had grown accustomed to regard him as a member of the family. Christian alone would often sit in a thoughtful mood; for it seemed to him as if he knew this traveller of old, and yet he could not think of any time when he had met with him. Three months had passed away, when the stranger at last took his leave, and said: "My dear friends, a wondrous destiny, and singular anticipations, drive me to the neighbouring mountains; a magic image, not to be withstood, allures me: I leave you now, and I know not whether I shall ever see you any more. I have a sum of money by me, which in your hands will be safer than in mine; so I ask you to take charge of it; and if within a year I come not back, then keep it, and accept my thanks along with it for the kindness you have shown me."

So the traveller went his way, and Christian took the money in charge. He locked it carefully up; and now and then, in the excess of his anxiety, looked over it; he counted it to see that none was missing, and in all respects took no little pains with it. "This sum might make us very happy," said he once to his father; "should the stranger not return, both we and our children were well provided for."

. "Heed not the gold," said the old man; "not in it can happiness be found: hitherto, thank God, we have never wanted aught; and do thou put away such thoughts far from thee."

Christian often rose in the night to set his servants to their labour, and look after everything himself: his father was afraid lest this excessive diligence might harm his youth and health; so one night he rose to speak with him about remitting such unreasonable efforts; when, to his astonishment, he found him sitting with a little lamp at his table, and counting, with the greatest eagerness, the stranger's gold. "My son," said the old man, full of sadness, "must it come to this with thee? Was this accursed metal brought beneath our roof to make us wretched? Bethink thee, my son, or the Evil One will consume thy blood and life out of thee."

"Yes," replied he; "it is true, I know myself no more; neither day nor night does it give me any rest: see how it looks on me even now, till the red glance of it goes into my very heart! Hark how it clinks, this golden stuff! It calls me when I sleep; I hear it when music sounds, when the wind blows, when people speak together on the street; if the sun shines, I see nothing but these yellow eyes, with which it beckons to me, as it were, to whisper words of love into my ear: and therefore I am forced to rise in the night-time, though it were but to satisfy its eagerness; and then I feel it triumphing and inwardly rejoicing when I touch it with my fingers; in its joy it grows still redder and lordlier. Do but look yourself at the glow of its rapture!" The old man, shuddering and weeping, took his son in his arms; he said a prayer, and then spoke: "Christel, thou must turn again to the Word of God; thou must go more zealously and reverently to church, or else, alas! my poor child, thou wilt droop and die away in the most mournful wretchedness."

The money was again locked up; Christian promised to take thought and change his conduct, and the old man was composed. A year and more had passed, and no tidings had been heard of the stranger: the old man at last gave in to the entreaties of his son; and the money was laid out in land, and other property. The young farmer's riches soon became the talk of the village; and Christian seemed contented and comfortable, and his father felt delighted at beholding him so well and cheerful; all fear had now vanished from his mind. What then must have been his consternation, when Elizabeth one evening took him aside; and told him, with tears, that she could no longer understand her husband; how he spoke so wildly, especially at night; how he dreamed strange dreams, and would often in his sleep walk long about the room, not knowing it; how he spoke strange things to her, at which she often shuddered. But what terrified her most, she said, was his pleasantry by day; for his laugh was wild and hollow, his look wandering and strange. The father stood amazed, and the sorrowing wife proceeded: "He is always talking of the traveller, and maintaining that he knew him formerly, and that the stranger man was in truth a woman of unearthly beauty; nor will he go any more into the fields or the garden to work, for he says he hears underneath the ground a fearful moaning when he but pulls out a root; he starts and seems to feel a horror at all plants and herbs."

"Good God!" exclaimed the father, "is the frightful hunger in him grown so rooted and strong, that it is come to this? Then is his spell-bound heart no longer human, but of cold metal; he who does not love a flower, has lost all love and fear of God."

Next day the old man went to walk with his son, and told him much of what Elizabeth had said; calling on him to be pious, and devote his soul to holy contemplations. "Willingly, my father," answered Christian; "and I often do so with success, and all is well with me: for long periods of time, for years, I can forget the true form of my inward man, and lead a life that is foreign to me, as it were, with cheerfulness: but then on a sudden, like a new moon, the ruling star, which I myself am, arises again in my heart, and conquers this other influence. I might be altogether happy; but once, in a mysterious night, a secret sign was imprinted through my hand deep on my soul; frequently the magic figure sleeps and is at rest; I imagine it has passed away; but in a moment, like a poison, it darts up and lives over all its lineaments. And then I can think or feel nothing else but it; and all around me is transformed, or rather swallowed up, by this subduing shape. As the rabid man recoils at the sight of water, and the poison in him grows more fell; so too it is with me at the sight of any cornered figure, any line, any gleam of brightness; anything will then rouse the form that dwells in me, and make it start into being; and my soul and body feel the throes of birth; for as my mind received it by a feeling from without, she strives in agony and bitter labour to work it forth again into an outward feeling, that she may be rid of it, and at rest."

"It was an evil star that took thee from us to the Mountains," said the old man; "thou wert born for calm life, thy mind inclined to peace and the love of plants; then thy impatience hurried thee away to the company of savage stones: the crags, the torn cliffs, with their jagged shapes, have overturned thy soul, and planted in thee the wasting hunger for metals. Thou shouldst still have been on thy guard, and kept thyself away from the view of mountains; so I meant to bring thee up, but it has not so been to be. Thy humility, thy peace, thy childlike feeling, have been thrust away by scorn, boisterousness and caprice."

"No," said the son; "I remember well that it was a plant which first made known to me the misery of the Earth; never, till then, did I understand the sighs and lamentations one may hear on every side, throughout the whole of Nature, if one but give ear to them. In plants and herbs, in trees and flowers, it is the painful writhing of one universal wound that moves and works; they are the corpse of foregone glorious worlds of rock, they offer to our eye a horrid universe of putrefaction. I now see clearly it was this, which the root with its deep-drawn sigh was saying to me; in its sorrow it forgot itself, and told me all. It is because of this that all green shrubs are so enraged at me, and lie in wait for my life; they wish to obliterate that lovely figure in my heart; and every spring, with their distorted deathlike looks, they try to win my soul. Truly it is piteous to consider how they have betrayed and cozened thee, old man; for they have gained complete possession of thy spirit. Do but question the rocks, and thou wilt be amazed when thou shalt hear them speak."

The father looked at him a long while, and could answer nothing. They went home again in silence, and the old man was as frightened as Elizabeth at Christian's mirth; for it seemed a thing quite foreign; and as if another being from within were working out of him, awkwardly and ineffectually, as out of some machine.

The harvest-home was once more to be held; the people went to church, and Elizabeth, with her little ones, set out to join the service; her husband also seemed intending to accompany them, but at the threshold of the church he turned aside; and with an air of deep thought, walked out of the village. He set himself on the height, and again looked over upon the smoking cottages; he heard the music of the psalm and organ coming from the little church; children, in holiday dresses, were dancing and sporting on the green. "How have I lost my life as in a dream!" said he to himself: "years have passed away since I went down this hill to the merry children; they who were then sportful on the green, are now serious in the church; I also once went into it, but Elizabeth is now no more a blooming childlike maiden; her youth is gone; I cannot seek for the glance of her eyes with the longing of those days; I have wilfully neglected a high eternal happiness, to win one which is finite and transitory."

With a heart full of wild desire, he walked to the neighbouring wood, and immersed himself in its thickest shades. A ghastly silence encompassed him; no breath of air was stirring in the leaves. Meanwhile he saw a man approaching him from a distance, whom he recognised for the stranger; he started in affright, and his first thought was, that the man would ask him for his money. But as the form came nearer, he perceived how greatly he had been mistaken; for the features, which he had imagined known to him, melted into one another; an old woman of the utmost hideousness approached; she was clad in dirty rags; a tattered clout bound up her few gray hairs; she was limping on a crutch. With a dreadful voice she spoke to him, and asked his name and situation; he replied to both inquiries, and then said, "But who art thou?"

"I am called the Woodwoman," answered she; "and every child can tell of me. Didst thou never see me before?" With the last words she whirled about, and Christian thought he recognised among the trees the golden veil, the lofty gait, the large stately form which he had once beheld of old. He turned to hasten after her, but nowhere was she to be seen.

Meanwhile something glittered in the grass, and drew his eye to it. He picked it up; it was the magic tablet with the coloured jewels, and the wondrous figure, which he had lost so many years before. The shape and the changeful gleams struck over all his senses with an instantaneous power. He grasped it firmly, to convince himself that it was really once more in his hands, and then hastened back with it to the village. His father met him. "See," cried Christian, "the thing which I was telling you about so often, which I thought must have been shown to me only in a dream, is now sure and true."

The old man looked a long while at the tablet, and then said: "My son, I am struck with horror in my heart when I view these stones, and dimly guess the meaning of the words on them. Look here, how cold they glitter, what cruel looks they cast from them, bloodthirsty, like the red eye of the tiger! Cast this writing from thee, which makes thee cold and cruel, which will turn thy heart to stone:

> See the flowers, when morn is beaming,
>   Waken in their dewy place;
> And, like children roused from dreaming,
>   Smiling look thee in the face.

By degrees, that way and this,
    To the golden Sun they're turning,
Till they meet his glowing kiss,
    And their hearts with love are burning:

For, with fond and sad desire,
    In their lover's looks to languish,
On his melting kisses to expire,
    And to die of love's sweet anguish:

This is what they joy in most;
    To depart in fondest weakness;
In their lover's being lost,
    Faded stand in silent meekness.

Then they pour away the treasure
    Of their perfumes, their soft souls,
And the air grows drunk with pleasure,
    As in wanton floods it rolls.

Love comes to us here below,
    Discord harsh away removing;
And the heart cries: Now I know
    Sadness, Fondness, Pain of Loving."

"What wonderful incalculable treasures," said the other, "must there still be in the depths of the Earth! Could one but sound into their secret beds and raise them up, and snatch them to one's-self! Could one but clasp this Earth like a beloved bride to one's bosom, so that in pain and love she would willingly grant one her costliest riches! The Woodwoman has called me; I go to seek for her. Near by is an old ruined shaft, which some miner has hollowed out many centuries ago; perhaps I shall find her there!"

He hastened off. In vain did the old man strive to detain him; in a few moments Christian had vanished from his sight. Some hours afterwards, the father, with a strong effort, reached the ruined shaft: he saw footprints in the sand at the entrance, and returned in tears; persuaded that his son, in a state of madness, had gone in and been drowned in the old collected waters and horrid caves of the mine.

From that day his heart seemed broken, and he was incessantly in tears. The whole neighbourhood deplored the fortune of the young farmer. Elizabeth was inconsolable, the children lamented aloud. In half a year the aged gardener died; the parents of Elizabeth soon followed him; and she was forced herself to take charge of everything. Her multiplied engagements helped a little to withdraw her from her sorrow; the education of her children, and the management of so much property, left little time for mourning. After two years, she determined on a new marriage; she bestowed her hand on a young light-hearted man, who had loved her from his youth. But, ere long, everything in their establishment assumed another form. The cattle died; men and maid servants proved dishonest; barns full of grain were burnt; people in the town who owed them sums of money, fled and made no payment. In a little while, the landlord found himself obliged to sell some fields and meadows; but a mildew, and a year of scarcity, brought new embarrassments. It seemed as if the gold, so strangely acquired, were taking speedy flight in all directions. Meanwhile the family was on the increase; and Elizabeth, as well as her husband, grew reckless and sluggish in this scene of despair: he fled for consolation to the bottle, he was often drunk, and therefore quarrelsome and sullen; so that frequently Elizabeth bewailed her state with bitter tears. As their fortune declined, their friends in the village stood aloof from them more and more; so that after some few years they saw themselves entirely forsaken, and were forced to struggle on, in penury and straits, from week to week.

They had nothing but a cow and a few sheep left them; these Elizabeth herself, with her children, often tended at their grass. She was sitting one day with her work in the field, Leonora at her side, and a sucking child on her breast, when they saw from afar a strange-looking shape approaching towards them. It was a man with a garment all in tatters, barefoot, sunburnt to a black-brown colour in the face, deformed still farther by a long matted beard: he wore no covering on his head; but had twisted a garland of green branches through his hair, which made his wild appearance still more strange and haggard. On his back he bore some heavy burden in a sack, very carefully tied, and as he walked he leaned upon a young fir.

On coming nearer, he put down his load, and drew deep draughts of breath. He bade Elizabeth good-day; she shuddered at the sight of him, the girl crouched close to her mother. Having rested for a little while, he said: "I am getting back from a very hard journey among the wildest mountains of the Earth; but to pay me for it, I have brought along with me the richest treasures which imagination can conceive, or heart desire. Look here, and wonder!" Thereupon he loosed his sack, and shook it empty: it was full of gravel, among which were to be seen large bits of chuck-stone, and other pebbles. "These jewels," he continued, "are not ground and polished yet, so they want the glance and the eye; the outward fire, with its glitter, is too deeply buried in their inmost heart; yet you have but to strike it out and frighten them, and show that no deceit will serve, and then you see what sort of stuff they are." So saying, he took a piece of flinty stone, and struck it hard against another, till they gave red sparks between them. "Did you see the glance?" cried he. "Ay, they are all fire and light; they illuminate the darkness with their laugh, though as yet it is against their will." With this he carefully repacked his pebbles in the bag, and tied it hard and fast. "I know thee very well," said he then, with a saddened tone; "thou art Elizabeth." The woman started.

"How comest thou to know my name?" cried she, with a forecasting shudder.

"Ah, good God!" said the unhappy creature, "I am Christian, he that was a hunter: dost thou not know me, then?"

She knew not, in her horror and deepest compassion, what to say. He fell upon her neck and kissed her. Elizabeth exclaimed: "O Heaven! my husband is coming!"

"Be at thy ease," said he; "I am as good as dead to thee: in the forest, there, my fair one waits for me; she that is tall and stately, with the black hair and the golden veil. This is my dearest child, Leonora. Come hither, darling: come, my pretty child; and give me a kiss, too; one kiss, that I may feel thy mouth upon my lips once again, and then I leave you."

Leonora wept; she clasped close to her mother, who, in sobs and tears, half held her towards the wanderer, while he half drew her towards him, took her in his arms, and pressed her to his breast. Then he went away in silence, and in the wood they saw him speaking with the hideous Woodwoman.

"What ails you?" said the husband, as he found mother and daughter pale and melting in tears. Neither of them answered.

The ill-fated creature was never seen again from that day.

THE ELVES

"WHERE IS OUR little Mary?" said the father.

"She is playing out upon the green there with our neighbour's boy," replied the mother.

"I wish they may not run away and lose themselves," said he; "they are so thoughtless."

The mother looked for the little ones, and brought them their evening luncheon. "It is warm," said the boy; "and Mary had a longing for the red cherries."

"Have a care, children," said the mother, "and do not run too far from home, and not into the wood; Father and I are going to the fields."

Little Andres answered: "Never fear, the wood frightens us; we shall sit here by the house, where there are people near us."

The mother went in, and soon came out again with her husband. They locked the door, and turned towards the fields to look after their labourers, and see their hay-harvest in the meadow. Their house lay upon a little green height, encircled by a pretty ring of paling, which likewise enclosed their fruit and flower garden. The hamlet stretched somewhat deeper down, and on the other side lay the castle of the Count. Martin rented the large farm from this nobleman; and was living in contentment with his wife and only child; for he yearly saved some money, and had the prospect of becoming a man of substance by his industry, for the ground was productive, and the Count not illiberal.

As he walked with his wife to the fields, he gazed cheerfully round, and said: "What a different look this quarter has, Brigitta, from the place we lived in formerly! Here it is all so green; the whole village is bedecked with thick-spreading fruit-trees; the ground is full of beautiful herbs and flowers; all the houses are cheerful and cleanly, the inhabitants are at their ease: nay I could almost fancy that the woods are greener here than elsewhere, and the sky bluer; and, so far as the eye can reach, you have pleasure and delight in beholding the bountiful Earth."

"And whenever you cross the stream," said Brigitta, "you are, as it were, in another world, all is so dreary and withered; but every traveller declares that our village is the fairest in the country far and near."

"All but that fir-ground," said her husband; "do but look back to it, how dark and dismal that solitary spot is lying in the gay scene: the dingy fir-trees with the smoky huts behind them, the ruined stalls, the brook flowing past with a sluggish melancholy."

"It is true," replied Brigitta; "if you but approach that spot, you grow disconsolate and sad, you know not why. What sort of people can they be that live there, and keep themselves so separate from the rest of us, as if they had an evil conscience?"

"A miserable crew," replied the young Farmer: "gipsies, seemingly, that steal and cheat in other quarters, and have their hoard and hiding-place here. I wonder only that his Lordship suffers them."

"Who knows," said the wife, with an accent of pity, "but perhaps they may be poor people, wishing, out of shame, to conceal their poverty; for, after all, no one can say aught ill of them; the only thing is, that they do not go to church, and none knows how they live; for the little garden, which indeed seems altogether waste, cannot possibly support them; and fields they have none."

"God knows," said Martin, as they went along, "what trade they follow; no mortal comes to them; for the place they live in is as if bewitched and excommunicated, so that even our wildest fellows will not venture into it."

Such conversation they pursued, while walking to the fields. That gloomy spot they spoke of lay aside from the hamlet. In a dell, begirt with firs, you might behold a hut, and various ruined office-houses; rarely was smoke seen to mount from it, still more rarely did men appear there; though at times curious people, venturing somewhat nearer, had perceived upon the bench before the hut, some hideous women, in ragged clothes, dandling in their arms some children equally dirty and ill-favoured; black dogs were running up and down upon the boundary; and, of an evening, a man of monstrous size was seen to cross the footbridge of the brook, and disappear in the hut; and, in the darkness, various shapes were observed, moving like shadows round a fire in the open air. This piece of ground, the firs and the ruined huts, formed in truth a strange contrast with the bright green landscape, the white houses of the hamlet, and the stately new-built castle.

The two little ones had now eaten their fruit; it came into their heads to run races; and the little nimble Mary always got the start of the less active Andres. "It is not fair," cried Andres at last: "let us try it for some length, then we shall see who wins."

"As thou wilt," said Mary; "only to the brook we must not run."

"No," said Andres; "but there, on the hill, stands the large pear-tree, a quarter of a mile from this. I shall run by the left, round past the fir-ground; thou canst try it by the right over the fields; so we do not meet till we get up, and then we shall see which of us is swifter."

"Done," cried Mary, and began to run; "for we shall not mar one another by the way, and my father says it is as far to the hill by that side of the Gipsies' house as by this."

Andres had already started, and Mary, turning to the right, could no longer see him. "It is very silly," said she to herself: "I have only to take heart, and run along the bridge, past the hut, and through the yard, and I shall certainly be first." She was already standing by the brook and the clump of firs. "Shall I? No; it is too frightful," said she. A little white dog was standing on the farther side, and barking with might and main. In her terror, Mary thought the dog some monster, and sprang back. "Fy! fy!" said she: "the dolt is gone half way by this time, while I stand here considering." The little dog kept barking, and, as she looked at it more narrowly, it seemed no longer frightful, but, on the contrary, quite pretty: it had a red collar round its neck, with a glittering bell; and as it raised its head, and shook itself in barking, the little bell sounded with the finest tinkle. "Well, I must risk it!" cried she: "I will run for life; quick, quick, I am through; certainly to Heaven, they cannot eat me up alive in half a minute!" And with this, the gay, courageous little Mary sprang along the footbridge; passed the dog, which ceased its barking and began to fawn on her; and in a moment she was standing on the other bank, and the black firs all round concealed from view her father's house, and the rest of the landscape.

But what was her astonishment when here! The loveliest, most variegated flower-garden, lay round her; tulips, roses and lilies were glittering in the fairest colours; blue and gold-red butterflies were wavering in the blossoms; cages of shining wire were hung on the espaliers, with many-coloured birds in them, singing beautiful songs; and children, in short white frocks, with flowing yellow hair and brilliant eyes, were frolicking about; some playing with lambkins, some feeding the birds, or gathering flowers, and giving them to one another; some, again, were eating cherries, grapes and ruddy apricots. No hut was to be seen; but instead of it, a large fair house, with a brazen door and lofty statues, stood glancing in the middle of the space. Mary was confounded with surprise, and knew not what to think; but, not being bashful, she went right up to the first of the children, held out her hand, and wished the little creature good-even.

"Art thou come to visit us, then?" said the glittering child; "I saw thee running, playing on the other side, but thou wert frightened at our little dog."

"So you are not gipsies and rogues," said Mary, "as Andres always told me? He is a stupid thing, and talks of much he does not understand."

"Stay with us," said the strange little girl; "thou wilt like it well."

"But we are running a race."

"Thou wilt find thy comrade soon enough. There, take and eat."

Mary ate, and found the fruit more sweet than any she had ever tasted in her life before; and Andres, and the race, and the prohibition of her parents, were entirely forgotten.

A stately woman, in a shining robe, came towards them, and asked about the stranger child. "Fairest lady," said Mary, "I came running hither by chance, and now they wish to keep me."

"Thou art aware, Zerina," said the lady, "that she can be here but for a little while; besides, thou shouldst have asked my leave."

"I thought," said Zerina, "when I saw her admitted across the bridge, that I might do it; we have often seen her running in the fields, and thou thyself hast taken pleasure in her lively temper. She will have to leave us soon enough."

"No, I will stay here," said the little stranger; "for here it is so beautiful, and here I shall find the prettiest playthings, and store of berries and cherries to boot. On the other side it is not half so grand."

The gold-robed lady went away with a smile; and many of the children now came bounding round the happy Mary in their mirth, and twitched her, and incited her to dance; others brought her lambs, or curious playthings; others made music on instruments, and sang to it.

She kept, however, by the playmate who had first met her; for Zerina was the kindest and loveliest of them all. Little Mary cried and cried again: "I will stay with you forever; I will stay with you, and you shall be my sisters;" at which the children all laughed, and embraced her. "Now we shall have a royal sport," said Zerina. She ran into the Palace, and returned with a little golden box, in which lay a quantity of seeds, like glittering dust. She lifted of it with her little hand, and scattered some grains on the green earth. Instantly the grass began to move, as in waves; and, after a few moments, bright rose-bushes started from the ground, shot rapidly up, and budded all at once, while the sweetest perfume filled the place. Mary also took a little of the dust, and, having scattered it, she saw white lilies, and the most variegated pinks, pushing up. At a signal from Zerina, the flowers disappeared, and others rose in their room. "Now," said Zerina, "look for something greater." She laid two pine-seeds in the ground, and stamped them in sharply with her foot. Two green bushes stood before them. "Grasp me fast," said she; and Mary threw her arms about the slender form. She felt herself borne upwards; for the trees were springing under them with the greatest speed; the tall pines waved to and fro, and the two children held each other fast embraced, swinging this way and that in the red clouds of the twilight, and kissed each other; while the rest were climbing up and down the trunks with quick dexterity, pushing and teasing one another with loud laughter when they met; if any one fell down in the press, it flew through the air, and sank slowly and surely to the ground. At length Mary was beginning to be frightened; and the other little child sang a few loud tones, and the trees again sank down, and set them on the ground as gradually as they had lifted them before to the clouds.

They next went through the brazen door of the palace. Here many fair women, elderly and young, were sitting in the round hall, partaking of the fairest fruits, and listening to glorious invisible music. In the vaulting of the ceiling, palms, flowers and groves stood painted, among which little figures of children were sporting and winding in every graceful posture; and with the tones of the music, the images altered and glowed with the most burning colours; now the blue and green were sparkling like radiant light, now these tints faded back in paleness, the purple flamed up, and the gold took fire; and then the naked children seemed to be alive among the flower-garlands, and to draw breath, and emit it through their ruby-coloured lips; so that by fits you could see the glance of their little white teeth, and the lighting up of their azure eyes.

From the hall, a stair of brass led down to a subterranean chamber. Here lay much gold and silver, and precious stones of every hue shone out between them. Strange vessels stood along the walls, and all seemed filled with costly things. The gold was worked into many forms, and glittered with the friendliest red. Many little dwarfs were busied sorting the pieces from the heap, and putting them in the vessels; others, hunchbacked and bandylegged, with long red noses, were tottering slowly along, half-bent to the ground, under full sacks, which they bore as millers do their grain; and, with much panting, shaking out the gold-dust on the ground. Then they darted awkwardly to the right and left, and caught the rolling balls that were like to run away; and it happened now and then that one in his eagerness overset the other, so that both fell heavily and clumsily to the ground. They made angry faces, and looked askance, as Mary laughed at their gestures and their ugliness. Behind them sat an old crumpled little man, whom Zerina reverently greeted; he thanked her with a grave inclination of his head. He held a sceptre in his hand, and wore a crown upon his brow, and all the other dwarfs appeared to regard him as their master, and obey his nod.

"What more wanted?" asked he, with a surly voice, as the children came a little nearer. Mary was afraid, and did not speak; but her companion answered, they were only come to look about them in the chambers. "Still your old child's tricks!" replied the dwarf: "Will there never be an end to idleness?" With this, he turned again to his employment, kept his people weighing and sorting the ingots; some he sent away on errands, some he chid with angry tones.

"Who is the gentleman?" said Mary.

"Our Metal-Prince," replied Zerina, as they walked along.

They seemed once more to reach the open air, for they were standing by a lake, yet no sun appeared, and they saw no sky above their heads. A little boat received them, and Zerina steered it diligently forwards. It shot rapidly along. On gaining the middle of the lake, the stranger saw that multitudes of pipes, channels and brooks, were spreading from the little sea in every direction. "These waters to the right," said Zerina, "flow beneath your garden, and this is why it blooms so freshly; by the other side we get down into the great stream." On a sudden, out of all the channels, and from every quarter of the lake, came a crowd of little children swimming up; some wore garlands of sedge and water-lily; some had red stems of coral, others were blowing on crooked shells; a tumultuous noise echoed merrily from the dark shores; among the children might be seen the fairest women sporting in the waters, and often several of the children sprang about some one of them, and with kisses hung upon her neck and shoulders. All saluted the strangers; and these steered onwards through the revelry out of the lake, into a little river, which grew narrower and narrower. At last the boat came aground. The strangers took their leave, and Zerina knocked against the cliff. This opened like a door, and a female form, all red, assisted them to mount. "Are you all brisk here?" inquired Zerina. "They are just at work," replied the other, "and happy as they could wish; indeed, the heat is very pleasant."

They went up a winding stair, and on a sudden Mary found herself in a most resplendent hall, so that as she entered, her eyes were dazzled by the radiance. Flame-coloured tapestry covered the walls with a purple glow; and when her eye had grown a little used to it, the stranger saw, to her astonishment, that, in the tapestry, there were figures moving up and down in dancing joyfulness; in form so beautiful, and of so fair proportions, that nothing could be seen more graceful; their bodies were as of red crystal, so that it appeared as if the blood were visible within them, flowing and playing in its courses. They smiled on the stranger, and saluted her with various bows; but as Mary was about approaching nearer them, Zerina plucked her sharply back, crying: "Thou wilt burn thyself, my little Mary, for the whole of it is fire."

Mary felt the heat. "Why do the pretty creatures not come out," said she, "and play with us?"

"As thou livest in the Air," replied the other, "so are they obliged to stay continually in Fire, and would faint and languish if they left it. Look now, how glad they are, how they laugh and shout; those down below spread out the fire-floods everywhere beneath the earth, and thereby the flowers, and fruits, and wine, are made to flourish; these red streams again, are to run beside the brooks of water; and thus the fiery creatures are kept ever busy and glad. But for thee it is too hot here; let us return to the garden."

In the garden, the scene had changed since they left it. The moonshine was lying on every flower; the birds were silent, and the children were asleep in complicated groups, among the green groves. Mary and her friend, however, did not feel fatigue, but walked about in the warm summer night, in abundant talk, till morning.

When the day dawned, they refreshed themselves on fruit and milk, and Mary said: "Suppose we go, by way of change, to the firs, and see how things look there?"

"With all my heart," replied Zerina; "thou wilt see our watchmen too, and they will surely please thee; they are standing up among the trees on the mound." The two proceeded through the flower-garden by pleasant groves, full of nightingales; then they ascended a vine-hill; and at last, after long following the windings of a clear brook, arrived at the firs, and the height which bounded the domain. "How does it come," said Mary, "that we have to walk so far here, when without, the circuit is so narrow?"

"I know not," said her friend; "but so it is."

They mounted to the dark firs, and a chill wind blew from without in their faces; a haze seemed lying far and wide over the landscape. On the top were many strange forms standing; with mealy, dusty faces; their misshapen heads not unlike those of white owls; they were clad in folded cloaks of shaggy wool; they held umbrellas of curious skins stretched out above them; and they waved and fanned themselves incessantly with large bat's wings, which flared out curiously beside the woollen roquelaures. "I could laugh, yet I am frightened," cried Mary.

"These are our good trusty watchmen," said her playmate; "they stand here and wave their fans, that cold anxiety and inexplicable fear may fall on every one that attempts to approach us. They are covered so, because without it is now cold and rainy, which they cannot bear. But snow, or wind, or cold air, never reaches down to us; here is an everlasting spring and summer: yet if these poor people on the top were not frequently relieved, they would certainly perish."

"But who are you, then?" said Mary, while again descending to the flowery fragrance; "or have you no name at all?"

"We are called the Elves," replied the friendly child; "people talk about us in the Earth, as I have heard."

They now perceived a mighty bustle on the green. "The fair Bird is come!" cried the children to them: all hastened to the hall. Here, as they approached, young and old were crowding over the threshold, all shouting for joy; and from within resounded a triumphant peal of music. Having entered, they perceived the vast circuit filled with the most varied forms, and all were looking upwards to a large Bird with glancing plumage, that was sweeping slowly round in the dome, and in its stately flight describing many a circle. The music sounded more gaily than before; the colours and lights alternated more rapidly. At last the music ceased; and the Bird, with a rustling noise, floated down upon a glittering crown that hung hovering in air under the high window, by which the hall was lighted from above. His plumage was purple and green, and shining golden streaks played through it; on his head there waved a diadem of feathers, so resplendent that they glanced like jewels. His bill was red, and his legs of a glancing blue. As he moved, the tints gleamed through each other, and the eye was charmed with their radiance. His size was as that of an eagle. But now he opened his glittering beak; and sweetest melodies came pouring from his moved breast, in finer tones than the lovesick nightingale gives forth; still stronger rose the song, and streamed like floods of Light, so that all, the very children themselves, were moved by it to tears of joy and rapture. When he ceased, all bowed before him; he again flew round the dome in circles, then darted through the door, and soared into the light heaven, where he shone far up like a red point, and then soon vanished from their eyes.

"Why are ye all so glad?" inquired Mary, bending to her fair playmate, who seemed smaller than yesterday.

"The King is coming!" said the little one; "many of us have never seen him, and whithersoever he turns his face, there is happiness and mirth; we have long looked for him, more anxiously than you look for spring when winter lingers with you; and now he has announced, by his fair herald, that he is at hand. This wise and glorious Bird, that has been sent to us by the King, is called Phœnix; he dwells far off in Arabia, on a tree, which there is no other that resembles on Earth, as in like manner there is no second Phœnix. When he feels himself grown old, he builds a pile of balm and incense, kindles it, and dies singing; and then from the fragrant ashes, soars up the renewed Phœnix with unlessened beauty. It is seldom he so wings his course that men behold him; and when once in centuries this does occur, they note it in their annals, and expect remarkable events. But now, my friend, thou and I must part; for the sight of the King is not permitted thee."

Then the lady with the golden robe came through the throng, and beckoning Mary to her, led her into a sequestered walk. "Thou must leave us, my dear child," said she; "the King is to hold his court here for twenty years, perhaps longer; and fruitfulness and blessings will spread far over the land, but chiefly here beside us; all the brooks and rivulets will become more bountiful, all the fields and gardens richer, the wine more generous, the meadows more fertile, and the woods more fresh and green; a milder air will blow, no hail shall hurt, no flood shall threaten. Take this ring, and think of us: but beware of telling any one of our existence; or we must fly this land, and thou and all around will lose the happiness and blessing of our neighbour-hood. Once more, kiss thy playmate, and farewell." They issued from the walk; Zerina wept, Mary stooped to embrace her, and they parted.

Already she was on the narrow bridge; the cold air was blowing on her back from the firs; the little dog barked with all its might, and rang its little bell; she looked round, then hastened over, for the darkness of the firs, the bleakness of the ruined huts, the shadows of the twilight, were filling her with terror.

"What a night my parents must have had on my account!" said she within herself, as she stept on the green; "and I dare not tell them where I have been, or what wonders I have witnessed, nor indeed would they believe me." Two men passing by saluted her; and as they went along, she heard them say: "What a pretty girl! Where can she come from?" With quickened steps she approached the house: but the trees which were hanging last night loaded with fruit, were now standing dry and leafless; the house was differently painted, and a new barn had been built beside it. Mary was amazed, and thought she must be dreaming. In this perplexity she opened the door; and behind the table sat her father, between an unknown woman and a stranger youth. "Good God! Father," cried she, "where is my mother?"

"Thy mother!" said the woman, with a forecasting tone, and sprang towards her: "Ha, thou surely canst not—Yes, indeed, indeed thou art my lost, long-lost dear, only Mary!" She had recognised her by a little brown mole beneath the chin, as well as by her eyes and shape. All embraced her, all were moved with joy, and the parents wept. Mary was astonished that she almost reached to her father's stature; and she could not understand how her mother had become so changed and faded; she asked the name of the stranger youth. "It is our neighbour's Andres," said Martin. "How comest thou to us again, so unexpectedly, after seven long years? Where hast thou been? Why didst thou never send us tidings of thee?"

"Seven years!" said Mary, and could not order her ideas and recollections. "Seven whole years?"

"Yes, yes," said Andres, laughing, and shaking her trustfully by the hand; "I have won the race, good Mary; I was at the pear-tree and back again seven years ago, and thou, sluggish creature, art but just returned!"

They again asked, they pressed her; but remembering her instruction, she could answer nothing. It was they themselves chiefly that, by degrees, shaped a story for her: How, having lost her way, she had been taken up by a coach, and carried to a strange remote part, where she could not give the people any notion of her parents' residence; how she was conducted to a distant town, where certain worthy persons brought her up and loved her; how they had lately died, and at length she had recollected her birthplace, and so returned. "No matter how it is!" exclaimed her mother; "enough, that we have thee again, my little daughter, my own, my all!"

Andres waited supper, and Mary could not be at home in anything she saw. The house seemed small and dark; she felt astonished at her dress, which was clean and simple, but appeared quite foreign; she looked at the ring on her finger, and the gold of it glittered strangely, enclosing a stone of burning red. To her father's question, she replied that the ring also was a present from her benefactors.

She was glad when the hour of sleep arrived, and she hastened to her bed. Next morning she felt much more collected; she had now arranged her thoughts a little, and could better stand the questions of the people in the village, all of whom came in to bid her welcome. Andres was there too with the earliest, active, glad, and serviceable beyond all others. The blooming maiden of fifteen had made a deep impression on him; he had passed a sleepless night. The people of the castle likewise sent for Mary, and she had once more to tell her story to them, which was now grown quite familiar to her. The old Count and his Lady were surprised at her good-breeding; she was modest, but not embarrassed; she made answer courteously in good phrases to all their questions; all fear of noble persons and their equipage had passed away from her; for when she measured these halls and forms by the wonders and the high beauty she had seen with the Elves in their hidden abode, this earthly splendour seemed but dim to her, the presence of men was almost mean. The young lords were charmed with her beauty.

It was now February. The trees were budding earlier than usual; the nightingale had never come so soon; the spring rose fairer in the land than the oldest men could recollect it. In every quarter, little brooks gushed out to irrigate the pastures and meadows; the hills seemed heaving, the vines rose higher and higher, the fruit-trees blossomed as they had never done; and a swelling fragrant blessedness hung suspended heavily in rosy clouds over the scene. All prospered beyond expectation: no rude day, no tempest injured the fruits; the wine flowed blushing in immense grapes; and the inhabitants of the place felt astonished, and were captivated as in a sweet dream. The next year was like its forerunner; but men had now become accustomed to the marvellous. In autumn, Mary yielded to the pressing entreaties of Andres and her parents; she was betrothed to him, and in winter they were married.

She often thought with inward longing of her residence behind the fir-trees; she continued serious and still. Beautiful as all that lay around her was, she knew of something yet more beautiful; and from the remembrance of this, a faint regret attuned her nature to soft melancholy. It smote her painfully when her father and mother talked about the gipsies and vagabonds, that dwelt in the dark spot of ground. Often she was on the point of speaking out in defence of those good beings, whom she knew to be the benefactors of the land; especially to Andres, who appeared to take delight in zealously abusing them: yet still she repressed the word that was struggling to escape her bosom. So passed this year; in the next, she was solaced by a little daughter, whom she named Elfrida, thinking of the designation of her friendly Elves.

The young people lived with Martin and Brigitta, the house being large enough for all; and helped their parents in conducting their now extended husbandry. The little Elfrida soon displayed peculiar faculties and gifts; for she could walk at a very early age, and could speak perfectly before she was a twelvemonth old; and after some few years, she had become so wise and clever, and of such wondrous beauty, that all people regarded her with astonishment; and her mother could not keep away the thought that her child resembled one of those shining little ones in the space behind the Firs. Elfrida cared not to be with other children; but seemed to avoid, with a sort of horror, their tumultuous amusements; and liked best to be alone. She would then retire into a corner of the garden, and read, or work diligently with her needle; often also you might see her sitting, as if deep sunk in thought; or violently walking up and down the alleys, speaking to herself. Her parents readily allowed her to have her will in these things, for she was healthy, and waxed apace; only her strange sagacious answers and observations often made them anxious. "Such wise children do not grow to age," her grandmother, Brigitta, many times observed; "they are too good for this world; the child, besides, is beautiful beyond nature, and will never find its proper place on Earth."

The little girl had this peculiarity, that she was very loath to let herself be served by any one, but endeavoured to do everything herself. She was almost the earliest riser in the house; she washed herself carefully, and dressed without assistance: at night she was equally careful; she took special heed to pack up her clothes and washes with her own hands, allowing no one, not even her mother, to meddle with her articles. The mother humoured her in this caprice,

not thinking it of any consequence. But what was her astonishment,
when, happening one holiday to insist, regardless of Elfrida's tears
and screams, on dressing her out for a visit to the castle, she found
upon her breast, suspended by a string, a piece of gold of a strange
form, which she directly recognised as one of that sort she had seen
in such abundance in the subterranean vault! The little thing was
greatly frightened; and at last confessed that she had found it in the
garden, and as she liked it much, had kept it carefully: she at the same
time prayed so earnestly and pressingly to have it back, that Mary
fastened it again on its former place, and, full of thoughts, went out
with her in silence to the castle.

Sidewards from the farmhouse lay some offices for the storing of
produce and implements; and behind these there was a little green,
with an old grove, now visited by no one, as, from the new arrangement of the buildings, it lay too far from the garden. In this solitude
Elfrida delighted most; and it occurred to nobody to interrupt her
here, so that frequently her parents did not see her for half a day.
One afternoon her mother chanced to be in these buildings, seeking
for some lost article among the lumber; and she noticed that a beam
of light was coming in, through a chink in the wall. She took a
thought of looking through this aperture, and seeing what her child
was busied with; and it happened that a stone was lying loose, and
could be pushed aside, so that she obtained a view right into the
grove. Elfrida was sitting there on a little bench, and beside her
the well-known Zerina; and the children were playing, and amusing
one another, in the kindliest unity. The Elf embraced her beautiful
companion, and said mournfully: "Ah! dear little creature, as I sport
with thee, so have I sported with thy mother, when she was a child;
but you mortals so soon grow tall and thoughtful! It is very hard:
wert thou but to be a child as long as I!"

"Willingly would I do it," said Elfrida; "but they all say, I shall
come to sense, and give over playing altogether; for I have great gifts,
as they think, for growing wise. Ah! and then I shall see thee no
more, thou dear Zerina! Yet it is with us as with the fruit-tree flowers:
how glorious the blossoming apple-tree, with its red bursting buds!
It looks so stately and broad; and every one, that passes under it,
thinks surely something great will come of it; then the sun grows
hot, and the buds come joyfully forth; but the wicked kernel is already
there, which pushes off and casts away the fair flower's dress; and
now, in pain and waxing, it can do nothing more, but must grow
to fruit in harvest. An apple, to be sure, is pretty and refreshing; yet

nothing to the blossom of spring. So is it also with us mortals: I am not glad in the least at growing to be a tall girl. Ah! could I but once visit you!"

"Since the King is with us," said Zerina, "it is quite impossible; but I will come to thee, my darling, often, often; and none shall see me either here or there. I will pass invisible through the air, or fly over to thee like a bird. O! we will be much, much together, while thou art still little. What can I do to please thee?"

"Thou must like me very dearly," said Elfrida, "as I like thee in my heart. But come, let us make another rose."

Zerina took the well-known box from her bosom, threw two grains from it on the ground; and instantly a green bush stood before them, with two deep-red roses, bending their heads, as if to kiss each other. The children plucked them smiling, and the bush disappeared. "O that it would not die so soon!" said Elfrida; "this red child, this wonder of the Earth!"

"Give it me here," said the little Elf; then breathed thrice upon the budding rose, and kissed it thrice. "Now," said she, giving back the rose, "it will continue fresh and blooming till winter."

"I will keep it," said Elfrida, "as an image of thee; I will guard it in my little room, and kiss it night and morning, as if it were thyself."

"The sun is setting," said the other; "I must home." They embraced again, and Zerina vanished.

In the evening, Mary clasped her child to her breast, with a feeling of alarm and veneration. She henceforth allowed the good little girl more liberty than formerly; and often calmed her husband, when he came to search for the child; which for some time he was wont to do, as her retiredness did not please him; and he feared that, in the end, it might make her silly, or even pervert her understanding. The mother often glided to the chink; and almost always found the bright Elf beside her child, employed in sport, or in earnest conversation.

"Wouldst thou like to fly?" inquired Zerina once.

"O well! How well!" replied Elfrida; and the fairy clasped her mortal playmate in her arms, and mounted with her from the ground, till they hovered above the grove. The mother, in alarm, forgot herself, and pushed out her head in terror to look after them; when Zerina, from the air, held up her finger, and threatened yet smiled; then descended with the child, embraced her, and disappeared. After this, it happened more than once that Mary was observed by her; and every time, the shining little creature shook her head, or threatened, yet with friendly looks.

Often, in disputing with her husband, Mary had said in her zeal: "Thou dost injustice to the poor people in the hut!" But when Andres pressed her to explain why she differed in opinion from the whole village, nay from his Lordship himself; and how she could understand it better than the whole of them, she still broke off embarrassed, and became silent. One day, after dinner, Andres grew more violent than ever; and maintained that, by one means or another, the crew must be packed away, as a nuisance to the country; when his wife, in anger, said to him: "Hush! for they are benefactors to thee and to everyone of us."

"Benefactors!" cried the other, in astonishment: "These rogues and vagabonds?"

In her indignation, she was now at last tempted to relate to him, under promise of the strictest secrecy, the history of her youth: and as Andres at every word grew more incredulous, and shook his head in mockery, she took him by the hand, and led him to the chink; where, to his amazement, he beheld the glittering Elf sporting with his child, and caressing her in the grove. He knew not what to say; an exclamation of astonishment escaped him, and Zerina raised her eyes. On the instant she grew pale, and trembled violently; not with friendly, but with indignant looks, she made the sign of threatening, and then said to Elfrida: "Thou canst not help it, dearest heart; but they will never learn sense, wise as they believe themselves." She embraced the little one with stormy haste; and then, in the shape of a raven, flew with hoarse cries over the garden, towards the Firs.

In the evening, the little one was very still; she kissed her rose with tears; Mary felt depressed and frightened, Andres scarcely spoke. It grew dark. Suddenly there went a rustling through the trees; birds flew to and fro with wild screaming, thunder was heard to roll, the Earth shook, and tones of lamentation moaned in the air. Andres and his wife had not courage to rise; they shrouded themselves within the curtains, and with fear and trembling awaited the day. Towards morning, it grew calmer; and all was silent when the Sun, with his cheerful light, rose over the wood.

Andres dressed himself; and Mary now observed that the stone of the ring upon her finger had become quite pale. On opening the door, the sun shone clear on their faces, but the scene around them they could scarcely recognise. The freshness of the wood was gone; the hills were shrunk, the brooks were flowing languidly with scanty streams, the sky seemed gray; and when you turned to the Firs, they were standing there no darker or more dreary than the other trees.

The huts behind them were no longer frightful; and several inhabitants of the village came and told about the fearful night, and how they had been across the spot where the gipsies had lived; how these people must have left the place at last, for their huts were standing empty, and within had quite a common look, just like the dwellings of other poor people: some of their household gear was left behind.

Elfrida in secret said to her mother: "I could not sleep last night; and in my fright at the noise, I was praying from the bottom of my heart, when the door suddenly opened, and my playmate entered to take leave of me. She had a travelling-pouch slung round her, a hat on her head, and a large staff in her hand. She was very angry at thee; since on thy account she had now to suffer the severest and most painful punishments, as she had always been so fond of thee; for all of them, she said, were very loath to leave this quarter."

Mary forbade her to speak of this; and now the ferryman came across the river, and told them new wonders. As it was growing dark, a stranger man of large size had come to him, and hired his boat till sunrise; and with this condition, that the boatman should remain quiet in his house, at least should not cross the threshold of his door. "I was frightened," continued the old man, "and the strange bargain would not let me sleep. I slipped softly to the window, and looked towards the river. Great clouds were driving restlessly through the sky, and the distant woods were rustling fearfully; it was as if my cottage shook, and moans and lamentations glided round it. On a sudden, I perceived a white streaming light, that grew broader and broader, like many thousands of falling stars; sparkling and waving, it proceeded forward from the dark Fir-ground, moved over the fields, and spread itself along towards the river. Then I heard a trampling, a jingling, a bustling, and rushing, nearer and nearer; it went forwards to my boat, and all stept into it, men and women, as it seemed, and children; and the tall stranger ferried them over. In the river were by the boat swimming many thousands of glittering forms; in the air white clouds and lights were wavering; and all lamented and bewailed that they must travel forth so far, far away, and leave their beloved dwelling. The noise of the rudder and the water creaked and gurgled between whiles, and then suddenly there would be silence. Many a time the boat landed, and went back, and was again laden; many heavy casks, too, they took along with them, which multitudes of horrid-looking little fellows carried and rolled; whether they were devils or goblins, Heaven only knows. Then came, in waving brightness, a stately freight; it seemed an old man, mounted on a small white horse, and all were crowding round him. I saw nothing of the horse but its head; for the rest of it was covered with costly glittering cloths and trappings: on his brow the old man had a crown, so bright that, as he came across, I thought the sun was rising there, and the redness of the dawn glimmering in my eyes. Thus it went on all night; I at last fell asleep in the tumult, half in joy, half in terror. In the morning all was still; but the river is, as it were, run off, and I know not how I am to steer my boat in it now."

The same year there came a blight; the woods died away, the springs ran dry; and the scene, which had once been the joy of every traveller, was in autumn standing waste, naked and bald; scarcely showing here and there, in the sea of sand, a spot or two where grass, with a dingy greenness, still grew up. The fruit-trees all withered, the vines faded away, and the aspect of the place became so melancholy, that the Count, with his people, next year left the castle, which in time decayed and fell to ruins.

Elfrida gazed on her rose day and night with deep longing, and thought of her kind playmate; and as it drooped and withered, so did she also hang her head; and before the spring, the little maiden had herself faded away. Mary often stood upon the spot before the hut, and wept for the happiness that had departed. She wasted herself away like her child, and in a few years she too was gone. Old Martin, with his son-in-law, returned to the quarter where he had lived before.

THE GOBLET

THE FORENOON BELLS were sounding from the high cathedral. Over the wide square in front of it were men and women walking to and fro, carriages rolling along, and priests proceeding to their various churches. Ferdinand was standing on the broad stair, with his eyes over the multitude, looking at them as they came up to attend the service. The sunshine glittered on the white stones, all were seeking shelter from the heat. He alone had stood for a long time leaning on a pillar, amid the burning beams, without regarding them; for he was lost in the remembrances which mounted up within his mind. He was calling back his bygone life; and inspiring his soul with the feeling which had penetrated all his being, and swallowed up every other wish in itself. At the same hour, in the past year, had he been standing here, looking at the women and the maidens coming to mass; with indifferent heart, and smiling face, he had viewed the variegated procession; many a kind look had roguishly met his, and many a virgin cheek had blushed; his busy eye had observed the pretty feet, how they mounted the steps, and how the wavering robe fell more or less aside, to let the dainty little ankles come to sight. Then a youthful form had crossed the square: clad in black; slender, and of noble mien, her eyes modestly cast down before her, carelessly she hovered up the steps with lovely grace; the silken robe lay round that fairest of forms, and rocked itself as in music about the moving limbs; she was mounting the highest step, when by chance she raised her head, and struck his eye with a ray of the purest azure. He was pierced as if by lightning. Her foot caught the robe; and quickly as he darted towards her, he could not prevent her having, for a moment, in the most charming posture, lain kneeling at his feet. He raised her; she did not look at him, she was all one blush; nor did she answer his inquiry whether she was hurt. He followed her into the church: his soul saw nothing but the image of that form kneeling before him, and that loveliest of bosoms bent towards him. Next day he visited the threshold of the church again; for him that spot was consecrated ground. He had been intending to pursue his travels, his friends were expecting him impatiently at home; but from henceforth his native country was here, his heart and its wishes were inverted. He saw her often, she did not shun him; yet it was but for a few separate and stolen moments; for her wealthy family observed her strictly, and still more a powerful and jealous bridegroom. They mutually confessed their love, but knew not what to do; for he was a stranger, and could offer his beloved no such splendid fortune as she was entitled to expect. He now felt his poverty; yet when he reflected on his former way of life, it seemed to him that he was passing rich; for his existence was rendered holy, his heart floated forever in the fairest emotion; Nature was now become his friend, and her beauty lay revealed to him; he felt himself no longer alien from worship and religion; and he now crossed this threshold, and the mysterious dimness of the temple, with far other feelings than in former days of levity. He withdrew from his acquaintances, and lived only to love. When he walked through her street, and saw her at the window, he was happy for the day. He had often spoken to her in the dusk of the evening; her garden was adjacent to a friend's, who, however, did not know his secret. Thus a year had passed away.

All these scenes of his new existence again moved through his remembrance. He raised his eyes; that noble form was even then gliding over the square; she shone out of the confused multitude like a sun. A lovely music sounded in his longing heart; and as she approached; he retired into the church. He offered her the holy water; her white fingers trembled as they touched his, she bowed with grateful kindness. He followed her, and knelt down near her. His whole heart was melting in sadness and love; it seemed to him as if, from the wounds of longing, his being were bleeding away in fervent prayers; every word of the priest went through him, every tone of the music poured new devotion into his bosom; his lips quivered, as the fair maiden pressed the crucifix of her rosary to her ruby mouth. How dim had been his apprehension of this Faith and this Love before! The priest elevated the Host, and the bell sounded; she bowed more humbly, and crossed her breast; and, like a flash, it struck through all his powers and feelings, and the image on the altar seemed alive, and the coloured dimness of the windows as a light of paradise; tears flowed fast from his eyes, and allayed the swelling fervour of his heart.

The service was concluded. He again offered her the consecrated font; they spoke some words, and she withdrew. He stayed behind, in order to excite no notice; he looked after her till the hem of her garment vanished round the corner; and he felt like the wanderer, weary and astray, from whom, in the thick forest, the last gleam of the setting sun departs. He awoke from his dream, as an old withered hand slapped him on the shoulder, and some one called him by name.

He started back, and recognised his friend, the testy old Albert, who lived apart from men, and whose solitary house was open to Ferdinand alone: "Do you remember our engagement?" said the hoarse husky voice. "O yes," said Ferdinand: "and will you perform your promise today?"

"This very hour," replied the other, "if you like to follow me."

They walked through the city to a remote street, and there entered a large edifice. "Today," said the old man, "you must push through with me into my most solitary chamber, that we may not be disturbed." They passed through many rooms, then along some stairs; they wound their way through passages: and Ferdinand, who had thought himself familiar with the house, was now astonished at the multitude of apartments, and the singular arrangement of the spacious building; but still more that the old man, a bachelor, and without family, should inhabit it by himself, with a few servants, and never let out any part of the superfluous room to strangers. Albert at length unbolted the door, and said: "Now, here is the place." They entered a large high chamber, hung round with red damask, which was trimmed with golden listings; the chairs were of the same stuff; and, through heavy red silk curtains covering the windows, came a purple light. "Wait a little," said the old man, and went into another room. Ferdinand took up some books: he found them to contain strange unintelligible characters, circles and lines, with many curious plates; and from the little he could read, they seemed to be works on alchemy; he was aware already that the old man had the reputation of a gold-maker. A lute was lying on the table, singularly overlaid with mother-of-pearl, and coloured wood; and representing birds and flowers in very splendid forms. The star in the middle was a large piece of mother-of-pearl, worked in the most skilful manner into many intersecting circular figures, almost like the centre of a window in a Gothic church. "You are looking at my instrument," said Albert, coming back; "it is two hundred years old: I brought it with me as a memorial of my journey into Spain. But let us leave all that, and do you take a seat."

They sat down beside the table, which was likewise covered with a red cloth; and the old man placed upon it something which was carefully wrapped up. "From pity to your youth," he began, "I promised lately to predict to you whether you could ever become happy or not; and this promise I will in the present hour perform, though you hold the matter only as a jest. You need not be alarmed; for what I purpose will take place without danger; no dread invocations shall be made by me, nor shall any horrid apparition terrify your senses. The business I am on may fail in two ways: either if you do not love so truly as you have been willing to persuade me; for then my labour is in vain, and nothing will disclose itself; or, if you shall disturb the oracle and destroy it by a useless question, or a hasty movement, should you leave your seat and dissipate the figure; you must therefore promise me to keep yourself quite still."

Ferdinand gave his word, and the old man unfolded from its cloths the packet he had placed on the table. It was a golden goblet, of very skilful and beautiful workmanship. Round its broad foot ran a garland of flowers, intertwined with myrtles, and various other leaves and fruits, worked out in high chasing with dim and with brilliant gold. A corresponding ring, but still richer, with figures of children, and wild little animals playing with them, or flying from them, wound itself about the middle of the cup. The bowl was beautifully turned; it bent itself back at the top as if to meet the lips; and within, the gold sparkled with a red glow. Old Albert placed the cup between him and the youth, whom he then beckoned to come nearer. "Do you not feel something," said he, "when your eye loses itself in this splendour?"

"Yes," answered Ferdinand, "this brightness glances into my inmost heart; I might almost say I felt it like a kiss in my longing bosom."

"It is right, then!" said the old man. "Now let not your eyes wander any more, but fix them steadfastly on the glittering of this gold, and think as intensely as you can of the woman whom you love."

Both sat quiet for a while, looking earnestly upon the gleaming cup. Ere long, however, Albert, with mute gestures, began, at first slowly, then faster, and at last in rapid movements, to whirl his outstretched finger in a constant circle round the glitter of the bowl. Then he paused, and recommenced his circles in the opposite direction. After this had lasted for a little, Ferdinand began to think he heard the sound of music; it came as from without, in some distant street, but soon the tones approached, they quivered more distinctly through the air; and at last no doubt remained with him that they were flowing from the hollow of the cup. The music became stronger, and of such piercing power, that the young man's heart was throbbing to the notes, and tears were flowing from his eyes. Busily old Albert's hand now moved in various lines across the mouth of the goblet; and it seemed as if sparks were issuing from his fingers, and darting in forked courses to the gold, and tinkling as they met it. The glittering points increased; and followed, as if strung on threads, the movements of his finger to and fro; they shone with various hues, and crowded more and more together till they joined in unbroken lines. And now it seemed as if the old man, in the red dusk, were stretching a wondrous net over the gleaming gold; for he drew the beams this way and that at pleasure, and wove up with them the opening of the bowl; they obeyed him, and remained there like a cover, wavering to and fro, and playing into one another. Having so fixed them, he again described the circle round the rim; the music then moved off, grew fainter and fainter, and at last died away. While the tones departed, the sparkling net quivered to and fro as in pain. In its increasing agitation it broke in pieces; and the beaming threads rained down in drops into the cup; but as the drops fell, there arose from them a ruddy cloud, which moved within itself in manifold eddies, and mounted over the brim like foam. A bright point darted with exceeding swiftness through the cloudy circle, and began to form the Image in the midst of it. On a sudden there looked out from the vapour as it were an eye; over this came a playing and curling as of golden locks; and soon there went a soft blush up and down the shadow, and Ferdinand beheld the smiling face of his beloved, the blue eyes, the tender cheeks, the fair red mouth. The head waved to and fro; rose clearer and more visible upon the slim white neck, and nodded towards the enraptured youth. Old Albert still kept casting circles round the cup; and out of it emerged the glancing shoulders; and as the fair form mounted more and more from its golden couch, and bent in lovely kindness this way and that, the soft curved parted breasts appeared, and on their summits two loveliest rose-buds glancing with sweet secret red. Ferdinand fancied he felt the breath, as the beloved form bent waving towards him, and almost touched him with its glowing lips; in his rapture he forgot his promise and himself; he started up and clasped that ruby mouth to him with a kiss, and meant to seize those lovely arms, and lift the enrapturing form from its golden prison. Instantly a violent trembling quivered through the lovely shape; the head and body broke away as in a thousand lines; and a rose was lying at the bottom of the goblet, in whose redness that sweet smile still seemed to play. The longing young man caught it and pressed it to his lips; and in his burning ardour it withered and melted into air.

"Thou hast kept thy promise badly," said the old man, with an angry tone; "thou hast none but thyself to blame." He again wrapped up the goblet, drew aside the curtains, and opened a window: the clear daylight broke in; and Ferdinand, in sadness, and with many fruitless excuses, left old Albert still in anger.

In an agitated mood, he hastened through the streets of the city. Without the gate, he sat down beneath the trees. She had told him in the morning that she was to go that night, with some relations, to the country. Intoxicated with love, he rose, he sat, he wandered in the wood: that fair kind form was still before him, as it flowed and mounted from the glowing gold; he looked that she would now step forth to meet him in the splendour of her beauty, and again that loveliest image broke away in pieces from his eyes; and he was indignant at himself that, by his restless passion and the tumult of his senses, he should have destroyed the shape, and perhaps his hopes, forever.

As the walk, in the afternoon, became crowded, he withdrew deeper into the thickets; but he still kept the distant highway in his eye; and every coach that issued from the gate was carefully examined by him.

The night approached. The setting sun was throwing forth its red splendour, when from the gate rushed out the richly gilded coach, gleaming with a fiery brightness in the glow of evening. He hastened towards it. Her eye had already seized him. Kindly and smilingly she leaned her glittering bosom from the window; he caught her soft salutation and signal; he was standing by the coach, her full look fell on his, and as she drew back to move away, the rose which had adorned her bosom flew out, and lay at his feet. He lifted it, and kissed it; and he felt as if it presaged to him that he should not see his loved one any more, that now his happiness had faded away from him forever.

Hurried steps were passing up stairs and down; the whole house was in commotion; all was bustle and tumult, preparing for the great festivities of the morrow. The mother was the gladdest and most active; the bride heeded nothing, but retired into her chamber to meditate upon her changing destiny. The family were still looking for their elder son, the captain, with his wife; and for two elder daughters, with their husbands: Leopold, the younger, was maliciously busied in increasing the disorder, and deepening the tumult; perplexing all, while he pretended to be furthering it. Agatha, his still unmarried sister, was in vain endeavouring to make him reasonable, and persuade him simply to do nothing, and to let the rest have peace; but her mother said: "Never mind him and his folly; for today a little more or less of it amounts to nothing; only this I beg of one and all of you, that as I have so much to think about already, you would trouble me with no fresh tidings, unless it be of something that especially concerns us. I care not whether any one have let some china fall, whether one spoon or two spoons are wanting, whether any of the stranger servants have been breaking windows; with all such freaks as these, I beg you would not vex me by recounting them. Were these days of tumult over, we will reckon matters; not till then."

"Bravely spoken, mother!" cried her son; "these sentiments are worthy of a governor. And if it chance that any of the maids should break her neck; the cook get tipsy, or set the chimney on fire; the butler, for joy, let all the malmsey run upon the floor, or down his throat, you shall not hear a word of such small tricks. If, indeed, an earthquake were to overset the house! that, my dear mother, could not be kept secret."

"When will he leave his folly!" said the mother: "What must thy sisters think, when they find thee every jot as riotous as when they left thee two years ago?"

"They must do justice to my force of character," said Leopold, "and grant that I am not so changeable as they or their husbands, who have altered so much within these few years, and so little to their advantage."

The bridegroom now entered, and inquired for the bride. Her maid was sent to call her. "Has Leopold made my request to you, my dear mother?" said he.

"I did, forsooth!" said Leopold. "There is such confusion here among us, not one of them can think a reasonable thought."

The bride entered, and the young pair joyfully saluted one another. "The request I meant," continued the bridegroom, "is this: That you would not take it ill, if I should bring another guest into your house, which, in truth, is full enough already."

"You are aware yourself," replied the mother, "that extensive as it is, I could scarcely find another chamber."

"Notwithstanding, I have partly managed it already," cried Leopold; "I have had the large apartment furbished up."

"Why, that is quite a miserable place," replied the mother; "for many years it has been nothing but a lumber-room."

"But it is splendidly repaired," said Leopold; "and our friend, for whom it is intended, does not mind such matters, he desires nothing but our love. Besides, he has no wife, and likes to be alone; it is the very place for him. We have had enough of trouble in persuading him to come, and show himself again among his fellow-creatures."

"Not your dismal conjuror and gold-maker, certainly?" cried Agatha.

"No other," said the bridegroom, "if you will still call him so."

"Then do not let him, mother," said the sister. "What should a man like that do here? I have seen him on the street with Leopold, and I was positively frightened at his face. The old sinner, too, almost never goes to church; he loves neither God nor man; and it cannot come to good to bring such infidels under the roof, on a solemnity like this. Who knows what may be the consequence!"

"To hear her talk!" said Leopold, in anger. "Thou condemnest without knowing him; and because the cut of his nose does not please thee, and he is no longer young and handsome, thou concludest him a wizard, and a servant of the Devil."

"Grant a place in your house, dear mother," said the bridegroom, "to our old friend, and let him take a part in our general joy. He seems, my dear Agatha, to have endured much suffering, which has rendered him distrustful and misanthropic; he avoids all society, his only exceptions are Leopold and myself. I owe him much; it was he that first gave my mind a good direction; nay, I may say, it is he alone that has rendered me perhaps worthy of my Julia's love."

"He lends me all his books," continued Leopold; "and, what is more, his old manuscripts; and what is more still, his money, on my bare word. He is a man of the most christian turn, my little sister. And who knows, when thou hast seen him better, whether thou wilt not throw off thy coyness, and take a fancy to him, ugly as he now appears to thee?"

"Well, bring him to us," said the mother; "I have had to hear so much of him from Leopold already, that I have a curiosity to be acquainted with him. Only you must answer for it, that I cannot lodge him better."

Meantime strangers were announced. They were members of the family, the married daughters, and the officer; they had brought their children with them. The good old lady was delighted to behold her grandsons; all was welcoming, and joyful talk; and Leopold and the bridegroom, having also given and received their greeting, went away to seek their ancient melancholic friend.

The latter lived most part of the year in the country, about a league from town; but he also kept a little dwelling for himself in a garden near the gate. Here, by chance, the young men had become acquainted with him. They now found him in a coffeehouse, where they had previously agreed to meet. As the evening had come on, they brought him, after some little conversation, directly to the house.

The stranger met a kindly welcome from the mother; the daughters stood a little more aloof from him. Agatha especially was shy, and carefully avoided his looks. But the first general compliments were scarcely over, when the old man's eye appeared to settle on the bride, who had entered the apartment later; he seemed as if transported, and it was observed that he was struggling to conceal a tear. The bridegroom rejoiced in his joy, and happening sometime after to be standing with him by a side at the window, he took his hand, and asked him: "Now, what think you of my lovely Julia? Is she not an angel?"

"O my friend!" replied the old man, with emotion, "such grace and beauty I have never seen; or rather, I should say (for that expression was not just), she is so fair, so ravishing, so heavenly, that I feel as if I had long known her; as if she were to me, utter stranger though she is, the most familiar form of my imagination, some shape which had always been an inmate of my heart."

"I understand you," said the young man: "yes, the truly beautiful, the great and sublime, when it overpowers us with astonishment and admiration, still does not surprise us as a thing foreign, never heard of, never seen; but, on the other hand, our own inmost nature in such moments becomes clear to us, our deepest remembrances are awakened, our dearest feelings made alive."

The stranger, during supper, mixed but little in the conversation; his looks were fixed on the bride, so earnestly and constantly, that she at last became embarrassed and alarmed. The captain told of a campaign which he had served in; the rich merchant of his speculations and the bad times; the country gentleman of the improvements which he meant to make in his estate.

Supper being done, the bridegroom took his leave, returning for the last time to his lonely chamber; for in future it was settled that the married pair were to live in the mother's house, their chambers were already furnished. The company dispersed, and Leopold conducted the stranger to his room. "You will excuse us," said he, as they went along, "for having been obliged to lodge you rather far away, and not so comfortably as our mother wished; but you see, yourself, how numerous our family is, and more relations are to come tomorrow. For one thing, you will not run away from us; there is no finding of your course through this enormous house."

They went through several passages, and Leopold at last took leave, and bade his guest good-night. The servant placed two wax-lights on the table; then asked the stranger whether he should help him to undress, and as the latter waived his help in that particular, he also went away, and the stranger found himself alone.

"How does it chance, then," said he, walking up and down, "that this Image springs so vividly from my heart today? I forgot the long past, and thought I saw herself. I was again young, and her voice sounded as of old; I thought I was awakening from a heavy dream; but no, I am now awake, and those fair moments were but a sweet delusion."

He was too restless to sleep; he looked at some pictures on the walls, and then round on the chamber. "Today," cried he, "all is so familiar to me, I could almost fancy I had known this house and this apartment of old." He tried to settle his remembrances, and lifted some large books which were standing in a corner. As he turned their leaves, he shook his head. A lute-case was leaning on the wall; he opened it, and found a strange old instrument, time-worn, and without the strings. "No, I am not mistaken!" cried he, in astonishment; "this lute is too remarkable; it is the Spanish lute of my long-departed friend, old Albert! Here are his magic books; this is the chamber where he raised for me that blissful vision; the red of the tapestry is faded, its golden hem is become dim; but strangely vivid in my heart is all pertaining to those hours. It was for this the fear went over me as I was coming hither, through these long complicated passages where Leopold conducted me. O Heaven! On this very table did the Shape rise budding forth, and grow up as if watered and refreshed by the redness of the gold. The same image smiled upon me here, which has almost driven me crazy in the hall tonight; in that hall where I have walked so often in trustful speech with Albert!"

He undressed, but slept very little. Early in the morning he was up, and looking at the room again; he opened the window, and the same gardens and buildings were lying before him as of old, only many other houses had been built since then. "Forty years have vanished," sighed he, "since that afternoon; and every day of those bright times has a longer life than all the intervening space."

He was called to the company. The morning passed in varied talk: at last the bride entered in her marriage-dress. As the old man noticed her, he fell into a state of agitation, such that every one observed it. They proceeded to the church, and the marriage-ceremony was performed. The party was again at home, when Leopold inquired: "Now, mother, how do you like our friend, the good morose old gentleman?"

"I had figured him, by your description," said she, "much more frightful; he is mild and sympathetic, and might gain from one an honest trust in him."

"Trust?" cried Agatha; "in these burning frightful eyes, these thousandfold wrinkles, that pale sunk mouth, that strange laugh of his, which looks and sounds so mockingly? No; God keep me from such friends! If evil spirits ever take the shape of men, they must assume some shape like this."

"Perhaps a younger and more handsome one," replied the mother; "but I cannot recognise the good old man in thy description. One easily observes that he is of a violent temperament, and has inured himself to lock up his feelings in his own bosom; perhaps, too, as Leopold was saying, he may have encountered many miseries; so he is grown mistrustful, and has lost that simple openness, which is especially the portion of the happy."

The rest of the party entered, and broke off their conversation. Dinner was served up; and the stranger sat between Agatha and the rich merchant. When the toasts were beginning, Leopold cried out: "Now, stop a little, worthy friends; we must have the golden goblet down for this, then let it travel round."

He was rising, but his mother beckoned him to keep his seat: "Thou wilt not find it," said she, "for the plate is all stowed elsewhere." She walked out rapidly to seek it herself.

"How brisk and busy is our good old lady still!" observed the merchant. "See how nimbly she can move, with all her breadth and weight, and reckoning sixty by this time of day. Her face is always bright and joyful, and today she is particularly happy, for she sees herself made young again in Julia."

The stranger gave assent, and the lady entered with the goblet. It was filled with wine, and began to circulate, each toasting what was dearest and most precious to him. Julia gave the welfare of her husband, he the love of his fair Julia; and thus did every one as it became his turn. The mother lingered, as the goblet came to her.

"Come, quick with it," said the captain, somewhat hastily and rudely; "we know, you reckon all men faithless, and not one among them worthy of a woman's love. What, then, is dearest to you?"

His mother looked at him, while the mildness of her brow was on a sudden overspread with angry seriousness. "Since my son," said she, "knows me so well, and can judge my mind so rigorously, let me be permitted *not* to speak what I was thinking of, and let him endeavour, by a life of constant love, to falsify what he gives out as my opinion." She pushed the goblet on, without drinking, and the company was for a while embarrassed and disturbed.

"It is reported," said the merchant, in a whisper, turning to the stranger, "that she did not love her husband; but another, who proved faithless to her. She was then, it seems, the finest woman in the city."

When the cup reached Ferdinand, he gazed upon it with astonishment; for it was the very goblet out of which old Albert had called forth to him the lovely shadow. He looked in upon the gold, and the waving of the wine; his hand shook; it would not have surprised him, if from the magic bowl that glowing Form had again mounted up, and brought with it his vanished youth. "No!" said he, after some time, half-aloud, "it is wine that is gleaming here!"

"Ay, what else?" cried the merchant, laughing: "Drink and be merry."

A thrill of terror passed over the old man; he pronounced the name "Francesca" in a vehement tone, and set the goblet to his lips. The mother cast upon him an inquiring and astonished look.

"Whence is this bright goblet?" said Ferdinand, who also felt ashamed of his embarrassment.

"Many years ago, long ere I was born," said Leopold, "my father bought it, with this house and all its furniture, from an old solitary bachelor; a silent man, whom the neighbours thought a dealer in the Black Art."

The stranger did not say that he had known this old man; for his whole being was too much perplexed, too like an enigmatic dream, to let the rest look into it, even from afar.

The cloth being withdrawn, he was left alone with the mother, as the young ones had retired to make ready for the ball. "Sit down by me," said the mother; "we will rest, for our dancing years are past; and if it is not rude, allow me to inquire whether you have seen our goblet elsewhere, or what it was that moved you so intensely?"

"O my lady," said the old man, "pardon my foolish violence and emotion; but ever since I crossed your threshold, I feel as if I were no longer myself; every moment I forget that my head is gray, that the hearts which loved me are dead. Your beautiful daughter, who is now celebrating the gladdest day of her existence, is so like a maiden whom I knew and adored in my youth, that I could reckon it a miracle. Like, did I say? No, she is not like; it is she herself! In this house, too, I have often been; and once I became acquainted with this cup in a manner I shall not forget." Here he told her his adventure. "On the evening of that day," concluded he, "in the park, I saw my loved one for the last time, as she was passing in her coach. A rose fell from her bosom; this I gathered; she herself was lost to me, for she proved faithless, and soon after married."

"God in Heaven!" cried the lady, violently moved, and starting up, "thou art not Ferdinand?"

"It is my name," replied he.

"I am Francesca," said the lady.

They sprang forward to embrace, then started suddenly back. Each viewed the other with investigating looks: both strove again to evolve from the ruins of Time those lineaments which of old they had known and loved in one another; and as, in dark tempestuous nights, amid the flight of black clouds, there are moments when solitary stars ambiguously twinkle forth, to disappear next instant, so to these two was there shown now and then from the eyes, from the brow and lips, the transitory gleam of some well-known feature; and it seemed as if their Youth stood in the distance, weeping smiles. He bowed down, and kissed her hand, while two big drops rolled from his eyes. They then embraced each other cordially.

"Is thy wife dead?" inquired she.

"I was never married," sobbed the other.

"Heavens!" cried she, wringing her hands, "then it is I who have been faithless! But no, not faithless. On returning from the country, where I stayed two months, I heard from every one, thy friends as well as mine, that thou wert long ago gone home, and married in thy own country. They showed me the most convincing letters, they pressed me vehemently, they profited by my despondency, my indignation; and so it was that I gave my hand to another, a deserving husband; but my heart and my thoughts were always thine."

"I never left this town," said Ferdinand; "but after a while I heard that thou wert married. They wished to part us, and they have succeeded. Thou art a happy mother; I live in the past, and all thy children I will love as if they were my own. But how strange that we should never once have met!"

"I seldom went abroad," said she; "and as my husband took another name, soon after we were married, from a property which he inherited, thou couldst have no suspicion that we were so near together."

"I avoided men," said Ferdinand, "and lived for solitude. Leopold is almost the only one that has attracted me, and led me out amongst my fellows. O my beloved friend, it is like a frightful spectre-story, to think how we lost, and have again found each other!"

As the young people entered, the two were dissolved in tears, and in the deepest emotion. Neither of them told what had occurred, the secret seemed too holy. But ever after, the old man was the friend of the house; and Death alone parted these two beings, who had found each other so strangely, to reunite them in a short time, beyond the power of separation.

JEAN PAUL RICHTER

ARMY-CHAPLAIN SCHMELZLE'S
JOURNEY TO FLÄTZ

WITH

A RUNNING COMMENTARY OF
NOTES BY JEAN PAUL[1]

PREFACE

THIS, I CONCEIVE, may be managed in two words.

The *first* word must relate to the Circular Letter of Army-chaplain Schmelzle, wherein he describes to his friends his Journey to the metropolitan city of Flätz; after having, in an Introduction, premised some proofs and assurances of his valour. Properly speaking, the *Journey* itself has been written purely with a view that his courageousness, impugned by rumour, may be fully evinced and demonstrated by the plain facts which he therein records. Whether, in the mean time, there shall not be found certain quick-scented readers, who may infer, directly contrariwise, that his breast is not everywhere bomb-proof, especially in the left side: on this point I keep my judgment suspended.

For the rest, I beg the judges of literature, as well as their satellites, the critics of literature, to regard this *Journey,* for whose literary contents I, as Editor, am answerable, solely in the light of a Portrait (in the French sense), a little Sketch of Character. It is a voluntary or involuntary comedy-piece, at which I have laughed so often, that I purpose in time coming to paint some similar Pictures of Character myself. And, for the present, when could such a little comic toy be

---

[1] Prefatory Introduction to Richter, *suprà,* at p. 354, Vol. VI. of *Works* (Vol. I. of *Miscellanies*).

more fitly imparted and set forth to the world, than in these very days, when the sound both of heavy money and of light laughter has died away from among us; when, like the Turks, we count and pay merely with sealed *purses,* and the coin within them has vanished?

Despicable would it seem to me, if any clownish squire of the goose-quill should publicly and censoriously demand of me, in what way this self-cabinet-piece of Schmelzle's has come into my hands? I know it well, and do not disclose it. This comedy-piece, for which I, at all events, as my Bookseller will testify, draw the profit myself, I got hold of so unblamably, that I await, with unspeakable composure, what the Army-chaplain shall please to say against the publication of it, in case he say anything at all. My conscience bears me witness, that I acquired this article, at least by more honourable methods than are those of the learned persons who steal with their ears, who, in the character of spiritual auditory-thieves, and classroom cutpurses and pirates, are in the habit of disloading their plundered Lectures, and vending them up and down the country as productions of their own. Hitherto, in my whole life, I have stolen little, except now and then in youth some—glances.

The *second* word must explain or apologise for the singular form of this little Work, standing as it does on a substratum of Notes. I myself am not contented with it. Let the World open, and look, and determine, in like manner. But the truth is, this line of demarcation, stretching through the whole book, originated in the following accident: certain thoughts (or digressions) of my own, with which it was not permitted me to disturb those of the Army-chaplain, and which could only be allowed to fight behind the lines, in the shape of Notes, I, with a view to conveniency and order, had written down in a separate paper; at the same time, as will be observed, regularly providing every Note with its Number, and thus referring it to the proper page of the main Manuscript. But, in the copying of the latter, I had forgotten to insert the corresponding numbers in the Text itself. Therefore, let no man, any more than I do, cast a stone at my worthy Printer, inasmuch as he (perhaps in the thought that it was my way, that I had some purpose in it) took these Notes, just as they stood, pell-mell, without arrangement of Numbers, and clapped them under the Text; at the same time, by a praiseworthy artful computation, taking care at least, that, at the bottom of every page in the Text, there should some portion of this glittering Note-precipitate make its appearance. Well, the thing at any rate is done, nay perpetuated, namely printed. After all, I might almost partly rejoice at it. For, in good truth, had I meditated for years (as I have done for the last twenty) how to provide for my digression-comets new orbits, if not focal suns, for my episodes new epopees,—I could scarce possibly have hit upon a better or more spacious Limbo for such Vanities than Chance and Printer here accidentally offer me ready-made. I have only to regret, that the thing has been printed, before I could turn it to account. Heavens! what remotest allusions (had I known it before printing) might not have been privily introduced in every Text-page and Note-number; and what apparent incongruity in the real congruity between this upper and under side of the cards! How vehemently and devilishly might one not have cut aloft, and to the right and left, from these impregnable casemates and covered ways; and what *læsio ultra dimidium* (injury beyond the half of the Text) might not, with these satirical injuries, have been effected and completed!

But Fate meant not so kindly with me: of this golden harvest-field of satire I was not to be informed till three days before the Preface.

Perhaps, however, the writing world, by the little blue flame of this accident, may be guided to a weightier acquisition, to a larger subterranean treasure, than I, alas, have dug up! For, to the writer, there is now a way pointed out of producing in one marbled volume a group of altogether different works; of writing in one leaf, for both sexes at the same time, without confounding them, nay, for the five faculties all at once, without disturbing their limitations; since now, instead of boiling up a vile fermenting shove-together, fit for nobody, he has nothing to do but draw his note-lines or partition-lines; and so on his five-story leaf give board and lodging to the most discordant heads. Perhaps one might then read many a book for the fourth time, simply because every time one had read but a fourth part of it.

On the whole, this Work has at least the property of being a short one; so that the reader, I hope, may almost run through it, and read it at the bookseller's counter, without, as in the case of thicker volumes, first needing to buy it. And why, indeed, in this world of Matter should anything whatever be great, except only what belongs not to it, the world of Spirit?

JEAN PAUL FR. RICHTER
Bayreuth, in the Hay and Peace Month, 1807

ARMY-CHAPLAIN SCHMELZLE'S
JOURNEY TO FLÄTZ

Circular Letter of the proposed Catechetical Professor ATTILA SCHMELZLE
*to his Friends; containing some Account of a Holidays' Journey to Flätz,
with an Introduction, touching his Flight, and his Courage as former
Army-chaplain*

NOTHING CAN BE more ludicrous, my esteemed Friends, than to hear
people stigmatising a man as cowardly and hare-hearted, who perhaps
is struggling all the while with precisely the opposite faults, those of
a lion; though indeed the African lion himself, since the time
of Sparrmann's Travels, passes among us for a poltroon. Yet this case
is mine, worthy Friends; and I purpose to say a few words thereupon,
before describing my Journey.

You in truth are all aware that, directly in the teeth of this calumny,
it is courage, it is desperadoes (provided they be not braggarts and
tumultuous persons), whom I chiefly venerate; for example, my
brother-in-law, the Dragoon, who never in his life bastinadoed one
man, but always a whole social circle at the same time. How truculent
was my fancy, even in childhood, when I, as the parson was toning
away to the silent congregation, used to take it into my head: "How
now, if thou shouldst start up from the pew, and shout aloud: I am
here too, Mr. Parson!" and to paint out this thought in such glowing
colours, that for very dread, I have often been obliged to leave
the church! Anything like Rugenda's battle-pieces; horrid murder-
tumults, sea-fights or Stormings of Toulon, exploding fleets; and,
in my childhood, Battles of Prague on the harpsichord; nay, in short,

---

103. Good princes easily obtain good subjects; not so easily good subjects good
princes: thus Adam, in the state of innocence, ruled over animals all tame and
gentle, till simply through his means they fell and grew savage.

5. For a good Physician saves, if not always from the disease, at least from a bad
Physician.

every map of any remarkable scene of war: these are perhaps too much my favourite objects; and I read—and purchase nothing sooner; and doubtless, they might lead me into many errors, were it not that my circumstances restrain me. Now, if it be objected that true courage is something higher than mere thinking and willing, then you, my worthy Friends, will be the first to recognise mine, when it shall break forth into, not barren and empty, but active and effective words, while I strengthen my future Catechetical Pupils, as well as can be done in a course of College Lectures, and steel them into Christian heroes.

It is well known that, out of care for the preservation of my life, I never walk within at least ten fields of any shore full of bathers or swimmers; merely because I foresee to a certainty, that in case one of them were drowning, I should that moment (for the heart over-balances the head) plunge after the fool to save him, into some bottomless depth or other, where we should both perish. And if dreaming is the reflex of waking, let me ask you, true Hearts, if you have forgotten my relating to you dreams of mine, which no Cæsar, no Alexander or Luther, need have felt ashamed of? Have I not, to mention a few instances, taken Rome by storm; and done battle with the Pope, and the whole elephantine body of the Cardinal College, at one and the same time? Did I not once on horseback, while simply looking at a review of military, dash headlong into a *bataillon quarré;* and then capture, in Aix-la-Chapelle, the Peruke of Charlemagne, for which the town pays yearly ten reichsthalers of barber-money; and carrying it off to Halberstadt and Herr Gleim's, there in like manner seize the Great Frederick's Hat; put both Peruke and Hat on my head, and yet return home, after I had stormed their batteries, and turned the cannon against the cannoneers themselves? Did I not once submit to be made a Jew of, and then be regaled with hams; though they were ape-hams on the Orinocco (see Humboldt)? And a thousand such things; for I have thrown the Consistorial President of Flätz out of the Palace window; those alarm-fulminators, sold by Heinrich Backofen in Gotha, at six groschen the dozen, and each going off like a cannon, I have listened to so calmly that the fulminators did not even awaken me; and more of the like sort.

---

100. In books lie the Phœnix-ashes of a past Millennium and Paradise; but War blows, and much ashes are scattered away.

102. Dear Political or Religions Inquisitor! art thou aware that Turin tapers never rightly begin shining, till thou breakest them, and then they take fire?

But enough! It is now time briefly to touch that farther slander of my chaplainship, which unhappily has likewise gained some circulation in Flätz, but which, as Cæsar did Alexander, I shall now by my touch dissipate into dust. Be what truth in it there can, it is still little or nothing. Your great Minister and General in Flätz (perhaps the very greatest in the world, for there are not many Schabackers) may indeed, like any other great man, be turned against me, but not with the Artillery of Truth; for this Artillery I here set before you, my good Hearts, and do you but fire it off for my advantage! The matter is this: Certain foolish rumours are afloat in the Flätz country, that I, on occasion of some important battles, took leg-bail (such is their plebeian phrase), and that afterwards, on the chaplain's being called-for to preach a Thanksgiving sermon for the victory, no chaplain whatever was to be found. The ridiculousness of this story will best appear, when I tell you that I never was in any action; but have always been accustomed, several hours prior to such an event, to withdraw so many miles to the rear, that our men, so soon as they were beaten, would be sure to find me. A good retreat is reckoned the masterpiece in the art of war; and at no time can a retreat be executed with such order, force and security, as just before the battle, when you are not yet beaten.

It is true, I might perhaps, as expectant Professor of Catechetics, sit still and smile at such nugatory speculations on my courage; for if by Socratic questioning I can hammer my future Catechist Pupils into the habit of asking questions in their turn, I shall thereby have tempered *them* into heroes, seeing they have nothing to fight with but children—(Catechists at all events, though dreading fire, have no reason to dread light, since in our days, as in London illuminations, it is only the *unlighted* windows that are battered in; whereas, in other ages, it was with nations and light, as it is with dogs and water; if you give them none for a long time, they at last get a horror at it);—and on the whole, for Catechists, any park looks kindlier, and smiles more sweetly, than a sulphurous park of artillery; and the Warlike Foot, which the age is placed on, is to them the true Devil's cloven-foot of human nature.

But for my part I think not so: almost as if the party-spirit influence of my christian name, Attila, had passed into me more strongly than

86. Very true! In youth we love and enjoy the most ill-assorted friends, perhaps more than, in old age, the best-assorted.

128. In Love there are Summer Holidays; but in Marriage also there are Winter Holidays, I hope.

was proper, I feel myself impelled still farther to prove my courageousness; which, dearest Friends! I shall here in a few lines again
do. This proof I could manage by mere inferences and learned citations.
For example, if Galen remarks that animals with large hind-quarters
are timid, I have nothing to do but turn round, and show the enemy
my back, and what is under it, in order to convince him that I am
not deficient in valour, but in flesh. Again, if by well-known expe-
riences it has been found that flesh-eating produces courage, I can
evince, that in this particular I yield to no officer of the service;
though it is the habit of these gentlemen not only to run up long
scores of roast-meat with their landlords, but also to leave them
unpaid, that so at every hour they may have an open document in
the hands of the enemy himself (the landlord), testifying that they
have eaten their own share (with some of other people's too), and
so put common butcher's-meat on a War-footing, living not like
others *by* bravery, but *for* bravery. As little have I ever, in my character
of chaplain, shrunk from comparison with any officer in the regiment,
who may be a true lion, and so snatch every sort of plunder, but yet,
like this King of the Beasts, is afraid of *fire;* or who,—like King James
of England, that scampered off at sight of drawn swords, yet so much
the more gallantly, before all Europe, went out against the storming
Luther with book and pen,[2]—does, from a similar idiosyncrasy, attack
all warlike armaments, both by word and writing. And here I recollect
with satisfaction a brave sub-lieutenant, whose confessor I was (he
still owes me the confession-money), and who, in respect of stout-
heartedness, had in him perhaps something of that Indian dog which
Alexander had presented to him, as a sort of Dog-Alexander. By way
of trying this crack dog, the Macedonian made various heroic or
heraldic beasts be let loose against him: first a stag; but the dog lay
still: then a sow; he lay still: then a bear; he lay still. Alexander was
on the point of condemning him; when a lion was let forth: the dog
rose, and tore the lion in pieces. So likewise the sub-lieutenant. A
challenger, a foreign enemy, a Frenchman, are to him only stag, and
sow, and bear, and he lies still in his place; but let his oldest enemy,

---

143. Women have weekly at least one active and passive day of glory, the holy
day, the Sunday. The higher ranks alone have more Sundays than workdays; as in
great towns, you can celebrate your Sunday on Friday with the Turks, on Saturday
with the Jews, and on Sunday with yourself.

---

[2] The good Professor of Catechetics is out here. *Indignor quandoque bonus dormitat
Schmelzlæus!*—ED.

his creditor, come and knock at his gate; and demand of him actual smart-money for long bygone pleasures, thus presuming to rob him both of past and present; the sub-lieutenant rises, and throws his creditor down stairs. I, alas, am still standing by the sow; and thus, naturally enough, misunderstood.

Quo, says Livy, xii. 5, and with great justice, *quo timoris minus est, eo minus ferme periculi est,* The less fear you have, the less danger you are likely to be in. With equal justice I invert the maxim, and say: The less the danger, the smaller the fear; nay, there may be situations, in which one has absolutely no knowledge of fear; and, among these, mine is to be reckoned. The more hateful, therefore, must that calumny about hare-heartedness appear to me.

To my Holidays' Journey I shall prefix a few facts, which prove how easily foresight—that is to say, when a person would not resemble the stupid marmot, that will even attack a man on horseback—may pass for cowardice. For the rest, I wish only that I could with equal ease wipe away a quite different reproach, that of being a foolhardy desperado; though I trust, in the sequel, I shall be able to advance some facts which invalidate it.

What boots the heroic arm, without a hero's eye? The former readily grows stronger and more nervous; but the latter is not so soon ground sharper, like glasses. Nevertheless, the merits of foresight obtain from the mass of men less admiration (nay, I should say, more ridicule) than those of courage. Whoso, for instance, shall see me walking under quite cloudless skies, with a wax-cloth umbrella over me, to him I shall probably appear ridiculous, so long as he is not aware that I carry this umbrella as a thunder-screen, to keep off any bolt out of the blue heaven (whereof there are several examples in the history of the Middle Ages) from striking me to death. My thunder-screen, in fact, is exactly that of Reimarus: on a long walking-stick, I carry the wax-cloth roof; from the peak of which depends a string of gold-lace as a conductor; and this, by means of a key fastened to it, which it trails along the ground, will lead off every possible bolt; and easily distribute it over the whole superficies of the Earth. With this *Paratonnerre Portatif* in my hand, I can walk about for weeks, under the clear sky, without the smallest danger. This Diving-bell, moreover, protects me against something else; against shot. For who, in the latter end of Harvest, will give me black on white that

---

21. Schiller and Klopstock are Poetic Mirrors held up to the Sun-god: the Mirrors reflect the Sun with such dazzling brightness, that you cannot find the Picture of the World imaged forth in them.

no lurking ninny of a sportsman somewhere, when I am out enjoying Nature, shall so fire off his piece, at an angle of 45°, that in falling down again, the shot needs only light directly on my crown, and so come to the same as if I had been shot through the brain from a side?

It is bad enough, at any rate, that we have nothing to guard us from the Moon; which at present is bombarding us with stones like a very Turk: for this paltry little Earth's trainbearer and errand-maid thinks, in these rebellious times, that she too must begin, forsooth, to sling somewhat against her Mother! In good truth, as matters stand, any young Catechist of feeling may go out o' nights, with whole limbs, into the moonshine, a-meditating; and ere long (in the midst of his meditation the villanous Satellite hits him) come home a pounded jelly. By heaven! new proofs of courage are required of us on every hand! No sooner have we, with great effort, got thunder-rods manufactured, and comet-tails explained away, than the enemy opens new batteries in the Moon, or somewhere else in the Blue!

Suffice one other story to manifest how ludicrous the most serious foresight, with all imaginable inward courage, often externally appears in the eyes of the many. Equestrians are well acquainted with the dangers of a horse that runs away. My evil star would have it, that I should once in Vienna get upon a hack-horse; a pretty enough honey-coloured nag, but old and hard-mouthed as Satan; so that the beast, in the next street, went off with me; and this in truth—only at a *walk*. No pulling, no tugging, took effect; I, at last, on the back of this Self-riding-horse, made signals of distress, and cried: "Stop him, good people, for God's sake stop him, my horse is off!" But these simple persons seeing the beast move along as slowly as a Reichshofrath law-suit, or the Daily Postwagen, could not in the least understand the matter, till I cried as if possessed: "Stop him then, ye blockheads and joltheads; don't you see that I cannot hold the nag?" But now, to these noodles, the sight of a hard-mouthed horse going off with its rider step by step, seemed ridiculous rather than otherwise; half Vienna gathered itself like a comet-tail behind my beast and me. Prince Kaunitz, the best horseman of the century (the last), pulled up to follow me. I myself sat and swam like a perpendicular piece of drift-ice on my honey-coloured nag, which stalked on, on, step by step: a many-cornered, red-coated letter-carrier, was delivering

---

34. Women are like precious carved works of ivory; nothing is whiter and smoother, and nothing sooner grows *yellow*.

72. The Half-learned is adored by the Quarter-learned; the latter by the Sixteenth-part-learned; and so on; but not the Whole-learned by the Half-learned.

his letters, to the right and left, in the various stories, and he still crossed over before me again, with satirical features, because the nag went along too slowly. The Schwanzschleuderer, or Train-dasher (the person, as you know, who drives along the streets with a huge barrel of water, and besplashes them with a leathern pipe of three ells long from an iron trough), came across the haunches of my horse, and, in the course of his duty, wetted both these and myself in a very cooling manner, though, for my part, I had too much cold sweat on me already, to need any fresh refrigeration. On my infernal Trojan Horse (only I myself was Troy, not beridden but riding to destruction), I arrived at Malzlein (a suburb of Vienna), or perhaps, so confused were my senses, it might be quite another range of streets. At last, late in the dusk, I had to turn into the Prater; and here, long after the Evening Gun, to my horror, and quite against the police-rules, keep riding to and fro on my honey-coloured nag; and possibly I might even have passed the night on him, had not my brother-in-law, the Dragoon, observed my plight, and so found me still sitting firm as a rock on my runaway steed. He made no ceremonies; caught the brute; and put the pleasant question: Why I had not vaulted, and come off by ground-and-lofty tumbling? though he knew full well, that for this a wooden-horse, which stands still, is requisite. However, he took me down; and so, after all this riding, horse and man got home with whole skins and unbroken bones.

But now at last to my Journey!

Journey to Flätz

You are aware, my friends, that this Journey to Flätz was necessarily to take place in Vacation time; not only because the Cattle-market, and consequently the Minister and General van Schabacker, was there then; but more especially, because the latter (as I had it positively from a private hand) did annually, on the 23d of July, the market-eve, about five o'clock, become so full of gaudium and graciousness, that in many cases he did not so much snarl on people, as listen to them, and grant their prayers. The cause of this gaudium I had rather not trust to paper. In short, my Petition, praying that he would be pleased to indemnify and reward me, as an unjustly deposed Army-

---

35. *Bien écouter c'est presque répondre,* says Marivaux justly of social circles: but I extend it to round Councillor-tables and Cabinet-tables, where reports are made, and the Prince listens.

chaplain, by a Catechetical Professorship, could plainly be presented to him at no better season, than exactly about five o'clock in the evening of the first dog-day. In less than a week, I had finished writing my Petition. As I spared neither summaries nor copies of it, I had soon got so far as to see the relatively best lying completed before me; when, to my terror, I observed, that, in this paper, I had introduced above thirty *dashes,* or breaks, in the middle of my sentences! Nowadays, alas, these stings shoot forth involuntarily from learned pens, as from the tails of wasps. I debated long within myself whether a private scholar could justly be entitled to approach a minister with dashes,—greatly as this level interlineation of thoughts, these horizontal note-marks of poetical *music*-pieces, and these rope-ladders or Achilles' tendons of philosophical *see*-pieces, are at present fashionable and indispensable: but, at last, I was obliged (as erasures may offend people of quality) to write my best proof-petition over again; and then to afflict myself for another quarter of an hour over the name Attila Schmelzle, seeing it is always my principle that this and the address of the letter, the two cardinal points of the whole, can never be written legibly enough.

First Stage; from Neusattel to Vierstädten

The 22d of July, or Wednesday, about five in the afternoon, was now, by the way-bill of the regular Post-coach, irrevocably fixed for my departure. I had still half a day to order my house; from which, for two nights and two days and a half, my breast, its breastwork and palisado, was now, along with my Self, to be withdrawn. Besides this, my good wife Bergelchen, as I call my Teutoberga, was immediately to travel after me, on Friday the 24th, in order to see and to make purchases at the yearly Fair; nay, she was ready to have gone along with me, the faithful spouse. I therefore assembled my little knot of domestics, and promulgated to them the Household Law and Valedictory Rescript, which, after my departure, in the first place *before* the outset of my wife, and in the second place *after* this outset, they had rigorously to obey; explaining to them especially whatever, in case of conflagrations, house-breakings, thunder-storms, or transits of troops, it would behove them to do. To my wife I

---

17. The Bed of Honour, since so frequently whole regiments lie on it, and receive their last unction, and last honour but one, really ought from time to time to be new-filled, beaten and sunned.

delivered an inventory of the best goods in our little Registership; which goods she, in case the house took fire, had, in the first place, to secure. I ordered her, in stormy nights (the peculiar thief-weather), to put our Eolian harp in the window, that so any villanous prowler might imagine I was fantasying on my instrument, and therefore awake: for like reasons, also, to take the house-dog within doors by day, that he might sleep then, and so be livelier at night. I farther counselled her to have an eye on the focus of every knot in the panes of the stable-window, nay, on every glass of water she might set down in the house; as I had already often recounted to her examples of such accidental burning-glasses having set whole buildings in flames. I then appointed her the hour when she was to set out on Friday morning to follow me; and recapitulated more emphatically the household precepts, which, prior to her departure, she must afresh inculcate on her domestics. My dear, heart-sound, blooming Berga answered her faithful lord, as it seemed very seriously: "Go thy ways, little old one; it shall all be done as smooth as velvet. Wert thou but away! There is no end of thee!" Her brother, my brother-in-law the Dragoon, for whom, out of complaisance, I had paid the coach-fare, in order to have in the vehicle along with me a stout swordsman and hector, as spiritual relative and bully-rock, so to speak; the Dragoon, I say, on hearing these my regulations, puckered up (which I easily forgave the wild soldier and bachelor) his sunburnt face considerably into ridicule, and said: "Were I in thy place, sister, I should do what I liked, and then afterwards take a peep into these regulation-papers of his."

"O!" answered I, "misfortune may conceal itself like a scorpion in any corner: I might say, we are like children, who, looking at their gaily painted toy-box, soon pull off the lid, and, pop! out springs a mouse who has young ones."

"Mouse, mouse!" said he, stepping up and down. "But, good brother, it is five o'clock; and you will find, when you return, that all looks exactly as it does today; the dog like the dog, and my sister like a pretty woman: *allons done!*" It was purely his blame that I, fearing his misconceptions, had not previously made a sort of testament.

I now packed-in two different sorts of medicines, heating as well as cooling, against two different possibilities; also my old splints for

---

120. Many a one becomes a free-spoken Diogenes, not when he dwells in the Cask, but when the Cask dwells in him.

3. Culture makes whole lands, for instance Germany, Gaul, and others, physically warmer, but spiritually colder.

arm or leg breakages, in case the coach overset; and (out of foresight) two times the money I was likely to need. Only here I could have wished, so uncertain is the stowage of such things, that I had been an Ape with cheek-pouches, or some sort of Opossum with a natural bag, that so I might have reposited these necessaries of existence in pockets which were sensitive. Shaving is a task I always go through before setting out on journeys; having a rational mistrust against stranger bloodthirsty barbers: but, on this occasion, I retained my beard; since, however close shaved, it would have grown again by the road to such a length that I could have fronted no Minister and General with it.

With a vehement emotion, I threw myself on the pith-heart of my Berga, and, with a still more vehement one, tore myself away: in her, however, this our first marriage-separation seemed to produce less lamentation than triumph, less consternation than rejoicing; simply because she turned her eye not half so much on the parting, as on the meeting, and the journey after me, and the wonders of the Fair. Yet she threw and hung herself on my somewhat long and thin neck and body, almost painfully, being indeed a too fleshy and weighty load, and said to me: "Whisk thee off quick, my charming Attel (Attila), and trouble thy head with no cares by the way, thou singular man! A whiff or two of ill luck we can stand, by God's help, so long as my father is no beggar. And for thee, Franz," continued she, turning with some heat to her brother, "I leave my Attel on thy soul: thou well knowest, thou wild fly, what I will do, if thou play the fool, and leave him anywhere in the lurch." Her meaning here was good, and I could not take it ill: to you also, my Friends, her wealth and her open-heartedness are nothing new.

Melted into sensibility, I said: "Now, Berga, if there be a reunion appointed for us, surely it is either in Heaven or in Flätz; and I hope in God, the latter." With these words, we whirled stoutly away. I looked round through the back-window of the coach at my good little village of Neusattel, and it seemed to me, in my melting mood, as if its steeples were rising aloft like an epitaphium over my life, or over my body, perhaps to return a lifeless corpse. "How will it all be," thought I, "when thou at last, after two or three days, comest back?" And now I noticed my Bergelchen looking after us from the garret-window. I leaned far out from the coach-door, and her falcon

---

1. The more Weakness the more Lying: Force goes straight; any cannon-ball with holes or cavities in it goes crooked.

eye instantly distinguished my head; kiss on kiss she threw with both hands after the carriage, as it rolled down into the valley. "Thou true-hearted wife," thought I, "how is thy lowly birth, by thy spiritual new-birth, made forgettable, nay remarkable!"

I must confess, the assemblage and conversational picnic of the stage-coach was much less to my taste: the whole of them suspicious, unknown rabble, whom (as markets usually do) the Flätz cattle-market was alluring by its scent. I dislike becoming acquainted with strangers: not so my brother-in-law, the Dragoon; who now, as he always does, had in a few minutes elbowed himself into close quarters with the whole ragamuffin posse of them. Beside me sat a person who, in all human probability, was a Harlot; on her breast, a Dwarf intending to exhibit himself at the Fair; on the other side was a Ratcatcher gazing at me; and a Blind Passenger,[3] in a red mantle, had joined us down in the valley. No one of them, except my brother-in-law, pleased me. That rascals among these people would not study me and my properties and accidents, to entangle me in their snares, no man could be my surety. In strange places, I even, out of prudence, avoid looking long up at any jail-window; because some losel, sitting behind the bars, may in a moment call down out of mere malice: "How goes it, comrade Schmelzle?" or farther, because any lurking catchpole may fancy I am planning a rescue for some confederate above. From another sort of prudence, little different from this, I also make a point of never turning round when any booby calls, Thief! behind me.

As to the Dwarf himself, I had no objection to his travelling with me whithersoever he pleased; but he thought to raise a particular delectation in our minds, by promising that his Pollux and Brother in Trade, an extraordinary Giant, who was also making for the Fair to exhibit himself, would by midnight, with his elephantine pace, infallibly overtake the coach, and plant himself among us, or behind on the outside. Both these noodles, it appeared, are in the

---

38. Epictetus advises us to travel, because our old acquaintances, by the influence of shame, impede our transition to higher virtues; as a bashful man will rather lay aside his provincial accent in some foreign quarter, and then return wholly purified to his own countrymen: in our days, people of rank and virtue follow this advice, but inversely; and travel because their old acquaintances, by the influence of shame, would too much deter them from new sins.

[3] 'Live Passenger,' 'Nip;' a passenger taken up only by Jarvie's authority, and for Jarvie's profit.—ED.

habit of going in company to fairs, as reciprocal exaggerators of opposite magnitudes: the Dwarf is the convex magnifying-glass of the Giant, the Giant the concave diminishing-glass of the Dwarf. Nobody expressed much joy at the prospective arrival of this Anti-dwarf, except my brother-in-law, who (if I may venture on a play of words) seems made, like a clock, solely for the purpose of *striking,* and once actually said to me: "That if in the Upper world he could not get a soul to curry and towzle by a time, he would rather go to the Under, where most probably there would be plenty of cuffing and to spare." The Ratcatcher, besides the circumstance that no man can prepossess us much in his favour, who lives solely by poisoning, like this Destroying Angel of rats, this mouse-Atropos; and also, which is still worse, that such a fellow bids fair to become an increaser of the vermin kingdom, the moment he may cease to be a lessener of it; besides all this, I say, the present Ratcatcher had many baneful features about him: first, his stabbing look, piercing you like a stiletto; then the lean sharp bony visage, conjoined with his enumeration of his considerable stock of poisons; then (for I hated him more and more) his sly stillness, his sly smile, as if in some corner he noticed a mouse, as he would notice a man! To me, I declare, though usually I take not the slightest exception against people's looks, it seemed at last as if his throat were a Dog-grotto, a *Grotta del cane,* his cheek-bones cliffs and breakers, his hot breath the wind of a calcining furnace, and his black hairy breast a kiln for parching and roasting.

Nor was I far wrong, I believe; for soon after this, he began quite coolly to inform the company, in which were a dwarf and a female, that, in his time, he had, not without enjoyment, run ten men through the body; had with great convenience hewed off a dozen men's arms; slowly split four heads, torn out two hearts, and more of the like sort; while none of them, otherwise persons of spirit, had in the least

---

32. Our Age (by some called the Paper Age, as if it were made from the rags of some better-dressed one) is improving in so far, as it now tears its rags rather into Bandages than into Papers; although, or because, the Rag-hacker (the Devil as they call it) will not altogether be at rest. Meanwhile, if Learned Heads transform themselves into Books, Crowned Heads transform and coin themselves into Government-paper: in Norway, according to the *Universal Indicator,* the people have even paper-houses; and in many good German States, the Exchequer Collegium (to say nothing of the Justice Collegium) keeps its own paper-mills, to furnish wrappage enough for the meal of its wind-mills. I could wish, however, that our Collegiums would take pattern from that Glass Manufactory at Madrid, in which (according to Baumgärtner) there were indeed nineteen clerks stationed, but also eleven workmen.

resisted: "but why?" added he, with a poisonous smile, and taking the hat from his odious bald pate: "I am invulnerable. Let any one of the company that chooses lay as much fire on my bare crown as he likes, I shall not mind it."

My brother-in-law, the Dragoon, directly kindled his tinder-box, and put a heap of the burning matter on the Ratcatcher's pole; but the fellow stood it, as if it had been a mere picture of fire, and the two looked expectingly at one another; and the former smiled very foolishly, saying: "It was simply pleasant to him, like a good warming-plaster; for this was always the wintry region of his body."

Here the Dragoon groped a little on the naked scull, and cried with amazement, that "it was as cold as a knee-pan."

But now the fellow, to our horror, after some preparations, actually lifted off the quarter-scull and held it out to us, saying: "He had sawed it off a murderer, his own having accidentally been broken;" and withal explained, that the stabbing and arm-cutting he had talked of was to be understood as a jest, seeing he had merely done it in the character of Famulus at an Anatomical Theatre. However, the jester seemed to rise little in favour with any of us; and for my part, as he put his brain-lid and sham-scull on again, I thought to myself; "This dungbed-bell has changed its place indeed, but not the hemlock it was made to cover."

Farther, I could not but reckon it a Suspicious circumstance, that he as well as all the company (the Blind Passenger too) were making for this very Flätz, to which I myself was bound: much good I could not expect of this; and, in truth, turning home again would have been as pleasant to me as going on, had I not rather felt a pleasure in defying the future.

I come now to the red-mantled Blind Passenger; most probably an *Emigre* or *Réfugié;* for he speaks German not worse than he does French; and his name, I think, was *Jean Pierre* or *Jean Paul,* or some such thing, if indeed he had any name. His red cloak, notwithstanding this his identity of colour with the Hangman, would in itself have remained heartily indifferent to me, had it not been for this singular circumstance, that he had already five times, contrary to all expectation, come upon me in five different towns (in great Berlin, in little Hof, in Coburg, Meiningen and Bayreuth), and each of these times had looked at me significantly enough, and then gone his ways. Whether this *Jean Pierre* is dogging me with hostile intent or not, I cannot say; but to our fancy, at any rate, no object can be gratifying that thus, with corps of observation, or out of loopholes, holds and aims at us with muskets, which for year after year it shall move to this side and that, without our knowing on whom it is to fire. Still more offensive did Redcloak become to me, when he began to talk about his soft mildness of soul; a thing which seemed either to betoken pumping you or undermining you.

I replied: "Sir, I am just come, with my brother-in-law here, from the field of battle (the last affair was at Pimpelstadt), and so perhaps am too much of a humour for fire, pluck and war-fury; and to many a one, who happens to have a roaring waterspout of a heart, it may be well if his clerical character (which is mine) rather enjoins on him mildness than wildness. However, all mildness has its iron limit. If any thoughtless dog chance to anger me, in the first heat of rage I kick my foot through him; and after me, my good brother here will perhaps drive matters twice as far, for he is the man to do it. Perhaps it may be singular; but I confess I regret to this day, that once when a boy I received three blows from another, without tightly returning them; and I often feel as if I must still pay them to his descendants. In sooth, if I but chance to see a child running off like a dastard from the weak attack of a child like himself, I cannot for my life understand his running, and can scarcely keep from interfering to save him by a decisive knock."

The Passenger meanwhile was smiling, not in the best fashion. He gave himself out for a Legations-Rath, and seemed fox enough for such a post; but a mad fox will, in the long-run, bite me as rabidly as a mad wolf will. For the rest, I calmly went on with my eulogy on courage; only that, instead of ludicrous gasconading, which directly betrays the coward, I purposely expressed myself in words at once cool, clear and firm.

"I am altogether for Montaigne's advice," said I: "Fear nothing but fear."

"I again," replied the Legations-man, with useless wiredrawing, "I should fear again that I did not sufficiently fear fear, but continued too dastardly."

"To this fear also," replied I coldly, "I set limits. A man, for instance, may not in the least believe in, or be afraid of ghosts; and yet by night may bathe himself in cold sweat, and this purely out of terror at the dreadful fright he should be in (especially with what whiffs of apoplexies, falling-sicknesses and so forth, he might be

---

2. In his Prince, a soldier reverences and obeys at once his Prince and his Generalissimo; a Citizen only his Prince.

visited), in case simply his own too vivid fancy should create any wild fever-image, and hang it up in the air before him."

"One should not, therefore," added my brother-in-law the Dragoon, contrary to his custom, moralising a little, "one should not bamboozle the poor sheep, man, with any ghost-tricks; the hen-heart may die on the spot."

A loud storm of thunder, overtaking the stage-coach, altered the discourse. You, my Friends, knowing me as a man not quite destitute of some tincture of Natural Philosophy, will easily guess my precautions against thunder. I place myself on a chair in the middle of the room (often, when suspicious clouds are out, I stay whole nights on it), and by careful removal of all conductors, rings, buckles, and so forth, I here sit thunder-proof, and listen with a cool spirit to this elemental music of the cloud-kettledrum. These precautions have never harmed me, for I am still alive at this date; and to the present hour I congratulate myself on once hurrying out of church, though I had confessed but the day previous; and running, without more ceremony, and before I had received the sacrament, into the charnel-house, because a heavy thunder-cloud (which did, in fact, strike the churchyard linden-tree) was hovering over it. So soon as the cloud had disloaded itself, I returned from the charnel-house into the church, and was happy enough to come in after the Hangman (usually the last), and so still participate in the Feast of Love.

Such, for my own part, is my manner of proceeding: but in the full stage-coach I met with men to whom Natural Philosophy was no philosophy at all. For when the clouds gathered dreadfully together over our coach-canopy, and sparkling, began to play through the air like so many fire-flies, and I at last could not but request that the sweating coach-conclave would at least bring out their watches, rings, money and suchlike, and put them all into one of the carriage-pockets, that none of us might have a conductor on his body; not only would no one of them do it, but my own brother-in-law the Dragoon even sprang out, with naked drawn sword, to the coach-box, and swore that he would conduct the thunder all away himself. Nor do I know whether this desperate mortal was not acting prudently; for our position within was frightful, and any one of us might every moment be a dead man. At last, to crown all, I got into a half altercation with two of the rude members of our leathern household, the Poisoner

---

45. Our present writers shrug their shoulders most at those on whose shoulders they stand; and exalt those most who crawl up along them.

and the Harlot; seeing, by their questions, they almost gave me to understand that, in our conversational picnic, especially with the Blind Passenger, I had not always come off with the best share. Such an imputation wounds your honour to the quick; and in my breast there was a thunder louder than that above us: however, I was obliged to carry on the needful exchange of sharp words as quietly and slowly as possible; and I quarrelled softly, and in a low tone, lest in the end a whole coachful of people, set in arms against each other, might get into heat and perspiration; and so, by vapour steaming through the coach-roof, conduct the too-near thunderbolt down into the midst of us. At last, I laid before the company the whole theory of Electricity, in clear words, but low and slow (striving to avoid all emission of vapour); and especially endeavoured to frighten them away from fear. For indeed, through fear, the stroke—nay two strokes, the electric or the apoplectic—might hit any one of us; since in Erxleben and Reimarus, it is sufficiently proved, that violent fear, by the transpiration it causes, may attract the lightning. I accordingly, in some fear of my own and other people's fear, represented to the passengers that now, in a coach so hot and crowded, with a drawn sword on the coach-box piercing the very lightning, with the thunder-cloud hanging over us, and even with so many transpirations from incipient fear; in short, with such visible danger on every hand, they must absolutely fear nothing, if they would not, all and sundry, be smitten to death in a few minutes.

"O Heaven!" cried I, "Courage! only courage! No fear, not even fear of fear! Would you have Providence to shoot you here sitting, like so many hares hunted into a pinfold? Fear, if you like, when you are out of the coach; fear to your heart's content in other places, where there is less to be afraid of; only not here, not here!"

I shall not determine—since among millions scarcely one man dies by thunder-clouds, but millions perhaps by snow-clouds, and rain-clouds, and thin mist—whether my Coach-sermon could have made any claim to a prize for man-saving; however, at last, all uninjured, and driving towards a rainbow, we entered the town of Vierstädten, where dwelt a Postmaster, in the only street which the place had.

---

103. The Great perhaps take as good charge of their posterity as the Ants: the eggs once laid, the male and female Ants fly about their business, and confide them to the trusty *working-Ants*.

10. And does Life offer us, in regard to our ideal hopes and purposes, anything but a prosaic, unrhymed, unmetrical Translation?

Second Stage; from Vierstädten to Niederschöna

The Postmaster was a churl and a striker; a class of mortals whom I inexpressibly detest, as my fancy always whispers to me, in their presence, that by accident or dislike I might happen to put on a scornful or impertinent look, and hound these mastiffs on my own throat; and so, from the very first, I must incessantly watch them. Happily, in this case (supposing I even had made a wrong face), I could have shielded myself with the Dragoon; for whose giant force such matters are a tidbit. This brother-in-law of mine, for example, cannot pass any tavern where he hears a sound of battle, without entering, and, as he crosses the threshold, shouting: "Peace, dogs!"— and therewith, under show of a peace-deputation, he directly snatches up the first chair-leg in his hand, as if it were an American peace-calumet, and cuts to the right and left among the belligerent powers, or he gnashes the hard heads of the parties together (he himself takes no side), catching each by the hind-lock; in such cases the rogue is in Heaven!

I, for my part, rather avoid discrepant circles than seek them; as I likewise avoid all dead or killed people: the prudent man easily foresees what is to be got by them; either vexatious and injurious witnessing, or often even (when circumstances conspire) painful investigation, and suspicions of your being an accomplice.

In Vierstädten, nothing of importance presented itself, except—to my horror—a dog without tail, which came running along the town or street. In the first fire of passion at this sight, I pointed it out to the passengers, and then put the question, Whether they could reckon a system of Medical Police well arranged, which, like this of Vierstädten, allowed dogs openly to scour about, when their tails were wanting? "What am I to do," said I, "when this member is cut away, and any such beast comes running towards me, and I cannot, either by the tail being cocked up or being drawn in, since the whole is snipt off, come to any conclusion whether the vermin is mad or

---

78. Our German frame of Government, cased in its harness, had much difficulty in moving, for the same reason why Beetles cannot fly, when their *wings* have *wing-shells,* of very sufficient strength, and—grown together.

8. Constitutions of Government are like highways: on a new and quite untrodden one, where every carriage helps in the process of bruising and smoothing, you are as much jolted and pitched as on an old worn-out one, full of holes? What is to be done then? Travel on.

3. In Criminal Courts, murdered children are often represented as still-born; in Anticritiques, still-born as murdered.

not? In this way, the most prudent man may be bit, and become rabid, and so make shipwreck purely for want of a tail-compass."

The Blind Passenger (he now got himself inscribed as a Seeing one, God knows for what objects) had heard my observation; which he now spun out in my presence almost into ridicule, and at last awakened in me the suspicion, that by an overdone flattery in imitating my style of speech, he meant to banter me. "The Dog-tail," said he, "is, in truth, an alarm-beacon, and fingerpost for us, that we come not even into the outmost precincts of madness: cut away from Comets their tails, from Bashaws theirs, from Crabs theirs (outstretched it denotes that they are burst); and in the most dangerous predicaments of life we are left without clew, without indicator, without hand *in margine;* and we perish, not so much as knowing how."

For the rest, this stage passed over without quarrelling or peril. About ten o'clock, the whole party, including even the Postillion, myself excepted, fell asleep. I indeed pretended to be sleeping, that I might observe whether some one, for his own good reasons, might not also be pretending it; but all continued snoring; the moon threw its brightening beams on nothing but down-pressed eyelids.

I had now a glorious opportunity of following Lavater's counsel, to apply the physiognomical ellwand specially to sleepers, since sleep, like death, expresses the genuine form in coarser lines. Other sleepers not in stage-coaches I think it less advisable to mete with this ellwand; having always an apprehension lest some fellow, but pretending to be asleep, may, the instant I am near enough, start up as in a dream, and deceitfully plant such a knock on the physiognomical mensurator's own facial structure, as to exclude it forever from appearing in any Physiognomical Fragments (itself being reduced to one), either in the stippled or line style. Nay, might not the most honest sleeper in the world, just while you are in hand with his physiognomical dissection, lay about him, spurred on by honour in some cudgelling-scene he may be dreaming; and in a few instants of clapperclawing, and kicking, and trampling, lull you into a much more lasting sleep than that out of which he was awakened?

---

101. Not only were the Rhodians, from their Colossus, called Colossians; but also innumerable Germans are, from their Luther, called Lutherans.

88. Hitherto I have always regarded the Polemical writings of our present philosophic and æsthetic Idealist Logic-buffers,—in which, certainly, a few contumelies, and misconceptions, and misconclusions do make their appearance,—rather on the fair side; observing in it merely an imitation of classical Antiquity, in particular of the ancient Athletes, who (according to Schöttgen) besmeared their

In my *Adumbrating Magic-lantern,* as I have named the Work, the whole physiognomical contents of this same sleeping stage-coach will be given to the world: there I shall explain to you at large how the Poisoner, with the murder-cupola, appeared to me devil-like; the Dwarf old-childlike; the Harlot languidly shameless; my Brother-in-law peacefully satisfied, with revenge or food; and the Legations-Rath, *Jean Pierre,* Heaven only knows why, like a half angel,—though, perhaps, it might be because only the fair body, not the other half, the soul, which had passed away in sleep, was affecting me.

I had almost forgotten to mention, that in a little village, while my Brother-in-law and the Postillion were sitting at their liquor, I happily fronted a small terror, Destiny having twice been on my side. Not far from a Hunting Box, beside a pretty clump of trees, I noticed a white tablet, with a black inscription on it. This gave me hopes that perhaps some little monumental piece, some pillar of honour, some battle memento, might here be awaiting me. Over an untrodden flowery tangle, I reach the black on white; and to my horror and amazement, I decipher in the moonshine: *Beware of Spring-guns!* Thus was I standing perhaps half a nail's breadth from the trigger, with which, if I but stirred my heel, I should shoot myself off like a forgotten ramrod, into the other world, beyond the verge of Time! The first thing I did was to cramp-down my toe-nails, to bite, and, as it were, eat myself into the ground with them; since I might at least continue in warm life so long as I pegged my body firmly in beside the Atropos-scissors and hangman's block, which lay beside me; then I endeavoured to recollect by what steps the fiend had let me hither unshot, but in my agony I had perspired the whole of it, and could remember nothing. In the Devil's village close at hand, there was no dog to be seen and called to, who might have plucked me from the water; and my Brother-in-law and the Postillion were both carousing with full can. However, I summoned my courage and determination; wrote down on a leaf of my pocket-book my last will, the accidental manner of my death,

---

bodies with *mud,* that they might not be laid hold of; and filled their hands with *sand,* that they might lay hold of their antagonists.

103. Or are all Mosques, Episcopal-churches, Pagodas, Chapels-of-Ease, Tabernacles and Pantheons, anything else than the Ethnic Forecourt of the Invisible Temple and its Holy of Holies?

40. The common man is copious only in narration, not in reasoning; the cultivated man is brief only in the former, not in the latter: because the common man's reasons are a sort of sensations, which, as well as things visible, he merely *looks at;* by the cultivated man, again, both reasons and things visible are rather *thought* than looked at.

and my dying remembrance of Berga; and then, with full sails, flew helterskelter through the midst of it the shortest way; expecting at every step to awaken the murderous engine, and thus to clap over my still long candle of life the *bonsoir,* or extinguisher, with my own hand. However, I got off without shot. In the tavern, indeed, there was more than one fool to laugh at me; because, forsooth, what none but a fool could know, this Notice had stood there for the last ten years, without any gun, as guns often do without any notice. But so it is, my Friends, with our game-police, which warns against all things, only not against warnings.

For the rest, throughout the whole stage, I had a constant source of altercation with the coachman, because he grudged stopping perhaps once in the quarter of an hour, when I chose to come out for a natural purpose. Unhappily, in truth, one has little reason to expect water-doctors among the postillion class, since Physicians themselves have so seldom learned from Haller's large *Physiology,* that a postponement of the above operation will precipitate devilish stoneware, and at last precipitate the proprietor himself; this stone-manufactory being generally concluded, not by the Lithotomist, but by Death. Had postillions read that Tycho Brahe died like a bombshell by bursting, they would rather pull up for a moment; with such unlooked-for knowledge, they would see it to be reasonable that a man, though expecting some time to carry his death-stone *on* him, should not incline, for the time being, to carry it *in* him. Nay, have I not often, at Weimar, in the longest concluding scenes of Schiller, run out with tears in my eyes; purely that, while his Minerva was melting me on the whole, I might not by the Gorgon's head on her breast be partially turned to stone? And did I not return to the weeping playhouse, and fall into the general emotion so much the more briskly, as now I had nothing to give vent to but my heart?

Deep in the dark we arrived at Niederschöna.

Third Stage; from Niederschöna to Flätz

While I am standing at the Posthouse musing, with my eye fixed on my portmanteau, comes a beast of a watchman, and bellows and

---

9. In any national calamity, the ancient Egyptians took revenge on the god Typhon, whom they blamed for it, by hurling his favourites, the Asses, down over rocks. In similar ways have countries of a different religion now and then taken their revenge.

brays in his night-tube so close by my ear, that I start back in trepidation, I whom even a too hasty accosting will vex. Is there no medical police, then, against such efflated hour fulminators and alarm-cannon, by which notwithstanding no gunpowder cannon are saved? In my opinion, nobody should be invested with the watchman-horn but some reasonable man, who had already blown himself into an asthma, and who would consequently be in case to sing out his hour-verse so low, that you could not hear it.

What I had long expected, and the Dwarf predicted, now took place: deeply stooping, through the high Posthouse door, issued the Giant, and raised, in the open air, a most unreasonably high figure, heightened by the ell-long bonnet and feather on his huge jobber-nowl. My Brother-in-law, beside him, looked but like his son of fourteen years; the Dwarf like his lap-dog waiting for him on its two hind legs. "Good friend," said my bantering Brother-in-law, leading him towards me and the stage-coach, "just step softly in, we shall all be happy to make room for you. Fold yourself neatly together, lay your head on your knee, and it will do." The unseasonable banterer would willingly have seen the almost stupid Giant (of whom he had soon observed that his brain was no active substance, but in the inverse ratio of his trunk) squeezed in among us in the post-chest, and lying kneaded together like a sand-bag before him. "Won't do! Won't do!" said the Giant, looking in. "The gentleman perhaps does not know," said the Dwarf, "how big the Giant is; and so he thinks that because *I* go in—But that is another story; *I* will creep into any hole, do but tell me where."

In short, there was no resource for the Postmaster and the Giant, but that the latter should plant himself behind, in the character of luggage, and there lie bending down like a weeping willow over the whole vehicle. To me such a back-wall and rearguard could not be particularly gratifying: and I may refer it, I hope, to any one of you, ye Friends, if with such ware at your back, you would not, as clearly and earnestly as I, have considered what manifold murderous projects a knave of a Giant behind you, a *pursuer* in all senses, might not maliciously attempt; say, that he broke in and assailed you by the back-window, or with Titanian strength laid hold of the coach-roof and demolished the whole party in a lump. However, this Elephant

---

70. Let Poetry veil itself in Philosophy, but only as the latter does in the former. Philosophy in poetised Prose resembles those tavern drinking-glasses, encircled with parti-coloured wreaths of figures, which disturb your enjoyment both of the drink, and (often awkwardly eclipsing and covering each other) of the carving also.

(who indeed seemed to owe the similarity more to his overpowering mass than to his quick light of inward faculty), crossing his arms over the top of the vehicle, soon began to sleep and snore above us; an Elephant, of whom, as I more and more joyfully observed, my Brother-in-law the Dragoon could easily be the tamer and bridle-holder, nay had already been so.

As more than one person now felt inclined to sleep, but I, on the contrary, as was proper, to wake, I freely offered my seat of honour, the front place in the coach (meaning thereby to abolish many little flaws of envy in my fellow-passengers), to such persons as wished to take a nap thereon. The Legations-man accepted the offer with eagerness, and soon fell asleep there sitting, under the Titan.[4] To me this sort of coach-sleeping of a diplomatic *chargé d'affaires* remained a thing incomprehensible. A man that, in the middle of a stranger and often barbarously-minded company, permits himself to slumber, may easily, supposing him to talk in his sleep and coach (think of the Saxon minister[5] before the Seven-Years War!), blab out a thousand secrets, and crimes, some of which, perhaps, he has not committed. Should not every minister, ambassador, or other man of honour and rank, really shudder at the thought of insanity or violent fevers; seeing no mortal can be his surety that he shall not in such cases publish the greatest scandals, of which, it may be, the half are lies?

At last, after the long July night, we passengers, together with Aurora, arrived in the precincts of Flätz. I looked with a sharp yet moistened eye at the steeples: I believe, every man who has anything decisive to seek in a town, and to whom it is either to be a judgment-seat of his hopes, or their anchoring-station, either a battle-field or a sugar-field, first and longest directs his eye on the steeples of the town, as upon the indexes and balance-tongues of his future destiny; these artificial peaks, which, like natural ones, are the thrones of our Future. As I happened to express myself on this point perhaps too poetically to *Jean Pierre,* he answered, with sufficient want of taste: "The steeples of such towns are indeed the Swiss Alpine peaks, on which we milk and manufacture the Swiss cheese of our Future." Did the Legations-Peter mean with this style to make me ridiculous, or only himself? Determine!

---

[4] *Titan* is also the title of this Legations-Rath Jean Pierre or Jean Paul (Friedrich Richter)'s chief novel.—ED.

[5] Brühl, I suppose; but the historical edition of the matter is, that Brühl's treasonable secrets were come at by the more ordinary means of wax impressions of his keys.—ED.

"Here is the place, the town," said I in secret, "where today much and for many years is to be determined; where thou, this evening, about five o'clock, art to present thy petition and thyself: May it prosper! May it be successful! Let Flätz, this arena of thy little efforts among the rest, become a building-space for fair castles and air-castles to two hearts, thy own and thy Berga's!"

At the Tiger Inn I alighted.

First Day in Flätz

No mortal, in my situation at this Tiger-hotel, would have triumphed much in his more immediate prospects. I, as the only man known to me, especially in the way of love (of the runaway Dragoon anon!), looked out from the windows of the overflowing Inn, and down on the rushing sea of marketers, and very soon began to reflect, that except Heaven and the rascals and murderers, none knew how many of the latter two classes were floating among the tide; purposing perhaps to lay hold of the most innocent strangers, and in part cut their purses, in part their throats. My situation had a special circumstance against it. My Brother-in-law, who still comes plump out with everything, had mentioned that I was to put up at the Tiger: O Heaven, when will such people learn to be secret, and to cover even the meanest pettinesses of life under mantles and veils, were it only that a silly mouse may as often give birth to a mountain, as a mountain to a mouse! The whole rabble of the stage-coach stopped at the Tiger; the Harlot, the Ratcatcher, *Jean Pierre,* the Giant, who had dismounted at the Gate of the town, and carrying the huge blockhead of the Dwarf on his shoulders as his own (cloaking over the deception by his cloak), had thus, like a ninny, exhibited himself gratis by half a dwarf more gigantic than he could be seen for money.

---

158. Governments should not too often change the penny-trumps and child's-drums of the Poets for the regimental trumpet and fire-drum: on the other hand, good subjects should regard many a princely drum-tendency simply as a disease, in which the patient, by air insinuating under the skin, has got dreadfully swoln.

89. In great towns, a stranger, for the first day or two after his arrival, lives purely at his own expense in an inn; afterwards, in the houses of his friends, without expense: on the other hand, if you arrive at the Earth, as, for instance, I have done, you are courteously maintained, precisely for the first few years, free of charges; but in the next and longer series—for you often stay sixty—you are actually obliged (I have the documents in my hands) to pay for every drop and morsel, as if you were in the great Earth Inn, which indeed you are.

And now for each of the Passengers, the question was, how he could make the Tiger, the heraldic emblem of the Inn, his prototype; and so, what lamb he might suck the blood of, and tear in pieces, and devour. My Brother-in-law too left me, having gone in quest of some horse-dealer; but he retained the chamber next mine for his sister: this, it appeared, was to denote attention on his part. I remained solitary, left to my own intrepidity and force of purpose.

Yet among so many villains, encompassing if not even beleaguering me, I thought warmly of one far distant, faithful soul, of my Berga in Neusattel; a true heart of pith, which perhaps with many a weak marriage-partner might have given protection rather than sought it.

"Appear, then, quickly tomorrow at noon, Berga," said my heart; "and if possible before noon, that I may lengthen thy market paradise so many hours as thou arrivest earlier!"

A clergyman, amid the tempests of the world, readily makes for a free harbour, for the church: the church-wall is his casemate-wall and fortification; and behind are to be found more peaceful and more accordant souls than on the market-place: in short, I went into the High Church. However, in the course of the psalm, I was somewhat disturbed by a Haiduc, who came up to a well-dressed young gentleman sitting opposite me, and tore the double opera-glass from his nose, it being against rule in Flätz, as it is in Dresden, to look at the Court with glasses which diminish and approximate. I myself had on a pair of spectacles, but they were magnifiers. It was impossible for me to resolve on taking them off; and here again, I am afraid, I shall pass for a foolhardy person and a desperado; so much only I reckoned fit, to look invariably into my psalm-book; not once lifting my eyes while the Court was rustling and entering, thereby to denote that my glasses were ground convex. For the rest, the sermon was good, if not always finely conceived for a Court-church; it admonished the hearers against innumerable vices, to whose counterparts, the

---

107. Germany is a long lofty mountain—under the sea.

144. The Reviewer does not in reality employ his pen for writing; but he burns it, to awaken weak people from their swoons, with the smell; he tickles with it the throat of the plagiary, to make him render back; and he picks with it his own teeth. He is the only individual in the whole learned lexicon that can never exhaust himself, never write himself out, let him sit before the ink-glass for centuries or tens of centuries. For while the Scholar, the Philosopher, and the Poet, produce their new book solely from new materials and growth, the Reviewer merely lays his old gage of taste and knowledge on a thousand now works; and his light, in the ever-passing, ever-differently-cut glass-world which he *elucidates,* is still refracted into new colours.

virtues, another preacher might so readily have exhorted us. During the whole service, I made it my business to exhibit true deep reverence, not only towards God, but also towards my illustrious Prince. For the latter reverence I had my private reason: I wished to stamp this sentiment strongly and openly as with raised letters on my countenance, and so give the lie to any malicious imp about Court, by whom my contravention of the *Panegyric on Nero,* and my free German satire on this real tyrant himself, which I had inserted in *the Flätz Weekly Journal,* might have been perverted into a secret characteristic portrait of my own Sovereign. We live in such times at present, that scarcely can we compose a pasquinade on the Devil in Hell, but some human Devil on Earth will apply it to an angel.

When the Court at last issued from church, and were getting into their carriages, I kept at such a distance that my face could not possibly be noticed, in case I had happened to assume no reverent look, but an indifferent or even proud one. God knows, who has kneaded into me those mad desperate fancies and crotchets, which perhaps would sit better on a Hero Schabacker than on an Army-chaplain under him. I cannot here forbear recording to you, my Friends, one of the maddest among them, though at first it may throw too glaring a light on me. It was at my ordination to be Army-chaplain, while about to participate in the Sacrament, on the first day of Easter. Now, here while I was standing, moved into softness, before the balustrade of the altar, in the middle of the whole male congregation,—nay, I perhaps more deeply moved than any among them, since, as a person going to war, I might consider myself a half-dead man, that was now partaking in the last Feast of Souls, as it were like a person to be hanged on the morrow,—here then, amid the pathetic effects of the organ and singing, there rose something—were it the first Easter-day which awoke in me what primitive Christians called their Easter-laughter, or merely the contrast between the most devilish predicaments and the most holy,—in short there rose something in me (for which reason, I have ever since taken the part of every simple person, who might ascribe such things to the Devil), and this something started the question: "Now, could there be aught more diabolical than if thou, just in receiving the Holy Supper, wert madly and blasphemously to begin laughing?" Instantly I took to wrestling with

---

71. The Youth is singular from caprice, and takes pleasure in it; the Man is so from constraint, unintentionally, and feels pain in it.

198. The Populace and Cattle grow giddy on the edge of no abyss; with the Man it is otherwise.

this hell-dog of a thought; neglected the most precious feelings, merely to keep the dog in my eye, and scare him away; yet was forced to draw back from him, exhausted and unsuccessful, and arrived at the step of the altar with the mournful certainty that in a little while I should, without more ado, begin laughing, let me weep and moan inwardly as I liked. Accordingly, while I and a very worthy old Bürgermeister were bowing down together before the long parson, and the latter (perhaps kneeling on the low cushion, I fancied him too long) put the wafer in my clenched mouth, I felt all the muscles of laughter already beginning sardonically to contract; and these had not long acted on the guiltless integument, till an actual smile appeared there; and as we bowed the second time, I was grinning like an ape. My companion the Bürgermeister justly expostulated with me, in a low voice, as we walked round behind the altar: "In Heaven's name, are you an ordained Preacher of the Gospel, or a Merry-Andrew? Is it Satan that is laughing out of you?"

"Ah, Heaven! who else?" said I; and this being over, I finished my devotions in a more becoming fashion.

From the church (I now return to the Flätz one), I proceeded to the Tiger Inn, and dined at the *table-d'hôte*, being at no time shy of encountering men. Previous to the second course, a waiter handed me an empty plate, on which, to my astonishment, I noticed a French verse scratched-in with a fork, containing nothing less than a lampoon on the Commandant of Flätz. Without ceremony, I held out the plate to the company; saying, I had just, as they saw, got this lampooning cover presented to me, and must request them to bear witness that I had nothing to do with the matter. An officer directly changed plates with me. During the fifth course, I could not but admire the chemico-medical ignorance of the company; for a hare, out of which a gentleman extracted and exhibited several grains of shot, that is to say, therefore, of lead alloyed with arsenic, and then cleaned by hot vinegar, did, nevertheless, by the spectators (I excepted) continue to be pleasantly eaten.

In the course of our table-talk, one topic seized me keenly by my weak side, I mean by my honour. The law custom of the city

---

11. The Golden Calf of Self-love soon waxes to be a burning Phalaris' Bull, which reduces its father and adorer to ashes.

103. The male Beau-crop which surrounds the female Roses and Lilies, must (if I rightly comprehend its flatteries) most probably presuppose in the fair the manners of the Spaniards and Italians, who offer any valuable, by way of present, to the man who praises it excessively.

happened to be mentioned, as it affects natural children; and I learned that here a loose girl may convert any man she pleases to select into the father of her brat, simply by her oath. "Horrible!" said I, and my hair stood on end. "In this way may the worthiest head of a family, with a wife and children, or a clergyman lodging in the Tiger, be stript of honour and innocence, by any wicked chambermaid whom he may have seen, or who may have seen him, in the course of her employment!"

An elderly officer observed: "But will the girl swear herself to the Devil so readily?"

What logic! "Or suppose," continued I, without answer, "a man happened to be travelling with that Vienna Locksmith, who afterwards became a mother, and was brought to bed of a baby son; or with any disguised Chevalier d'Eon, who often passes the night in his company, whereby the Locksmith or the Chevalier can swear to their private interviews: no delicate man of honour will in the end risk travelling with another; seeing he knows not how soon the latter may pull off his boots, and pull on his women's-pumps, and swear his companion into fatherhood, and himself to the Devil!"

Some of the company, however, misunderstood my oratorical fire so much, that they, sheep-wise, gave some insinuations as if I myself were not strict in this point, but lax. By Heaven! I no longer knew what I was eating or speaking. Happily, on the opposite side of the table, some lying story of a French defeat was started: now, as I had read on the street-corners that French and German Proclamation, calling before the Court Martial any one who had heard war-rumours (disadvantageous, namely), without giving notice of them,—I, as a man not willing ever to forget himself, had nothing more prudent to do in this case, than to withdraw with empty ears, telling none but the landlord why.

It was no improper time; for I had previously determined to have my beard shaven about half-past four, that so, towards five I might present myself with a chin just polished by the razor smoothing-iron,

---

199. But not many existing Governments, I believe, do behead under pretext of trepanning; or sew (in a more choice allegory) the people's lips together, under pretence of sewing the harelips in them.

67. Hospitable Entertainer, wouldst thou search into thy guest? Accompany him to another Entertainer, and listen to him. Just so: Wouldst thou become better acquainted with Mistress in an hour, than by living with her for a month? Accompany her among her female friends and female enemies (if that is no pleonasm), and look at her!

and sleek as wove-paper, without the smallest root-stump of a hair left on it. By way of preparation, like Pitt before Parliamentary debates, I poured a devilish deal of Pontac into my stomach, with true disgust, and contrary to all sanitary rules: not so much for fronting the light stranger Barber, as the Minister and General von Schabacker, with whom I had it in view to exchange perhaps more than one fiery statement.

The common Hotel Barber was ushered in to me; but at first view you noticed in his polygonal zigzag visage, more of a man that would finally go mad, than of one growing wiser. Now, madmen are a class of persons whom I hate incredibly; and nothing can take me to see any madhouse, simply because the first maniac among them may clutch me in his giant fists if he like; and because, owing to infection, I cannot be sure that I shall ever get out again with the sense which I brought in. In a general way, I sit (when once I am lathered) in such a posture on my chair as to keep both my hands (the eyes I fix intently on the barbering countenance) lying clenched along my sides, and pointed directly at the midriff of the barber; that so, on the smallest ambiguity of movement, I may dash in upon him, and overset him in a twinkling.

I scarce know rightly how it happened; but here, while I am anxiously studying the foolish twisted visage of the shaver, and he just then chanced to lay his long-whetted weapon a little too abruptly against my bare throat, I gave him such a sudden bounce on the abdominal viscera, that the silly varlet had well-nigh suicidally slit his own windpipe. For me, truly, nothing remained but to indemnify the man; and then, contrary to my usual principles, to tie round a broad stuffed cravat, by way of cloak to what remained unshorn.

And now at last I sallied forth to the General, drinking out the remnant of the Pontac, as I crossed the threshold. I hope, there were plans lying ready within me for answering rightly, nay for asking. The Petition I carried in my pocket, and in my right hand. In the left I had a duplicate of it. My fire of spirit easily helped over the

---

80. In the summer of life, men keep digging and filling ice-pits as well as circumstances will admit; that so, in their Winter, they may have something in store to give them coolness.

28. It is impossible for me, amid the tendril-forest of allusions (even this again is a tendril-twig), to state and declare on the spot whether all the Courts or Heights, the (Bougouer) *Snowline* of Europe, have ever been mentioned in my Writings or not; but I could wish for information on the subject, that if not, I may try to do it still.

living fence of ministerial obstructions; and soon I unexpectedly found myself in the ante-chamber, among his most distinguished lackeys; persons, so far as I could see, not inclined to change flour for bran with any one. Selecting the most respectable individual of the number, I delivered him my paper request, accompanied with the verbal one that he would hand it in. He took it, but ungraciously: I waited in vain till far in the sixth hour, at which season alone the gay General can safely be applied to. At last I pitch upon another lackey, and repeat my request: he runs about seeking his runaway brother, or my Petition; to no purpose, neither of them could be found. How happy was it that in the midst of my Pontac, before shaving, I had written out the duplicate of this paper; and therefore—simply on the principle that you should always keep a second wooden leg packed into your knapsack when you have the first on your body—and out of fear that if the original petition chanced to drop from me in the way between the Tiger and Schabacker's, my whole journey and hope would melt into water—and therefore, I say, having stuck the repeating work of that original paper into my pocket, I had, in any case, something to hand in, and that something truly a Ditto. I handed it in.

Unhappily six o'clock was already past. The lackey, however, did not keep me long waiting; but returned with—I may say, the text of this whole Circular—the almost rude answer (which you, my Friends, out of regard for me and Schabacker, will not divulge) that: "In case I were the Attila Schmelzle of Schabacker's Regiment, I might lift my pigeon-liver flag again, and fly to the Devil, as I did at Pimpelstadt." Another man would have dropt dead on the spot: I, however, walked quite stoutly off, answering the fellow: "With great pleasure indeed. I fly to the Devil; and so Devil a fly I care." On the road home I examined myself whether it had not been the Pontac that spoke out of me (though the very examination contradicted this, for Pontac never examines); but I found that nothing but I, my heart, my courage perhaps, had spoken: and why,

---

36. And so I should like, in all cases, to be the First, especially in Begging. The first prisoner-of-war, the first cripple, the first man ruined by burning (like him who brings the first fire-engine), gains the head-subscription and the heart; the next-comer finds nothing but Duty to address; and at last, in this melodious *mancando* of sympathy, matters sink so far, that the last (if the last but one may at least have retired laden with a rich "God help you!") obtains from the benignant hand nothing more than its fist. And as in Begging the first, so in Giving I should like to be the last: one obliterates the other, especially the last the first. So, however, is the world ordered.

after all, any whimpering? Does not the patrimony of my good wife endow me better than ten Catechetical Professorships? And has she not furnished all the corners of my book of Life with so many golden clasps, that I can open it forever without wearing it? Let henhearts cackle and pip; I flapped my pinions, and said: "Dash boldly through it, come what may!" I felt myself excited and exalted; I fancied Republics, in which I, as a hero, might be at home; I longed to be in that noble Grecian time, when one hero readily put up with bastinadoes from another, and said: "Strike, but hear!" and out of this ignoble one, where men will scarcely put up with hard words, to say nothing of more. I painted out to my mind how I should feel, if, in happier circumstances, I were uprooting hollow Thrones, and before whole nations mounting on mighty deeds as on the Temple-steps of Immortality; and in gigantic ages, finding quite other men to outman and outstrip, than the mite-populace about me, or, at the best, here and there a Vulcanello. I thought and thought, and grew wilder and wilder, and intoxicated myself (no Pontac intoxication therefore, which, you know, increases more by continuance than cessation of drinking), and gesticulated openly, as I put the question to myself: "Wilt thou be a mere state-lapdog? A dog's-dog, a *pium desiderium* of an *impium desiderium,* an Ex-Ex, a Nothing's-Nothing?—Fire and Fury!" With this, however, I dashed down my hat into the mud of the market. On lifting and cleaning this old servant, I could not but perceive how worn and faded it was; and I therefore determined instantly to purchase a new one, and carry the same home in my hand.

I accomplished this; I bought one of the finest cut. Strangely enough, by this hat, as if it had been a graduation-hat, was my head tried and examined, in the Ziegengasse or Goat-gate of Flätz. For as General Schabacker came driving along that street in his carriage, and I (it need not be said) was determined to avenge myself, not by vulgar clownishness, but by courtesy, I had here got one of the most ticklish problems imaginable to solve on the spur of the instant. You observe, if I swung only the fine hat which I carried in my hand, and kept the faded one on my head,—I might have the appearance of a perfect clown, who does not doff at all: if, on the other hand, I pulled the old hat from my head, and therewith

---

136. If you mount too high above your time, your ears (on the side of Fame) are little better off than if you sink too deep below it: in truth, Charles up in his Balloon, and Halley down in his Diving-bell, felt equally the same strange pain in their ears.

did my reverence, then two hats, both in play at once (let me swing the other at the same time or not), brought my salute within the verge of ridicule. Now do you, my Friends, before reading farther, bethink you how a man was to extricate himself from such a plight, without losing head! I think, perhaps, by this means: by merely losing hat. In one word, then, I simply dropped the new bat from my hand into the mud, to put myself in a condition for taking off the old hat by itself, and swaying it in needful courtesy, without any shade of ridicule.

Arrived at the Tiger,—to avoid misconstructions, I first had the glossy, fine and superfine hat cleaned, and some time afterwards the mud-hat or rubbish-hat.

And now, weighing my momentous Past in the adjusting balance within me, I walked in fiery mood to and fro. The Pontac must—I know that there is no unadulterated liquor here below—have been more than usually adulterated; so keenly did it chase my fancy out of one fire into the other. I now looked forth into a wide glittering life, in which I lived without post, merely on money; and which I beheld, as it were, sowed with the Delphic caves, and Zenonic walks, and Muse-hills of all the Sciences, which I might now cultivate at my ease. In particular, I should have it in my power to apply more diligently to writing Prize-essays for Academies; of which (that is to say, of the Prize-essays) no author need ever be ashamed, since, in all cases, there is a whole crowning Academy to stand and blush for the crownee. And even if the Prize-marksman does not hit the crown, he still continues more unknown and more anonymous (his Device not being unsealed) than any other author, who indeed can publish some nameless Long-ear of a book, but not hinder it from being, by a Literary Ass-burial (*sepultura asinina*), publicly interred, in a short time, before half the world.

Only one thing grieved me by anticipation; the sorrow of my Berga, for whom, dear tired wayfarer, I on the morrow must overcloud her arrival, and her shortened market-spectacle, by my negatory intelligence. She would so gladly (and who can take it ill of a rich farmer's daughter?) have made herself somebody in Neusattel, and overshone many a female dignitary! Every mortal

---

25. In youth, like a blind man just couched (and what is birth but a couching of the sight?), you take the Distant for the Near, the starry heaven for tangible room-furniture, pictures for objects; and, to the young man, the whole world is sitting on his very nose, till repeated bandaging and unbandaging have at last taught him, like the blind patient, to estimate *Distance* and *Appearance*.

longs for his parade-place, and some earlier living honour than the last honours. Especially so good a lowly-born housewife as my Berga, conscious perhaps rather of her metallic than of her spiritual treasure, would still wish at banquets to be mistress of some seat or other, and so in place to overtop this or that plucked goose of the neighbourhood.

It is in this point of view that husbands are so indispensable. I therefore resolved to purchase for myself, and consequently for her, one of the best of those titles, which our Courts in Germany (as in a Leipzig sale-room) stand offering to buyers, in all sizes and sorts, from Noble and Half-noble down to Rath or Councillor; and once invested therewith, to reflect from my own Quarter-nobility such an Eighth-part-nobility on this true soul, that many a Neusattelitess (I hope) shall half burst with envy, and say and cry: "Pooh, the stupid farmer thing! See how it wabbles and bridles! It has forgot how matters stood when it had no moneybag, and no Hofrath!" For to the Hofrathship I shall before this have attained.

But in the cold solitude of my room, and the fire of my remembrances, I longed unspeakably for my Bergelchen: I and my heart were wearied with the foreign busy day; no one here said a kind word to me, which he did not hope to put in the bill. Friends! I languished for my friend, whose heart would pour out its blood as a balsam for a second heart; I cursed my over-prudent regulations, and wished that, to have the good Berga at my side, I had given up the stupid houseware to all thieves and fires whatsoever: as I walked to and fro, it seemed to me easier and easier to become all things, an Exchequer-Rath, an Excise-Rath, any Rath in the world, and whatever she required when she came.

"See thou take thy pleasure in the town!" had Bergelchen kept saying the whole week through. But how, without her, can I take any? Our tears of sorrow friends dry up, and accompany with their own: but our tears of joy we find most readily repeated in the eyes of our wives. Pardon me, good Friends, these libations of my sensibility; I am but showing you my heart and my Berga. If I need an Absolution-merchant, the Pontac-merchant is the man.

---

125. In the long-run, out of mere fear and necessity, we shall become the warmest cosmopolites I know of; so rapidly do ships shoot to and fro, and, like shuttles, weave Islands and Quarters of the World together. For, let but the political weatherglass fall today in South America, tomorrow we in Europe have storm and thunder.

First Night in Flätz

Yet the wine did not take from me the good sense to look under the bed, before going into it, and examine whether any one was lurking there; for example, the Dwarf, or the Ratcatcher, or the Legations-Rath; also to shove the key under the latch (which I reckon the best bolting arrangement of all), and then, by way of farther assurance, to bore my night-screws into the door, and pile all the chairs in a heap behind it; and, lastly, to keep on my breeches and shoes, wishing absolutely to have no care upon my mind.

But I had still other precautions to take in regard to sleepwalking. To me it has always been incomprehensible how so many men can go to bed, and lie down at their ease there, without reflecting that perhaps, in the first sleep, they may get up again as Somnambulists, and crawl over the tops of roofs and the like; awakening in some spot where they may fall in a moment and break their necks. While at home, there is little risk in my sleep: because, my right toe being fastened every night with three ells of tape (I call it in jest our marriage-tie) to my wife's left hand, I feel a certainty that, in case I should start up from this bed-arrest, I must with the tether infallibly awaken her, and so by my Berga, as by my living bridle, be again led back to bed. But here in the Inn, I had nothing for it but to knot myself once or

---

19. It is easier, they say, to climb a hill when you ascend back foremost. This, perhaps, might admit of application to political eminences; if you still turned towards them that part of the body on which you sit, and kept your face directed down to the people; all the while, however, removing and mounting.

26. Few German writers are not original, if we may ascribe originality (as is at least the conversational practice of all people) to a man, who merely dishes out his own thoughts without foreign admixture. For as, between their Memory, where their reading or foreign matter dwells, and their Imagination or Productive Power, where their writing or own peculiar matter originates, a sufficient space intervenes, and the boundary stones are fixed-in so conscientiously and firmly that nothing foreign may pass over into their own, or inversely, so that they may really read a hundred works without losing their own primitive flavour, or even altering it,—their individuality may, I believe, be considered as secured; and their spiritual nourishment, their pancakes, loaves, fritters, caviare and meat-balls, are not assimilated to their system, but given back pure and unaltered. Often in my own mind I figure such writers as living but thousandfold more artificial Ducklings from Vaucanson's Artificial Duck of Wood. For in fact they are not less cunningly put together than this timber Duck, which will gobble meat, and apparently void it again, under show of having digested it, and derived from it blood and juices; though the secret of the business is, the artist has merely introduced an ingenious compound ejective matter behind, with which concoction and nourishment have nothing to do, but which the Duck illusorily gives forth and publishes to the world.

twice to the bed-foot, that I might not wander; though in this way, an irruption of villains would have brought double peril with it.— Alas! so dangerous is sleep at all times, that every man, who is not lying on his back a corpse, must be on his guard lest with the general system some limb or other also fall asleep; in which case the sleeping limb (there are not wanting examples of it in Medical History) may next morning be lying ripe for amputation. For this reason, I have myself frequently awakened, that no part of me fall asleep.

Having properly tied myself to the bed-posts, and at length got under the coverlid, I now began to be dubious about my Pontac Fire-bath, and apprehensive of the valorous and tumultuous dreams too likely to ensue; which, alas, did actually prove to be nothing better than heroic and monarchic feats, castle-stormings, rock-throwings, and the like. This point also I am sorry to see so little attended to in medicine. Medical gentlemen, as well as their customers, all stretch themselves quietly in their beds, without one among them considering whether a furious rage (supposing him also directly after to drink cold water in his dream), or a heart-devouring grief, all which he may undergo in vision, does harm to life or not.

Shortly before midnight, I awoke from a heavy dream, to encounter a ghost-trick much too ghostly for my fancy. My Brother-in-law, who manufactured it, deserves for such vapid cookery to be named before you without reserve, as the malt-master of this washy brewage. Had suspicion been more compatible with intrepidity, I might perhaps, by his moral maxim about this matter, on the road, as well as by his taking up the side-room, at the middle door of which stood my couch, have easily divined the whole. But now, on awakening, I felt myself blown upon by a cold ghost-breath, which I could nowise deduce from the distant bolted window; a point I had rightly decided, for the Dragoon was producing the phenomenon, through the keyhole, by a pair of bellows. Every sort of coldness, in the night-season, reminds you of clay-coldness and spectre-coldness. I summoned my resolution, however, and abode the issue: but now the very coverlid began to get in motion; I pulled it towards me; it would not stay; sharply I sit upright in my bed, and cry: "What is that?" No answer; everywhere silence in the Inn; the whole room full of moonshine. And now my drawing-plaster, my coverlid, actually rose up, and let in the air; at which I felt like a wounded man whose

---

15. After the manner of the fine polished English folding-knives, there are now also folding-war-swords, or in other words—Treaties of Peace.

cataplasm you suddenly pull off. In this crisis, I made a bold leap from this Devil's-torus, and, leaping, snapped asunder my somnambulist tether. "Where is the silly human fool," cried I, "that dares to ape the unseen sublime world of Spirits, which may, in the instant, open before him?" But on, above, under the bed, there was nothing to be heard or seen. I looked out of the window: everywhere spectral moonlight and street-stillness; nothing moving except (probably from the wind), on the distant Gallows-hill, a person lately hanged.

Any man would have taken it for self-deception as well as I: therefore I again wrapped myself in my passive *lit de justice* and air-bed, and waited with calmness to see whether my fright would subside or not.

In a few minutes, the coverlid, the infernal Faust's-mantle, again began flying and towing; also, by way of change, the invisible bed-maker again lifted me up. Accursed hour!—I should beg to know whether, in the whole of cultivated Europe, there is one cultivated or uncultivated man, who, in a case of this kind, would not have lighted on ghost-devilry? I lighted on it, under my piece of (self) movable property, my coverlid: and thought Berga had died suddenly, and was now, in spirit, laying hold of my bed. However, I could not speak to her, nor as little to the Devil, who might well be supposed to have a hand in the game; but I turned myself solely to Heaven, and prayed aloud: "To thee I commit myself; thou alone heretofore hast cared for thy weak servant; and I swear that I will turn a new leaf,"—a promise which shall be kept nevertheless, though the whole was but stupid treachery and trick.

My prayer had no effect with the unchristian Dragoon, who now, once for all, had got me prisoner in the dragnet of a coverlid; and heeded little whether a guest's bed were, by his means, made a

---

13. *Omnibus una* SALUS *Sanctis, sed* GLORIA *dispar:* that is to say (as Divines once taught) according to Saint Paul, we have all the same Beatitude in Heaven, but different degrees of Honour. Here, on Earth, we find a shadow of this in the writing world; for the Beatitude of authors once beatified by Criticism, whether they be genial, good, mediocre, or poor, is the same throughout; they all obtain the same pecuniary Felicity, the same slender profit. But, Heavens! in regard to the degrees of Fame, again, how far (in spite of the same emolument and sale) will a Dunce, even in his lifetime, be put below a Genius! Is not a shallow writer frequently forgotten in a single Fair, while a deep writer, or even a writer of genius, will blossom through fifty Fairs, and so may celebrate his Twenty-five Years' Jubilee, before, late forgotten, he is lowered into the German Temple of Fame; a Temple imitating the peculiarity of the *Padri Lucchesi* churches in Naples, which (according to Volkmann) permit *burials* under their roofs, but no *tombstone*.

state-bed and death-bed or not. He span out my nerves, like gold-wire through smaller and smaller holes, to utter inanition and evanition; for the bed-clothes at last literally marched off to the door of the room.

Now was the moment to rise into the sublime; and to trouble myself no longer about aught here below, but softly to devote myself to death. "Snatch me away," cried I, and, without thinking, cut three crosses; "quick, dispatch me, ye ghosts: I die more innocent than thousands of tyrants and blasphemers, to whom ye yet appear not, but to unpolluted me." Here I heard a sort of laugh, either on the street or in the side-room: at this warm human tone, I suddenly bloomed up again, as at the coming of a new Spring, in every twig and leaf. Wholly despising the winged coverlid, which was not now to be picked from the door, I laid myself down uncovered, but warm and perspiring from other causes, and soon fell asleep. For the rest, I am not the least ashamed, in the face of all refined capital cities,—though they were standing here at my hand,—that by this Devil-belief and Devil-address I have attained some likeness to our great German Lion, to Luther.

Second Day in Flätz

Early in the morning, I felt myself awakened by the well-known coverlid; it had laid itself on me like a nightmare: I gaped up; quiet, in a corner of the room, sat a red, round, blooming, decorated girl, like a full-blown tulip in the freshness of life, and gently rustling with gay ribbons as with leaves.

"Who's there—how came you in?" cried I, half-blind.

"I covered thee softly, and thought to let thee sleep," said Bergelchen; "I have walked all night to be here early; do but look!"

She showed me her boots, the only remnant of her travelling-gear, which, in the moulting process of the toilette, she had not stript at the gate of Flätz.

"Is there," said I, alarmed at her coming six hours sooner, and the more, as I had been alarmed all night and was still so, at her mysterious

---

79. Weak and wrong heads are the hardest to change; and their inward man acquires a scanty covering: thus capons never moult.

89. In times of misfortune, the Ancients supported themselves with Philosophy or Christianity; the moderns again (for example, in the reign of Terror), take to Pleasure; as the wounded Buffalo, for bandage and salve, rolls himself in the mire.

entrance,—"is there some fresh woe come over us, fire, murder, robbery?"

She answered: "The old Rat thou hast chased so long died yesterday; farther, there was nothing of importance."

"And all has been managed rightly, and according to my Letter of Instructions, at home?" inquired I.

"Yes, truly," answered she; "only I did not see the Letter; it is lost; thou hast packed it among thy clothes."

Well, I could not but forgive the blooming brave pedestrian all omissions. Her eye, then her heart was bringing fresh cool morning air and morning red into my sultry hours. And yet, for this kind soul, looking into life with such love and hope, I must in a little while overcloud the merited Heaven of today, with tidings of my failure in the Catechetical Professorship! I dallied and postponed to the utmost. I asked how she had got in, as the whole *chevaux-de-frise* barricado of chairs was still standing fast at the door. She laughed heartily, curtseying in village fashion, and said, she had planned it with her brother the day before yesterday, knowing my precautions in locking, that he should admit her into my room, that so she might cunningly awaken me. And now bolted the Dragoon with loud laughter into the apartment, and cried: "Slept well, brother?"

In this wise truly the whole ghost-story was now solved and expounded, as if by the pen of a Biester or a Hennings; I instantly saw through the entire ghost-scheme, which our Dragoon had executed. With some bitterness I told him my conjecture, and his sister my story. But he lied and laughed; nay, attempted shamelessly enough to palm spectre-notions on me a second time, in open day. I answered coldly, that in me he had found the wrong man, granting even that I had some similarity with Luther, with Hobbes, with Brutus, all of whom had seen and dreaded ghosts. He replied, tearing the facts away from their originating causes: "All he could say was, that last night he had heard some poor sinner creaking and lamenting

---

181. God be thanked that we live nowhere forever except in Hell or Heaven; on Earth otherwise we should grow to be the veriest rascals, and the World a House of Incurables, for want of the dog-doctor (the Hangman), and the issue-cord (on the Gallows), and the sulphur and chalybeate medicines (on Battlefields). So that we too find our gigantic moral force dependent on the *Debt of Nature* which we have to pay, exactly as your politicians (for example, the Author of the *New Leviathan*) demonstrate that the English have their *National Debt* to thank for their superiority.

dolefully enough; and from this he had inferred, it must be an unhappy brother set upon by goblins."

In the end, his sister's eyes also were opened to the low character which he had tried to act with me: she sharply flew at him, pushed him with both hands out of his and my door, and called after him: "Wait, thou villain, I will mind it!"

Then hastily turning round, she fell on my neck, and (at the wrong place) into laughter, and said: "The wild fool! But I could not keep my laugh another minute, and he was not to see it. Forgive the ninny, thou a learned man, his ass pranks: what can one expect?"

I inquired whether she, in her nocturnal travelling, had not met with any spectral persons; though I knew that to her, a wild beast, a river, a half abyss, are nothing. No, she had not; but the gay-dressed town's-people, she said, had scared her in the morning. O! how I do love these soft Harmonica-quiverings of female fright!

At last, however, I was forced to bite or cut the coloquinta-apple, and give her the half of it; I mean the news of my rejected petition for the Catechetical Professorship. Wishing to spare this joyful heart the rudeness of the whole truth, and to subtract something from a heavy burden, more fit for the shoulders of a man, I began: "Bergelchen, the Professorship affair is taking another, though still a good enough course: the General, whom may the Devil and his Grandmother teach sense, will not be taken except by storm; and storm he shall have, as certainly as I have on my nightcap."

"Then, thou art nothing yet?" inquired she.

"For the moment, indeed, not!" answered I.

"But before Saturday night?" said she.

"Not quite," said I.

"Then am I sore stricken, and could leap out of the window," said she, and turned away her rosy face, to hide its wet eyes, and was silent very long. Then, with painfully quivering voice, she began: "Good Christ stand by me at Neusattel on Sunday, when these high-prancing prideful dames look at me in church, and I grow scarlet for shame!"

Here in sympathetic woe I sprang out of bed to the dear soul, over whose brightly blooming cheeks warm tears were rolling, and cried: "Thou true heart, do not tear me in pieces so! May I die, if yet in these dog-days I become not all and everything that thou wishest!

63. To apprehend danger from the Education of the People, is like fearing lest the thunderbolt strike into the house because it has *windows;* whereas the lightning never comes through these, but through their *lead* framing, or down by the *smoke* of the chimney.

Speak, wilt thou be Mining-räthin, Build-räthin, Court-räthin, War-räthin, Chamber-räthin, Commerce-räthin, Legations-räthin, or Devil and his Dam's räthin: I am here, and will buy it, and be it. Tomorrow I send riding posts to Saxony and Hessia, to Prussia and Russia, to Friesland and Katzenellenbogen, and demand patents. Nay, I will carry matters farther than another, and be all things at once, Flachsenfingen Court-rath, Scheerau Excise-rath, Haarhaar Building-rath, Pestitz[6] Chamber-rath (for we have the cash); and thus, alone and single-handed, represent with one *podex* and *corpus* a whole Rath-session of select Raths; and stand, a complete Legion of Honour, on one single pair of legs: the like no man ever did."

"O! now thou art angel-good!" said she, and gladder tears rolled down; "thou shalt counsel me thyself which are the finest Raths, and these we will be."

"No," continued I, in the fire of the moment, "neither shall this serve us: to me it is not enough that to Mrs. Chaplain thou canst announce thyself as Building-räthin, to Mrs. Town-parson as Legations-räthin, to Mrs. Bürgermeister as Court-räthin, to Mrs. Road-and-toll-surveyor as Commerce-räthin, or how and where thou pleasest———"

"Ah! my own too good Attelchen!" said she.

"———But," continued I, "I shall likewise become corresponding member of the several Learned Societies in the several best capital cities (among which I have only to choose); and truly no common actual member, but a whole honorary member; then thee, as another honorary member, growing out of my honorary membership, I uplift and exalt."

Pardon me, my Friends, this warm cataplasm, or deception-balsam for a wounded breast, whose blood is so pure and precious, that one may be permitted to endeavour, with all possible stanching-lints and spider-webs, to drive it back into the fair heart, its home.

But now came bright and brightest hours. I had conquered Time, I had conquered myself and Berga: seldom does a conqueror, as I did, bless both the victorious and the vanquished party. Berga called back her former Heaven, and pulled off her dusty boots, and on her flowery shoes. Precious morning beverage, intoxicating to a heart that loves! I felt (if the low figure may be permitted) a double-beer of courage in me, now that I had one being more to protect. In

---

[6] Cities of Richter's romance kingdom. Flachsenfingen he sometimes calls *Klein-Wien*, Little Vienna.—ED.

general it is my nature—which the honourable Premier seems not to be fully aware of—to grow bolder not among the bold, but fastest among poltroons, the bad example acting on me by the rule of contraries. Little touches may in this case shadow forth man and wife, without casting them into the shade: When the trim waiter with his green silk apron brought up cracknels for breakfast, and I told him: "Johann, for two!" Berga said: "He would oblige her very much," and called him Herr Johann.

Bergelchen, more familiar with rural burghs than capital cities, felt a good deal amazed and alarmed at the coffee-trays, dressing-tables, paper-hangings, sconces, alabaster inkholders, with Egyptian emblems, as well as at the gilt bell-handle, lying ready for any one to pull out or to push in. Accordingly, she had not courage to walk through the hall, with its lustres, purely because a whistling, whiffling Cap-and-feather was gesturing up and down in it. Nay, her poor heart was like to fail when she peeped out of the window at so many gay promenading town's-people (I was briskly whistling a Gascon air down over them); and thought that in a little while, at my side, she must break into the middle of this dazzling courtly throng. In a case like this, reasons are of less avail than examples. I tried to elevate my Bergelchen, by reciting some of my nocturnal dream-feats; for example, how, riding on a whale's back, with a three-pronged fork, I had pierced and eaten three eagles; and by more of the like sort: but I produced no effect; perhaps, because to the timid female heart the battlefield was presented rather than the conqueror, the abyss rather than the overleaper of it.

At this time a sheaf of newspapers was brought me, full of gallant decisive victories. And though these happen only on one side, and on the other arc just so many defeats, yet the former somehow assimilate more with my blood than the latter, and inspire me (as Schiller's *Robbers* used to do) with a strange inclination to lay hold of some one, and thrash and curry him on the spot. Unluckily for the waiter, he had chanced, even now, like a military host, to stand a triple bell-order for march, before he would leave his ground and come up. "Sir," began I, my head full of battle-fields, and my arm of inclination to baste him; and Berga feared the very worst, as I gave her the well-known anger and alarm signal, namely, shoved up my cap to my hindhead—"Sir, is this your way of treating guests? Why

---

76. Your economical, preaching Poetry, apparently supposes that a surgical Stone-cutter is an Artistical one; and a Pulpit or a Sinai a Hill of the Muses.

don't you come promptly? Don't come so again; and now be going, friend!" Although his retreat was my victory, I still kept briskly cannonading on the field of action, and fired the louder (to let him hear it), the more steps he descended in his flight. Bergelchen,—who felt quite horrorstruck at my fury, particularly in a quite strange house, and at a quality waiter with silk apron,—mustered all her soft words against the wild ones of a man-of-war, and spoke of dangers that might follow. "Dangers," answered I, "are just what I seek; but for a man there are none; in all cases he will either conquer or evade them, either show them front or back."

I could scarcely lay aside this indignant mood, so sweet was it to me, and so much did I feel refreshed by the fire of rage, and quickened in my breast as by a benignant stimulant. It belongs certainly to the class of Unrecognised Mercies (on which, in ancient times, special sermons were preached), that one is never more completely in his Heaven and *Monplaisir* (a pleasure-palace) than while in the midst of right hearty storming and indignation. Heavens! what might not a man of weight accomplish in this new walk of charity! The gall-bladder is for us the chief swimming-bladder and Montgolfier; and the filling of it costs us nothing but a contumelious word or two from some bystander. And does not the whirlwind Luther, with whom I nowise compare myself, confess, in his *Table-talk,* that he never preached, sung, or prayed so well, as while in a rage? Truly, he was a man sufficient of himself to rouse many others into rage.

The whole morning till noon now passed in viewing sights, and trafficking for wares; and indeed, for the greatest part, in the broad street of our Hotel. Berga needed but to press along with me into the market throng; needed but to look, and see that she was decorated more according to the fashion than hundreds like her. But soon, in her care for household gear, she forgot that of dress, and in the potter-market the toilette-table faded from her thoughts.

---

115. According to Smith, the universal measure of economical value is *Labour.* This fact, at least in regard to spiritual and poetical value, we Germans had discovered before Smith; and to my knowledge we have always preferred the learned poet to the poet of genius, and the heavy book full of labour to the light one full of sport.

4. The Hypocrite does not imitate the old practice, of cutting fruit by a knife poisoned only on the one side, and giving the poisoned side to the victim, the cutter eating the sound side himself; on the contrary, he so disinterestedly inverts this practice, that to others he shows and gives the sound moral half, or side, and retains for himself the poisoned one. Heavens! compared with such a man, how wicked does the Devil seem!

I, for my share, full of true tedium, while gliding after her through her various marts, with their long cheapenings and chafferings, merely acted the Philosopher hid within me: I weighed this empty Life, and the heavy value which is put upon it, and the daily anxiety of man lest it, this lightest down-feather of the Earth, fly off, and feather him, and take him with it. These thoughts, perhaps, I owe to the street-fry of boys, who were turning their market-freedom to account, by throwing stones at one another all round me: for, in the midst of this tumult, I vividly figured myself to be a man who had never seen war; and who, therefore, never having experienced, that often of a thousand bullets not one will hit, feels apprehensive of these few silly stones lest they beat-in his nose and eyes. O! it is the battle-field alone that sows, manures and nourishes true courage, courage even for daily, domestic and smallest perils. For not till he comes from the battle-field can a man both sing and cannonade; like the canary-bird, which, though so melodious, so timid, so small, so tender, so solitary, so soft-feathered, can yet be trained to fire off cannon, though cannon of smaller calibre.

After dinner (in our room), we issued from the Purgatory of the market-tumult,—where Berga, at every booth, had something to order, and load her attendant maid with,—into Heaven, into the Dog Inn, as the best Flätz public and pleasure-house without the gates is named, where, in market-time, hundreds turn in, and see thousands going by. On the way thither, my little wife, my elbow-tendril, as it were, had extracted from me such a measure of courage, that, while going through the Gate (where I, aware of the military order that you must not pass _near_ the sentry, threw myself over to the other side), she quietly glided on, close by the very guns and fixed bayonets of the City Guard. Outside the wall, I could direct her with my finger, to the bechained, begrated, gigantic Schabacker-Palace, mounting up even externally on stairs, where I last night had called and (it may be) stormed: "I had rather take a peep at the Giant," said she, "and the Dwarf: why else are we under one roof with them?"

In the pleasure-house itself we found sufficient pleasure; encircled, as we were, with blooming faces and meadows. In my secret heart, I all along kept looking down, with success, on Schabacker's refusal;

---

67. Individual Minds, nay Political Bodies, are like organic bodies: extract the _interior_ air from them, the atmosphere crushes them together; pump off under the bell the _exterior_ resisting air, the interior inflates and bursts them. Therefore, let every State keep up its internal and its external resistance both at once.

and till midnight made myself a happy day of it: I had deserved it, Berga still more. Nevertheless, about one in the morning, I was destined to find a windmill to tilt with; a windmill, which truly lays about it with somewhat longer, stronger and more numerous arms than a giant, for which Don Quixote might readily enough have taken it. On the market-place, for reasons more easily fancied than specified in words, I let Berga go along some twenty paces before me; and I myself, for these foresaid reasons, retire without malice behind a covered booth, the tent most probably of some rude trader; and linger there a moment according to circumstances: lo! steering hither with dart and spear, comes the Booth-watcher, and coins and stamps me, on the spot, into a filcher and housebreaker of his Booth-street; though the simpleton sees nothing but that I am standing in the corner, and doing anything but—taking. A sense of honour without callosity is never blunted for such attacks. But how in the dead of night was a man of this kind, who had nothing in his head—at the utmost beer, instead of brains—to be enlightened on the truth of the matter?

I shall not conceal my perilous resource: I seized the fox by the tail, as we say; in other words, I made as if I had been muddled, and knew not rightly, in my liquor, what I was about: I therefore mimicked everything I was master of in this department; staggered hither and thither; splayed out my feet like a dancing-master; got into zigzag in spite of all efforts at the straight line; nay, I knocked my good head (perhaps one of the clearest and emptiest of the night), like a full one, against real posts.

However, the Booth-bailiff, who probably had been oftener drunk than I, and knew the symptoms better, or even felt them in himself at this moment, looked upon the whole exhibition as mere craft, and shouted dreadfully: "Stop, rascal; thou art no more drunk than I! I know thee of old. Stand, I say, till I speak to thee! Wouldst have thy long finger in the market, too? Stand, dog, or I'll make thee!"

You see the whole *nodus* of the matter: I whisked away zigzag among the booths as fast as possible, from the claws of this rude Tosspot; yet he still hobbled after me. But my Teutoberga. who had

---

8. In great Saloons, the real stove is masked into a pretty ornamented sham stove; so likewise, it is fit and pretty that a virgin *Love* should always hide itself in an interesting virgin *Friendship*.

12. Nations—unlike rivers, which precipitate their impurities in level places and when at rest—drop their baseness just whilst in the most violent motion; and become the dirtier the farther they flow along through lazy flats.

heard somewhat of it, came running back; clutched the tipsy market-warder by the collar, and said (shrieking, it is true, in village-wise): "Stupid sot, go sleep the drink out of thy head, or I'll teach thee! Dost know, then, whom thou art speaking to? My husband, Army-chaplain Schmelzle under General and Minister von Schabacker at Pimpelstadt, thou blockhead!—Fye! Take shame, fellow!" The watchman mumbled: "Meant no harm," and reeled about his business. "O thou Lioness!" said I, in the transport of love, "why hast thou never been in any deadly peril, that I might show thee the Lion in thy husband?"

Thus lovingly we both reached home; and perhaps in the sequel of this Fair day might still have enjoyed a glorious after-midnight, had not the Devil led my eye to the ninth volume of Lichtenberg's Works, and the 206th page, where this passage occurs: "It is not impossible that at a future period, our Chemists may light on some means of suddenly decomposing the Atmosphere by a sort of Ferment. In this way the world may be destroyed." Ah! true indeed! Since the Earth-ball is lapped up in the larger Atmospheric ball, let but any chemical scoundrel, in the remotest scoundrel-island, say in New Holland, devise some decomposing substance for the Atmosphere, like what a spark of fire would be for a powder-wagon: in a few seconds, the monstrous devouring world-storm catches me and you in Flätz by the throat; my breathing, and the like, in this choke-air is over, and the whole game ended! The Earth becomes a boundless gallows, where the very cattle are hanged: worm-powder, and bug-liquor, Bradly ant-ploughs, and rat-poison, and wolf-traps are, in this universal world-trap and world-poison, no longer specially needful; and the Devil takes the whole, in the Bartholomew-night, when this cursed "Ferment" is invented.

From the true soul, however, I concealed these deadly Night Thoughts; seeing she would either painfully have sympathised in them, or else mirthfully laughed at them. I merely gave orders that next morning (Saturday) she was to be standing booted and ready, at the outset of the returning coach; if so were she would have me

---

28. When Nature takes the huge old Earth-round, the Earth-loaf, and kneads it up again, for the purpose of introducing under this pie-crust new stuffing and Dwarfs,—she then, for most part, as a mother when baking will do to her daughters, gives in jest a little fraction of the dough (two or three thousand square leagues of such dough are enough for a child) to some Poetical or Philosophical, or Legislative polisher, that so the little elf may have something to he shaping and manufacturing beside its mother. And when the other young ones get a taste of sisterkin's baking, they all clap hands, and cry: "Aha, Mother! canst bake like *Suky* here?"

speedily fulfil her wishes in regard to that stock of Rathships which lay so near her heart. She rejoiced in my purpose, gladly surrendering the market for such prospects. I too slept sound, my great toe tied to her finger, the whole night through.

The Dragoon, next morning, twitched me by the ear, and secretly whispered into it that he had a pleasant fairing to give his sister; and so would ride off somewhat early, on the nag he had yesterday purchased of the horse-dealer. I thanked him beforehand.

At the appointed hour, all gaily started from the Staple, I excepted; for I still retained, even in the fairest daylight, that nocturnal Devil's–Ferment and Decomposition (of my cerebral globe as well as of the Earth-globe) fermenting in my head; a proof that the night had not affected me, or exaggerated my fear. The Blind Passenger, whom I liked so ill, also mounted along with us, and looked at me as usual, but without effect; for on this occasion, when the destruction not of myself only, but of worlds, was occupying my thoughts, the Passenger was nothing to me but a joke and a show: as a man, while his leg is being sawed off, does not feel the throbbing of his heart; or amid the humming of cannon, does not guard himself from that of wasps; so to me any Passenger, with all the fire-brands he might throw into my near or distant Future, could appear but ludicrous, at a time when I was reflecting that the "Ferment" might, even in my journey between Flätz and Neusattel, be, by some American or European man of science, quite guiltlessly experimenting and decomposing, hit upon by accident and let loose. The question, nay prize-question now, however, were this: "In how far, since Lichtenberg's threatening, it may not appear world-murderous and self-murderous, if enlightened Potentates of chemical nations do not enjoin it on their chemical subjects, who in their decompositions and separations may so easily separate the soul from their body, and unite Heaven with Earth,—not in future to make any other chemical experiments than those already made, which hitherto have profited the State rather than harmed it?"

Unfortunately, I continued sunk in this Domsday of the Ferment with all my thoughts and meditations, without, in the whole course of our return from Flätz to Neusattel, suffering or observing anything, except that I actually arrived there, and at the same time saw the Blind Passenger once more go his ways.

My Bergelchen alone had I constantly looked at by the road, partly that I might still see her, so long as life and eyes endured; partly that, even at the smallest danger to her, be it a great, or even all-over-sweeping Deluge and World's-doom, I might die, if not *for* her, at least *by* her, and so united with that stanch true heart, cast away a plagued and plaguing life, in which, at any rate, not half of my wishes for her have been fulfilled.

So then were my Journey over,—crowned with some *Historiolæ;* and in time coming, perhaps, still more rewarded through you, ye Friends about Flätz, if in these pages you shall find any well-ground pruning-knives, whereby you may more readily out-root the weedy tangle of Lies, which for the present excludes me from the gallant Schabacker:—Only this cursed Ferment still sits in my head. Farewell then, so long as there are Atmospheres left us to breathe. I wish I had that Ferment out of my head.

Yours always,
ATTILA SCHMELZLE

P.S.—My Brother-in-law has kept his promise well, and Berga is dancing. Particulars in my next!

LIFE OF QUINTUS FIXLEIN

DOWN TO OUR OWN TIMES

EXTRACTED FROM

FIFTEEN LETTER-BOXES BY JEAN PAUL

LETTER TO MY FRIENDS

INSTEAD OF PREFACE

MERCHANTS, AUTHORS, YOUNG Ladies and Quakers, call all persons, with whom they have any business, Friends; and my readers accordingly are my table and college Friends. Now, at this time, I am about presenting so many hundred Friends with just as many hundred gratis copies; and my Bookseller has orders to supply each on request, after the Fair, with his copy—in return for a trifling consideration and *don gratuit* to printers, pressmen and other such persons. But as I could not, like the French authors, send the whole Edition to the binder, the blank leaf in front was necessarily wanting; and thus to write a complimentary word or two upon it was out of my power. I have therefore caused a few white leaves to be inserted directly after the title-page: on these we are now printing.

My Book contains the Life of a Schoolmaster, extracted and compiled from various public and private documents. With this Biography, dear Friends, it is the purpose of the Author not so much to procure you a pleasure, as to teach you how to enjoy one. In truth, King Xerxes should have offered his prize-medals not for the invention of new pleasures, but for a good methodology and directory to use the old ones.

Of ways for becoming happier (not happy) I could never inquire out more than three. The first, rather an elevated road, is this: To soar away so far above the clouds of life, that you see the whole external world, with its wolf-dens, charnel-houses and thunder-rods, lying far down beneath you, shrunk into a little child's garden. The second is: Simply to sink down into this little garden; and there to nestle yourself so snugly, so homewise, in some furrow, that in looking out from your warm lark-nest, you likewise can discern no wolf-dens, charnel-houses or thunder-rods, but only blades and ears, every one of which, for the nest-bird, is a tree, and a sun-screen, and rain-screen. The third, finally, which I look upon as the hardest and cunningest, is that of alternating between the other two.

This I shall now satisfactorily expound to men at large.

The Hero, the Reformer, your Brutus, your Howard, your Republican, he whom civic storm, or genius, poetic storm, impels; in short, every mortal with a great Purpose, or even a perennial Passion (were it but that of writing the largest folios), all these men fence themselves in by their internal world against the frosts and heats of the external, as the madman in a worse sense does: every *fixed* idea, such as rules every genius, every enthusiast, at least periodically, separates and elevates a man above the bed and board of this Earth, above its Dog's-grottoes, buckthorns and Devil's-walls; like the Bird of Paradise, he slumbers flying; and on his outspread pinions, oversleeps unconsciously the earthquakes and conflagrations of Life; in his long fair dream of his ideal Motherland.—Alas! to few is this dream granted; and these few are so often awakened by Flying Dogs!

This skyward track, however, is fit only for the winged portion of the human species, for the smallest. What can it profit poor quill-driving brethren, whoso souls have not even wing-shells, to say nothing of wings? Or these tethered persons with the best back, breast and neck fins, who float motionless in the wicker Fish-box of the State, and are not allowed to swim, because the Box or State, long ago tied to the shore, itself swims in the name of the Fishes? To the whole standing and writing host of heavy-laden State-domestics, Purveyors, Clerks of all departments, and all the lobsters packed together heels over head into the Lobster-basket of the Government office-rooms, and for refreshment, sprinkled over with a few nettles;

So are the Vampires called.

to these persons, what way of becoming happy *here*, can I possibly point out?

My *second* merely; and that is as follows: To take a compound microscope, and with it to discover, and convince themselves, that their drop of Burgundy is properly a Red Sea, that butterfly-dust is peacock-feathers, mouldiness a flowery-field, and sand a heap of jewels. These microscopic recreations are more lasting than all costly watering-place recreations.—But I must explain these metaphors by new ones. The purpose, for which I have sent *Fixlein's Life* into the Messrs. Lübeks' Warehouse, is simply that in this same *Life*,—therefore in this Preface it is less needful,—I may show to the whole Earth that we ought to value little joys more than great ones, the nightgown more than the dresscoat; that Plutus' heaps are worth less than his handfuls, the plum than the penny for a rainy day; and that not great, but little good-haps can make us happy.—Can I accomplish this, I shall, through means of my Book, bring up for Posterity, a race of men finding refreshment in all things; in the warmth of their rooms and of their nightcaps; in their pillows; in the three High Festivals; in mere Apostles' days; in the Evening Moral Tales of their wives, when these gentle persons have been forth as ambassadresses visiting some Dowager Residence, whither the husband could not be persuaded; in the bloodletting-day of these their news-bringers; in the day of slaughtering, salting, potting against the rigour of grim winter; and in all such days. You perceive, my drift is that man must become a little Tailor-bird, which, not amid the crashing boughs of the storm-tost, roaring, immeasurable tree of Life, but on one of its leaves, sews itself a nest together, and there lies snug. The most essential sermon one could preach to our century, were a sermon on the duty of staying at home.

The *third* skyward road is the alternation between the other two. The foregoing *second* way is not good enough for man, who here on Earth should take into his hand not the Sickle only, but also the Plough. The *first* is too good for him. He has not always the force, like Rugendas, in the midst of the Battle to compose Battle-pieces; and, like Backhuysen in the Shipwreck, to clutch at no board but the drawing-board to paint it on. And then his *pains* are not less lasting than his *fatigues*. Still oftener is Strength denied its Arena: it is but the smallest portion of life that, to a working soul, offers Alps, Revolutions, Rhine-falls, Worms Diets, and Wars with Xerxes; and for the whole it is better so: the longer portion of life is a field beaten flat as a threshing-floor, without lofty Gothard Mountains; often it is a tedious ice-field, without a single glacier tinged with dawn.

But even by walking, a man rests and recovers himself for climbing; by little joys and duties, for great. The victorious Dictator must contrive to plough down his battle Mars-field into a flax and carrot field; to transform his theatre of war into a parlour theatre, on which his children may enact some good pieces from the *Children's Friend*. Can he accomplish this, can he turn so softly from the path of poetical happiness into that of household happiness,—then is he little different from myself, who even now, though modesty might forbid me to disclose it—who even now, I say, amid the creation of this Letter, have been enabled to reflect, that when it is done, so also will the Roses and Elder-berries of pastry be done, which a sure hand is seething in butter for the Author of this Work.

As I purpose appending to this Letter a Postscript (at the end of the Book), I reserve somewhat which I had to say about the Third half-satirical half-philosophical part of the Work, till that opportunity.

Here, out of respect for the rights of a Letter, the Author drops his half anonymity, and for the first time subscribes himself with his *whole* true name,

JEAN PAUL FRIEDRICH RICHTER
Hof in Voigtland, 29th June 1795

Fixlein stands in the middle of the volume; preceded by *Einer Mustheil, für Mädchen* (A Jelly-course for Young Ladies); and followed by *Some* Jus DE TABLETTE *for Men*. A small portion of the Preface relating to the first I have already omitted. Neither of the two has the smallest relation to *Fixlein*.—ED.

J. P. H., Jean Paul HASUS, *Jean Paul*, &c. have in succession been Richter's signatures. At present even, his German designation, either in writing or speech, is never *Richter*, but *Jean Paul*.—ED.

LIFE OF QUINTUS FIXLEIN

FIRST LETTER-BOX

Dog-days Vacation. Visits. An Indigent of Quality.

EGIDIUS ZEBEDÆUS FIXLEIN had just for eight days been Quintus, and fairly commenced his teaching duties, when Fortune tabled out for him four refreshing courses and collations, besprinkled with flowers and sugar. These were the four canicular weeks. I could find in my heart, at this hour, to pat the cranium of that good-man who invented the Dog-days Vacation: I never go to walk in that season, without thinking how a thousand down-pressed pedagogic persons are now erecting themselves in the open air; and the stiff knapsack is lying unbuckled at their feet, and they can seek whatsoever their soul desires; butterflies,—or roots of numbers,—or roots of words,— or herbs,—or their native villages.

The last did our Fixlein. He moved not, however, till Sunday,— for you like to know how holidays taste in the city; and then, in company with his Shock and a Quintaner, or Fifth-Form boy, who carried his Green nightgown, he issued through the gate in the morning. The dew was still lying; and as he reached the back of the gardens, the children of the Orphan Hospital were uplifting with

---

For understanding many little hints which occur in this *Life of Fixlein,* it will be necessary to bear in mind the following particulars: A German *Gymnasium,* in its complete state, appears to include eight Masters; Rector, Conrector, Subrector, Quintus, Quartus, Tertius, &c., to the *first* or lowest. The *forms,* or classes, again, are arranged in an inverse order; the *Primaner* (boys of the *Prima,* or first form) being the most advanced, and taught by the Rector; the *Secundaner,* by the Conrector, &c., and therefore the *Quartaner* by the Quintus. In many cases, it would seem, the number of Teachers is only six; but, in this Flachsenfingen Gymnasium, we have express evidence that there was no curtailment.—ED.

clear voices their morning hymn. The city was Flachsenfingen, the village Hukelum, the dog Schil, and the year of Grace 1791.

"Manikin," said he to the Quintaner, for he liked to speak as Love, children, and the people of Vienna do, in diminutives, "Manikin, give me the bundle to the village: run about, and seek thee a little bird, as thou art thyself, and so have something to pet too in vacation-time." For the manikin was at once his page, lackey, room-comrade, train-bearer and gentleman-in-waiting; and the Shock also was his manikin.

He stept slowly along, through the crisped cole-beds, overlaid with coloured beads of dew; and looked at the bushes, out of which, when the morning wind bent them asunder, there seemed to start a flight of jewel-colibri, so brightly did they glitter. From time to time he drew the bell-rope of his—whistle, that the manikin might not skip away too far; and he shortened his league and half of road, by measuring it not in leagues, but in villages. It is more pleasant for pedestrians—for geographers it is not—to count by wersts than by miles. In walking, our Quintus farthermore got by heart the few fields, on which the grain was already reaped.

But now roam slower, Fixlein, through his Lordship's garden of Hukelum; not, indeed, lest thy coat sweep away any tulip-stamina, but that thy good mother may have time to lay her Cupid's-band of black taffeta about her smooth brow. I am grieved to think my fair readers take it ill of her, that she means first to iron this same band: they cannot know that she has no maid; and that today the whole Preceptorial dinner—the money purveyances the guest has made over to her three days before—is to be arranged and prepared by herself, without the aid of any Mistress of the Household whatever; for indeed she belongs to the *Tiers Etat,* being neither more nor less than a gardener's widow.

You can figure how this true, warm-hearted mother may have lain in wait all morning for her Schoolman, whom she loved as the apple of her eye; since, on the whole populous Earth, she had not (her first son, as well as her husband, was dead) any other for her soul, which indeed overflowed with love; not any other but her Zebedäus. Could she ever tell you aught about him, I mean aught joyful, without ten times wiping her eyes? Nay, did she not once divide her solitary Kirmes (or Churchale) cake between two mendicant students, because she thought Heaven would punish her for so feasting, while her boy in Leipzig had nothing to feast on, and must pass the cake-garden like other gardens, merely smelling at it?

"Dickens! Thou already, Zebedäus!" said the mother, giving an embarrassed smile, to keep from weeping, as the son, who had ducked past the window, and crossed the grassy threshold without knocking, suddenly entered. For joy she forgot to put the heater into the smoothing-iron, as her illustrious scholar, amid the loud boiling of the soup, tenderly kissed her brow, and even said Mamma; a name which lighted on her breast like downy silk. All the windows were open; and the garden, with its flower-essences, and bird-music, and butterfly-collections, was almost half within the room: but I suppose I have not yet mentioned that the little garden-house, rather a chamber than a house, was situated on the western cape of the Castle garden. The owner had graciously allowed the widow to retain this dowager-mansion; as indeed the mansion would otherwise have stood empty, for he now kept no gardener.

But Fixlein, in spite of his joy, could not stay long with her; being bound for the Church, which, to his spiritual appetite, was at all times a king's kitchen; a mother's. A sermon pleased him simply because it was a sermon, and because he himself had once preached one. The mother was contented he should go: these good women think they enjoy their guests, if they can only give them aught to enjoy.

In the choir, this Free-haven and Ethnic Forecourt of stranger church-goers, he smiled on all parishioners; and, as in his childhood, standing under the wooden wing of an archangel, he looked down on the coifed *parterre*. His young years now enclosed him like children in their smiling circle; and a long garland wound itself in rings among them, and by fits they plucked flowers from it, and threw them in his face: Was it not old Senior Astman that stood there on the pulpit Parnassus, the man by whom he had been so often flogged, while acquiring Greek with him from a grammar written in Latin, which he could not explain, yet was forced to walk by the light of? Stood there not behind the pulpit-stairs the sacristy-cabin, and in this was there not a church-library of consequence—no schoolboy could have buckled it wholly in his book-strap—lying under the minever cover of pastil dust? And did it not consist of the Polyglott in folio, which he, spurred on by Pfeiffer's *Critica Sacra,* had turned up leaf by leaf, in his early years, excerpting therefrom the *literæ inversæ, majusculæ, minusculæ,* and so forth, with an immensity of toil? And could he not at present, the sooner the more readily, have wished to cast this alphabetic soft-fodder into the Hebrew letter-trough, whereto your Oriental Rhizophagi (Root-eaters) are tied, especially

as here they get so little vowel hard-fodder to keep them in heart?—
Stood there not close by him the organ-stool, the throne to which,
every Apostle-day, the Schoolmaster had by three nods elevated him,
thence to fetch down the sacred hyssop, the sprinkler of the Church?

My readers themselves will gather spirits when they now hear that
our Quintus, during the outshaking of the poor-bag, was invited by
the Senior to come over in the afternoon; and to them, it will be
little less gratifying than if he had invited themselves But what will
they say, when they get home with him to mother and dinner-table,
both already clad in their white Sunday dress; and behold the large
cake which Fräulein Thiennette (Stephanie) has rolled from her peel?
In the first place, however, they will wish to know who *she* is?

She is,—for if (according to Lessing) in the very excellence of the
Iliad, we neglect the personalities of its author; the same thing will
apply to the fate of several authors, for instance to my own; but an
authoress of cakes must not be forgotten in the excellence of her
baking,—Thiennette is a poor, indigent, insolvent young lady; has
not much, except years, of which she counts five-and-twenty; no
near relations living now; no acquirements (for in literature she
does not even know *Werter*) except economical; reads no books, not
even mine; inhabits, that is, watches like a wardeness, quite alone,
the thirteen void disfurnished chambers of the Castle of Hukelum,
which belongs to the Dragoon Rittmeister Aufhammer, at present
resident in his other mansion of Schadeck: on occasion, she commands
and feeds his soccagers and handmaids; and can write herself By the
grace of God,—which, in the thirteenth century, the country nobles
did as well as princes,—for she lives by the grace of man, at least of
woman, the Lady Rittmeisterinn Aufhammer's grace, who, at all
times, blesses those vassals whom her husband curses. But, in the
breast of the orphaned Thiennette lay a sugared marchpane heart,
which, for very love, you could have devoured: her fate was hard,
but her soul was soft; she was modest, courteous and timid, but too
much so;—cheerfully and coldly she received the most cutting
humiliations in Schadeck, and felt no pain, and not till some days
after did she see it all clearly, and then these cuts began sharply to
bleed, and she wept in her loneliness over her lot.

It is hard for me to give a light tone, after this deep one, and to
add, that Fixlein had been almost brought up beside her, and that
she, his school-moiety over with the Senior, while the latter was
training him for the dignities of the Third Form, had learned the
Verba Anomala along with him.

The Achilles'-shield of the cake, jagged and embossed with carved work of brown scales, was whirling round in the Quintus like a swing-wheel of hungry and thankful ideas. Of that philosophy which despises eating, and of that high breeding which wastes it, he had not so much about him as belongs to the ungratefulness of such cultivated persons; but for his platter of meat, for his dinner of herbs, he could never give thanks enough.

Innocent and contented, the quadruple dinner-party,—for the Shock with his cover under the stove cannot be omitted,—now began their Feast of Sweet Bread, their Feast of Honour for Thiennette, their Grove-feast in the garden. It may truly be a subject of wonder how a man who has not, like the King of France, four hundred and forty-eight persons (the hundred and sixty-one *Garçons de la Maison-bouche* I do not reckon) in his kitchen, nor a *Fruiterie* of thirty-one human bipeds, nor a Pastry-cookery of three-and-twenty, nor a daily expenditure of 387 livres 21 sous,—how such a man, I say, can eat with any satisfaction. Nevertheless, to me, a cooking mother is as dear as a whole royal cooking household, given rather to feed upon me than to feed me.—The most precious fragments which the Biographer and the World can gather from this meal, consist of here and there an edifying piece of table-talk. The mother had much to tell. Thiennette is this night, she mentions, for the first time, to put on her morning promenade-dress of white muslin, as also a satin girdle and steel buckle: but, adds she, it will not sit her; as the Rittmeisterinn (for this lady used to hang her cast clothes on Thiennette, as Catholics do their cast crutches and sores on their patron Saints) was much thicker. Good women grudge each other nothing, save only clothes, husbands and flax. In the fancy of the Quintus, by virtue of this apparel, a pair of angel pinions were sprouting forth from the shoulder-blades of Thiennette: for him a garment was a sort of hollow half-man, to whom only the nobler parts and the first principles were wanting: he honoured these wrappages and hulls of our interior, not as an Elegant, or a Critic of Beauty, but because it was not possible for him to despise aught which he saw others honouring. Farther, the good mother read to him, as it were, the monumental inscription of his father, who had sunk into the arms of Death in the thirty-second year of his age, from a cause which I explain not here, but in a future Letter-box, having too much affection for the reader. Our Quintus could not sate himself with hearing of his father.

The fairest piece of news was, that Fräulein Thiennette had sent word today: "he might visit Her Ladyship tomorrow, as My Lord, his godfather, was to be absent in town." This, however, I must explain. Old Aufhammer was called *Egidius,* and was Fixlein's godfather: but he,—though the Rittmeisterinn duly covered the cradle of the child with nightly offerings, with flesh-tithes and grain-tithes,—had frugally made him no christening present, except that of his name, which proved to be the very balefulest. For, our *Egidius* Fixlein, with his Shock, which, by reason of the French convulsions, had, in company with other emigrants, run off from Nantes, was but lately returned from college,—when he and his dog, as ill luck would have it, went to walk in the Hukelum wood. Now, as the Quintus was ever and anon crying out to his attendant: "Coosh, Schil" (*Couche, Gilles*), it must apparently have been the Devil that had just then planted the Lord of Aufhammer among the trees and bushes in such a way, that this whole travestying and docking of his name,—for Gilles means Egidius,—must fall directly into his ear. Fixlein could neither speak French, nor any offence to mortal: he knew not head or tail of what *couche* signified; a word, which, in Paris, even the plebeian dogs are now in the habit of saying to their *valets de chiens.* But there were three things which Von Aufhammer never recalled; his error, his anger and his word. The provokee, therefore, determined that the plebeian provoker and honour-stealer should never more speak to him, or—get a doit from him.

I return. After dinner he gazed out of the little window into the garden, and saw his path of life dividing into four branches, leading towards just as many skyward Ascensions; towards the Ascension into the Parsonage, and that into the Castle to Thiennette, for this day; and towards the third into Schadeck for the morrow; and lastly, into every house in Hukelum as the fourth. And now when the mother had long enough kept cheerfully gliding about on tiptoe, "not to disturb him in studying his Latin Bible" (the *Vulgata*), that is, in reading the *Litteratur-zeitung,* he at last rose to his own feet; and the humble joy of the mother ran long after the courageous son, who dared to go forth and speak to a Senior, quite unappalled. Yet it was not without reverence that he entered the dwelling of his old, rather gray than bald-headed teacher, who was not only Virtue itself, but also Hunger, eating frequently, and with the appetite of Pharaoh's lean kine. A schoolman, that expects to become a professor, will scarcely deign to cast an eye on a pastor; but one, who is himself looking up to a parsonage as to his working-house and breeding-house, knows how to value such a character. The new parsonage,—as if it had, like a *Casa Santa,* come flying out of Erlangen, or the

Berlin Friedrichs-strasse, and alighted in Hukelum,—was for the Quintus a Temple of the Sun, and the Senior a Priest of the Sun. To be Parson there himself, was a thought overlaid with virgin honey; such a thought as occurs but one other time in History, namely, in the head of Hannibal, when he projected stepping over the Alps, that is to say, over the threshold of Rome.

The landlord and his guest formed an excellent *bureau d'esprit,* people of office, especially of the same office, have more to tell each other, namely, their own history, than your idle May-chafers and Court-celestials, who must speak only of other people's.—The Senior made a soft transition from his iron-ware (in the stable furniture), to the golden age of his Academic life, of which such people like as much to think, as poets do of their childhood. So good as he was, he still half joyfully recollected that he had once been less so: but joyful remembrances of wrong actions are their half repetition, as repentant remembrances of good ones are their half abolishment.

Courteously and kindly did Zebedäus (who could not even enter in his Notebook the name of a person of quality without writing an H. for Herr before it) listen to the Academic Saturnalia of the old gentleman, who in Wittenberg had toped as well as written, and thirsted not more for the Hippocrene than for Gukguk.

Herr Jerusalem has observed, that the barbarism which often springs up, close on the brightest efflorescence of the sciences, is a sort of strengthening mudbath, good for averting the over-refinement, wherewith such efflorescence always threatens us. I believe that a man who considers how high the sciences have mounted with our upper classes,—for instance with every Patrician's son in Nürnberg, to whom the public must present 1000 florins for studying with,—I believe that such a man will not grudge the Son of the Muses a certain barbarous Middle-age (the Burschen or Student Life, as it is called), which may again so case-harden him that his refinement shall not go beyond the limits. The Senior, while in Wittenberg, had protected the one hundred and eighty Academic Freedoms,—so many of them has Petrus Rebuffus summed up, —against prescription, and lost

---

A university beer.

From Peter I will copy one or two of these privileges; the whole of which were once, at the origin of universities, in full force. For instance, a student can compel a citizen to let him his house and his horse; an injury, done even to his relations, must be made good fourfold; he is not obliged to fulfil the written commands of the Pope; the neighbourhood must indemnify him for what is stolen from him; if he and a non-student are living at variance, the latter only

none except his moral one, of which truly a man, even in a convent, can seldom make much. This gave our Quintus courage to relate certain pleasant somersets of his own, which at Leipzig, under the Incubus-pressure of poverty, he had contrived to execute. Let us hear him: His landlord, who was at the same time Professor and Miser, maintained in his enclosed court a whole community of hens: Fixlein, in company with three room-mates, without difficulty mastered the rent of a chamber, or closet: in general their main equipments, like Phoenixes, existed but in the singular number; one bed, in which always the one pair slept before midnight, the other after midnight, like nocturnal watchmen; one coat, in which one after the other they appeared in public, and which, like a watch-coat, was the national uniform of the company; and several other *ones*, Unities both of Interest and Place. Nowhere can you collect the stress-memorials and siege-medals of Poverty more pleasantly and philosophically than at College; the Academic burgher exhibits to us how many humorists and Diogeneses Germany has in it. Our Unitarians had just one thing four times, and that was hunger. The Quintus related, perhaps with a too pleasurable enjoyment of the recollection, how one of this famishing *coro* invented means of appropriating the Professor's hens as just tribute, or subsidies. He said (he was a Jurist), they must once for all borrow a legal fiction from the Feudal code, and look on the Professor as the soccage tenant, to whom the usufruct of the hen-yard and hen-house belonged; but on themselves, as the feudal superiors of the same, to whom accordingly the vassal was bound to pay his feudal dues. And now, that the Fiction might follow Nature, continued he,—"*fictio sequitur naturam*,"—it behoved them to lay hold of said Yule-hens, by direct personal distraint. But into the court-yard there was no getting. The feudalist, therefore, prepared a fishing-line; stuck a bread-pill on the hook, and lowered his fishing-tackle, anglerwise, down into the court. In a few seconds the barb stuck in a hen's throat, and the hen now communicating with its feudal superior, could silently, like ships by Archimedes, be heaved aloft to the hungry air-fishing society, where, according to circumstances, the proper feudal name and title of possession failed not to be awaiting her: for the updrawn fowls were now denominated Christmas-fowls, now Forest-hens, Bailiff-hens, Pentecost and Summer-hens. "I begin," said the angling lord of the

---

can be expelled from the boarding-house; a Doctor is obliged to support a poor student; if he is killed, the next ten houses are laid under interdict till the murderer is discovered; his legacies are not abridged by *falcidia*, &c. &c.

manor, "with taking *Rutcher-dues,* for so we call the triple and quintuple of the original quit-rent, when the vassal, as is the case here, has long neglected payment." The Professor, like any other prince, observed with sorrow the decreasing population of his hen-yard, for his subjects, like the Hebrews, were dying by enumeration. At last he had the happiness, while reading his lecture,—he was just come to the subject of *Forest Salt and Coin Regalities,*—to descry, through the window of his auditorium, a quit-rent hen suspended, like Ignatius Loyola in prayer, or Juno in her punishment, in middle air: he followed the incomprehensible direct ascension of the aeronautic animal, and at last descried at the upper window the attracting artist, and animal-magnetiser, who had drawn his lot for dinner from the hen-yard below. Contrary to all expectation, he terminated this fowling sport sooner than his Lecture on Regalities.

Fixlein walked home, amid the vesperal melodies of the steeple sounding-holes; and by the road, courteously took off his hat before the empty windows of the Castle: houses of quality were to him like persons of quality, as in India the Pagoda at once represents the temple and the god. To the mother he brought feigned compliments, which she repaid with authentic ones; for this afternoon she had been over, with her historical tongue and nature-interrogating eye, visiting the white-muslin Thiennette. The mother was wont to show her every spare penny which he dropped into her large empty purse, and so raise him in the good graces of the Fräulein; for women feel their hearts much more attracted towards a son, who tenderly reserves for a mother some of his benefits, than we do to a daughter anxiously caring for her father; perhaps from a hundred causes, and this among the rest, that in their experience of sons and husbands they are more used to find these persons mere six-feet thunder-clouds, forked waterspouts, or even reposing tornadoes.

Blessed Quintus! on whose Life this other distinction like an order of nobility does also shine, that thou canst tell it over to thy mother; as, for example, this past afternoon in the parsonage. Thy joy flows into another heart, and streams back from it, redoubled, into thy own. There is a closer approximating of hearts, and also of sounds, than that of the *Echo;* the highest approximation melts Tone and Echo into *Resonance* together.

It is historically certain that both of them supped this evening; and that instead of the whole dinner fragments which tomorrow might themselves represent a dinner, nothing but the cake-offering or pudding was laid upon the altar of the table. The mother, who for her own child would willingly have neglected not herself only, but all other people, now made a motion that to the Quintaner, who was sporting out of doors and baiting a bird instead of himself, there should no crum of the precious pastry be given, but only table-bread without the crust. But the Schoolman had a Christian disposition, and said that it was Sunday, and the young man liked something delicate to eat as well as he. Fixlein,—the counterpart of great men and geniuses,—was inclined to treat, to gift, to gratify a serving house-mate, rather than a man who is for the first time passing through the gate, and at the next post-stage will forget both his hospitable landlord and the last postmaster. On the whole, our Quintus had a touch of honour in him, and notwithstanding his thrift and sacred regard for money, he willingly gave it away in cases of honour, and unwillingly in cases of overpowering sympathy, which too painfully filled the cavities of his heart, and emptied those of his purse. Whilst the Quintaner was exercising the *jus compascui* on the cake, and six arms were peacefully resting on Thiennette's free-table, Fixlein read to himself and the company the Flachs-enfingen Address-calendar; any higher thing, except Meusel's *Gelehrtes Deutschland,* he could not figure: the Kammerherrs and Raths of the Calendar went tickling over his tongue like the raisins of the cake; and of the more rich church-livings he, by reading, as it were levied a tithe.

He purposely remained his own Edition in Sunday Wove-paper; I mean, he did not lay away his Sunday coat, even when the Prayer-bell tolled; for he had still much to do.

After supper, he was just about visiting the Fräulein, when he descried her in person, like a lily dipt in the red twilight, in the Castle-garden, whose western limit his house constituted, the southern one being the Chinese wall of the Castle . . . . By the way, how I got to the knowledge of all this, what Letter-boxes are, whether I myself was ever there, &c. &c.,—the whole of this shall, upon my life, be soon and faithfully communicated to the reader, and that too in the present Book.

Fixlein hopped forth like a Will-o'-wisp into the garden, whose flower-perfume was mingling with his supper-perfume. No one bowed lower to a nobleman than he, not out of plebeian servility, nor of self-interested cringing, but because he thought "a nobleman was a nobleman." But in this case his bow, instead of falling forwards,

---

Literary Germany; a work (I believe of no great merit) which Richter often twitches in the same style.—ED.

fell obliquely to the right, as it were after his hat: for he had not risked taking a stick with him; and hat and stick were his proppage and balance-wheel, in short, his bowing-gear, without which it was out of his power to produce any courtly bow, had you offered him the High Church of Hamburg for so doing. Thiennette's mirthfulness soon unfolded his crumpled soul into straight form, and into the proper tone. He delivered her a long neat Thanksgiving and Harvest sermon for the scaly cake; which appeared to her at once kind and tedious. Young women without the polish of high life reckon tedious pedantry, merely like snuffing, one of the necessary ingredients of a man: they reverence us infinitely; and as Lambert could never speak to the King of Prussia, by reason of his sun-eyes, except in the dark, so they, I believe, often like better,—also by reason of our sublime air,—if they can catch us in the dark too. *Him* Thiennette edified by the Imperial History of Herr von Aufhammer and Her Ladyship his spouse, who meant to put him, the Quintus, in her will: *her* he edified by his Literary History, as relating to himself and the Subrector; how, for instance, he was at present vicariating in the Second Form, and ruling over scholars as long in stature as himself. And thus did the two in happiness, among red bean-blossoms, red may-chafers, before the red of the twilight burning lower and lower on the horizon, walk to and fro in the garden; and turn always with a smile as they approached the head of the ancient gardeneress, standing like a window-bust through the little lattice, which opened in the bottom of a larger one.

To me it is incomprehensible he did not fall in love. I know his reasons, indeed: in the first place, she had nothing; secondly, he had nothing, and school-debts to boot; thirdly, her genealogical tree was a boundary-tree and warning-post; fourthly, his hands were tied up by another nobler thought, which, for good cause, is yet reserved from the reader. Nevertheless—Fixlein! I durst not have been in thy place! I should have looked at her, and remembered her virtues and our school-years, and then have drawn forth my too fusible heart, and presented it to her as a bill of exchange, or insinuated it as a summons. For I should have considered that she resembled a nun in two senses, in her good heart and in her good pastry; that, in spite of her intercourse with male vassals, she was no Charles Genevieve Louise Auguste Timothé Eon de Beaumont, but a smooth, fair-haired, white-capped dove; that she sought more to please her own

See *Schmelzle's Journey*. p. 131.—ED.

sex than ours; that she showed a melting heart, not previously borrowed from the Circulating Library, in tears, for which in her innocence she rather took shame than credit.—At the very first cheapening, I should, on these grounds, have been out with my heart.—Had I fully reflected, Quintus! that I knew her as myself; that her hands and mine (to wit, had I been thou) had both been guided by the same Senior to Latin penmanship; that we two, when little children, had kissed each other before the glass, to see whether the two image-children would do it likewise in the mirror; that often we had put hands of both sexes into the same muff, and there played with them in secret; had I, lastly, considered that we were here standing before the glass-house, now splendent in the enamel of twilight, and that on the cold panes of this glass-house we two (she within, I without) had often pressed our warm cheeks together, parted only by the thickness of the glass,—then had I taken this poor gentle soul, pressed asunder by Fate, and seeing, amid her thunder-clouds, no higher elevation to part them and protect her than the grave, and had drawn her to my own soul, and warmed her on my heart, and encompassed her about with my eyes.

In truth, the Quintus would have done so too, had not the above-mentioned nobler thought, which I yet disclose not, kept him back. Softened, without knowing the cause—(accordingly he gave his mother a kiss)—and blessed without having had a literary conversation; and dismissed with a freight of humble compliments, which he was to disload on the morrow before the Dragoon Rittmeisterinn, he returned to his little cottage, and looked yet a long while out of its dark windows, at the light ones of the Castle. And then, when the first quarter of the moon was setting, that is, about midnight, he again, in the cool sigh of a mild, fanning, moist and directly heart-addressing night-breeze, opened the eyelids of a sight already sunk in dreaming. . . . .

Sleep, for today thou hast done naught ill! I, whilst the drooping shut flower-bell of thy spirit sinks on thy pillow, will look forth into the breezy night over thy morning footpath, which, through the translucent little wood, is to lead thee to Schadeck, to thy patroness. All prosperity attend thee, thou foolish Quintus!—

SECOND LETTER-BOX

Frau von Aufhammer. Childhood-Resonance. Authorcraft.

The early piping which the little thrush last night adopted by the Quintaner from its nest, started for victual about two o'clock, soon drove our Quintus into his clothes; whose calender-press and parallel-ruler the hands of his careful mother had been, for she would not send him to the Rittmeisterinn "like a runagate dog." The Shock was incarcerated, the Quintaner taken with him, as likewise many wholesome rules from Mother Fixlein, how to conduct himself towards the Rittmeisterinn. But the son answered: "Mamma, when a man has been in company, like me, with high people, with a Fräulein Thiennette, he soon knows whom he is speaking to, and what polished manners and Saver di veaver (*Savoir vivre*) require."

He arrived with the Quintaner, and green fingers (dyed with the leaves he had plucked on the path), and with a half-nibbled rose between his teeth, in presence of the sleek lackeys of Schadeck.—If women are flowers,—though as often silk and Italian and gum-flowers as botanical ones,—then was Frau von Aufhammer a ripe flower, with (adipose) neck-bulb, and tuberosity (of lard). Already, in the half of her body, cut away from life by the apoplexy, she lay upon her lard-pillow but as on a softer grave: nevertheless, the portion of her that remained was at once lively, pious and proud. Her heart was a flowing cornucopia to all men, yet this not from philanthropy, but from rigid devotion: the lower classes she assisted, cherished and despised, regarding nothing in them, except it were their piety. She received the bowing Quintus with the back-bowing air of a patroness; yet she brightened into a look of kindliness at his disloading of the compliments from Thiennette.

She began the conversation, and long continued it alone, and said,—yet without losing the inflation of pride from her countenance: "She should soon die; but the god-children of her husband she would remember in her will." Farther, she told him directly in the face, which stood there all over-written with the Fourth Commandment before her, that "he must not build upon a settlement in Hukelum; but to the Flachsenfingen Conrectorate (to which the Bürgermeister and Council had the right of nomination), she hoped to promote him, as it was from the then Bürgermeister that she bought her coffee, and from the Town-Syndic (he drove a considerable wholesale and retail trade in Hamburg candles) that she bought both her wax and tallow lights."

And now by degrees he arrived at his humble petition, when she asked him sick-news of Senior Astmann, who guided himself more by Luther's Catechism than by the Catechism of Health. She was Astmann's patroness in a stricter than ecclesiastical sense; and she even confessed that she would soon follow this true shepherd of souls, when she heard, here at Shadeck, the sound of his funeral-bell. Such strange chemical affinities exist between our dross and our silver veins; as, for example, here between Pride and Love: and I could wish that we would pardon this hypostatic union in all persons, as readily as we do it in the fair, who, with all their faults, are nevertheless by us,—as, according to Du Fay, iron, though mixed with any other metal, is, by the magnet,—attracted and held fast.

Supposing even that the Devil *had,* in some idle minute, sown a handful or two of the seeds of Envy in our Quintus' soul, yet they had not sprouted; and today especially they did not, when he heard the praises of a man who had been his teacher, and who,—what he reckoned a Titulado of the Earth, not from vanity but from piety,— was a clergyman. So much, however, is, according to History, not to be denied: That he now straightway came forth with his petition to the noble lady, signifying that "indeed he would cheerfully content himself for a few years in the school; but yet in the end he longed to be in some small quiet priestly office." To her question, "But was he orthodox?" he answered, that "he hoped so; he had in Leipzig, not only attended all the public lectures of Dr. Burscher, but also had taken private instructions from several sound teachers of the faith, well knowing that the Consistorium, in its examinations as to purity of doctrine, was now more strict than formerly."

The sick lady required him to make a proof-shot, namely, to administer to her a sick-bed exhortation. By Heaven! he administered to her one of the best. Her pride of birth now crouched before his pride of office and priesthood; for though he could not, with the Dominican monk, Alanus de Rupe, believe that a priest was greater than God, inasmuch as the latter could only make a World, but the former a God (in the mass); yet he could not but fall-in with Hostiensis, who shows that the priestly dignity is seven thousand six hundred and forty-four times greater than the kingly, the Sun being just so many times greater than the Moon.—But a Rittmeisterinn—*she* shrinks into absolute nothing before a parson.

In the servants' hall he applied to the lackeys for the last annual series of the *Hamburg Political Journal;* perceiving, that with these historical documents of the time, they were scandalously papering the buttons of travelling raiment. In gloomy harvest evenings, he could now sit down and read for himself what good news were transpiring in the political world—twelve months ago.

On a Triumphal Car, full-laden with laurel, and to which Hopes alone were yoked, he drove home at night, and by the road advised the Quintaner not to be puffed up with any earthly honour, but silently to thank God, as himself was now doing.

The thickset blooming grove of his four canicular weeks, and the flying tumult of blossoms therein, are already painted on three of the sides. I will now clutch blindfold into his days, and bring out one of them: one smiles and sends forth its perfumes like another.

Let us take, for instance, the Saint's day of his mother, *Clara,* the twelfth of August. In the morning, he had perennial, fireproof joys, that is to say, Employments. For he was writing, as I am doing. Truly, if Xerxes proposed a prize for the invention of a new pleasure, any man who had sat down to write his thoughts on the prize-question, had the new pleasure already among his fingers. I know only one thing sweeter than making a book, and that is, to project one. Fixlein used to write little works, of the twelfth part of an alphabet in size, which in their manuscript state he got bound by the bookbinder in gilt boards, and betitled with printed letters, and then inserted them among the literary ranks of his book-board. Every one thought they were novelties printed in writing types. He had laboured,—I shall omit his less interesting performances,—at a *Collection of Errors of the Press,* in German writings: he compared *Errata* with each other; showed which occurred most frequently; observed that important results were to be drawn from this, and advised the reader to draw them.

Moreover, he took his place among the German *Masorites.* He observes with great justice in his Preface: "The Jews had their *Masora* to show, which told them how often every letter was to be found in their Bible; for example, the Aleph (the A) 42,377 times; how many verses there are in which all the consonants appear (there are 26 verses), or only eighty (there are 3); how many verses we have into which 42 words and 160 consonants enter (there is just one, Jeremiah xxi. 7); which is the middle letter in certain books (in the

Pentateuch, it is in Leviticus xi. 42, the noble V), or in the whole Bible itself. But where have we Christians any similar Masora for Luther's Bible to show? Has it been accurately investigated which is the middle word, or the middle letter here, which vowel appears seldomest, and how often each vowel? Thousands of Bible-Christians go out of the world, without ever knowing that the German A occurs 323,015 times (therefore above 7 times oftener than the Hebrew one) in their Bible."

I could wish that inquirers into Biblical Literature among our Reviewers would publicly let me know, if on a more accurate summation they find this number incorrect.

Much also did the Quintus *collect*: he had a fine *Almanac Collection*, a *Catechism* and *Pamphlet Collection;* also a *Collection of Advertisements,* which he began, is not so incomplete as you most frequently see such things. He puts high value on his *Alphabetical Lexicon of German Subscribers for Books,* where my name also occurs among the J's.

But what he liked best to produce were Schemes of Books. Accordingly, he sewed together a large work, wherein he merely advised the Learned of things they ought to introduce in Literary History, which History he rated some ells higher than Universal or Imperial History. In his Prolegomena to this performance, he transiently submitted to the Literary republic that Hommel had given a register of Jurists who were sons of wh——, of others who had become Saints; that Baillet enumerates the Learned who *meant* to write something; and Ancillon those who wrote nothing at all; and the Lübeck Superintendent Götze, those who were shoemakers, those who were drowned; and Bernhard those whose fortunes and history before birth were interesting. This (he could now continue) should, as it seems, have excited us to similar muster-rolls and matriculations of other kinds of Learned; whereof he proposed a few: for example, of the Learned, who were unlearned; of those who were entire rascals; of such as wore their own hair,—of cue-preachers, cue-psalmists, cue-annalists, and so forth; of the Learned who had worn black leather

---

As in the State.—[V. or Von, *de, of,* being the symbol of the nobility, the middle order of the State.—Ed.]

In Erlang, my petition has been granted. The *Bible Institution* of that town have found instead of the 116,301 A's, which Fixlein at first pretended with such certainty to find in the Bible-books (which false number was accordingly given in the first Edition of this Work, p. 81), the above-mentioned 323,015; which (uncommonly singular) is precisely the sum of all the letters in the Koran put together. See *Lüdeke's Beschr. des Türk. Reichs* (Lüdeke's Description of the Turkish Empire. New edition, 1780).

breeches, of others who had worn rapiers; of the Learned who had died in their eleventh year,—in their twentieth—twenty-first, &c.,—in their hundred and fiftieth, of which he knew no instance, unless the Beggar Thomas Parr might be adduced; of the Learned who wrote a more abominable hand than the other Learned (whereof we know only Rolfinken and his letters, which were as long as his hands); or of the Learned who had clipt nothing from each other but the beard (whereof no instance is known, save that of Philelphus and Timotheus).

Such by-studies did he carry on along with his official labours: but I think the State in viewing these matters is actually mad; it compares the man who is great in Philosophy and Belles Lettres at the expense of his jog-trot officialities, to *concert-clocks,* which, though striking their hours in flute-melodies, are worse timekeepers than your gross stupid *steeple-clocks*.

To return to St. Clara's day. Fixlein, after such mental exertions, bolted out under the music-bushes and rustling-trees; and returned not again out of warm Nature, till plate and chair were already placed at the table. In the course of the repast, something occurred which a Biographer must not omit: for his mother had, by request, been wont to map out for him, during the process of mastication, the chart of his child's-world, relating all the traits which in any way prefigured what he had now grown to. This perspective sketch of his early Past, he committed to certain little leaves, which merit our undivided attention. For such leaves exclusively, containing scenes, acts, plays of his childhood, he used chronologically to file and arrange in separate drawers in a little child's-desk of his; and thus to divide his Biography, as Moser did his Publicistic Materials, into separate *letter-boxes*. He had boxes or drawers for memorial-letters of his twelfth, of his thirteenth, fourteenth, &c. of his twenty-first year, and so on. Whenever he chose to conclude a day of pedagogic drudgery by an evening of peculiar rest, he simply pulled out a letter-drawer, a register-bar in his Life-hand-organ, and recollected the whole.

And here must I in reference to those reviewing Mutes, who may be for casting the noose of strangulation round my neck, most particularly beg, that, before doing so on account of my Chapters being called Letter-boxes, they would have the goodness to look whose blame it was, and to think whether I could possibly help it,

---

Paravicini Singularia de viris claris. Cent. I.?
  Ejusd. Cent. II. Philelphus quarrelled with the Greek about the quantity of a
  syllable: the prize or bet was the beard of the vanquished. Timotheus lost his.

seeing the Quintus had divided his Biography into such Boxes himself:
they have Christian bowels.

But about his elder brother he put no saddening question to his
mother: this poor boy a peculiar Fate had laid hold of, and with all
his genial endowment, dashed to pieces on the iceberg of Death. For
he chanced to leap on an ice-board that had jammed itself among
several others; but these recoiled, and his shot forth with him; melted
away as it floated under his feet, and so sunk his heart of fire amid
the ice and waves. It grieved his mother that he was not found, that
her heart had not been harrowed by the look of the swoln corpse.—O
good mother, rather thank God for it!—

After breakfast, to fortify himself with new vigour for his desk, he
for some time strolled idly over the house, and, like a Police Fire-
inspector, visited all the nooks of his cottage, to gather from them
here and there a live ember from the ash-covered rejoicing-fire of
his childhood. He mounted to the garret, to the empty bird-coops
of his father, who in winter had been a birder; and he transiently
reviewed the lumber of his old playthings, which were lying in the
netted enclosure of a large canary breeding-cage. In the minds of
children, it is regular *little* forms, such as those of balls and dies, that
impress and express themselves most forcibly. From this may the
reader explain to himself Fixlein's delight in the red acorn-blockhouse,
in the sparwork glued together out of white chips and husks of
potato-plums, in the cheerful glasshouse of a cube-shaped lantern,
and other the like products of his early architecture. The following,
however, I explain quite differently: he had ventured, without leave
given from any lord of the manor, to build a clay house; not for
cottagers, but for flies; and which, therefore, you could readily enough
have put in your pocket. This fly-hospital had its glass windows, and
a red coat of colouring, and very many alcoves, and three balconies:
balconies, as a sort of house within a house, he had loved from of
old so much, that he could scarcely have liked Jerusalem well, where
(according to Lightfoot) no such thing is permitted to be built. From
the glistening eyes, with which the architect had viewed his tenantry
creeping about the windows or feeding out of the sugar-trough,—for,
like the Count St. Germain, they ate nothing but sugar,—from this
joy an adept in the art of education might easily have prophesied his
turn for household contraction; to his fancy, in those times, even
gardeners'-huts were like large waste Arks and Halls, and nothing
bigger than such a fly-Louvre seemed a true, snug, citizen's-house.

He now felt and handled his old high child's-stool, which had, in former days, resembled the *Sedes Exploratoria* of the Pope; he gave his child's-coach a tug and made it run; but he could not understand what balsam and holiness so much distinguished it from all other child's-coaches. He wondered that the real sports of children should not so delight him, as the emblems of these sports, when the child that had carried them on was standing grown up to manhood in his presence.

Before one article in the house he stood heart-melted and sad; before a little angular clothes-press, which was no higher than my table, and which had belonged to his poor drowned brother. When the boy with the key of it was swallowed by the waves, the excruciated mother had made a vow that this toy-press of his should never be broken up by violence. Most probably there is nothing in it, but the poor soul's playthings. Let us look away from this bloody urn.——

Bacon reckons the remembrances of childhood among wholesome medicinal things; naturally enough, therefore, they acted like a salutary digestive on the Quintus. He could now again betake him with new heart to his desk, and produce something quite peculiar—petitions for church-livings. He took the Address-calendar, and for every country parish that he found in it, got a petition in readiness; which he then laid aside, till such time as the present incumbent should decease. For Hukelum alone he did not solicit.—It is a pretty custom in Flachsenfingen that for every office which is vacant, you are required, if you want it, to sue. As the higher use of Prayer consists not in its fulfilment, but in its accustoming you to pray; so likewise petitionary papers ought to be given in, not indeed that you may get the office,—this nothing but your money can do,—but that you may learn to write petitions. In truth, if among the Calmucks, the turning of a calabash stands in the place of Prayer, a slight movement of the purse may be as much as if you supplicated in words.

Towards evening—it was Sunday—he went out roving over the village; he pilgrimed to his old sporting-places, and to the common where he had so often driven his snails to pasture; visited the peasant, who, from school-times upwards, had been wont, to the amazement

---

Their prayer-barrel, Kürüdu, is a hollowed shell, a calabash, full of unrolled formulas of prayer; they sway it from side to side, and then it works. More philosophically viewed, since in prayer the feeling only is of consequence, it is much the same whether this express itself by motion of the mouth or of the calabash.

of the rest, to *thou* him; went, an Academic Tutor, to the Schoolmaster; then to the Senior; then to the Episcopal-barn or church. This last no mortal understands, till I explain it. The case was this: some three-and-forty years ago, a fire had destroyed the church (not the steeple), the parsonage, and—what was not to be replaced—the church-records. (For this reason, it was only the smallest portion of the Hukelum people that knew exactly how old they were; and the memory of our Quintus himself vibrated between adopting the thirty-third year and the thirty-second.) In consequence, the preaching had now to be carried on where formerly there had been thrashing; and the seed of the divine word to be turned over on the same threshing-floor with natural corn-seed. The Chanter and the Schoolboys took up the threshing-floor; the female mother-church-people stood on the one sheaves-loft, the Schadeck womankind on the other; and their husbands clustered pyramidically, like groschen and farthing-gallery men, about the barn-stairs; and far up on the straw-loft, mixed souls stood listening. A little flute was their organ, an upturned beer-cask their altar, round which they had to walk. I confess, I myself could have preached in such a place, not without humour. The Senior (at that time still a Junior), while the parsonage was building, dwelt and taught in the Castle: it was here, accordingly, that Fixlein had learned the *Irregular Verbs* with Thiennette.

These voyages of discovery completed, our Hukelum voyager could still, after evening prayers, pick leaf-insects, with Thiennette, from the roses; worms from the beds, and a Heaven of joy from every minute. Every dew-drop was coloured as with oil of cloves and oil of gladness; every star was a sparkle from the sun of happiness; and in the closed heart of the maiden, there lay near to him, behind a little wall of separation (as near to the Righteous man behind the thin wall of Life), an outstretched blooming Paradise . . . . . I mean, she loved him a little.

He might have known it, perhaps. But to his compressed delight he gave freer vent, as he went to bed, by early recollections on the

---

In German, as in some other languages, the common mode of address is by the *third* person: plural, it indicates respect; singular, command: the *second* person is also used; plural, it generally denotes indifference; singular, great familiarity, and sometimes its product, contempt. *Dutzenfreund, Thouing-friend,* is the strictest term of intimacy; and among the wild *Burschen* (Students) many a duel (happily, however, often ending like the *Polem-Midinia* in *one* drop of blood) has
been fought, in consequence of saying *Du* (th u) and *Sie* (they) in the wrong place.—ED.

stair. For in his childhood he had been accustomed, by way of evening-prayer, to go over, under his coverlid, as it were, a rosary, including fourteen Bible Proverbs, the first verse of the Psalm, "All people that on Earth," the Tenth Commandment, and, lastly, a long blessing. To get the sooner done with it, he had used to begin his devotion, not only on the stair, but before leaving that place where Alexander studied men, and Semler stupid books. Moored in the haven of the down-waves, he was already over with his evening supplication, and could now, without farther exertion, shut his eyes and plump into sleep.——Thus does there lurk, in the smallest *homunculus,* the model of—the Catholic Church.

So far the Dog-days of Quintus Zebedäus Egidius Fixlein.—I, for the second time, close a Chapter of this *Life,* as Life itself is closed, with a sleep.

THIRD LETTER-BOX

Christmas Recollections. New Occurrence.

For all of us the passage to the grave is, alas! a string of empty insipid days, as of glass pearls, only here and there divided by an orient one of price. But you die murmuring, unless, like the Quintus, you regard your existence as a drum: this has only one single *tone,* but variety of *time* gives the sound of it cheerfulness enough. Our Quintus taught in the Fourth Class; vicariated in the Second; wrote at his desk by night; and so lived on in the usual monotonous fashion—all the time from the Holidays—till Christmas-eve, 1791; and nothing was remarkable in his history except this same eve, which I am now about to paint.

But I shall still have time to paint it, after, in the first place, explaining shortly how, like birds of passage, he had contrived to soar away over the dim cloudy Harvest. The secret was, he set upon the *Hamburg Political Journal,* with which the lackeys of Schadeck had been for papering their buttons. He could now calmly, with his back at the stove, accompany the winter campaigns of the foregoing year; and fly after every battle, as the ravens did after that of Pharsalia. On the printed paper he could still, with joy and admiration, walk round our German triumphal arches and scaffoldings for fireworks: while to the people in the town, who got only the newest newspapers, the very fragments of these our trophies, maliciously torn down by the French, were scarcely discernible; nay, with old plans he could drive back and discomfit the enemy, while later readers in vain tried to resist them with new ones.

Moreover, not only did the facility of conquering the French prepossess him in favour of this journal; but also the circumstance that it—cost him nothing. His attachment to gratis reading was decided. And does not this throw light on the fact, that he, as Morhof advised, was wont sedulously to collect the separate leaves of waste-paper books as they came from the grocer, and to rake among the same, as Virgil did in Ennius? Nay, for him the grocer was a Fortius (the scholar), or a Frederick (the king), both which persons were in the habit of simply cutting from complete books such leaves as contained anything. It was also this respect for all waste-paper that inspired him with such esteem for the aprons of French cooks, which it is well known consist of printed paper; and he often wished some German would translate these aprons: indeed I am willing to believe that a good version of more than one of such paper aprons might contribute to elevate our Literature (this Muse à *belles fesses*), and serve her in place of drivel-bib.—On many things a man puts a *pretium affectionis,* simply because he hopes he may have half stolen them: on this principle, combined with the former, our Quintus adopted into his belief anything he could snap away from an open Lecture, or as a visitor in class-rooms; opinions only for which the Professor must be paid, he rigorously examined.—I return to the Christmas-eve.

At the very first, Egidius was glad, because out of doors millers and bakers were at fisty-cuffs (as we say of drifting snow in large flakes), and the ice-flowers of the window were blossoming; for external frost, with a snug warm room, was what he liked. He could now put fir-wood into his stove, and Mocha coffee into his stomach; and shove his right foot (not into the slipper, but) under the warm side of his Shock, and also on the left keep swinging his pet Starling, which was pecking at the snout of old Schil; and then with the right hand—with the left he was holding his pipe—proceed, so undisturbed, so intrenched, so cloud-capt, without the smallest breath of frost, to the highest enterprise which a Quintus can attempt,—to writing the Class-prodromus of the Flachsenfingen Gymnasium, namely, the eighth part thereof. I hold the *first printing* in the history of a literary man to be more important than the *first printing* in the history of Letters: Fixlein could not sate himself with specifying what he purposed, God willing, in the following year, to treat of; and accordingly, more for the sake of printing than of use, he farther inserted three or four pedagogic glances at the plan of operations to be followed by his schoolmaster colleagues as a body.

He lastly introduced a few dashes, by way of booking his thoughts together; and then laid aside the *Opus,* and would no longer look at it, that so, when printed, he might stand astonished at his own thoughts. And now he could take the Leipzig Fair Catalogue, which he purchased yearly, instead of the books therein, and open it without a sigh: he too was in print, as well as I am.

The happy fool, while writing, had shaken his head, rubbed his hands, hitched about on his chair, puckered his face, and sucked the end of his cue.—He could now spring up about five o'clock in the evening, to recreate himself; and across the magic vapour of his pipe, like a new-caught bird, move up and down in his cage. On the warm smoke, the long galaxy of street-lamps was gleaming; and red on his bed-curtains lay the fitful reflection of the blazing windows, and illuminated trees in the neighbourhood. And now he shook away the snow of Time from the winter-green of Memory; and beheld the fair years of his childhood, uncovered, fresh, green and balmy, standing afar off before him. From his distance of twenty years, he looked into the quiet cottage of his parents, where his father and his brother had not yet been reaped away by the sickle of Death. He said to himself: "I will go through the whole Christmas-eve from the very dawn, as I had it of old."

At his very rising he finds spangles on the table; sacred spangles from the gold-leaf and silver-leaf, with which the Christ-child has been emblazoning and coating his apples and nuts, the presents of the night.—On the mint-balance of joy, this metallic foam pulls heavier than the golden calves, and golden Pythagoras'-legs, and golden Philistine-mice of wealthier capitalists.—Then came his mother, bringing him both Christianity and clothes: for in drawing on his trousers, she easily recapitulated the Ten Commandments, and, in tying his garters, the Apostles' Creed. So soon as candle-light was over, and day-light come, he clambers to the arm of the settle, and then measures the nocturnal growth of the yellow wiry grove

---

These antique Christmas festivities Richter describes with equal *gusto* in another work (*Briefe und Zukünftige Lebenslemf*); where the Christ-child (falsely reported to the young ones, to have been seen flying through the air, with gold wings); the Birch-bough fixed in a corner of the room, and by him made to grow; the fruit, of gilt sweetmeats, apples, nuts, which (for good boys) it suddenly produces, &c. &c. are specified with the same fidelity as here.—ED.

of Christmas-Birch; and devotes far less attention than usual to the little white winter-flowerage, which the seeds shaken from the bird-cage are sending forth in the wet joints of the window-panes.—I nowise grudge J. J. Rousseau his *Flora Petrinsularis;* but let him also allow our Quintus his *Window-flora.*—There was no such thing as school all day; so he had time enough to seek his Butcher (his brother), and commence (when could there be finer frost for it?) the slaughtering of their winter-meat. Some days before, the brother, at the peril of his life and of a cudgelling, had caught their stalled-beast—so they called the sparrow—under a window-sill in the Castle. Their slaughtering wants not an axe (of wood), nor puddings, nor potted meat.—About three o'clock the old Gardener, whom neighbours have to call the Professor of Gardening, takes his place on his large chair, with his Cologne tobacco-pipe; and after this no mortal shall work a stroke. He tells nothing but lies; of the aeronautic Christ-child, and the jingling Ruprecht with his bells. In the dusk, our little Quintus takes an apple; divides it into all the figures of stereometry, and spreads the fragments in two heaps on the table: then as the lighted candle enters, he starts up in amazement at the unexpected present, and says to his brother: "Look what the good Christ-child has given thee and me; and I saw one of his wings glittering." And for this same glittering he himself lies in wait the whole evening.

About eight o'clock,—here he walks chiefly by the chronicle of his letter-drawer,—both of them, with necks almost excoriated with washing, and in clean linen, and in universal anxiety lest the Holy Christ-child find them up, are put to bed. What a magic night!—What tumult of dreaming hopes!—The populous, motley, glittering cave of Fancy opens itself, in the length of the night, and in the exhaustion of dreamy effort, still darker and darker, fuller and more grotesque; but the awakening gives back to the thirsty heart its hopes. All accidental tones, the cries of animals, of watchmen, are, for the timidly devout Fancy, sounds out of Heaven; singing voices of Angels in the air, church-music of the morning worship.

Ah! it was not the mere Lubberland of sweetmeats and playthings which then, with its perspective, stormed like a river of joy against the chambers of our hearts; and which yet, in the moonlight of memory, with its dusky landscapes, melts our souls in sweetness. Ah! this was it, that then for our boundless wishes there were still boundless

---

Which he purposed to make for his Island of St. Pierre in the Bienne Lake.

hopes: but now reality is round us, and the wishes are all that we have left!

At last came rapid lights from the neighbourhood playing through the window on the walls, and the Christmas trumpets, and the crowing from the steeple, hurries both the boys from their bed. With their clothes in their hands, without fear for the darkness, without feeling for the morning-frost, rushing, intoxicated, shouting, they hurry down-stairs into the dark room. Fancy riots in the pastry and fruit-perfume of the still eclipsed treasures, and paints her air-castles by the glimmering of the Hesperides-fruit with which the Birch-tree is loaded. While their mother strikes a light, the falling sparks sportfully open and shroud the dainties on the table, and the many-coloured grove on the wall; and a single atom of that fire bears on it a hanging garden of Eden.——

——On a sudden all grew light; and the Quintus got——the Conrectorship, and a table-clock.

FOURTH LETTER-BOX

Office-brokage. Discovery of the promised Secret. Hans von Füchslein.

For while the Quintus, in his vapoury chamber, was thus running over the sounding-board of his early years, the Rathsdiener, or City-officer, entered with a lantern and the Presentation; and behind him the courier of the Frau von Aufhammer with a note and a table-clock. The Rittmeisterinn had transformed her payment for the Dog-days sickbed-exhortation into a Christmas present; which consisted, *first,* of a table-clock, with a wooden ape thereon, starting out when the hours struck, and drumming along with every stroke; *secondly,* of the Conrectorate, which she had procured for him.

As in the public this appointment from the private Flachsenfingen Council has not been judged of as it deserved, I consider it my duty to offer a defence for the body corporate; and that rather here, than in the *Reichsanzeiger,* or *Imperial Indicator.*——I have already mentioned, in the Second Letter-Box, that the Town-Syndic drove a trade in Hamburg candles; and the then Bürgermeister in coffee-beans, which he sold as well whole as ground. Their joint traffic, however, which they carried on exclusively, was in the eight School-offices of Flachsenfingen: the other members of the Council acting only as bale-wrappers, shopmen and accountants in the Council wareroom.

A Council-house, indeed, is like an India-house, where not only resolutions or appointments, but also shoes and cloth, are exposed to sale. Properly speaking, the Councillor derives his freedom of office-trading from that principle of the Roman law: *Cui jus est donandi, eidem et vendendi jus est,* that is to say, He who has the right of giving anything away, has also a right to dispose of it for money, if he can. Now as the Council-members have palpably the right of conferring offices gratis, the right of selling them must follow of course.

Short Extra-word on Appointment-brokers in general

My chief anxiety is lest the Academy-product-sale-Commission of the State carry on its office-trade too slackly. And what but the commonweal must suffer in the long-run, if important posts are distributed, not according to the current cash, which is laid down for them, but according to connexions, relationships, party recommendations, and bowings and cringings? Is it not a contradiction, to charge titulary offices dearer than real ones? Should not one rather expect that the real Hofrath would pay higher by the *alterum tantum* than the mere titulary Hofrath?—Money, among European nations, is now the equivalent and representative of value in all things, and consequently in understanding; the rather as a *head* is stamped on it: to pay down the purchase-money of an office is therefore neither more nor less than to stand an *examen rigorosum,* which is held by a good *schema examinandi.* To invert this, to pretend exhibiting your qualifications, in place of these their surrogates, and assignates and *monnoie de confiance,* is simply to resemble the crazy philosophers in *Gulliver's Travels,* who, for social converse, instead of names of things, brought the things themselves tied up in a bag; it is, indeed, plainly as much as trying to fall back into the barbarous times of trade by barter, when the Romans, instead of the figured cattle on their leather money, drove forth the beeves themselves.

From all such injudicious notions I myself am so far removed, that often when I used to read that the King of France was devising new offices, to stand and sell them under the booth of his Baldaquin, I have set myself to do something of the like. This I shall now at least calmly propose; not vexing my heart whether Governments choose

---

Borrowed from the "Imperial Mine-product-sale-Commissiou," in Vienna: in their very names these Vienna people show taste.

to adopt it or not. As our Sovereign will not allow us to multiply offices purely for sale, nay, on the contrary, is day and night (like managers of strolling companies) meditating how to give more parts to one State-actor; and thus to the Three Stage Unities to add a Fourth, that of Players; as the above French method, therefore, will not apply, could not we at least contrive to invent some Virtues harmonising with the offices, along with which they might be sold as titles? Might we not, for instance, with the office of a Referendary, put off at the same time a titular Incorruptibility, for a fair consideration; and so that this virtue, as not belonging to the office, must be separately paid for by the candidate? Such a market-title and patent of nobility could not but be ornamental to a Referendary. We forget that in former times such high titles were appended to all posts whatsoever: the scholastic Professor then wrote himself (besides his official designation) "The Seraphic," "The Incontrovertible," "The Penetrating;" the King wrote himself "The Great," "The Bald," "The Bold," and so also did the Rabbins. Could it be unpleasant to gentlemen in the higher stations of Justice, if the titles of Impartiality, Rapidity, &c. might be conferred on them by sale, as well as the posts themselves? Thus with the appointment of a Kammerrath, or Councillor of Revenue, the virtue of Patriotism might fitly be conjoined; and I believe, few Advocates would grudge purchasing the title of Integrity (as well as their common one of Government-advocacy), were it to be had in the market. If, however, any candidate chose to take his post without the virtues, then it would stand with himself to do so, and in the adoption of this reflex morality, Government should not constrain him.

It might be that, as, according to Tristram Shandy, clothes; according to Walter Shandy and Lavater, proper names exert an influence on men, appellatives would do so still more; since, on us, as on testaceous animals, *the foam so often hardens into shell*: but such internal morality is not a thing the State can have an eye to; for, as in the fine arts, it is not this, but the *representation* of it, which forms her true aim.

I have found it rather difficult to devise for our different offices different verbal-virtues; but I should think there might many such divisions of Virtue (at this moment, Love of Freedom, Public-spirit, Sincerity and Uprightness occur to me) be hunted out; were but some well-disposed minister of state to appoint a Virtue-board or Moral Address Department, with some half dozen secretaries, who, for a small salary, might devise various virtues for the various posts. Were I in their place, I should hold a good prism before the white ray of Virtue, and divide it completely. Pity that it were not crimes we wanted—their subdivision I mean;—our country Judges might then be selected for this purpose. For in their tribunals, where only inferior jurisdiction, and no penalty above five florins Frankish, is admitted, they have a daily training how out of every mischief to make several small ones, none of which they ever punish to a greater amount than their five florins. This is a precious moral *Rolfinkenism,* which our Jurists have learned from the great Sin-cutters, St. Augustin and his Sorbonne, who together have carved more sins on Adam's Sin-apple than ever Rolfinken did faces on a cherrystone. How different one of our Judges from a Papal Casuist, who, by side-scrapings, will rasp you down the best deadly sin into a venial!—

School-offices (to come to these) are a small branch of traffic certainly; yet still they are monarchies,—school-monarchies, to wit,—resembling the Polish crown, which, according to Pope's verse, is twice exposed to sale in the century; a statement, I need hardly say, arithmetically false, Newton having settled the average duration of a reign at twenty-two years. For the rest, whether the city Council bring the young of the community a Hameln *Rat*-and-Child-*catcher;* or a Weisse's *Child's-friend,*—this to the Council can make no difference; seeing the Schoolmaster is not a horse, for whose secret defects the horse-dealer is to be responsible. It is enough if Town-Syndic and Co. cannot reproach themselves with having picked out any fellow of genius; for a genius, as he is useless to the State, except for recreation and ornament, would at the very least exclude the duller, cooler head, who properly forms the true care and profit of the State; as your costly carat-pearl is good for show alone, but coarse grain-pearls for medicine. On the whole, if a schoolmaster be adequate to flog his scholars, it should suffice; and I cannot but blame our Commission of Inspectors when they go examining schools, that they do not make the schoolmaster go through the duty of firking one or two young persons of his class in their presence, by way of trial, to see what is in him.

End of the Extra-word on Appointment-brokers in general

Now again to our history! The Councillor Heads of the Firm had conferred the Conrectorate on my hero, not only with a view to the continued consumpt of candles and beans, but also on the strength of a quite mad notion: they believed, the Quintus would very soon die.

—And here I have reached a most important circumstance in this History, and one into which I have yet let no mortal look: now, however, it no longer depends on my will whether I shall shove aside the folding-screen from it or not; but I must positively lay it open, nay hang a reverberating-lamp over it.

In medical history, it is a well-known fact that in certain families the people all die precisely at the same age, just as in these families they are all born at the same age (of nine months); nay, from Voltaire, I recollect one family, the members of which at the same age all killed themselves. Now, in the Fixleinic lineage, it was the custom that the male ascendants uniformly on Cantata-Sunday, in their thirty-second year, took to bed and died: every one of my readers would do well to insert in his copy of the *Thirty-Years War,* Schiller having entirely omitted it, the fact, that in the course thereof, one Fixlein died of the plague, another of hunger, another of a musket-bullet; all in their thirty-second year. True Philosophy explains the matter thus: "The first two or three times, it happened purely by accident; and the other times, the people died of sheer fright: if not so, the whole fact is rather to be questioned."

But what did Fixlein make of the affair? Little or nothing: the only thing he did was, that he took little or no pains to fall in love with Thiennette; that so no other might have cause for fear on his account. He himself, however, for five reasons, minded it so little, that he hoped to be older than Senior Astmann before he died: First, because three Gipsies, in three different places and at three different times, had each shown him the same long vista of years in her magic mirror. Secondly, because he had a sound constitution. Thirdly, because his own brother had formed an exception, and perished before the thirties. Fourthly, on this ground: When a boy he had fallen sick of sorrow, on the very Cantata-Sunday when his father was lying in the winding-sheet, and only been saved from death by his playthings; and with this Cantata-sickness, he conceived that he had given the murderous Genius of his race the slip. Fifthly, the church-books being destroyed, and with them the certainty of his age, he could never fall into a right definite deadly fear: "It may be," said he, "that I have got whisked away over this whoreson year, and no one the wiser." I will not deny that last year he had fancied he was two-and-thirty: "however," said he, "if I am not to be so till, God willing, the next (1792), it may run away as smoothly as the last; am I not always in *His* keeping? And were it unjust if the pretty years that were broken off from the life of my brother should be added to mine?"—Thus, under the cold snow of the Present, does poor man strive to warm himself, or to mould out of it a fair snow-man.

The Councillor Oligarchy, however, built upon the opposite opinion; and, like a Divinity, elevated our Quintus all at once from the Quintusship to the Conrectorate; swearing to themselves, that he would soon vacate it again. Properly speaking, by school-seniority, this holy chair should have belonged to the Subrector Hans von Füchslein; but he wished it not; being minded to become Hukelum Parson; especially, as Astmann's Death-angel, according to sure intelligence, was opening more and more widely the door of this spiritual sheepfold. "If the fellow weather another year, 'tis more than I expect," said Hans.

This Hans was such a churl, that it is pity he had not been a Hanoverian Postboy; that so, by the Mandate of the Hanoverian Government, enjoining on all its Post-officers an elegant style of manners, he might have somewhat refined himself. To our poor Quintus, whom no mortal disliked, and who again could hate no mortal, he alone bore a grudge; simply because *Fixlein* did not write himself *Füchslein,* and had not chosen along with him to purchase a Patent of Nobility. The Subrector, on this his Patent triumphal chariot, drawn by a team of four specified ancestors, was obliged to see the Quintus, who was related to him, clutching by the lackey-straps behind the carriage; and to hear him, in the most despicable raiment, saying to the train: "He that rides there is my cousin, and a mortal, and I always remind him of it." The mild compliant Quintus never noticed this large wasp-poisonbag in the Subrector, but took it for a honeybag; nay, by his brotherly warmness, which the nobleman regarded as mere show, he concreted these venomous juices into still feller consistency. The Quintus, in his simplicity, took Füchslein's contempt for envy of his pedagogic talents.

A Catherinenhof, an Annenhof, an Elizabethhof, Stralenhof and Petershof, all these Russian pleasure palaces, a man can dispense with (if not despise), who has a room, in which on Christmas-eve he walks about with a Presentation in his hand. The new Conrector now longed for nothing but—daylight: joys always (cares never) nibbled from him, like sparrows, his sleep-grains; and tonight, moreover, the registrator of his glad time, the clock-ape, drummed out every hour to him, which, accordingly, he spent in gay dreaming, rather than in sound snoring.

On Christmas-morn, he looked at his Class-prodromus, and thought but little of it; he scarcely knew what to make of his last night's foolish inflation about his Quintusship: "the Quintus-post," said he to himself, "is not to be named in the same day with the Conrectorate; I wonder how I could parade so last night before my promotion; at present, I had more reason." Today he ate, as on all Sundays and holydays, with the Master-Butcher Steinberger, his former Guardian. To this man, Fixlein was, what common people arc *always,* but polished philosophical and sentimental people very *seldom* are,—*thankful*: a man thanks you the less for presents, the more inclined he is to give presents of his own; and the beneficent is rarely a grateful person. Meister Steinberger, in the character of store-master, had introduced into the wire-cage of a garret, where Fixlein, while a Student at Leipzig, was suspended, many a well-filled trough with good canary-meat, of hung-beef, of household bread and *Sauerkraut.* Money indeed was never to be wrung from him: it is well known that he often sent the best calfskins gratis to the tanner, to be boots for our Quintus; but the tanning-charges the Ward himself had to bear.—On Fixlein's entrance, as was at all times customary, a smaller damask table-cloth was laid upon the large coarser one; the armchair; silver implements, and a wine-stoup were handed him: mere waste, which, as the Guardian used to say, suited well enough for a Scholar; but for a Flesher not at all. Fixlein first took his victuals, and then signified that he was made Conrector. "Ward," said Steinberger, "if you are made that, it is well.—Seest thou, Eva, I cannot buy a tail of thy cows now; I must have smelt it beforehand." He was hereby informing his daughter that the cash set apart for the fatted cattle must now be applied to the Conrectorate; for he was in the habit of advancing all instalment-dues to his ward, at an interest of four and a half per cent. Fifty gulden he had already lent the Quintus on his advancement to the Quintusship: of these the interest had to be duly paid; yet, on the day of payment, the Quintus always got some abatement; being wont every Sunday after dinner to instruct his guardian's daughter in arithmetic, writing and geography. Steinberger with justice required of his own grown-up daughter that she should know all the towns, where he in his wanderings as a journeyman had slain fat oxen; and if she slipped, or wrote crookedly, or subtracted wrong, he himself, as Academical Senate and Justiciary, was standing behind her chair, ready, so to speak, with the forge-hammer of his fist to beat out the dross from her brain, and at a few strokes hammer it into right ductility. The soft Quintus, for his part, had never struck her. On this account she had perhaps, with a few glances, appointed him executor and assignee of her heart. The old Flesher—simply because his wife was dead—had constantly been in the habit of searching with mine-lamps and pokers into all the corners of Eva's heart; and had in consequence long ago observed—what the Quintus never did—that she had a mind for the said Quintus. Young women conceal their sorrows more easily than their joys: today at the mention of this Conrectorate, Eva had become unusually *red*.

When she went after breakfast to bring in coffee, which the Ward had to drink down to the grounds: "I beat Eva to death if she but look at him," said he. Then addressing Fixlein: "Hear you, Ward, did you never cast an eye on my Eva? She can suffer you, and if you want her, you get her; but *we* have done with one another: for a learned man needs quite another sort of thing."

"Herr Regiments-Quartermaster," said Fixlein (for this post Steinberger filled in the provincial Militia), "such a match were far too rich, at any rate, for a Schoolman." The Quartermaster nodded fifty times; and then said to Eva, as she returned,—at the same time taking down from the shelf a wooden crook, on which he used to rack out and suspend his slain calves: "Stop!—Hark, dost wish the present Herr Conrector here for thy husband?"

"Ah, good Heaven!" said Eva.

"Mayst wish him or not," continued the Flesher; "with this crook, thy father knocks thy brains out, if thou but think of a learned man. Now make his coffee." And so by the dissevering stroke of this wooden crook was a love easily smitten asunder, which in a higher rank, by such cutting through it with the sword, would only have foamed and hissed the keenlier.

Fixlein might now, at any hour he liked, lay hold of fifty florins Frankish, and clutch the pedagogic sceptre, and become coadjutor of the Rector, that is, Conrector. We may assert, that it is with debts, as with proportions in Architecture; of which Wolf has shown that those are the best, which can be expressed in the smallest numbers. Nevertheless, the Quartermaster cheerfully took learned men under his arm: for the notion that his debtor would decease in his thirty-second year, and that so Death, as creditor in the first rank, must be paid his Debt of Nature, before the other creditors could come forward with their debts—this notion he named stuff and oldwifery; he was neither superstitious nor fanatical, and he walked by firm principles of action, such as the common man much oftener has than your vapouring man of letters, or your empty dainty man of rank.

As it is but a few clear Ladydays, warm Mayday-nights, at the most a few odorous Rose-weeks, which I am digging from this Fixleinic Life, embedded in the dross of week-day cares; and as if they were so many veins of silver, am separating, stamping, smelting and burnishing for the reader,—I must now travel on with the stream of his history to Cantata-Sunday, 1792, before I can gather a few handfuls of this gold-dust, to carry in and wash in my biographical gold-hut. That Sunday, on the contrary, is very metalliferous: do but consider that Fixlein is yet uncertain (the ashes of the Church-books not being legible) whether it is conducting him into his thirty-second or his thirty-third year.

From Christmas till then he did nothing, but simply became Conrector. The new chair of office was a Sun-altar, on which, from his Quintus-ashes, a young Phoenix combined itself together. Great changes—in offices, marriages, travels—make us younger; we always date our history from the last revolution, as the French have done from theirs. A colonel, who first set foot on the ladder of seniority as corporal, is five times younger than a king, who in his whole life has never been aught else except a—crown-prince.

FIFTH LETTER-BOX

Cantata-Sunday. Two Testaments. Pontac; Blood; Love.

The Spring months clothe the earth in new variegated hues; but man they usually dress in black. Just when our icy regions are becoming fruitful, and the flower-waves of the meadows are rolling together over our quarter of the globe, we on all hands meet with men in sables, the beginning of whose Spring is full of tears. But, on the other hand, this very upblooming of the renovated earth is itself the best balm for sorrow over those who lie under it; and graves are better hid by blossoms than by snow.

In April, which is no less deadly than it is fickle, old Senior Astmann, our Conrector's teacher, was overtaken by death. His departure it was meant to hide from the Rittmeisterinn; but the unusual ringing of funereal peals carried his swan-song to her heart; and gradually set the curfew-bell of her life into similar movement. Age and sufferings had already marked out the first incisions for Death, so that he required but little effort to cut her down; for it is with men as with trees, they are notched long before felling, that their life-sap may exude. The second stroke of apoplexy was soon followed by the last: it is strange that Death, like criminal courts, cites the apoplectic thrice.

Men are apt to postpone their *last* will as long as their *better* one: the Rittmeisterinn would perhaps have let all her hours, till the speechless and deaf one, roll away without testament, had not Thiennette, during the last night, before from sick-nurse she became corpse-watcher, reminded the patient of the poor Conrector, and of his meagre hunger-bitten existence, and of the scanty aliment and board-wages which Fortune had thrown him, and of his empty Future, where, like a drooping yellow plant in the parched deal-box of the schoolroom between scholars and creditors, he must languish to the end. Her own poverty offered her a model of his; and her inward tears were the fluid tints with which she coloured her picture. As the Rittmeisterinn's testament related solely to domestics and dependents, and as she began with the male ones, Fixlein stood at the top; and Death, who must have been a special friend of the Conrector's, did not lift his scythe and give the last stroke till his protegee had been with audible voice declared testamentary heir; then he cut all away, life, testament and hopes.

When the Conrector, in a wash-bill from his mother, received these two Death's-posts and Job's-posts in his class, the first thing he did was to dismiss his class-boys, and break into tears before reaching home. Though the mother had informed him that he had been remembered in the will (I could wish, however, that the Notary had blabbed how much it was), yet almost with every O which he masoretically excerpted from his German Bible, and entered in his Masoretic Work, great drops fell down on his pen, and made his black ink pale. His sorrow was not the gorgeous sorrow of the Poet, who veils the gaping wounds of the departed in the winding-sheet, and breaks the cry of anguish in soft tones of plaintiveness; nor the sorrow of the Philosopher, who, through one open grave, must look into the whole catacomb-Necropolis of the Past, and before whom the spectre of a friend expands into the spectral Shadow of this whole Earth: but it was the woe of a child, of a mother, whom this thought itself, without subsidiary reflections, bitterly cuts asunder: "So I shall never more see thee; so must thou moulder away, and I shall never see thee, thou good soul, never, never any more!"—And even because he neither felt the philosophical nor the poetical sadness, every trifle could make a division, a break in his mourning; and, like a woman, he was that very evening capable of sketching some plans for the future employment of his legacy.

Four weeks after, to wit, on the 5th of May, the testament was unsealed; but not till the 6th (Cantata-Sunday) did he go down to Hukelum. His mother met his salutations with tears; which she shed, over the corpse for grief, over the testament for joy.—To the now Conrector Egidius Zebedäus was left: *In the first place,* a large sumptuous bed, with a mirror-tester, in which the giant Goliath might have rolled at his ease, and to which I and my fair readers will by and by approach nearer, to examine it; *secondly,* there was devised to him, as unpaid Easter-godchild-money, for every year that he had lived, one ducat; *thirdly,* all the admittance and instalment dues, which his elevation to the Quintate and Conrectorate had cost him, were to be made good to the utmost penny. "And dost thou know, then," proceeded the mother, "what the poor Fräulein has got? Ah Heaven! Nothing! Not one brass farthing!" For Death had stiffened the hand which was just stretching itself out to reach the poor Thiennette a little rain-screen against the foul weather of life. The mother related this perverse trick of Fortune with true condolence; which in women dissipates envy, and comes easier to them than congratulation, a feeling belonging rather to men. In many female hearts sympathy and envy are such near door-neighbours that they could be virtuous nowhere except in Hell, where men have such frightful times of it; and vicious nowhere except in Heaven, where people have more happiness than they know what to do with.

The Conrector was now enjoying on Earth that Heaven to which his benefactress had ascended. First of all, he started off—without so much as putting up his handkerchief, in which lay his emotion—up-stairs to see the legacy-bed unshrouded; for he had a *female* predilection for furniture. I know not whether the reader ever looked at or mounted any of these ancient chivalric beds, into which, by means of a little stair without balustrades, you can easily ascend; and in which you, properly speaking, sleep always at least one story above ground. Nazianzen informs us (*Orat. XVI.*) that the Jews, in old times, had high beds with cock-ladders of this sort; but simply because of vermin. The legacy bed-Ark was quite as large as one of these; and a flea would have measured it not in Diameters of the Earth, but in Distances of Sirius. When Fixlein beheld this colossal dormitory, with the curtains drawn asunder, and its canopy of looking-glass, he could have longed to be in it; and had it been in his power to cut from the opaque hemisphere of Night, at that time in America, a small section, he would have established himself there along with it, just to swim about, for one half hour, with his thin lath figure, in this sea of down. The mother, by longer chains of reasoning and chains of calculation than the bed was, had not succeeded in persuading him to have the broad mirror on the top cut in pieces, though his large dressing-table had nothing to see itself in but a mere shaving-glass: he let the mirror lie where it was for this reason: "Should I ever, God willing, get married," said he, "I shall then, towards morning, be able to look at my sleeping wife, without sitting up in bed."

As to the second article of the testament, the godchild Easterpence, his mother had, last night, arranged it perfectly. The Lawyer took her evidence on the years of the heir; and these she had stated at exactly the teeth-number, two-and-thirty. She would willingly have lied, and passed off her son, like an Inscription, for older than he was: but against this *venia ætatis,* she saw too well, the authorities would have taken exception, "that it was falsehood and cozenage; had the son been two-and-thirty, he must have been dead some time ago, as it could not but be presumed that he then was."

And just as she was recounting this, a servant from Schadeck called, and delivered to the Conrector, in return for a discharge and ratification of the birth-certificate given out by his mother, a gold bar of two-and-thirty ducat age-counters, like a helm-bar for the voyage of his life: Herr von Aufhammer was too proud to engage in any pettifogging discussion over a plebeian birth-certificate.

And thus, by a proud open-handedness, was one of the best lawsuits thrown to the dogs: seeing this gold bar might, in the wire-mill of the judgment-bench, have been drawn out into the finest threads. From such a tangled lock, which was not to be unravelled—for, in the first place, there was no document to prove Fixlein's age; in the second place, so long as he lived, the necessary conclusion was, that he was not yet thirty-two —from such a lock, might not only silk and hanging-cords, but whole dragnets have been spun and twisted. Clients in general would have less reason to complain of their causes, if these lasted longer: Philosophers contend for thousands of years over philosophical questions; and it seems an unaccountable thing, therefore, that Advocates should attempt to end their juristical questions in a space of eighty, or even sometimes of sixty years. But

---

As, by the evidence at present before us, we can found on no other presumption, than that he must die in his thirty-second year; it would follow, that, in case he died two-and-thirty years after the death of the testatrix, no farthing could be claimed by him; since, according to our fiction, at the making of the testament he was not even one year old.

the professors of law are not to blame for this: on the other hand, as Lessing asserts of Truth, that not the *finding* but the *seeking* of it profits men, and that he himself would willingly make over his claim to all truths in return for the sweet labour of investigation, so is the professor of Law not profited by the finding and deciding, but by the investigation of a juridical truth,—which is called pleading and practising,—and he would willingly consent to approximate to Truth forever, like an hyperbola to its asymptote, without ever meeting it, seeing he can subsist as an honourable man with wife and child, let such approximation be as tedious as it likes.

The Schadeck servant had, besides the gold legacy, a farther commission from the Lawyer, whereby the testamentary heir was directed to sum up the mint-dues which he had been obliged to pay while lying under the coining-press of his superiors, as Quintus and Conrector; the which, properly documented and authenticated, were forthwith to be made good to him.

Our Conrector, who now rated himself among the great capitalists of the world, held his short gold-roll like a sceptre in his hand; like a basket-net lifted from the sea of the Future, which was now to run on, and bring him all manner of fed-fishes, well-washed, sound and in good season.

I cannot relate all things at once; else I should ere now have told the reader, who must long have been waiting for it, that to the moneyed Conrector his two-and-thirty godchild-pennies but too much prefigured the two-and-thirty years of his age; besides which, today the Cantata-Sunday, this Bartholomew-night and Second of September of his family, came in as a farther aggravation. The mother, who should have known the age of her child, said she had forgotten it; but durst wager he was thirty-two a year ago; only the Lawyer was a man you could not speak to. "I could swear it myself," said the capitalist; "I recollect how stupid I felt on Cantata-Sunday last year." Fixlein beheld Death, not as the poet does, in the up-towering, asunder-driving concave-mirror of Imagination; but as the child, as the savage, as the peasant, as the woman does, in the plane octavo-mirror on the board of a Prayer-book; and Death looked to him like an old white-headed man, sunk down into slumber in some latticed pew.—

And yet he thought oftener of him than last year: for joy readily melts us into softness; and the lackered Wheel of Fortune is a cistern-wheel that empties its water in our eyes . . . . . But the friendly Genius of this terrestrial, or rather aquatic Ball,—for, in the physical and in the moral world, there are more tear-seas than firm land,—has provided for the poor water-insects that float about in it, for us namely, a quite special elixir against spasms in the soul: I declare this same Genius must have studied the whole pathology of man with care; for to the poor devil who is no Stoic, and can pay no Soul-doctor, that for the fissures of his cranium and his breast might prepare costly prescriptions of simples, he has stowed up cask-wise in all cellarages a precious wound-water, which the patient has only to take and pour over his slashes and bone-breakages—gin-twist, I mean, or beer, or a touch of wine. . . . . By Heaven! it is either stupid ingratitude towards this medicinal Genius on the one hand, or theological confusion of permitted tippling with prohibited drunkenness on the other, if men do not thank God that they have something at hand, which, in the nervous vertigos of life, will instantly supply the place of Philosophy, Christianity, Judaism, Paganism and *Time;*—liquor, as I said.

The Conrector had long before sunset given the village post three groschens of post-money, and commissioned,—for he had a whole cabinet of ducats in his pocket, which all day he was surveying in the dark with his hand,—three thalers' worth of Pontac from the town. "I must have a Cantata merrying-making," said he; "if it be my last day, let it be my gayest too!" I could wish he had given a larger order; but he kept the bit of moderation between his teeth at all times; even in a threatened sham-death-night, and in the midst of jubilee. The question is, Whether he would not have restricted himself to a single bottle, if he had not wished to treat his mother and the Fräulein. Had he lived in the tenth century, when the Day of Judgment was thought to be at hand, or in other centuries, when new Noah's Deluges were expected, and when, accordingly, like sailors in a shipwreck, people bouzed up all,—he would not have spent one kreutzer more on that account. His joy was, that with his legacy he could now satisfy his head-creditor Steinberger, and leave the world an honest man: just people, who make much of money, pay their debts the most punctually.

The purple Pontac arrived at a time when Fixlein could compare the red-chalk-drawings and red-letter-titles of joy, which it would bring out on the cheeks of its drinker and drinkeresses,—with the Evening-carnation of the last clouds about the Sun. . . .

I declare, among all the spectators of this History, no one can be thinking more about poor Thiennette than I; nevertheless, it is not permitted me to bring her out from her tiring-room to my historical scene, before the time. Poor girl! The Conrector cannot wish more warmly than his Biographer, that, in the Temple of Nature as in that of Jerusalem, there were a special door—besides that of Death—standing open, through which only the afflicted entered, that a Priest might give them solace. But Thiennette's heart-sickness over all her vanished prospects, over her entombed benefactress, over a whole life enwrapped in the pall, had hitherto, in a grief which the stony Rittmeister rather made to bleed than alleviated, swept all away from her, occupations excepted; had fettered all her steps which led not to some task, and granted to her eyes nothing to dry them or gladden them, save down-falling eyelids full of dreams and sleep.

All sorrow raises us above the civic Ceremonial-law, and makes the Prosaist a Psalmist: in sorrow alone have women courage to front opinion. Thiennette walked out only in the evening, and then only in the garden.

The Conrector could scarcely wait for the appearance of his fair friend, to offer his thanks,—and tonight also—his Pontac. Three Pontac decanters and three wine-glasses were placed outside on the projecting window-sill of his cottage; and every time he returned from the dusky covered-way amid the flower-forests, he drank a little from his glass,—and the mother sipped now and then from within through the opened window.

I have already said, his Life-laboratory lay in the south west corner of the garden or park, over against the Castle-Escurial, which stretched back into the village. In the north-west corner bloomed an acacia-grove, like the floral crown of the garden. Fixlein turned his steps in that direction also; to see if, perhaps, he might not cast a happy glance through the wide-latticed grove over the intervening meads to Thiennette. He recoiled a little before two stone steps leading down into a pond before this grove, which were sprinkled with fresh blood. On the flags, also, there was blood hanging. Man shudders at this oil of our life's lamp where he finds it shed: to him it is the red death-signature of the Destroying Angel. Fixlein hurried apprehensively into the grove; and found here his paler benefactress leaning on the flower-bushes; her hands with their knitting-ware sunk into her bosom, her eyes lying under their lids as if in the bandage of slumber; her left arm in the real bandage of blood-letting; and with cheeks to which the twilight was lending as much red, as late woundings—this day's included—had taken from them. Fixlein, after his first terror—not at this flower's-sleep, but at his own abrupt entrance—began to unrol the spiral butterfly's-sucker of his vision, and to lay it on the motionless leaves of this same sleeping flower. At bottom, I may assert, that this was the first time he had ever looked at her: he was now among the thirties; and he still continued to believe, that, in a young lady, he must look at the clothes only, not the person, and wait on her with his ears, not with his eyes.

I impute it to the elevating influences of the Pontac, that the Conrector plucked up courage to—turn, to come back, and employ the resuscitating means of coughing, sneezing, trampling and calling to his Shock, in stronger and stronger doses on the fair sleeper. To take her by the hand, and, with some medical apology, gently pull her out of sleep, this was an audacity of which the Conrector, so long as he could stand for Pontac, and had any grain of judgment left, could never dream.

However, he did awake her, by those other means.

Wearied, heavy-laden Thiennette! how slowly does thy eye open! The warmest balsam of this earth, soft sleep has shifted aside, and the night-air of memory is again blowing on thy naked wounds!—And yet was the smiling friend of thy youth the fairest object which thy eye could light on, when it sank from the hanging garden of Dreams into this lower one round thee.

She herself was little conscious,—and the Conrector not at all,— that she was bending her flower-leaves imperceptibly towards a terrestrial body, namely towards Fixlein: she resembled an Italian flower, that contains cunningly concealed within it a newyear's gift, which the receiver knows not at first how to extract. But now the golden chain of her late kind deed attracted her as well towards him, as him towards her.—She at once gave her eye and her voice a mask of joy; for she did not put her tears, as Catholics do those of Christ, in relic-vials, upon altars to be worshiped. He could very suitably preface his invitation to the Pontac festival, with a long acknowledgment of thanks for the kind intervention which had opened to him the sources for procuring it. She rose slowly, and walked with him to the banquet of wine; but he was not so discreet, as at first to attempt leading her, or rather not so courageous; he could more easily have offered a young lady his hand (that is, with marriage ring) than offered her his arm. One only time in his life had he escorted a female, a Lombard Countess from the theatre; a thing truly not to be believed, were not this the secret of it, that he was obliged; for the lady, a foreigner, parted in the press from all her people, in a bad night, had laid hold of him as a sable Abbé by the arm, and requested him to take her to her inn. He, however, knew the fashions of society, and attended her no farther than the porch of his Quintus-mansion, and there directed her with his finger to her inn, which, with thirty blazing windows, was looking down from another street.

These things he cannot help. But tonight he had scarcely, with his fair faint companion, reached the bank of the pond, into which some superstitious dread of water-sprites had lately poured the pure blood of her left arm,—when, in his terror lest she fell in, with the rest of her blood, over the brink, he quite valiantly laid hold of the sick arm. Thus will much Pontac and a little courage at all times put a Conrector in case to lay hold of a Fräulein. I aver, that, at the banquet-board of the wine, at the window-sill, he continued in the same conducting position. What a soft group in the penumbra of the Earth, while Night, with its dusky waters, was falling deeper and deeper, and the silver-light of the Moon was already glancing back from the copper-ball of the steeple! I call the group soft, because it consists of a maiden that in two senses has been bleeding; of a mother again with tears giving her thanks for the happiness of her child; and of a pious, modest man, pouring wine, and drinking health to both, and who traces in his veins a burning lava-stream, which is boiling through his heart, and threatening piece by piece to melt it and bear it away.—A candle stood without among the three bottles, like Reason among the Passions; on this account the Conrector looked without intermission at the window-panes, for on them (the darkness of the room served as mirror-foil) was painted, among other faces which Fixlein liked, the face he liked best of all, and which he dared to look at only in reflection, the face of Thiennette.

Every minute was a Federation-festival, and every second a Preparation-Sabbath for it. The Moon was gleaming from the evening dew, and the Pontac from their eyes, and the bean-stalks were casting a shorter grating of shadow.—The quicksilver-drops of stars were hanging more and more continuous in the sable of night.—The warm vapour of the wine set our two friends (like steam-engines) again in motion.

Nothing makes the heart fuller and bolder than walking to and fro in the night. Fixlein now led the Fräulein in his arm without scruple. By reason of her lancet-wound, Thiennette could only put her hand, in a clasping position, in his arm; and he, to save her the trouble of holding fast, held fast himself, and pressed her fingers as well as might be with his arm to his heart. It would betray a total want of polished manners to censure his. At the same time, trifles are the provender of Love; the fingers are electric dischargers of a fire sparkling along every fibre; sighs are the guiding tones of two approximating hearts; and the worst and most effectual thing of all in such a case is some misfortune; for the fire of Love, like that of naphtha, likes to swim on water. Two teardrops, one in another's, one in your own eyes, compose, as with two convex lenses, a microscope which enlarges everything, and changes all sorrows into charms. Good sex! I too consider every sister in misfortune as fair; and perhaps thou wouldst deserve the name of the Fair, even because thou art the Suffering sex!

And if Professor Hunczogsky in Vienna modelled all the wounds of the human frame in wax, to teach his pupils how to cure them, I also, thou good sex, am representing in little figures the cuts and scars of thy spirit, though only to keep away rude hands from inflicting new ones. . . . .

Thiennette felt not the loss of the inheritance, but of her that should have left it; and this more deeply for one little trait, which she had already told his mother, as she now told him: In the last two nights of the Rittmeisterinn, when the feverish watching was holding up to Thiennette's imagination nothing but the winding-sheet and the mourning-coaches of her protectress; while she was sitting at the foot of the bed, looking on those fixed eyes, unconsciously quick drops often trickled over her cheeks, while in thought she prefigured the heavy, cumbrous dressing of her benefactress for the coffin. Once, after midnight, the dying lady pointed with her finger to her own lips. Thiennette understood her not; but rose and bent over her face. The Enfeebled tried to lift her head, but could not,—and only rounded her lips. At last, a thought glanced through Thiennette, that the Departing, whose dead arms could now press no beloved heart to her own, wished that she herself should embrace her. O then, that instant, keen and tearful she pressed her warm lips on the colder,— and she was silent like her that was to speak no more,—and she embraced alone and was not embraced. About four o'clock, the finger waved again;—she sank down on the stiffened lips—but this had been no signal, for the lips of her friend under the long kiss had grown stiff and cold. . . . .

How deeply now, before the infinite Eternity's-countenance of Night, did the cutting of this thought pass through Fixlein's warm soul: "O thou forsaken one beside me! No happy accident, no twilight hast thou, like that now glimmering in the heavens, to point to the prospect of a sunny day: without parents art thou, without brother, without friend; here alone on a disblossomed, emptied corner of the Earth; and thou, left Harvest-flower, must wave lonely and frozen over the withered stubble of the Past." That was the meaning of his thoughts, whose internal words were: "Poor young lady! Not so much as a half-cousin left; no nobleman will seek her, and she grows old so forgotten, and she is so good from the very heart—Me she has made happy—Ah, had I the presentation to the parish of Hukelum in my pocket, I should make a trial." . . . . Their mutual lives, which a straitcutting bond of Destiny was binding so closely together, now rose before him overhung with sable,—and he forthwith conducted his friend (for a bashful man may in an hour and a half be transformed into the boldest, and then continues so) back to the last flask, that all these upsprouting thistles and passion-flowers of sorrow might therewith be swept away. I remark, in passing, that this was stupid: the torn vine is full of water-veins as well as grapes; and a soft oppressed heart the beverage of joy can melt only into tears.

If any man disagree with me, I shall desire him to look at the Conrector, who demonstrates my experimental maxim like a very syllogism.—One might arrive at some philosophic views, if one traced out the causes, why liquors—that is to say, in the long-run, more plentiful secretion of the nervous spirits—make men at once pious, soft and poetical. The Poet, like Apollo his father, is *forever a youth;* and is, what other men are only once, namely in love,—or only after Pontac, namely intoxicated,—all his life long. Fixlein, who had been no poet in the morning, now became one at night: wine made him pious and soft; the Harmonica-bells in man, which sound to the tones of a higher world, must, like the glass Harmonica-bells, if they are to act, be kept *moist.*

He was now standing with her again beside the wavering pond, in which the second blue hemisphere of heaven, with dancing stars and amid quivering trees, was playing; over the green hills ran the white crooked footpaths dimly along; on the one mountain was the twilight sinking together, on the other was the mist of night rising up; and over all these vapours of life, hung motionless and flaming the thousand-armed lustre of the starry heaven, and every arm held in it a burning galaxy. . . . .

It now struck eleven. . . . . Amid such scenes, an unknown hand stretches itself out in man, and writes in foreign language on his heart, a dread *Mene Mene Tekel Upharsin.* "Perhaps by twelve I am dead," thought our friend, in whose soul the Cantata-Sunday, with all its black funeral piles, was mounting up.

The whole future Crucifixion-path of his friend lay prickly and bethorned before him; and he saw every bloody trace from which she lifted her foot,—she who had made his own way soft with flowers and leaves. He could no longer restrain himself; trembling in his whole frame, and with a trembling voice, he solemnly said to her: "If the Lord this night call me away, let the half of my fortune be yours; for it is your goodness I must thank that I am free of debts, as few Teachers are."

Thiennette, unacquainted with our sex, naturally mistook this speech for a proposal of marriage; and the fingers of her wounded arm, tonight for the first time, pressed suddenly against the arm in which they lay; the only living mortal's arm, by which Joy, Love and the Earth, were still united with her bosom. The Conrector, rapturously terrified at the first pressure of a female hand, bent over his right to take hold of her left; and Thiennette, observing his unsuccessful movement, lifted her fingers, and laid her whole wounded arm in his, and her whole left hand in his right. Two lovers dwell in the Whispering-gallery, where the faintest breath bodies itself forth into a sound. The good Conrector received and returned this blissful love-pressure, wherewith our poor powerless soul, stammering, hemmed in, longing, distracted, seeks for a warmer language, which exists not: he was overpowered; he had not the courage to look at her; but he looked into the gleam of the twilight, and said (and here for unspeakable love the tears were running warm over his cheeks): "Ah, I will give you all; fortune, life and all that I have, my heart and my hand."

She was about to answer, but casting a side-glance, she cried, with a shriek: "Ah, Heaven!" He started round; and perceived the white muslin sleeve all dyed with blood; for in putting her arm into his, she had pushed away the bandage from the open vein. With the speed of lightning, he hurried her into the acacia-grove; the blood was already running from the muslin; he grew paler than she, for every drop of it was coming from his heart. The blue-white arm was bared; the bandage was put on; he tore a piece of gold from his pocket; clapped it, as one does with open arteries, on the spouting fountain, and bolted with this golden bar, and with

---

In St. Paul's Church at London, where the slightest whisper sounds over across a space of 143 feet.

the bandage over it, the door out of which her afflicted life was hurrying.—

When it was over, she looked up to him; pale, languid, but her eyes were two glistening fountains of an unspeakable love, full of sorrow and full of gratitude.—The exhausting loss of blood was spreading her soul asunder in sighs. Thiennette was dissolved into inexpressible softness; and the heart, lacerated by so many years, by so many arrows, was plunging with all its wounds in warm streams of tears, to be healed; as chapped flutes close together by lying in water, and get back their tones.—Before such a magic form, before such a pure heavenly love, her sympathising friend was melted between the flames of joy and grief; and sank, with stifled voice, and bent down by love and rapture, on the pale angelic face, the lips of which he timidly pressed, but did not kiss, till all-powerful Love bound its girdles round them, and drew the two closer and closer together, and their two souls, like two tears, melted into one. O now, when it struck twelve, the hour of death, did not the lover fancy that her lips were drawing his soul away, and all the fibres and all the nerves of his life closed spasmodically round the last heart in this world, round the last rapture of existence? . . . . Yes, happy man, thou didst express thy love; for in thy love thou thoughtest to die. . . . .

However, he did not die. After midnight, there floated a balmy morning air through the shaken flowers, and the whole spring was breathing. The blissful lover, setting bounds even to his sea of joy, reminded his delicate beloved, who was now his bride, of the dangers from night-cold; and himself of the longer night-cold of Death, which was now for long years passed over.—Innocent and blessed, they rose from the grove of their betrothment, from its dusk broken by white acacia-flowers and straggling moonbeams. And without, they felt as if a whole wide Past had sunk away in a convulsion of the world; all was new, light and young. The sky stood full of glittering dewdrops from the everlasting Morning; and the stars quivered joyfully asunder, and sank, resolved into beams, down into the hearts of men.—The Moon, with her fountain of light, had overspread and kindled all the garden; and was hanging above in a starless Blue, as if she had consumed the nearest stars; and she seemed like a smaller wandering Spring, like a Christ's-face smiling in love of man.—

Under this light they looked at one another for the first time, after the first words of love; and the sky gleamed magically down on the disordered features with which the first rapture of love was still standing written on their faces. . . . .

Dream, ye beloved, as ye wake, happy as in Paradise, innocent as in Paradise!

SIXTH LETTER-BOX

Office-impost. One of the most important of Petitions.

The finest thing was his awakening in his European Settlement in the giant Schadeck bed!—With the inflammatory, tickling, eating fever of love in his breast; with the triumphant feeling, that he had now got the introductory program of love put happily by; and with the sweet resurrection from his living prophetic burial; and with the joy that now, among his thirties, he could, for the first time, cherish hopes of a longer life (and did not longer mean at least till seventy?) than he could ten years ago;—with all this stirring life-balsam, in which the living fire-wheel of his heart was rapidly revolving, he lay here, and laughed at his glancing portrait in the bed-canopy; but he could not do it long, he was obliged to move. For a less happy man, it would have been gratifying to have measured,—as pilgrims measure the length of their pilgrimage,—not so much by steps as by body-lengths, like Earth-diameters, the superficial content of the bed. But Fixlein, for his own part, had to launch from his bed into warm billowy Life, he had now his dear good Earth again to look after, and a Conrectorship thereon, and a bride to boot. Besides all this, his mother downstairs now admitted that he had last night actually glided through beneath the scythe of Death, like supple-grass, and that yesterday she had not told him merely out of fear of his fear. Still a cōld shudder went over him,—especially as he was sober now,—when he looked round at the high Tarpeian Rock, four hours' distance behind him, on the battlements of which he had last night walked hand in hand with Death.

The only thing that grieved him was, that it was Monday, and that he must back to the Gymnasium. Such a freightage of joys he had never taken with him on his road to town. After four he issued from his house, satisfied with coffee (which he drank in Hukelum merely for his mother's sake, who, for two days after, would still have portions of this woman's-wine to draw from the lees of the pot-sediment) into the *cooling* dawning May-morning (for joy needs coolness, sorrow sun); his Betrothed comes—not indeed to meet him, but still—into his hearing, by her distant morning hymn; he makes but one momentary turn into the blissful haven of the blooming acacia-grove, which still, like the covenant sealed in it, has no thorns; he dips his warm hand in the cold-bath of the dewy leaves; he wades with pleasure through the beautifying-water of the dew, which, as it imparts colour to faces, eats it away from boots ("but with thirty ducats, a Conrector may make shift to keep two pairs of boots on the hook").—And now the Moon, as it were the hanging seal of his last night's happiness, dips down into the West, like an emptied bucket of light, and in the East the other overrunning bucket, the Sun, mounts up, and the gushes of light flow broader and broader.—

The city stood in the celestial flames of Morning. Here his divining-rod (his gold-roll, which, excepting one sixteenth of an inch broken off from it, he carried along with him) began to quiver over all the spots where booty and silver-veins of enjoyment were concealed; and our rod-diviner easily discovered that the city and the future were a true entire Potosi of delights.

In his Conrectorate closet he fell upon his knees, and thanked God—not so much for his heritage and bride as—for his life: for he had gone away on Sunday morning with doubts whether he should ever come back; and it was purely out of love to the reader, and fear lest he might fret himself too much with apprehension, that I cunningly imputed Fixlein's journey more to his desire of knowing what was in the will, than of making his own will in presence of his mother. Every recovery is a bringing back and palingenesia of our youth: one loves the Earth and those that are on it with a new love.—The Conrector could have found in his heart to take all his class by the locks, and press them to his breast; but he only did so to his adjutant, the Quartaner, who, in the first Letter-box, was still sitting in the rank of a Quintaner. . . . .

His first expedition, after school-hours, was to the house of Meister Steinberger, where, without speaking a word, he counted down fifty florins cash, in ducats, on the table: "At last I repay you," said Fixlein, "the moiety of my debt, and give you many thanks."

"Ey, Herr Conrector," said the Quartermaster, and continued calmly stuffing puddings as before, "in my bond it is said, *payable at three months' mutual notice*. How could a man like me go on, else?— However, I will change you the gold pieces." Thereupon he advised him that it might be more judicious to take back a florin or two, and buy himself a better hat, and whole shoes: "if you like," added he, "to get a calfskin and half a dozen hareskins dressed, they are lying upstairs."—I should think, for my own part, that to the reader it must be as little a matter of indifference as it was to the Butcher, whether the hero of such a History appear before him with an old tattered potlid of a hat, and a pump-sucker and leg-harness pair of boots, or in suitable apparel.—In short, before St. John's day, the man was dressed with taste and pomp.

But now came two most peculiarly important papers—at bottom only one, the Petition for the Hukelum parsonship—to be elaborated; in regard to which I feel as if I myself must assist. . . . It were a simple turn, if now at least the assembled public did not pay attention.

In the first place, the Conrector searched out and sorted all the Consistorial and Councillor quittances, or rather the toll-bills of the road-money, which he had been obliged to pay, before the toll-gates at the Quintusship and Conrectorship had been thrown open: for the executor of the Schadeck testament had to reimburse him the whole, as his discharge would express it, "to penny and farthing." Another would have summed up this post-excise much more readily; by merely looking what he—owed; as these debt-bills and those toll-bills, like parallel passages, elucidate and confirm each other. But in Fixlein's case, there was a small circumstance of peculiarity at work; which I cannot explain till after what follows.

It grieved him a little that for his two offices he had been obliged to pay and to borrow no larger a sum than 135 florins, 41 kreutzers and one halfpenny. The legacy, it is true, was to pass directly from the hands of the testamentary executor into those of the Regiments-Quartermaster; but yet he could have liked well, had he—for man is a fool from the very foundation of him—had more to pay, and therefore to inherit. The whole Conrectorate he had, by a slight deposit of 90 florins, plucked, as it were, from the Wheel of Fortune; and so small a sum must surprise my reader: but what will he say, when I tell him that there are countries where the entry-money into schoolrooms is even more moderate? In Scherau, a Conrector is charged only 88 florins, and perhaps he may have an income triple of this sum. Not to speak of Saxony (what, in truth, was to be expected from the cradle of the Reformation, in Religion and Polite Literature), where a schoolmaster and a parson have *nothing* to pay,—even in Bayreuth, for example, in Hof, the progress of improvement has been such, that a Quartus—a Quartus do I say,—a Tertius—a Tertius do I say,—a Conrector, at entrance on his post, is not required to pay down more than:

Fl. rhen.	Kr. rhen.	
30	49	For taking the oaths at the Consistorium.
4	0	To the Syndic for the Presentation.
2	0	To the then Bürgermeister.
45	7½	For the Government sanction.

Total 81 fl.   56½ kr.

If the printing-charges of a Rector do stand a little higher in some points, yet, on the other hand, a Tertius, Quartus &c. come cheaper from the press than even a Conrector. Now it is clear that in this case a schoolmaster can subsist; since, in the course of the very first year, he gets an overplus beyond this *dock-money* of his office. A schoolmaster must, like his scholars, have been advanced from class to class, before these his loans to Government, together with the interest for delay of payment, can jointly amount to so much as his yearly income in the highest class. Another thing in his favour is, that our institutions do not—as those of Athens did—prohibit people from entering on office while in debt; but every man, with his debt-knapsack on his shoulders, mounts up, step after step, without obstruction. The Pope, in large benefices, appropriates the income of the first year under the title of *Annates,* or First Fruits; and accordingly he, in all cases, bestows any large benefice on the possessor of a smaller one, thereby to augment both his own revenues and those of others; but it shows, in my opinion, a bright distinction between Popery and Lutheranism, that the Consistoriums of the latter abstract from their school-ministers and church-ministers not perhaps above two-thirds of their first yearly income; though they too, like the Pope, must naturally have an eye to vacancies.

It may be that I shall here come in collision with the Elector of Mentz, when I confess, that in Schmausen's *Corp. Jur. Pub. Germ.* I have turned up the Mentz-Imperial-Court-Chancery-tax-ordinance of the 6th January 1659; and there investigated how much this same Imperial-Court-Chancery demands, as contrasted with a Consistorium. For example, any man that wishes to be baked or sodden into a *Poet Laureate,* has 50 florins tax-dues, and 20 florins Chancery-dues to pay down; whereas, for 20 florins more, he might have been made a Conrector, who is a poet of this species, as it were by the by and *ex officio.*—The institution of a Gymnasium is permitted for 1000 florins; an extraordinary sum, with which the whole body of the teachers in the instituted Gymnasium might with us clear off the entrymoneys of their schoolrooms. Again, a Freiherr, who, at any rate, often enough grows old without knowing how, must purchase the *venia ætatis* with 200 hard florins; while with the half sum he might have become a schoolmaster, and here *age* would have come of its own accord.—And a thousand such things!—They prove, however, that matters can be at no bad pass in our Governments and Circles, where promotions are sold dearer to Folly than to Diligence, and where it costs more to institute a school than to serve in one.

The remarks I made on this subject to a Prince, as well as the remarks a Town-Syndic made on it to myself, are too remarkable to be omitted for mere dread of digressiveness.

The Syndic—a man of enlarged views, and of fiery patriotism, the warmth of which was the more beneficent that he collected all the beams of it into one focus, and directed them to himself and his family—gave me (I had perhaps been comparing the School-bench and the School-stair to the *bench* and the *ladder*, on which people are laid when about to be tortured) the best reply: "If a schoolmaster consume nothing but 30 reichsthalers; if he annually purchase manufactured goods, according as Political Economists have calculated for each individual, namely, to the amount of 5 reichsthalers; and no more hundredweights of victual than these assume, namely 10; in short, if he live like a substantial wood-cutter,—then the Devil must be in it, if he cannot yearly lay by so much net profit, as shall, in the long-run, pay the interest of his entry-debts."

The Syndic must have failed to convince me at the time, since I afterwards told the Flachsenfingen Prince: "Illustrious Sir, you know not, but I do—not a player in your Theatre would act the Schoolmaster in Engel's *Prodigal Son*, three nights running, for such a sum as every real Schoolmaster has to take for acting it all the days of the year.— In Prussia, Invalids are made Schoolmasters; with us, Schoolmasters are made Invalids." . . .

So much, according to Political Economists, a man yearly requires in Germany. This singular tone of my address to a Prince can only be excused by the equally singular relation, wherein the Biographer stands to the Flachsenfingen Sovereign, and which I would willingly unfold here, were it not that, in my Book, which, under the title of *Dog-post-days*, I mean to give to the world at Easter-fair 1795, I hoped to expound the matter to universal satisfaction.

But to our story! Fixlein wrote out the inventory of his Crown-debts; but with quite a different purpose than the reader will guess, who has still the Schadeck testament in his head. In one word, he wanted to be Parson of Hukelum. To be a clergyman, and in the place where his cradle stood, and all the little gardens of his childhood, his mother also, and the grove of betrothment,—this was an open gate into a New Jerusalem, supposing even that the living had been nothing but a meagre penitentiary. The main point was, he might marry, if he were appointed. For, in the capacity of lank Conrector, supported only by the strengthening-girth of his waistcoat, and with emoluments whereby scarcely the purchase-money of a—purse was to be come at; in this way he was more like collecting wick and tallow for his burial-torch than for his bridal one.

For the Schoolmaster class are, in well-ordered States, as little permitted to marry as the Soldiery. In *Conringius de Antiquitatibus Academicis,* where in every leaf it is proved that all cloisters were originally schools, I hit upon the reason. Our schools are now cloisters, and consequently we endeavour to maintain in our teachers at least an imitation of the Three Monastic Vows. The vow of Obedience might perhaps be sufficiently enforced by School-Inspectors; but the second vow, that of Celibacy, would be more hard of attainment, were it not that, by one of the best political arrangements, the third vow, I mean a beautiful equality in Poverty, is so admirably attended to, that no man who has made it needs any farther *testimonium paupertatis;*—and now *let* this man, if he likes, lay hold of a matrimonial half, when of the two halves each has a whole stomach, and nothing for it but half-coins and half-beer! . . . .

I know well, millions of my readers would themselves compose this Petition for the Conrector, and ride with it to Schadeck to his Lordship, that so the poor rogue might get the sheepfold, with the annexed wedding-mansion: for they see clearly enough, that directly thereafter one of the best Letter-Boxes would be written that ever came from such a repository.

Fixlein's Petition was particularly good and striking: it submitted to the Rittmeister four grounds of preference: 1. "He was a native of the parish: his parents and ancestors had already done Hukelum service; therefore he prayed," &c.

2. "The here-documented official debts of 135 florins, 41 kreutzers and one halfpenny, the cancelling of which a never-to-be-forgotten testament secured him, he himself could clear, in case he obtained the living, and so hereby give up his claim to the legacy," &c.

Voluntary Note by me. It is plain he means to bribe his Godfather, whom the lady's testament has put into a fume. But, gentle reader, blame not without mercy a poor, oppressed, heavy-laden school-man and school-horse for an indelicate insinuation, which truly was never mine. Consider, Fixlein knew that the Rittmeister was a cormorant towards the poor, as he was a squanderer towards the rich. It may be, too, the Conrector might once or twice have heard, in the Law Courts, of patrons, by whom not indeed the church and churchyard— though these things are articles of commerce in England—so much as the true management of them had been sold, or rather farmed to farming-candidates. I know from Lange, that the Church must support its patron, when he has nothing to live upon: and might not a nobleman, before he actually began begging, be justified in taking a little advance, a fore-payment of his alimentary moneys, from the hands of his pulpit-farmer?—

3. "He had lately betrothed himself with Fräulein von Thiennette, and given her a piece of gold, as marriage-pledge; and could therefore wed the said Fräulein were he once provided for," &c.

Voluntary Note by me. I hold this ground to be the strongest in the whole Petition. In the eyes of Herr von Aufhammer, Thiennette's genealogical tree was long since stubbed, disleaved, worm-eaten and full of millepedes: she was his Œconoma, his Castle-Stewardess and Legatess *a Latere* for his domestics; and with her pretensions for an alms-coffer, was threatening in the end to become a burden to him. His indignant wish that she had been provided for with Fixlein's legacy might now he fulfilled. In a word, if Fixlein become Parson, he will have the third ground to thank for it; not at all the mad fourth. . . . .

4. "He had learned with sorrow, that the name of his Shock, which he had purchased from an Emigrant at Leipzig, meant Egidius in German; and that the dog had drawn upon him the displeasure of his Lordship. Far be it from him so to designate the Shock in future; but he would take it as a special grace, if for the dog, which he at present called without any name, his Lordship would be pleased to appoint one himself."

My Voluntary Note. The dog then, it seems, to which the nobleman has hitherto been godfather, is to receive its name a *second* time from him!—But how can the famishing gardener's son, whose career never mounted higher than from the school-bench to the school-chair, and who never spoke with polished ladies, except singing, namely in the church, how can he be expected, in fingering such a string,

His *Clerical Law*, p. 551.

to educe from it any finer tone than the pedantic one? And yet the source of it lies deeper: not the contracted *situation,* but the contracted *eye,* not a favourite science, but a narrow plebeian soul, makes us pedantic, a soul that cannot *measure* and *separate* the *concentric* circles of human knowledge and activity, that confounds the focus of universal human life, by reason of the focal distance, with every two or three converging rays; and that cannot see all, and tolerate all——In short, the true Pedant is the Intolerant.

The Corrector wrote out his petition splendidly in five propitious evenings; employed a peculiar ink for the purpose; worked not indeed so long over it as the stupid Manucius over a Latin letter, namely, some months, if Scioppius' word is to be taken; still less so long as another scholar at a Latin epistle, who—truly we have nothing but Morhof's word for it—hatched it during four whole months; inserting his variations, adjectives, feet, with the authorities for his phrases, accurately marked between the lines. Fixlein possessed a more thorough-going genius, and had completely mastered the whole enterprise in sixteen days. While sealing, he thought, as we all do, how this cover was the seed-husk of a great entire Future, the rind of many sweet or bitter fruits, the swathing of his whole after-life.

Heaven bless his cover; but I let you throw me from the Tower of Babel, if he get the parsonage: can't you see, then, that Aufhammer's hands are tied? In spite of all his other faults, or even because of them, he will stand like iron by his word, which he has given so long ago to the Subrector. It were another matter had he been resident at Court; for there, where old German manners still are, no promise is kept; for as, according to Möser, the Ancient Germans kept only such promises as they made in the *forenoon* (in the afternoon they were all dead drunk),—so the Court Germans likewise keep no afternoon promise; forenoon ones they would keep if they made any, which, however, cannot possibly happen, as at those hours they are—sleeping.

SEVENTH LETTER-BOX

Sermon. School-Exhibition. Splendid Mistake.

The Corrector received his 135 florins, 43 kreutzers, one halfpenny Frankish; but no answer: the clog remained without name, his master without parsonage. Meanwhile the summer passed away; and the Dragoon Rittmeister had yet drawn out no pike from the Candidate *breeding-pond,* and thrown him into the *feeding-pond* of the Hukelum parsonage. It gratified him to be behung with prayers like a Spanish guardian Saint; and he postponed (though determined to prefer the Subrector) granting any one petition, till he had seven-and-thirty dyers', buttonmakers', tinsmiths' sons, whose petitions he could at the same time refuse. Grudge not him of Aufhammer this out-lengthening of his electorial power! He knows the privileges of rank; feels that a nobleman is like Timoleon, who gained his greatest victories on his birthday, and had nothing more to do than name some squiress, countess, or the like, as his mother. A man, however, who has been exalted to the Peerage, while still a fœtus, may with more propriety be likened to the *spinner,* which, contrariwise to all other insects, passes from the chrysalis state, and becomes a perfect insect in its mother's womb.—

But to proceed! Fixlein was at present not without cash. It will be the same as if I made a present of it to the reader, when I reveal to him, that of the legacy, which was clearing off old scores, he had still thirty-five florins left to himself, as *allodium* and pocket-money, wherewith he might purchase whatsoever seemed good to him. And how came he by so large a sum, by so considerable a competence? Simply by this means: Every time he changed a piece of gold, and especially at every payment he received, it had been his custom to throw in, blindly at random, two, three, or four small coins, among the papers of his trunk. His purpose was to astonish himself one day, when he summed up and took possession of this sleeping capital. And, by Heaven! he reached it too, when on mounting the throne of his Conrectorate, he drew out these funds from among his papers, and applied them to the coronation charges. For the present, he sowed them in again among his waste letters. Foolish Fixlein! I mean, had he not luckily exposed his legacy to jeopardy, having offered it as bounty-money, and luck-penny to the patron, this false clutch of his at the knocker of the Hukelum church-door would certainly have vexed him; but now if he had missed the knocker, he had the luck-penny again, and could be merry.

I now advance a little way in his History, and hit, in the rock of his Life, upon so fine a vein of silver, I mean upon so fine a day, that I must (I believe) content myself even in regard to the twenty-third of Trinity-term, when he preached a vacation sermon in his dear native village, with a brief transitory notice.

In itself the sermon was good and glorious; and the day a rich day of pleasure; but I should really need to have more hours at my disposal than I can steal from May, in which I am at present living and writing; and more strength than wandering through this fine weather has left me for landscape pictures of the same, before I could attempt, with any well-founded hope, to draw out a mathematical estimate of the length and thickness, and the vibrations and accordant relations to each other, of the various strings, which combined together to form for his heart a Music of the Spheres, on this day of Trinity-term, though such a thing would please myself as much as another. . . . . Do not ask me! In my opinion, when a man preaches on Sunday before all the peasants, who had carried him in their arms when a gardener's boy; farther, before his mother, who is leading off her tears through the conduit of her satin muff; farther, before his Lordship, whom he can positively command to be blessed; and finally, before his muslin bride, who is already blessed, and changing almost into stone, to find that the same lips can both kiss and preach: in my opinion, I say, when a man effects all this, he has some right to require of any Biographer who would paint his situation, that he—hold his jaw; and of the reader who would sympathise with it, that he open his, and preach himself.——

But what I must *ex officio* depict, is the day to which this Sunday was but the prelude, the vigil and the whet; I mean the prelude, the vigil and the whet to the *Martini Actus,* or *Martinmas Exhibition,* of his school. On Sunday was the Sermon, on Wednesday the Actus, on Tuesday the Rehearsal. This Tuesday shall now be delineated to the universe.

I count upon it that I shall not be read by mere people of the world alone, to whom a School-Actus cannot truly appear much better, or more interesting, than some Investiture of a Bishop, or the *opera seria* of a Frankfort Coronation; but that I likewise have people before me, who have been at schools, and who know how the school-drama of an Actus, and the stage-manager, and the playbill (the Program) thereof are to be estimated, still without overrating their importance.

Before proceeding to the Rehearsal of the *Martini Actus,* I impose upon myself, as dramaturgist of the play, the duty, if not of extracting, at least of recording the Conrector's Letter of Invitation. In this composition he said many things; and (what an author likes so well) made proposals rather than reproaches; interrogatively reminding the public, Whether in regard to the well-known head-breakages of Priscian on the part of the Magnates in Pest and Poland, our school-houses were not the best quarantine and lazar-houses to protect us against infectious *barbarisms?* Moreover, he defended in schools what

could be defended (and nothing in the world is sweeter or easier than
a defence); and said, Schoolmasters, who not quite justifiably, like
certain Courts, spoke nothing, and let nothing be spoken to them
but Latin, might plead the Romans in excuse, whose subjects, and
whose kings, at least in their epistles and public transactions, were
obliged to make use of the Latin tongue. He wondered why only
our Greek, and not also our Latin Grammars, were composed in
Latin, and put the pregnant question: Whether the Romans, when
they taught their little children the Latin tongue, did it in any other
than in this same? Thereupon he went over to the Actus, and said
what follows, in his own words:

"I am minded to prove, in a subsequent Invitation, that everything
which can be said or known about the great founder of the
Reformation, the subject of our present Martini Prolusions, has been
long ago exhausted, as well by Seckendorf as others. In fact, with
regard to Luther's personalities, his table-talk, incomes, journeys,
clothes, and so forth, there can now nothing new be brought forward,
if at the same time it is to be true. Nevertheless, the field of the
Reformation history is, to speak in a figure, by no means wholly
cultivated; and it does appear to me as if the inquirer even of the
present day might in vain look about for correct intelligence respecting
the children, grandchildren and children's children, down to our
own times, of this great Reformer; all of whom, however, appertain,
in a more remote degree, to the Reformation history, as he himself
in a nearer. Thou shalt not perhaps be threshing, said I to myself,
altogether empty straw, if, according to thy small ability, thou bring
forward and cultivate this neglected branch of History. And so have
I ventured, with the last male descendant of Luther, namely, with
the Advocate Martin Gottlob Luther, who practised in Dresden, and
deceased there in 1759, to make a beginning of a more special
Reformation history. My feeble attempt, in regard to this
Reformationary Advocate, will be sufficiently rewarded, should it
excite to better works on the subject: however, the little which I
have succeeded in digging up and collecting with regard to him I
here submissively, obediently, and humbly request all friends and
patrons of the Flachsenfingen Gymnasium to listen to, on the 14th
of November, from the mouths of six well-conditioned perorators.
In the first place, shall

"*Gottlieb Spiesglass,* a Flachsenfinger, endeavour to show, in a Latin
oration, that Martin Gottlob Luther was certainly descended of the
Luther family. After him strives

"*Friedrich Christian Krabbler,* from Hukelum, in German prose, to appreciate the influence which Martin Gottlob Luther exercised on the then existing Reformation; whereupon, after him, will

"*Daniel Lorenz Stenzinger* deliver, in Latin verse, an account of Martin Gottlob Luther's lawsuits; embracing the probable merits of Advocates generally, in regard to the Reformation. Which then will give opportunity to

"*Nikol Tobias Pfizman* to come forward in French, and recount the most important circumstances of Martin Gottlob Luther's school-years, university-life and riper age. And now, when

"*Andreas Eintarm* shall have endeavoured, in German verse, to apologise for the possible failings of this representative of the great Luther, will

"*Justus Strobel,* in Latin verse according to ability, sing his uprightness and integrity in the Advocate profession; whereafter I myself shall mount the cathedra, and most humbly thank all the patrons of the Flachsenfingen School, and then farther bring forward those portions in the life of this remarkable man, of which we yet know absolutely nothing, they being spared *Deo volente* for the speakers of the next *Martini Actus.*"

The day before the Actus offered as it were the proof-shot and sample-sheet of the Wednesday. Persons who on account of dress could not be present at the great school-festival, especially ladies, made their appearance on Tuesday, during the six proof-orations. No one can be readier than I to subordinate the proof-Actus to the Wednesday-Actus; and I do anything but need being stimulated suitably to estimate the solemn feast of a School; but on the other hand I am equally convinced that no one, who did not go to the real Actus of Wednesday, could possibly figure anything more splendid than the proof-day preceding; because he could have no object wherewith to compare the pomp in which the Primate of the festival drove in with his triumphal chariot and six—to call the six brethren-speakers coach-horses—next morning in presence of ladies and Councillor gentlemen. Smile away, Fixlein, at this astonishment over thy today's *Ovation,* which is leading on tomorrow's *Triumph*: on thy dissolving countenance quivers happy Self, feeding on these incense-fumes; but a vanity like thine, and that only, which enjoys without comparing or despising, can one tolerate, will one foster. But what flowed over all his heart, like a melting sunbeam over wax, was his mother, who after much persuasion had ventured in her

Sunday clothes humbly to place herself quite low down, beside the door of the Prima class-room. It were difficult to say who is happier, the mother, beholding how he whom she has borne under her heart can direct such noble young gentlemen, and hearing how he along with them can talk of these really high things and understand them too;—or the son, who, like some of the heroes of Antiquity, has the felicity of triumphing in the lifetime of his mother. I have never in my writings or doings cast a stone upon the late Burchardt Grossmann, who under the initial letters of the stanzas in his song, "*Brich an, du liebe Morgenröthe.*" inserted the letters of his own name; and still less have I ever censured any poor herbwoman for smoothing out her winding-sheet, while still living, and making herself one-twelfth of a dozen of grave-shifts. Nor do I regard the man as wise—though indeed as very clever and pedantic—who can fret his gall-bladder full because every one of us leaf-miners views the leaf whereon he is mining as a park-garden, as a fifth Quarter of the World (so near and rich is it); the leaf-pores as so many Valleys of Tempe, the leaf-skeleton as a Liberty-tree, a Bread-tree and Life-tree, and the dew-drops as the Ocean. We poor day-moths, evening-moths and night-moths, fall universally into the same error, only on different leaves; and whosoever (as I do) laughs at the important airs with which the schoolmaster issues his programs, the dramaturgist his playbills, the classical variation-alms-gatherer his alphabetic letters,—does it, if he is wise (as is the case here), with the consciousness of his own *similar* folly; and laughs in regard to his neighbour, at nothing but mankind and himself.

The mother was not to be detained; she must off, this very night, to Hukelum, to give the Fräulein Thiennette at least some tidings of this glorious business.—

And now the World will bet a hundred to one, that I forthwith take biographical wax, and emboss such a wax-figure cabinet of the Actus itself as shall be single of its kind.

But on Wednesday morning, while the hope-intoxicated Conrector was just about putting on his fine raiment, something knocked.——

It was the well-known servant of the Rittmeister, carrying the Hukelum Presentation for the Subrector *Füchs*lein in his pocket. To the last-named gentleman he had been sent with this call to the parsonage: but he had distinguished ill betwixt *Sub* and *Con*rector; and had besides his own good reasons for directing his steps to the latter; for he thought: "Who can it be that gets it, but the parson that preached last Sunday, and that comes from the village, and is engaged to our Fräulein Thiennette, and to whom I brought a clock and a roll of ducats already?" That his Lordship could pass over his own godson, never entered the man's head.

Fixlein read the address of the Appointment: "To the Reverend the Parson *Fixlein* of Hukelum." He naturally enough made the same mistake as the lackey; and broke up the Presentation as his own: and finding moreover in the body of the paper no special mention of persons, but only of a *Schul-unter-befehlshaber* or School-undergovernor (instead of Subrector), he could not but persist in his error. Before I properly explain why the Rittmeister's Lawyer, the framer of the Presentation, had so designated a Subrector—we two, the reader and myself, will keep an eye for a moment on Fixlein's joyful saltations—on his gratefully-streaming eyes—on his full hands so laden with bounty—on the present of two ducats, which he drops into the hands of the mitre-bearer, as willingly as he will soon drop his own pedagogic office. Could he tell what to think (of the Rittmeister), or to write (to the same), or to table (for the lackey)? Did he not ask tidings of the noble health of his benefactor over and over, though the servant answered him with all distinctness at the very first? And was not this same man, who belonged to the nose-upturning, shoulder-shrugging, shoulder-knotted, toad-eating species of men, at last so moved by the joy which he had imparted, that he determined on the spot, to bestow his presence on the new clergyman's School-Actus, though no person of quality whatever was to be there? Fixlein, in the first place, sealed his letter of thanks; and courteously invited this messenger of good news to visit him frequently in the Parsonage; and to call this evening in passing at his mother's, and give her a lecture for not staying last night, when she might have seen the Presentation from his Lordship arrive today.

The lackey being gone, Fixlein for joy began to grow sceptical—and timorous (wherefore, to prevent filching, he stowed his Presentation securely in his coffer, under keeping of two padlocks); and devout and softened, since he thanked God without scruple for all good that happened to him, and never wrote this Eternal Name but in pulpit characters and with coloured ink, as the Jewish copyists never wrote it except in ornamental letters and when newly washed; —and deaf also did the parson grow, so that he scarcely heard the soft wooing-hour of the Actus—for a still softer one beside

Thiennette, with its rose-bushes and rose-honey, would not leave his thoughts. He who of old, when Fortune made a wry face at him, was wont, like children in their sport at one another, to laugh at her so long till she herself was obliged to begin smiling,—he was now flying as on a huge seesaw higher and higher, quicker and quicker aloft.

But before the Actus, let us examine the Schadeck Lawyer. *Fixlein* instead of *Füchslein* he had written from uncertainty about the spelling of the name; the more naturally as in transcribing the Rittmeisterinn's will, the former had occurred so often. *Von,* this triumphal arch he durst not set up before Füchslein's new name, because Aufhammer forbade it, considering Hans Füchslein as a mushroom who had no right to *vons* and titles of nobility, for all his patents. In fine, the Presentation-writer was possessed with Campe's whim of Germanising everything, minding little though when Germanised it should cease to be intelligible;—as if a word needed any better act of naturalisation than that which universal intelligibility imparts to it. In itself it is the same—the rather as all languages, like all men, are cognate, intermarried and intermixed—whether a word was invented by a savage or a foreigner; whether it grew up like moss amid the German forests, or like street-grass, in the pavement of the Roman forum. The Lawyer, on the other hand, contended that it was different; and accordingly he hid not from any of his clients that *Tagefarth* (Day-turn) meant *Term,* and that *Appealing* was *Berufen* (Becalling). On this principle he dressed the word *Subrector* in the new livery of *School-undergovernor.* And this version farther converted the Schoolmaster into Parson: to such a degree does our *civic* fortune—not our *personal* well-being, which supports itself on our own internal soil and resources—grow merely on the *drift-mould* of accidents, connexions, acquaintances, and Heaven or the Devil knows what!—

By the by, from a Lawyer, at the same time a Country Judge, I should certainly have looked for more sense; I should (I may be

---

Both have the same sound. *Füchslein* means Foxling, Foxwhelp.—Ed.

Campe, a German philologist, who, along with several others of that class, has really proposed, as represented in the Text, to substitute for all Greek or Latin derivatives corresponding German terms of the like import. *Geography,* which may be *Erdbeschreibung* (Earth-description), was thenceforth to be nothing else; a *Geometer* became an *Earthmeasurer,* &c. &c. *School-undergovernor,* instead of *Subrector,* is by no means the happiest example of the system, and seems due rather to the Schadeck Lawyer than to Campe, whom our Author has elsewhere more than once eulogised for his project in similar style.—Ed.

mistaken) have presumed he knew that the *Acts* or Reports, which in former times (see Hoffmann's *German or un-German Law-practice*) were written in Latin, as before the times of Joseph the Hungarian,— are now, if we may say so without offence, perhaps written fully more in the German dialect than in the Latin; and in support of this opinion, I can point to whole lines of German language, to be found in these Imperial-Court-Confessions. However, I will not believe that the Jurist is endeavouring, because Imhofer declares the Roman tongue to be the mother tongue in the other world, to disengage himself from a language, by means of which, like the Roman *Eagle,* or later, like the Roman *Fish-heron* (Pope), he has clutched such abundant booty in his talons.——

Toll, toll your bell for the Actus; stream in, in to the ceremony: who cares for it? Neither I nor the Ex-Conrector. The six pigmy Ciceros will in vain set forth before us in sumptuous dress their thoughts and bodies. The draught-wind of Chance has blown away from the Actus its powder-nimbus of glory; and the Conrector that was has discovered how small a matter a cathedra is, and how great a one a pulpit: "I should not have thought," thought he now, "when I became Conrector, that there could be anything grander, I mean a Parson." Man, behind his everlasting blind, which he only colours differently, and makes no thinner, carries his pride with him from one step to another; and, on the higher step, blames only the pride of the lower.

The best of the Actus was, that the Regiments-Quartermaster, and Master Butcher, Steinberg, attended there, embaled in a long woollen shag. During the solemnity, the Subrector Hans von Füchslein cast several gratified and inquiring glances on the Schadeck servant, who did not once look at him: Hans would have staked his head, that after the Actus, the fellow would wait upon him. When at last the sextuple cockerel-brood had on their dunghill done crowing, that is to say, had perorated, the scholastic cocker, over whom a higher banner was now waving, himself came upon the stage; and delivered to the School-Inspectorships, to the Subrectorship, to the Guardianship and the Lackeyship, his most grateful thanks for their attendance; shortly announcing to them at the same time, "that Providence had now called him from his post to another; and committed to him, unworthy as he was, the cure of souls in the Hukelum parish, as well as in the Schadeck chapel of ease."

This little address, to appearance, well-nigh blew up the then Subrector Hans von Füchslein from his chair; and his face looked of a mingled colour, like red bole, green chalk, tinsel-yellow and *vomissement de la reine*.

The tall Quartermaster erected himself considerably in his shag, and hummed loud enough in happy forgetfulness: "The Dickens!—Parson?"——

The Subrector dashed-by like a comet before the lackey: ordered him to call and take a letter for his master; strode home, and prepared for his patron, who at Schadeck was waiting for a long thanksgiving psalm, a short satirical epistle, as nervous as haste would permit, and mingled a few nicknames and verbal injuries along with it.

The courier handed in, to his master, Fixlein's song of gratitude, and Füchslein's invectives, with the same hand. The Dragoon Rittmeister, incensed at the ill-mannered churl, and bound to his word, which Fixlein had publicly announced in his Actus, forthwith wrote back to the new Parson an acceptance and ratification; and Fixlein is and remains, to the joy of us all, incontestable ordained parson of Hukelum.

His disappointed rival has still this consolation, that he holds a seat in the wasp-nest of the *Neue Allgemeine Deutsche Bibliothek*. Should the Parson ever chrysalise himself into an author, the watch-wasp may then buzz out, and dart its sting into the chrysalis, and put its own brood in the room of the murdered butterfly. As the Subrector everywhere went about, and threatened in plain terms that he would review his colleague, let not the public be surprised that Fixlein's *Errata,* and his Masoretic *Exercitationes,* are to this hour withheld from it.

In spring, the widowed church receives her new husband; and how it will be, when Fixlein, under a canopy of flower-trees, takes the *Sponsa Christi* in one hand, and his own *Sponsa* in the other,—this, without an Eighth Letter-Box, which, in the present case, may be a true jewel-box and rainbow-key, can no mortal figure, except the *Sponsus* himself.

New Universal German Library, a reviewing periodical; in those days conducted by Nicolai, a sworn enemy to what has since been called the New School. (See Tieck, *ante*)—Ed.

Superstition declares, that on the spot where the rainbow rises, a golden key is left.

EIGHTH LETTER-BOX

Instalment in the Parsonage

On the 15th of April 1793, the reader may observe, far down in the hollow, three baggage-wagons groaning along. These baggage-wagons are transporting the house-gear of the new Parson to Hukelum: the proprietor himself, with a little escort of his parishioners, is marching at their side, that of his china sets and household furniture there may be nothing broken in the eighteenth century, as the whole came down to him unbroken from the seventeenth. Fixlein hears the School-bell ringing behind him; but this chime now sings to him, like a curfew, the songs of future rest: he is now escaped from the Death-valley of the Gymnasium, and admitted into the abodes of the Blessed. Here dwells no envy, no colleague, no Subrector; here in the heavenly country, no man works in the *New Universal German Library;* here, in the heavenly Hukelumic Jerusalem, they do nothing but sing praises in the church; and here the Perfected requires no more increase of knowledge . . . . Here too one need not sorrow that Sunday and Saint's day so often fall together into one.

Truth to tell, the Parson goes too far: but it was his way from of old never to paint out the whole and half shadows of a situation, till he was got into a new one; the beauties of which he could then enhance by contrast with the former. For it requires little reflection to discover that the torments of a schoolmaster are nothing so extraordinary; but, on the contrary, as in the Gymnasium, he mounts from one degree to another, not very dissimilar to the common torments of Hell, which, in spite of their eternity, grow weaker from century to century. Moreover, since, according to the saying of a Frenchman, *deux afflictions mises ensemble peuvent devenir une consolation,* a man gets afflictions enow in a school to console him; seeing out of eight combined afflictions—I reckon only one for every teacher—certainly more comfort is to be extracted than out of two. The only pity is, that school-people will never act towards each other as court-people do: none but polished men and polished glasses will readily cohere. In addition to all this, in schools—and in offices generally—one is always recompensed: for, as in the second life, a greater virtue is the recompense of an earthly one, so, in the Schoolmaster's case, his merits are always rewarded by more opportunities for new merits; and often enough he is not dismissed from his post at all.—

Eight Gymnasiasts are trotting about in the Parsonage, setting up, nailing to, hauling in. I think, as a scholar of Plutarch, I am right to introduce such seeming *minutiæ*. A man whom grown-up people love, children love still more. The whole school had smiled on the smiling Fixlein, and liked him in their hearts, because he did not thunder, but sport with them; because he said *Sie* (They) to the Secundaners, and the Subrector said *Ihr* (Ye); because his uprearing forefinger was his only sceptre and baculus; because in the Secunda he had interchanged Latin epistles with his scholars; and in the Quinta, had taught not with Napier's Rods (or rods of a sharper description), but with sticks of barley-sugar.

Today his churchyard appeared to him so solemn and festive, that he wondered (though it was Monday) why his parishioners were not in their holiday, but merely in their weekday drapery. Under the door of the Parsonage stood a weeping woman; for she was too happy, and he was her—son. Yet the mother, in the height of her emotion, contrives quite readily to call upon the carriers, while disloading, not to twist off the four corner globes from the old Frankish chest of drawers. Her son now appeared to her as venerable, as if he had sat for one of the copperplates in her pictured Bible; and that simply, because he had cast off his pedagogue hair-cue, as the ripening tadpole does its tail; and was now standing in a clerical periwig before her: he was now a Comet, soaring away from the profane Earth, and had accordingly changed from a *stella caudata* into a *stella crinita*.

His bride also had, on former days, given sedulous assistance in this new improved edition of his house, and laboured faithfully among the other furnishers and furbishers. But today she kept aloof; for she was too good to forget the maiden in the bride. Love, like men, dies oftener of excess than of hunger; it lives on love, but it resembles those Alpine flowers, which feed themselves by *suction* from the wet clouds, and die if you *besprinkle* them.—

At length the Parson is settled, and of course he must—for I know my fair readers, who are bent on it as if they were bride-maids— without delay get married. But he may not: before Ascension-day there can nothing be done, and till then are full four weeks and a half. The matter was this: He wished in the first place to have the murder-Sunday, the Cantata, behind him; not indeed because he doubted of his earthly continuance, but because he would not (even for the bride's sake) that the slightest apprehension should mingle with these weeks of glory.

The main reason was, He did not wish to marry till he were betrothed: which latter ceremony was appointed, with the Introduction Sermon, to take place next Sunday. It is the Cantata-Sunday. Let not the reader afflict himself with fears. Indeed, I should not have molested an enlightened century with this Sunday-*Wauwau* at all, were it not that I delineate with such extreme fidelity. Fixlein himself—especially as the Quartermaster asked him if he was a baby—at last grew so sensible, that he saw the folly of it; nay, he went so far, that he committed a greater folly. For as dreaming that you die signifies, according to the exegetic *rule of false,* nothing else than long life and welfare, so did Fixlein easily infer that his death-imagination was just such a lucky dream; the rather as it was precisely on this Cantata-Sunday that Fortune had turned up her cornucopia over him, and at once showered down out of it a bride, a presentation and a roll of ducats. Thus can Superstition imp its wings, let Chance favour it or not.

A Secretary of State, a Peace-treaty writer, a Notary, any such incarcerated Slave of the Desk, feels excellently well how far he is beneath a Parson composing his inaugural sermon. The latter (do but look at my Fixlein) lays himself heartily over the paper—injects the venous system of his sermon-preparation with coloured ink—has a Text-Concordance on the right side, and a Song-Concordance on the left; is there digging out a marrowy sentence, here clipping off a song-blossom, with both to garnish his homiletic pastry;—sketches out the finest plan of operations, not, like a man of the world, to subdue the heart of one woman, but the hearts of all women that hear him, and of their husbands to boot;—draws every peasant passing by his window into some niche of his discourse, to coöperate with the result;—and, finally, scoops out the butter of the smooth soft hymn-book, and therewith exquisitely fattens the black broth of his sermon, which is to feed five thousand men.——

At last, in the evening, as the red sun is dazzling him at the desk, he can rise with heart free from guilt; and, amid twittering sparrows and finches, over the cherry-trees encircling the parsonage, look toward the west, till there is nothing more in the sky but a faint gleam among the clouds. And then when Fixlein, amid the tolling of the evening prayer-bell, *slowly* descends the stair to his cooking mother, there must be some miracle in the case, if for him whatever has been done or baked, or served up in the lower regions, is not right and good. . . . . . . A bound, after supper, into the Castle; a look into a pure loving eye; a word without falseness to a bride without falseness;

and then under the coverlid, a soft-breathing breast, in which there is nothing but Paradise, a sermon and evening prayer . . . . . . I swear, with this I will satisfy a Mythic God, who has left his Heaven, and is seeking a new one among us here below!

Can a mortal, can a Me in the wet clay of Earth, which Death will soon dry into dust, ask more in one week than Fixlein is gathering into his heart? I see not how: At least I should suppose, if such a dust-framed being, after such a twenty-thousand prize from the Lottery of Chance, could require aught more, it would at most be the twenty-one-thousand prize, namely, the inaugural discourse itself.

And this prize our Zebedäus actually drew on Sunday: he preached—he preached with unction,——he did it before the crowding, rustling press of people; before his Guardian, and before the Lord of Aufhammer, the godfather of the priest and the dog;—a flock with whom in childhood he had driven out the Castle herds about the pasture, he was now, himself a spiritual sheep-smearer, leading out to pasture;—he was standing to the ankles among Candidates and Schoolmasters, for today (what none of them could) at the altar, with the nail of his finger, he might scratch a large cross in the air, baptisms and marriages not once mentioned . . . . . I believe, I should feel less scrupulous than I do to chequer this sunshiny esplanade with that thin shadow of the grave, which the preacher threw over it, when, in the application, with wet heavy eyes, he looked round over the mute attentive church, as if in some corner of it he would seek the mouldering teacher of his youth and of this congregation, who without, under the white tombstone, the wrong-side of life, had laid away the garment of his pious spirit. And when he, himself hurried on by the internal stream, inexpressibly softened by the farther recollections of his own fear of death on this day, of his life now overspread with flowers and benefits, of his entombed benefactress resting here in her narrow bed—when he now—before the dissolving countenance of her friend, his Thiennette—overpowered, motionless and weeping, looked down from the pulpit to the door of the Schadeck vault, and said: "Thanks, thou pious soul, for the good thou hast done to this flock and to their new teacher; and, in the fulness of time, may the dust of thy god-fearing and man-loving breast gather itself, transfigured as gold-dust, round thy reawakened heavenly heart,"—was there an eye in the audience dry? Her husband sobbed aloud; and Thiennette, her beloved, bowed her head, sinking down with inconsolable remembrances, over the front of the seat, like kindred mourners in a funeral train.

No fairer forenoon could prepare the way for an afternoon in which a man was to betroth himself forever, and to unite the exchanged rings with the Ring of Eternity. Except the bridal pair, there was none present but an ancient pair; the mother and the long Guardian. The bridegroom wrote out the marriage-contract or marriage-charter with his own hand; hereby making over to his bride, from this day, his whole moveable property (not, as you may suppose, his pocket-library, but his whole library; whereas, in the Middle Ages, the daughter of a noble was glad to get one or two books for marriage-portion);—in return for which, she liberally enough contributed—a whole nuptial coach or car, laden as follows: with nine pounds of feathers, not feathers for the cap such as we carry, but of the lighter sort such as carry us;—with a sumptuous dozen of godchild-plates and godchild-spoons (gifts from Schadeck), together with a fish-knife;—of silk, not only stockings (though even King Henri II. of France could dress no more than his legs in silk), but whole gowns;—with jewels and other furnishings of smaller value. Good Thiennette! in the chariot of thy spirit lies the true dowry; namely, thy noble, soft, modest heart, the morning-gift of Nature!

The Parson,—who, not from mistrust but from "the uncertainty of life," could have wished for a notary's seal on everything; to whom no security but a hypothecary one appeared sufficient, and who, in the depositing of every barleycorn, required quittances and contracts,—had now, when the marriage-charter was completed, a lighter heart; and through the whole evening the good man ceased not to thank his bride for what she had given him. To me, however, a marriage-contract were a thing as painful and repulsive,—I confess it candidly, though you should in consequence upbraid me with my great youth,—as if I had to take my love-letter to a Notary Imperial, and make him docket and countersign it before it could be sent. Heavens! to see the light flower of Love, whose perfume acts not on the balance, so laid like tulip-bulbs on the hay-beam of Law; two hearts on the cold councillor- and flesh-beam of relatives and advocates, who are heaping on the scales nothing but houses, fields and tin—this, to the interested party, may be as delightful as, to the intoxicated suckling and nursling of the Muses and Philosophy, it is to carry the evening and morning sacrifices he has offered up to his goddess into the book-shop, and there to change his devotions into money, and sell them by weight and measure.——

From Cantata-Sunday to Ascension, that is, to marriage-day, are one and a half weeks—or one and a half blissful eternities. If it is pleasant that nights or winter separate the days and seasons of joy to a comfortable distance; if, for example, it is pleasant that birthday, Saint's-day, betrothment, marriage and baptismal day, do not all occur on the same day (for with very few do those festivities, like Holiday and Apostle's day, commerge),—then is it still more pleasant to make the interval, the flower-border, between betrothment and marriage, of an extraordinary breadth. Before the marriage-day are the true honey-weeks; then come the wax-weeks; then the honey-vinegar-weeks.

In the Ninth Letter-Box, our Parson celebrates his wedding; and here, in the Eighth, I shall just briefly skim over his way and manner of existence till then; an existence, as might have been expected, celestial enough. To few is it allotted, as it was to him, to have at once such wings and such flowers (to fly over) before his nuptials; to few is it allotted, I imagine, to purchase flour and poultry on the same day, as Fixlein did;—to stuff the wedding-turkey with hangman-meals;—to go every night into the stall, and see whether the wedding-pig, which his Guardian has given him by way of marriage-present, is still standing and eating;—to spy out for his future wife the flax-magazines and clothes-press-niches in the house;—to lay in new wood-stores in the prospect of winter;—to obtain from the Consistorium directly, and for little smart-money, their Bull of Dispensation, their remission of the threefold proclamation of banns;—to live not in a city, where you must send to every fool (because you are one yourself), and disclose to him that you are going to be married; but in a little angular hamlet, where you have no one to tell aught, but simply the Schoolmaster that he is to ring a little later, and put a knee-cushion before the altar.——

O! if the Ritter Michaelis maintains that Paradise was little, because otherwise the people would not have found each other,—a hamlet and its joys are little and narrow, so that some shadow of Eden may still linger on our Ball.——

I have not even hinted that, the day before the wedding, the Regiments-Quartermaster came uncalled, and killed the pig, and made puddings gratis, such as were never eaten at any Court.

And besides, dear Fixlein, on this soft rich oil of joy there was also floating gratis a vernal sun,—and red twilights,—and flower-garlands,—and a bursting half world of buds! . . . .

How didst thou behave thee in these hot whirlpools of pleasure?—Thou movedst thy Fishtail (Reason), and therewith describedst for thyself a rectilineal course through the billows. For even half as much would have hurried another Parson from his study; but the very crowning felicity of ours was, that he stood as if rooted to the boundary-hill of Moderation, and from thence looked down on what thousands flout away. Sitting opposite the Castle-windows, he was still in a condition to reckon up that *Amen* occurs in the Bible one hundred and thirty times. Nay, to his old learned laboratory he now appended a new chemical stove: he purposed writing to Nürnberg and Bayreuth, and there offering his pen to the Brothers Senft, not only for composing practical *Receipts* at the end of their *Almanacs,* but also for separate *Essays* in front under the copperplate title of each Month, because he had a thought of making some reformatory cuts at the common people's mental habitudes. . . . . . And now, when in the capacity of Parson he had less to do, and could add to the holy resting-day of the congregation six literary creating-days, he determined (even in these Carnival weeks) to strike his plough into the hitherto quite fallow History of Hukelum, and soon to follow the plough with his drill. . . . .

Thus roll his minutes, on golden wheels-of-fortune, over the twelve days, which form the glancing star-paved road to the third heaven of the thirteenth, that is to the

NINTH LETTER-BOX

Or to the Marriage

Rise, fair Ascension and Marriage day, and gladden readers also! Adorn thyself with the fairest jewel, with the bride, whose soul is as pure and glittering as its vesture; like pearl and pearl-muscle, the one as the other, lustrous and ornamental! And so over the espalier, whose fruit-hedge has hitherto divided our darling from his Eden, every reader now presses after him!—

On the 9th of May 1793, about three in the morning, there came a sharp peal of trumpets, like a light-beam, through the dim-red May-dawn: two twisted horns, with a straight trumpet between them, like a note of admiration between interrogation-points, were clanging from a house in which only a parishioner (not the Parson) dwelt and blew: for this parishioner had last night been celebrating the same ceremony which the pastor had this day before him. The joyful tallyho raised our Parson from his broad bed (and the Shock from beneath it, who some weeks ago had been exiled from the white sleek coverlid), and this so early, that in the portraying tester, where on every former morning he had observed his ruddy visage and his white bedclothes, all was at present dim and crayonned.

I confess, the new-painted room, and a gleam of dawn on the wall, made it so light, that he could see his knee-buckles glancing on the chair. He then softly awakened his mother (the other guests were to lie for hours in the sheets), and she had the city cookmaid to awaken, who, like several other articles of wedding-furniture, had been borrowed for a day or two from Flachsenfingen. At two doors he knocked in vain, and without answer; for all were already down at the hearth, cooking, blowing and arranging.

How softly does the Spring day gradually fold back its nunveil, and the Earth grow bright, as if it were the morning of a Resurrection!—The quicksilver-pillar of the barometer, the guiding Fire-pillar of the weather-prophet, rests firmly on Fixlein's Ark of the Covenant. The Sun raises himself, pure and cool, into the morning-blue, instead of into the morning-red. Swallows, instead of clouds, shoot skimming through the melodious air . . . O, the good Genius of Fair Weather, who deserves many temples and festivals (because without him no festival could be held), lifted an ethereal azure Day, as it were, from the well-clear atmosphere of the Moon, and sent it down, on blue butterfly-wings—as if it were a *blue* Monday—glittering below the Sun, in the zigzag of joyful quivering descent, upon the narrow spot of Earth, which our heated fancies are now viewing. . . . . . . And on this balmy vernal spot, stand amid flowers, over which the trees are shaking blossoms instead of leaves, a bride and a bridegroom. . . . Happy Fixlein! how shall I paint thee without deepening the sighs of longing in the fairest souls?—

But soft! we will not drink the magic cup of Fancy to the bottom at six in the morning; but keep sober till towards night!

At the sound of the morning prayer-bell, the bridegroom, for the din of preparation was disturbing his quiet orison, went out into the churchyard, which (as in many other places), together with the church, lay round his mansion like a court, Here on the moist green, over whose closed flowers the churchyard-wall was still spreading broad shadows, did his spirit cool itself from the warm dreams of Earth: here, where the white flat grave-stone of his Teacher lay before him like the fallen-in door on the Janus'-temple of Life, or like the windward side of the narrow house, turned towards the tempests of the world: here, where the little shrunk metallic door on the grated cross of his father uttered to him the inscriptions of death, and the year when his parent departed, and all the admonitions and mementos, graven on the lead;—there, I say, his mood grew softer and more solemn; and he now lifted up by heart his morning prayer, which usually he read; and entreated God to bless him in his office, and to spare his mother's life; and to look with favour and acceptance on the purpose of today.—Then over the graves he walked into his fenceless little angular flower-garden; and here, composed and confident in the divine keeping, he pressed the stalks of his tulips deeper into the mellow earth.

But on returning to the house, he was met on all hands by the bell-ringing and the janissary-music of wedding-gladness;—the marriage-guests had all thrown off their nightcaps, and were drinking diligently;—there was a clattering, a cooking, a frizzling;—tea-services, coffee-services and warm-beer-services, were advancing in succession; and plates full of bride-cakes were going round like potter's frames or cistern-wheels.—The Schoolmaster, with three young lads, was heard rehearsing from his own house an *Arioso*, with which, so soon as they were perfect, he purposed to surprise his clerical superior.—But now rushed all the arms of the foaming joy-streams into one, when the sky-queen besprinkled with blossoms, the bride, descended upon Earth in her timid joy, full of quivering humble love;—when the bells began;—when the procession-column set forth with the whole village round and before it;—when the organ, the congregation, the officiating priest and the sparrows on the trees of the church-window, struck louder and louder their rolling peals on the drum of the jubilee-festival. . . . The heart of the singing bridegroom was like to leap from its place for joy, "that on his bridal-day it was all so respectable and grand."—Not till the marriage-benediction could he pray a little.

Still worse and louder grew the business during dinner, when pastry-work and marchpane-devices were brought forward,—when glasses and slain fishes (laid under the napkins to frighten the guests) went round;—and when the guests rose, and themselves rent round, and at length danced round: for they had instrumental music from the city there.

One minute handed over to the other the sugar-bowl and bottle-case of joy: the guests heard and saw less and less, and the villagers began to see and hear more and more, and towards night they penetrated like a wedge into the open door,—nay two youths ventured even in the middle of the parsonage-court, to mount a plank over a beam, and commence seesawing.—Out of doors, the gleaming vapour of the departed Sun was encircling the Earth, the evening-star was glittering over parsonage and churchyard; no one heeded it.

However, about nine o'clock,—when the marriage-guests had well-nigh forgotten the marriage-pair, and were drinking or dancing along for their own behoof; when poor mortals, in this sunshine of Fate, like fishes in the sunshine of the sky, were leaping up from their wet cold element; and when the bridegroom under the star of happiness and love, casting like a comet its long train of radiance over all his heaven, had in secret pressed to his joy-filled breast his bride and his mother,—then did he lock a slice of wedding-bread privily into a press, in the old superstitious belief that this residue secured continuance of bread for the whole marriage. As he returned, with greater love for the sole partner of his life, she herself met him with his mother, to deliver him in private the bridal-nightgown and bridal-shirt, as is the ancient usage. Many a countenance grows pale in violent emotions, even of joy: Thiennette's wax-face was bleaching still whiter under the sunbeams of Happiness. O never fall, thou lily of Heaven, and may four springs instead of four seasons open and shut thy flower-bells to the sun!—All the arms of his soul, as he floated on the sea of joy, were quivering to clasp the soft warm heart of his beloved, to encircle it gently and fast, and draw it to his own. . . . .

He led her from the crowded dancing-room into the cool evening. Why does the evening, does the night put warmer love in our hearts? Is it the nightly pressure of helplessness; or is it the exalting separation from the turmoil of life; that veiling of the world, in which for the soul nothing more remains but souls;—is it therefore, that the letters in which the loved name stands written on our spirit appear, like phosphorus-writing, by night *in fire,* while by day in their *cloudy* traces they but smoke?

He walked with his bride into the Castle-garden: she hastened quickly through the Castle, and past its servants'-hall, where the fair flowers of her young life had been crushed broad and dry, under a long dreary pressure; and her soul expanded and breathed in the free open garden, on whose flowery soil destiny had cast forth the first seeds of the blossoms which today were gladdening her existence. Still Eden! green flower-chequered *chiaroscuro!* —The moon is sleeping underground like a dead one; but beyond the garden the sun's red evening-clouds have fallen down like rose-leaves; and the evening-star, the brideman of the sun, hovers, like a glancing butterfly, above the rosy red, and, modest as a bride, deprives no single starlet of its light.

The wandering pair arrived at the old gardener's hut; now standing locked and dumb, with dark windows in the light garden, like a fragment of the Past surviving in the Present. Bared twigs of trees were folding, with clammy half-formed leaves, over the thick inter-twisted tangles of the bushes.—The Spring was standing, like a conqueror, with Winter at his feet.—In the blue pond, now bloodless, a dusky evening-sky lay hollowed out, and the gushing waters were moistening the flower-beds.—The silver sparks of stars were rising on the altar of the East, and falling down extinguished in the red sea of the West.

The wind whirred, like a night-bird, louder through the trees; and gave tones to the acacia-grove, and the tones called to the pair who had first become happy within it: "Enter, new mortal pair, and think of what is past, and of my withering and your own; and be holy as Eternity, and weep not only for joy, but for gratitude also!"— And the wet-eyed bridegroom led his wet-eyed bride under the blossoms, and laid his soul, like a flower, on her heart, and said: "Best Thiennette, I am unspeakably happy, and would say much, and cannot.—Ah, thou Dearest, we will live like angels, like children together! Surely I will do all that is good to thee; two years ago I had nothing, no nothing; ah, it is through thee, best Love, that I am happy. I call thee Thou, now, thou dear good soul!" She drew him closer to her, and said, though without kissing him: "Call me Thou always, Dearest!"

And as they stept forth again from the sacred grove into the magic-dusky garden, he took off his hat; first, that he might internally thank God, and secondly, because he wished to look into this fairest evening sky.

They reached the blazing, rustling marriage-house, but their softened hearts sought stillness; and a foreign touch, as in the blossoming vine, would have disturbed the flower-nuptials of their souls. They turned rather, and winded up into the churchyard to preserve their mood. Majestic on the groves and mountains stood the Night before man's heart, and made it also great. Over the *white* steeple-obelisk the sky rested *bluer* and *darker;* and behind it wavered the withered summit of the May-pole with faded flag. The son noticed his father's grave, on which the wind was opening and shutting, with harsh noise, the little door of the metal cross, to let the year of his death be read on the brass plate within. An overpowering sadness seized his heart with violent streams of tears, and drove him to the sunk hillock, and he led his bride to the grave, and said: "Here sleeps he, my good father; in his thirty-second year, he was carried hither to his long rest. O thou good, dear father, couldst thou today but see the happiness of thy son, like my mother! But thy eyes are empty, and thy breast is full of ashes, and thou seest us not."—He was silent. The bride wept aloud; she saw the mouldering coffins of her parents open, and the two dead arise and look round for their daughter, who had stayed so long behind them, forsaken on the Earth. She fell upon his heart, and faltered: "O beloved, I have neither father nor mother, do not forsake me!"

O thou who hast still a father and a mother, thank God for it, on the day when thy soul is full of joyful tears, and needs a bosom wherein to shed them. . . . .

And with this embracing at a father's grave, let this day of joy be holily concluded.—

TENTH LETTER-BOX

St. Thomas's Day and Birthday

An Author is a sort of bee-keeper for his reader-swarm; in whose behalf he separates the Flora kept for their use into different seasons, and here accelerates, and there retards, the blossoming of many a flower, that so in all chapters there be blooming.

The goddess of Love and the angel of Peace conducted our married pair on tracks running over full meadows, through the Spring; and on footpaths hidden by high cornfields, through the Summer; and Autumn, as they advanced towards Winter, spread her marbled leaves under their feet. And thus they arrived before the low dark gate of Winter, full of life, full of love, trustful, contented, sound and ruddy.

On St. Thomas's day was Thiennette's birthday as well as Winter's. About a quarter past nine, just when the singing ceases in the church, we shall take a peep through the window into the interior of the parsonage. There is nothing here but the old mother, who has all day (the son having restricted her to rest, and not work) been gliding about, and brushing, and burnishing, and scouring, and wiping: every carved chair-leg, and every brass nail of the waxcloth-covered table, she has polished into brightness;—everything hangs, as with all married people who have no children, in its right place, brushes, fly-flaps and almanacs;—the chairs are stationed by the room-police in their ancient corners;—a flax-rock, encircled with a diadem, or scarf of azure ribbon, is lying in the Schadeck bed, because, though it is a half holiday, some spinning may go on;—the narrow slips of paper, whereon heads of sermons are to be arranged, lie white beside the sermons themselves, that is, beside the octavo paper-book which holds them, for the Parson and his work-table, by reason of the cold, have migrated from the study to the sitting-room;—his large furred doublet is hanging beside his clean bridegroom nightgown: there is nothing wanting in the room but He and She. For he had preached her with him tonight into the empty Apostle's-day church, that so her mother, without witnesses—except the two or three thousand readers who are peeping with me through the window—might arrange the provender-baking, and whole commissariat department of the birthday-festival, and spread out her best table-gear and victual-stores without obstruction.

The soul-curer reckoned it no sin to admonish, and exhort, and encourage, and threaten his parishioners, till he felt pretty certain that the soup must be smoking on the plates. Then he led his birthday helpmate home, and suddenly placed her before the altar of meat-offering, before a sweet title-page of bread-tart, on which her name stood baked, in true *monastic characters,* in tooth-letters of almonds. In the background of time and of the room, I yet conceal two—bottles of Pontac. How quickly, under the sunshine of joy, do thy cheeks grow ripe, Thiennette, when thy husband solemnly says: "This is thy birthday; and may the Lord bless thee and watch over thee, and cause his countenance to shine on thee, and send thee, to the joy of our mother and thy husband especially, a happy glad *recovery.* Amen!"—And when Thiennette perceived that it was the old mistress who had cooked and served up all this herself, she fell upon her neck, as if it had been not her husband's mother, but her own.

Emotion conquers the appetite. But Fixlein's stomach was as strong as his heart; and with him no species of movement could subdue the peristaltic. Drink is the friction-oil of the tongue, as eating is its drag. Yet, not till he had eaten and spoken much, did the pastor fill the glasses. Then indeed he drew the cork-sluice from the bottle, and set forth its streams. The sickly mother, of a being still hid beneath her heart, turned her eyes, in embarrassed emotion, on the old woman only; and could scarcely chide him for sending to the city wine-merchant on her account. He took a glass in each hand, for each of the two whom he loved, and handed them to his mother and his wife, and said: "To thy long, long life, Thiennette!—And your health and happiness, Mamma!—And a glad arrival to our little one, if God so bless us!"—"My son," said the gardeneress, "it is to thy long life that we must drink; for it is by thee we are supported. God grant thee length of days!" added she, with stifled voice, and her eyes betrayed her tears.

I nowhere find a livelier emblem of the female sex in all its boundless levity, than in the case where a woman is carrying the angel of Death beneath her heart, and yet in these nine months full of mortal tokens thinks of nothing more important, than of who shall be the gossips, and what shall be cooked at the christening. But thou, Thiennette, hadst nobler thoughts, though these too along with them. The still-hidden darling of thy heart was resting before thy eyes like a little angel sculptured on a grave-stone, and pointing with its small finger to the hour when thou shouldst die; and every morning and every evening, thou thoughtest of death, with a certainty, of which I yet knew not the reasons; and to thee it was as if the Earth were a dark mineral cave where man's blood like stalactitic water drops down, and in dropping raises shapes which gleam so transiently, and so quickly fade away! And that was the cause why tears were continually trickling from thy soft eyes, and betraying all thy anxious thoughts about thy child: but thou repaidst these sad effusions of thy heart by the embrace in which, with new-awakened love, thou fellest on thy husband's neck, and saidst: "Be as it may, God's will be done, so thou and my child are left alive!—But I know well that thou, Dearest, lovest me as I do thee." . . . . Lay thy hand, good mother, full of blessings, on the two; and thou kind Fate, never lift thine away from them!—

It is with emotion and good wishes that I witness the kiss of two fair friends, or the embracing of two virtuous lovers; and from the fire of their altar sparks fly over to me: but what is this to our sympathetic exaltation, when we see two mortals, bending under the same burden, bound to the same duties, animated by the same care for the same little darlings—fall on one another's overflowing hearts, in some fair hour? And if these, moreover, are two mortals who already wear the mourning-weeds of life, I mean old age, whose hair and cheeks are now grown colourless, and eyes grown dim, and whose faces a thousand thorns have marred into images of Sorrow;— when these two clasp each other with such wearied aged arms, and so near to the precipice of the grave, and when they say or think: "All in us is dead, but not our love—O, we have lived and suffered long together, and now we will hold out our hands to Death together also, and let him carry us away together,"—does not all within us cry: O Love, thy spark is superior to Time; it burns neither in joy nor in the cheek of roses; it dies not, neither under a thousand tears, nor under the snow of old age, nor under the ashes of thy—beloved? It never dies: and Thou, All-good! if there were no eternal love, there were no love at all. . . . .

To the Parson it was easier than it is to me to pave for himself a transition from the heart to the digestive faculty. He now submitted to Thiennette (whoso voice at once grew cheerful, while her eyes time after time began to sparkle) his purpose to take advantage of the frosty weather, and have the winter meat slaughtered and salted: "the pig can scarcely rise," said he; and forthwith he fixed the determination of the women, farther the butcher, and the day, and all *et ceteras;* appointing everything with a degree of punctuality, such as the war-college (when it applies the cupping-glass, the battle-sword, to the overfull system of mankind) exhibits on the previous day, in its arrangements, before it drives a province into the baiting-ring and slaughterhouse.

This settled, he began to talk and feel quite joyously about the course of winter, which had commenced today at two-and-twenty minutes past eight in the morning: "for," said he, "new-year is close at hand; and we shall not need so much candle tomorrow night as tonight." His mother, it is true, came athwart him with the weapons of her five senses: but he fronted her with his Astronomical Tables, and proved that the lengthening of the day was no less undeniable than imperceptible. In the last place, like most official and married persons, heeding little whether his women took him or not, he informed them in juristico-theological phrase: "That he would put off no longer, but write this very afternoon to the venerable Consistorium, in whose hands lay the *jus circa sacra,* for a new Ball to the church-steeple; and the rather, as he hoped before newyear's day to raise a bountiful subscription from the parish for this purpose.—If God spare us till Spring," added he with peculiar cheerfulness, "and thou wert happily recovered, I might so arrange the whole that the Ball should be set up at thy first church-going, dame!"

Thereupon he shifted his chair from the dinner and dessert table to the work-table; and spent the half of his afternoon over the petition for the steeple-ball. As there still remained a little space till dusk, he clapped his tackle to his new learned *Opus,* of which I must now afford a little glimpse. Out of doors among the snow, there stood near Hukelum an old Robber-Castle, which Fixlein, every day in Autumn, had hovered round like a *revenant,* with a view to gauge it, ichnographically to delineate it, to put every window-bar and every bridle-hook of it correctly on paper. He believed he was not expecting too much, if thereby—and by some drawings of the not so much vertical as horizontal walls—he hoped to impart to his *"Architectural Correspondence of two Friends concerning the Hukelum Robber-Castle"* that last polish and *labor limæ* which contents Reviewers. For towards the critical Starchamber of the Reviewers he entertained not that contempt which some authors actually feel—or only affect, as for instance, I. From this mouldered Robber-*Louvre,* there grew for him more flowers of joy, than ever in all probability had grown from it of old for its owners.—To my knowledge, it is an anecdote not hitherto made public, that for all this no man but *Büsching* has to answer. Fixlein had not long ago, among the rubbish of the church letter-room, stumbled on a paper wherein the Geographer had been requesting special information about the statistics of the village. Büsching, it is true, had picked up nothing—accordingly, indeed, Hukelum, in his *Geography,* is still omitted altogether;—but this pestilential letter had infected Fixlein with the spring-fever of Ambition, so that his palpitating heart was no longer to be stilled or held in cheek, except by the assafœtida-emulsion of a review. It is with authorcraft as with love: both of them for decades long one may equally desire and forbear: but is the first spark once thrown into the powder-magazine, it burns to the end of the chapter.

Simply because winter had commenced by the Almanac, the fire must be larger than usual; for warm rooms, like large furs and bearskin-caps, were things which he loved more than you would figure. The dusk, this fair *chiaroscuro* of the day, this coloured foreground of the night, he lengthened out as far as possible, that he might study Christmas discourses therein: and yet could his wife, without scruple, just as he was pacing up and down the room, with the sowing-sheet full of divine word-seeds hung round his shoulder,—hold up to him a spoonful of alegar, that he might try the same in his palate, and decide whether she should yet draw it off. Nay, did he not in all cases, though fonder of roe-fishes himself, order a milter to be drawn from the herring-barrel, because his good-wife liked it better?—

Here light was brought in; and as Winter was just now commencing his glass-painting on the windows, his ice flower-pieces, and his snow-foliage, our Parson felt that it was time to read something cold, which he pleasantly named his cold collation; namely, the description of some unutterably frosty land. On the present occasion, it was the winter history of the four Russian sailors on Nova Zembla. I, for my share, do often in summer, when the sultry zephyr is inflating the flower-bells, append certain charts and sketches of Italy, or the East, as additional landscapes to those among which I am sitting. And yet tonight he farther took up the *Weekly Chronicle* of Flachsenfingen; and amid the bombshells, pestilences, famines, comets with long tails, and the roaring of all the Hell-floods of another Thirty-Years War, he could still listen with the one ear towards the kitchen, where the salad for his roast-duck was just a-cutting.

Good-night, old Fixlein! I am tired. May kind Heaven send thee with the young year 1794, when the Earth shall again carry her people, like precious night-moths, on leaves and flowers, the new steeple-ball, and a thick handsome—boy to boot!

ELEVENTH LETTER-BOX

Spring; Investiture; and Childbirth

I have just risen from a singular dream; but the foregoing Box makes it natural. I dreamed that all was verdant, all full of odours; and I was looking up at a steeple-ball glittering in the sun, from my station in the window of a little white garden-house, my eyelids full of flower-pollen, my shoulders full of thin cherry-blossoms, and my ears full of humming from the neighbouring bee-hives. Then, methought, advancing slowly through the beds, came the Hukelum Parson, and stept into the garden-house, and solemnly said to me: "Honoured Sir, my wife has just brought me a little boy; and I make bold to solicit *your Honour* to do the holy office for the same, when it shall be received into the bosom of the church."

I naturally started up, and there was—Parson Fixlein standing bodily at my bedside, and requesting me to be godfather: for Thiennette had given him a son last night about one o'clock. The confinement had been as light and happy as could be conceived; for this reason, that the father had, some months before, been careful to provide one of those *Klappersteins,* as we call them, which are found in the aerie of the eagle, and therewith to alleviate the travail: for this stone performs, in its way, all the service which the bonnet of that old Minorite monk in Naples, of whom Gorani informs us, could accomplish for people in such circumstances, who put it on. . . . .

—I might vex the reader still longer; but I willingly give up, and show him how the matter stood.

Such a May as the present (of 1794), Nature has not, in the memory of man—begun: for this is but the fifteenth of it. People of reflection have for centuries been vexed once every year, that our German singers should indite May-songs, since several other months deserve such a poetical night-music much better; and I myself have often gone so far as to adopt the idiom of our market-women, and instead of May butter, to say June butter, as also June, March, April songs.— But thou, kind May of this year, thou deservest to thyself all the songs which were ever made on thy rude namesakes! By Heaven! when I now issue from the wavering chequered acacia-grove of the Castle-garden, in which I am writing this Chapter, and come forth into the broad living day, and look up to the warming Heaven, and over its Earth budding out beneath it,—the Spring rises before me like a vast full cloud, with a splendour of blue and green. I see the Sun standing amid roses in the western sky, into which he has thrown his ray-brush, wherewith he has today been painting the Earth;—and when I look round a little in our picture-exhibition, his enamelling is still hot on the mountains; on the moist chalk of the moist Earth, the flowers full of sap-colours are laid out to dry, and the forget-me-not with miniature colours; under the varnish of the streams, the skyey Painter has pencilled his own eye; and the clouds, like a decoration-painter, he has touched off with wild outlines and single tints: and so he stands at the border of the Earth, and looks back upon his stately Spring, whose robe-folds are valleys, whose breast-bouquet is gardens, and whose blush is a vernal evening, and who, when she arises, shall be—Summer.

But to proceed! Every spring—and especially in such a spring—I imitate on foot our birds of passage; and travel off the hypochondriacal sediment of winter: but I do not think I should have seen even the steeple-ball of Hukelum, which is to be set up one of these days, to say nothing of the Parson's family, had not I happened to be visiting the Flachsenfingen Superintendent and Consistorialrath. From him I got acquainted with Fixlein's history (every Candidatus must deliver an account of his life to the Consistorium), and with his still madder petition for a steeple-ball. I observed, with pleasure, how gaily the cob was diving and swashing about in his duck-pool and milk-bath of life; and forthwith determined on a journey to his shore. It is singular, that is to say, manlike, that when we have for years kept prizing and describing some original person or original book, yet the moment we see such, they anger us: we would have them fit us and delight us in all points, as if any originality could do this but our own.

It was Saturday the third of May, when I, with the Superintendent, the *Senior Capituli,* and some temporal Baths, mounted and rolled off, and in two carriages were driven to the Parson's door. The matter was, he was not yet—*invested,* and tomorrow this was to be done. I little thought, while we whirled by the white espalier of the Castle-garden, that there I was to write another book.

I still see the Parson, in his peruke-minever and head-case, come springing to the coach-door and lead us out; so smiling—so courteous—so vain of the disloaded freight, and so attentive to it. He looked as if in the journey of life he had never once put on the *travelling-gauze* of Sorrow: Thiennette again seemed never to have thrown hers back. How neat was everything in the house, how dainty, decorated and polished! And yet so quiet, without the cursed alarm-ringing of servants' bells, and without the bass-drum tumult of stair-pedaling. Whilst the gentlemen, my road-companions, were sitting in state in the upper room, I flitted, as my way is, like a smell, over the whole house, and my path led me through the sitting-room over the kitchen, and at last into the churchyard beside the house. Good Saturday! I will paint thy hours as I may, with the black asphaltos of ink, on the tablets of other souls! In the sitting-room, I lifted from the desk a volume gilt on the back and edges, and bearing this title: "*Holy Sayings, by Fixlein. First Collection.*" And as I looked to see where it had been printed, the Holy Collection turned out to be in writing. I handled the quills, and dipped into the negro-black of the ink, and I found that all was right and good: with your fluttering gentlemen of letters, who hold only a department of the foreign, and none of the home affairs, nothing (except some other things about them) can be worse than their ink and pens. I also found a little copperplate, to which I shall in due time return.

In the kitchen, a place not more essential for the writing of an English novel, than for the acting of a German one, I could plant myself beside Thiennette, and help her to blow the fire, and look at once into her face and her burning coals. Though she was in wedlock, a state in which white roses on the cheeks are changed for red ones,

and young women are similar to a similitude given in my Note; —
and although the blazing wood threw a false rouge over her, I guessed
how pale she must have been; and my sympathy in her paleness rose
still higher at the thought of the burden which Fate had now not so
much taken from her, as laid in her arms and nearer to her heart. In
truth, a man must never have reflected on the Creation-moment,
when the Universe first rose from the bosom of an Eternity, if he
does not view with philosophic reverence a woman, whose thread
of life a secret all-wondrous Hand is spinning to a second thread, and
who veils within her the transition from Nothingness to Existence,
from Eternity to Time;—but still less can a man have any heart of
flesh, if his soul, in presence of a woman, who, to an unknown unseen
being, is sacrificing more than we will sacrifice when it is seen and
known, namely, her nights, her joys, often her life, does not bow
lower, and with deeper emotion, than in presence of a whole nun-
orchestra on their Sahara-desert;—and worse than either is the man
for whom his own mother has not made all other mothers venerable.

"It is little serviceable to thee, poor Thiennette," thought I, "that
now, when thy bitter cup of sickness is made to run over, thou must
have loud festivities come crowding round thee." I meant the
Investiture and the Ball-raising. My rank, the diploma of which the
reader will find stitched in with the *Dog-post-days,* and which had
formerly been hers, brought about my ears a host of repelling,
embarrassed, wavering titles of address from her; which people, to
whom they have once belonged, are at all times apt to parade before
superiors or inferiors, and which it now cost me no little trouble to
disperse. Through the whole Saturday and Sunday, I could never get
into the right track either with her or him, till the other guests were
gone. As for the mother, she acted, like obscure ideas, powerfully
and constantly, but out of view: this arose in part from her idolatrous
fear of us; and partly also from a slight shade of care (probably springing
from the state of her daughter), which had spread over her like a
little cloud.

I cruised about, so long as the moon-crescent glimmered in the
sky, over the churchyard; and softened my fantasies, which are at
any rate too prone to paint with the brown of crumbling mummies,
not only by the red of twilight, but also by reflecting how easily our
eyes and our hearts can become reconciled even to the ruins of Death;

To the Spring, namely, which begins with snowdrops, and ends with roses and
pinks.—

a reflection which the Schoolmaster, whistling as he arranged the charnel-house for the morrow, and the Parson's maid singing, as she reaped away the grass from the graves, readily enough suggested to me. And why should not this habituation to all forms of Fate in the other world, also, be a gift reserved for us in our nature by the bounty of our great Preserver?—I perused the grave-stones; and I think even now that Superstition is right in connecting with the reading of such things a loss of *memory;* at all events, one does *forget* a thousand things belonging to this world. . . . .

The Investiture on Sunday (whose Gospel, of the good shepherd, suited well with the ceremony) I must dispatch in few words; because nothing truly sublime can bear to be treated of in many. However, I shall impart the most memorable circumstances, when I say that there was—drinking (in the Parsonage),—music-making (in the Choir),—reading (of the Presentation by the Senior, and of the Ratification-rescript by the lay Rath),—and preaching, by the Consistorialrath, who took the soul-curer by the hand, and presented, made over and guaranteed him to the congregation, and them to him. Fixlein felt that he was departing as a high-priest from the church, which he had entered as a country parson; and all day he had not once the heart to ban. When a man is treated with solemnity, he looks upon himself as a higher nature, and goes through his solemn feasts devoutly.

This indenturing, this monastic profession, our Head–Rabbis and Lodge-masters (our Superintendents) have usually a taste for putting off till once the pastor has been some years ministering among the people, to whom they hereby present him; as the early Christians frequently postponed their consecration and investiture to Christianity, their baptism namely, till the day when they died: nay, I do not even think this clerical Investiture would lose much of its usefulness, if it and the declaring-vacant of the office were reserved for the same day; the rather as this usefulness consists entirely in two items; what the Superintendent and his Raths can eat, and what they can pocket.

Not till towards evening did the Parson and I get acquainted. The Investiture officials, and elevation pulley-men, had, throughout the whole evening, been very violently—breathing. I mean thus: as these gentlemen could not but be aware, by the most ancient theories and the latest experiments, that air was nothing else than a sort of

---

This Christian superstition is not only a Rabbinical, but also a Roman one. *Cicero de Senectute.*

rarefied and exploded water, it became easy for them to infer that, conversely, water was nothing else than a denser sort of air. Wine-drinking, therefore, is nothing else but the breathing of an air pressed together into proper spissitude, and sprinkled over with a few perfumes. Now, in our days, by clerical persons too much (fluid) breath can never be inhaled through the mouth; seeing the dignity of their station excludes them from that breathing through the *smaller* pores, which Abernethy so highly recommends under the name of *air-bath*: and can the Gullet in their case be aught else than door-neighbour to the Windpipe, the *consonant* and fellow-shoot of the Windpipe?—I am running astray: I meant to signify, that I this evening had adopted the same opinion; only that I used this air or ether, not like the rest for loud laughter, but for the more quiet contemplation of life in general. I even shot forth at my gossip certain speeches, which betrayed devoutness: these he at first took for jests, being aware that I was from Court, and of quality. But the concave mirror of the wine-mist at length suspended the images of my soul, enlarged and embodied like spiritual shapes, in the air before me.—Life shaded itself off to my eyes like a hasty summer night, which we little fire-flies shoot across with transient gleam;—I said to him that man must turn himself like the leaves of the great mallow, at the different day-seasons of his life, now to the rising sun, now to the setting, now to the night, towards the Earth and its graves;—I said, the omnipotence of Goodness was driving us and the centuries of the world towards the gates of the City of God, as, according to Euler, the resistance of the *Ether* leads the circling Earth towards the Sun, &c. &c.

On the strength of these entremets, he considered me the first theologian of his age; and had he been obliged to go to war, would previously have taken my advice on the matter, as belligerent powers were wont of old from the theologians of the Reformation. I hide not from myself, however, that what preachers call vanity of the world, is something altogether different from what philosophy so calls. When I, moreover, signified to him that I was not ashamed to be an Author; but had a turn for working up this and the other biography; and that I had got a sight of his *Life* in the hands of the Superintendent; and might be in case to prepare a printed one therefrom, if so were he would assist me with here and there a tint of flesh-colour,—then was my silk, which, alas! not only isolates one from electric fire, but also from a kindlier sort of it, the only grate which rose between his arms and me; for, like the most part of poor country parsons, it was not in his power to forget the rank of any man, or to vivify his own on a higher one. He said: "He would acknowledge it with veneration, if I should mention him in print; but he was much afraid his life was too common and too poor for a biography." Nevertheless, he opened me the drawer of his Letter-boxes; and said, perhaps, he had hereby been paving the way for me.

The main point, however, was, he hoped that his *Errata,* his *Exercitationes,* and his *Letters on the Robber-Castle,* if I should previously send forth a Life of the Author, might be better received; and that it would be much the same as if I accompanied them with a Preface.

In short, when on Monday the other dignitaries with their nimbus of splendour had dissipated, I alone, like a precipitate, abode with him; and am still abiding, that is, from the fifth of May (the Public should take the Almanac of 1794, and keep it open beside them) to the fifteenth: today is Thursday, tomorrow is the sixteenth and Friday, when comes the Spinat-Kirmes, or Spinage-Wake, as they call it, and the uplifting of the steeple-ball, which I just purposed to await before I went. Now, however, I do not go so soon; for on Sunday I have to assist at the baptismal ceremony, as baptismal agent for my little future godson. Whoever pays attention to me, and keeps the Almanac open, may readily guess why the christening is put off till Sunday: for it is that memorable Cantata-Sunday, which once, for its mad narcotic hemlock-virtues, was of importance in our History; but is now so only for the fair betrothment, which after two years we mean to celebrate with a baptism.

Truly it is not in my power—for want of colours and presses—to paint or print upon my paper the soft balmy flower-garland of a fortnight which has here wound itself about my sickly life; but with a single day I shall attempt it. Man, I know well, cannot prognosticate either his joys or his sorrows, still less repeat them, either in living or writing.

The black hour of coffee has gold in its mouth for us and honey; here, in the morning coolness, we are all gathered; we maintain popular conversation, that so the parsoness and the gardeneress may be able to take share in it. The morning-service in the church, where often the whole people are sitting and singing, divides us. While the bell is sounding, I march with my writing-gear into the singing Castle-garden; and seat myself in the fresh acacia-grove, at the dewy two-legged table. Fixlein's Letter-boxes I keep by me in my pocket; and I have only to look and abstract from his what can be of use in

---

For according to the Jurists, fifteen persons make a people.

my own.—Strange enough! so easily do we forget a thing in describing it, I really did not recollect for a moment that I am now sitting at the very grove-table, of which I speak, and writing all this.—

My gossip in the mean time is also labouring for the world. His study is a sort of sacristy, and his printing-press a pulpit, wherefrom he preaches to all men; for an Author is the Town-chaplain of the Universe. A man, who is making a Book, will scarcely hang himself; all rich Lords'-sons, therefore, should labour for the press; for, in that case, when you awake too early in bed, you have always a *plan,* an aim, and therefore a cause before you why you should get out of it. Better off too is the author who collects rather than invents,— for the latter with its eating fire calcines the heart: I praise the Antiquary, the Heraldist, Notemaker, Compiler; I esteem the *Title-perch* (a fish called *Perca-Diagramma,* because of the letters on its scales), and the *Printer* (a chafer, called *Scarabæus Typographus,* which eats letters in the bark of fir),—neither of them needs any greater or fairer arena in the world than a piece of rag-paper, or any other laying-apparatus than a pointed pencil, wherewith to lay his four-and-twenty letter-eggs.—In regard to the *catalogue raisonné,* which my gossip is now drawing up of German *Errata,* I have several times suggested to him, "that it were good if he extended his researches in one respect, and revised the rule, by which it has been computed, that *e.g.* for a hundredweight of pica black-letter, four hundred and fifty semicolons, three hundred periods, &c. are required; and to recount, and see whether in Political writings and Dedications the fifty notes of admiration for a hundredweight of pica black-letter were not far too small an allowance, and if so, what the real quantity was?"

Several days he wrote nothing; but wrapped himself in the slough of his parson's-cloak; and so in his canonicals, beside the Schoolmaster, put the few A-b-c shooters, which were not, like forest-shooters, absent on furlough by reason of the spring,—through their platoon firing in the Hornbook. He never did more than his duty, but also never less. It brought a soft benignant warmth over his heart, to think that he, who had once ducked under a School-inspectorship, was now one himself.

About ten o'clock, we meet from our different museums, and examine the village, especially the Biographical furniture and holy places, which I chance that morning to have had under my pen or pantagraph; because I look at them with more interest *after* my description than *before* it.

Next comes dinner.—

After the concluding grace, which is too long, we both of us set to entering the charitable subsidies, and religious donations, which our parishioners have remitted to the sinking or rather rising fund of the church-box for the purchase of the new steeple-globe, into two ledgers: the one of these, with the names of the subscribers, or (in case they have subscribed for their children) with their children's names also, is to be inurned in a leaden capsule, and preserved in the steeple-ball; the other will remain below among the parish Registers. You cannot fancy what contributions the ambition of getting into the Ball brings us in; I declare, several peasants who had given and well once already, contributed again when they had baptisms: must not little Hans be in the Ball too?

After this book-keeping by double-entry, my gossip took to engraving on copper. He had been so happy as to elicit the discovery, that from a certain stroke resembling an inverted Latin S, the capital letters of our German Chancery-hand, beautiful and intertwisted as you see them stand in Law-deeds and Letters-of-nobility, may every one of them be composed and spun out.

"Before you can count sixty," said he to me, "I take my fundamental-stroke and make you any letter out of it."

I merely inverted this fundamental-stroke, that is, gave him a German S, and counted sixty till he had it done. This line of beauty, when once it has been twisted and flourished into all the capitals, he purposes by copperplates which he is himself engraving, to make more common for the use of Chanceries; and I may take upon me to give the Russian, the Prussian, and a few other smaller Courts, hopes of proof impressions from his hand: to under-secretaries they are indispensable.

Now comes evening; and it is time for us both, here forking about with our fruit-hooks on the literary Tree of Knowledge, at the risk of our necks, to clamber down again into the meadow-flowers and pasturages of rural joy. We wait, however, till the busy Thiennette, whom we are now to receive into our communion, has no more walks to take but the one between us. Then slowly we stept along (the sick lady was weak) through the office-houses; that is to say, through stalls and their population, and past a horrid lake of ducks, and past a little milk-pond of carps, to both of which colonies, I and the rest, like princes, gave bread, seeing we had it in view on the Sunday after the christening, to—take them for bread ourselves.

The sky is still growing kindlier and redder, the swallows and the blossom-trees louder, the house-shadows broader, and men more happy. The clustering blossoms of the acacia-grove hang down over our cold collation; and the ham is not stuck (which always vexes me) with flowers, but beshaded with them from a distance. . . . .

And now the deeper evening and the nightingale conspire to soften me; and I soften in my turn the mild beings round me; especially the pale Thiennette, to whom, or to whose heart, after the apoplectic crushings of a downpressed youth, the most violent pulses of joy are heavier than the movements of pensive sadness. And thus beautifully runs our pure transparent life along, under the blooming curtains of May; and in our modest pleasures we look with timidity neither behind us nor before; as people who are lifting treasure gaze not round at the road they came, or the road they are going.

So pass our days. Today, however, it was different: by this time, usually, the evening meal is over; and the Shock has got the osseous preparation of our supper between his jaws; but tonight I am still sitting here alone in the garden, writing the Eleventh Letter-Box, and peeping out every instant over the meadows, to see if my gossip is not coming.

For he is gone to town, to bring a whole magazine of spiceries: his coat-pockets are wide. Nay, it is certain enough that oftentimes he brings home with him, simply in his coat-pocket, considerable flesh-tithes from his Guardian, at whose house he alights; though truly intercourse with the polished world and city, and the refinement of manners thence arising,—for he calls on the bookseller, on school-colleagues, and several respectable shopkeepers,—does, much more than flesh-fetching, form the object of these journeys to the city. This morning he appointed me regent head of the house, and delivered me the *fasces* and *curule chair*. I sat the whole day beside the young pale mother; and could not but think, simply because the husband had left me there as his representative, that I liked the fair soul better. She had to take dark colours, and paint out for me the winter landscape and ice region of her sorrow-wasted youth; but often, contrary to my intention, by some simple elegiac word, I made her still eye wet; for the too full heart, which had been crushed with other than sentimental woes, overflowed at the smallest pressure. A hundred times in the recital I was on the point of saying: "O yes, it was with winter that your life began, and the course of it has resembled winter!"—Windless, cloudless day! Three more words about thee, the world will still not take amiss from me!

I advanced nearer and nearer to the heart-central-fire of the women; and at last they mildly broke forth in censure of the Parson; the best wives will complain of their husbands to a stranger, without in the smallest liking them the less on that account. The mother and the wife, during dinner, accused him of buying lots at every book-auction; and, in truth, in such places, he does strive and bid not so much for good or for bad books—or old ones—or new ones—or such as he likes to read—or any sort of favourite books—but simply for books. The mother blamed especially his squandering so much on copperplates; yet some hours after, when the Schultheis, or Mayor, who wrote a beautiful hand, came in to subscribe for the steeple-ball, she pointed out to him how finely her son could engrave, and said that it was well worth while to spend a groschen or two on such capitals as these.

They then handed me,—for when once women are in the way of a full open-hearted effusion, they like (only you must not turn the stop-cock of inquiry) to pour out the whole,—a ring-case, in which he kept a Chamberlain's key that he had found, and asked me if I knew who had lost it. Who could know such a thing, when there are almost more Chamberlains than picklocks among us?—

At last I took heart, and asked after the little toy-press of the drowned son, which hitherto I had sought for in vain over all the house. Fixlein himself had inquired for it, with as little success. Thiennette gave the old mother a persuading look full of love; and the latter led me up-stairs to an outstretched hoop-petticoat, covering the poor press as with a dome. On the way thither the mother told me, she kept it hid from her son, because the recollection of his brother would pain him. When this deposit-chest of Time (the lock had fallen off) was laid open to me, and I had looked into the little charnel-house, with its wrecks of a childlike sportful Past, I, without saying a word, determined, some time ere I went away, to unpack these playthings of the lost boy, before his surviving brother: Can there be aught finer than to look at these ash-buried, deep-sunk Herculanean ruins of childhood, now dug up and in the open air?

Thiennette sent twice to ask me whether he was come. He and she, precisely because they do not give their love the weakening expression of phrases, but the strengthening one of actions, have a boundless feeling of it towards one another. Some wedded pairs eat each other's lips and hearts and love away by kisses,—as in Rome, the statues of Christ (by Angelo) have lost their feet by the same process of kissing, and got leaden ones instead; in other couples, again, you may see, by mere inspection, the number of their conflagrations and eruptions, as in Vesuvius you can discover his, of which there are now forty-three: but in these two beings rose the Greek fire of a moderate and everlasting love, and gave warmth without casting forth sparks, and flamed straight up without crackling. The evening-red is flowing back more magically from the windows of the gardener's cottage into my grove; and I feel as if I must say to Destiny: "Hast thou a sharp sorrow, then throw it rather into my breast, and strike not with it three good souls, who are too happy not to bleed by it, and too sequestered in their little dim village not to shrink back at the thunderbolt which hurries a stricken spirit from its earthly dwelling."——

Thou good Fixlein! Here comes he hurrying over the parsonage-green. What languishing looks full of love already rest in the eye of thy Thiennette!—What news wilt thou bring us tonight from the town!—How will the ascending steeple-ball refresh thy soul tomorrow!—

TWELFTH LETTER-BOX

Steeple-ball-Ascension. The Toy-press.

How, on this sixteenth of May, the old steeple-ball was twisted-off from the Hukelum steeple, and a new one put on in its stead, will I now describe to my best ability; but in that simple historical style of the Ancients, which, for great events, is perhaps the most suitable.

At a very early hour, a coach arrived containing Messrs. Court-Guilder Zeddel and Locksmith Wächser, and the new Peter's-cupola of the steeple. Towards eight o'clock the community, consisting of subscribers to the Globe, was visibly collecting. A little later came the Lord Dragoon Rittmeister von Aufhammer, as Patron of the church and steeple, attended by Mr. Church-Inspector Streichert. Hereupon my Reverend Cousin Fixlein and I repaired, with the other persons whom I have already named, into the Church, and there celebrated before innumerable hearers a weekday prayer-service. Directly afterwards, my Reverend Friend made his appearance above in the pulpit, and endeavoured to deliver a speech which might correspond to the solemn transaction;—and immediately thereafter, he read aloud the names of the patrons and charitable souls, by whose donations the Ball had been put together; and showed to the congregation the leaden box in which they were specially recorded; observing, that the book from which he had recited them was to be reposited in the Parish Register-office. Next he held it necessary to thank them and God, that he, above his deserts, had been chosen as the instrument and undertaker of such a work. The whole he concluded with a short prayer for Mr. Stechmann the Slater (who was already hanging on the outside on the steeple, and loosening the old shaft); and entreated that he might not break his neck, or any of his members. A short hymn was then sung, which the most of those assembled without the church-doors sang along with us, looking up at the same time to the steeple.

All of us now proceeded out likewise; and the discarded ball, as it were the amputated cock's-comb of the church, was lowered down and untied. Church-Inspector Streichert drew a leaden case from the crumbling ball, which my Reverend Friend put into his pocket, purposing to read it at his convenience; I, however, said to some peasants: "See, thus will your names also be preserved in the new Ball, and when, after long years, it shall be taken down, the box lies within it, and the then parson becomes acquainted with you all."— And now was the new steeple-globe, with the leaden cup in which lay the names of the bystanders, at length full-laden so to speak, and saturated, and fixed to the pulley-rope;—and so did this the whilom cupping-glass of the community ascend aloft. . . . .

By heaven! the unadorned style is here a thing beyond my power: for when the Ball moved, swung, mounted, there rose a drumming in the centre of the steeple; and the Schoolmaster, who, till now, had looked down through a sounding-hole directed towards the congregation, now stept out with a trumpet at a side sounding-hole, which the mounting Ball was not to cross.—But when the whole Church rung and pealed, the nearer the capital approached its crown,—and when the Slater clutched it and turned it round, and happily incorporated the spike of it, and delivered down, between Heaven and Earth, and leaning on the Ball, a Topstone-speech to this and all of us,—and when my gossip's eyes, in his rapture at being Parson on this great day, were running over, and the tears trickling down his priestly garment;—I believe I was the only man,—as his mother was the only woman,—whose souls a common grief laid hold of to press them even to bleeding; for I and the mother had yesternight, as I shall tell more largely afterwards, discovered in the little chest of the drowned boy, from a memorial in his father's hand, that, on the day after the morrow, on Cantata-Sunday and his baptismal-Sunday, he would be—two-and-thirty years of age. "O!" thought I, while I looked at the blue heaven, the green graves, the glittering ball, the weeping priest, "so, at all times, stands poor man with bandaged eyes before thy sharp sword, incomprehensible Destiny! And when thou drawest it and brandishest it aloft, he listens with pleasure to the whizzing of the stroke before it falls!"—

Last night I was aware of it; but to the reader, whom I was preparing for it afar off, I would toll nothing of the mournful news, that, in the press of the dead brother, I had found an old Bible which the boys had used at school, with a white blank leaf in it, on which the father had written down the dates of his children's birth. And even this it was that raised in thee, thou poor mother, the shade of sorrow which of late we have been attributing to smaller causes; and thy heart was still standing amid the rain, which seemed to us already past over and changed into a rainbow!—Out of love to him, she had yearly told one falsehood, and concealed his age. By extreme good luck, he had not been present when the press was opened. I still purpose, after this fatal Sunday, to surprise him with the parti-coloured reliques of his childhood, and so of these old Christmas-presents to make him new ones. In the mean while, if I and his mother can but follow him incessantly, like fish-hook-floats and foot-clogs, through tomorrow and next day, that no murderous accident lift aside the curtain from his birth-certificate,—all may yet be well. For now, in truth, to his eyes, this birthday, in the metamorphotic mirror of his superstitious imagination, and behind the magnifying magic vapour of his present joys, would burn forth like a red death-warrant. . . . . But besides all this, the leaf of the Bible is now sitting higher than any of us, namely, in the new steeple-ball, into which I this morning prudently introduced it. Properly speaking there is indeed no danger.

THIRTEENTH LETTER-BOX

Christening

Today is that stupid Cantata-Sunday; but nothing now remains of it save an hour.—By heaven! in right spirits were we all today. I believe I have drunk as faithfully as another.—In truth, one should be moderate in all things, in writing, in drinking, in rejoicing; and as we lay straws into the honey for our bees that they may not drown in their sugar, so ought one at all times to lay a few firm Principles, and twigs from the tree of Knowledge, into the Syrup of life, instead of those same bee-straws, that so one may cling thereto, and not drown like a rat. But now I do purpose in earnest to—write (and also live) with steadfastness; and therefore, that I may record the christening ceremony with greater coolness,—to besprinkle my fire with the night-air, and to roam out for an hour into the blossom-and-wave-embroidered night, where a lukewarm breath of air, intoxicated with soft odours, is sinking down from the blossom-peaks to the low-bent flowers, and roaming over the meadows, and at last launching on a wave, and with it sailing down the moonshiny brook. O, without, under the stars, under the tones of the nightingale, which seem to reverberate, not from the echo, but from the far-off down-glancing worlds; beside that moon, which the gushing brook in its flickering watery band is carrying away, and which creeps under the little shadows of the bank as under clouds,—O, amid such forms and tones, the heart of man grows serious; and as of old an evening bell was rung to direct the wanderer through the deep forests to his nightly home, so in our Night are such voices within us and about us, which call to us in our strayings, and make us calmer, and teach us to moderate our own joys, and to conceive those of others.

I return, peaceful and cool enough, to my narrative. All yesternight I left not the worthy Parson half an hour from my sight, to guard him from poisoning the well of his life. Full of paternal joy, and with the skeleton of the sermon (he was committing it to memory) in his hand, he set before me all that he had; and pointed out to me the fruit-baskets of pleasures which Cantata-Sunday always plucked and filled for him. He recounted to me, as I did not go away, his baptisms, his accidents of office; told me of his relatives; and removed my uncertainty with regard to the public revenues—of his parish, to the number of his communicants and expected catechumens. At this point, however, I am afraid that many a reader will in vain endeavour to transport himself into my situation, and still be unable to discover why I said to Fixlein: "Worthy gossip, better no man could wish himself." I lied not, for so it is . . . . But look in the Note.

At last rose the Sunday, the present; and on this holy day, simply because my little godson was for going over to Christianity, there

---

A long philosophical elucidation is indispensably requisite: which will be found in this Book, under the title: *Natural Magic of the Imagination.* [A part of the *Jus de Tablette* appended to this Biography, unconnected with it, and not given here.—ED.]

was a vast racket made: every time a conversion happens, especially of nations, there is an uproaring and a shooting; I refer to the two Thirty-Years Wars, to the more recent one, and to the earlier, which Charlemagne so long carried on with the heathen Saxons: thus, in the *Palais Royal,* the Sun, at his transit over the meridian, fires off a cannon. But this morning the little Unchristian, my godson, was precisely the person least attended to; for, in thinking of the conversion, they had no time left to think of the convert. Therefore I strolled about with him myself half the forenoon; and, in our walk, hastily conferred on him a private-baptism; having named him *Jean Paul* before the priest did so. At midday, we sent the beef away as it had come; the Sun of happiness having desiccated all our gastric juices. We now began to look about us for pomp; I for scientific decorations of my hair, my godson for his christening-shirt, and his mother for her dress-cap. Yet before the child's-rattle of the christening-bell had been jingled, I and the midwife, in front of the mother's bed, instituted Physiognomical Travels on the countenance of the small Unchristian, and returned with the discovery, that some features had been embossed by the pattern of the mother, and many firm portions resembled me; a double similarity, in which my readers can take little interest. *Jean Paul* looks very sensible for his years, or rather for his minutes, for it is the small one I am speaking of.——

But now I would ask, what German writer durst take it upon him to spread out and paint a large historic sheet, representing the whole of us as we went to church? Would he not require to draw the father, with swelling canonicals, moving forward slowly, devoutly, and full of emotion? Would he not have to sketch the godfather, minded this day to lend out his names, which he derived from two Apostles (John and Paul), as Julius Cæsar lent out his names to two things still living even now (to a month, and a throne)?—And must he not put the godson on his sheet, with whom even the Emperor Joseph (in his need of nurse-milk) might become a foster-brother, in his old days, if he were still in them?——

In my chamber, I have a hundred times determined to smile at solemnities, in the midst of which I afterwards, while assisting at them, involuntarily wore a petrified countenance, full of dignity and

---

This pigmy piece of ordnance, with its cunningly devised burning-glass, is still
    to be seen on the south side of the Paris Vanity-Fair; and in fine weather, to
    be heard, on all sides thereof, proclaiming the *conversion* (so it seems to Richter)
    of the Day from Forenoon to Afternoon.—Ed.
See *Musäus,* ante.—Ed.

seriousness. For, as the Schoolmaster, just before the baptism, began to sound the organ,—an honour never paid to any other child in Hukelum,—and when I saw the wooden christening-angel, like an alighted Genius, with his painted timber arm spread out under the baptismal ewer, and I myself came to stand close by him, under his gilt wing, I protest the blood went slow and solemn, warm and close, through my pulsing head, and my lungs full of sighs; and, to the silent darling lying in my arms, whose unripe eyes Nature yet held closed from the full perspective of the Earth, I wished, with more sadness than I do to myself, for his Future also as soft a sleep as today; and as good an angel as today, but a more living one, to guide him into a more living religion, and, with invisible hand, conduct him unlost through the forest of Life, through its falling trees, and Wild Hunters, and all its storms and perils. . . . . Will the world not excuse me, if when, by a side-glance, I saw on the paternal countenance prayers for the son, and tears of joy trickling down into the prayer; and when I noticed on the countenance of the grandmother far darker and fast-hidden drops, which she could not restrain, while I, in answer to the ancient question, engaged to provide for the child if its parents died,—am I not to be excused if I then cast my eyes deep down on my little godson, merely to hide their running over?— For I remembered that his father might perhaps this very day grow pale and cold before a suddenly arising mask of Death; I thought how the poor little one had only changed his bent posture in the womb with a freer one, to bend and cramp himself ere long more harshly in the strait arena of life; I thought of his inevitable follies and errors and sins; of these soiled steps to the Grecian Temple of our Perfection; I thought that one day his own fire of genius might reduce himself to ashes, as a man that is electrified can kill himself with his own lightning. . . . . All the theological wishes, which, on the godson-billet printed over with them, I placed in his young bosom, were glowing written in mine. . . . . But the white feathered-pink of my joy had then, as it always has, a bloody point within it,—I again, as it always is, went to nest, like a woodpecker, in a skull. . . . . And as I am doing so even now, let the describing of the baptism be over for today, and proceed again tomorrow. . . . .

The Wild Hunter, *Wilde Jäger*, is a popular spectre of Germany.—ED.

FOURTEENTH LETTER-BOX

O, so is it ever! So does Fate set fire to the theatre of our little plays, and our bright-painted curtain of Futurity! So does the Serpent of Eternity wind round us and our joys, and crush, like the royal-snake, what it does not poison! Thou good Fixlein!—Ah! last night, I little thought that thou, mild soul, while I was writing beside thee, wert already journeying into the poisonous Earth-shadow of Death.

Last night, late as it was, he opened the lead box found in the old steeple-ball; a catalogue of those who had subscribed to the last repairing of the church was there; and he began to read it now; my presence and his occupations having prevented him before. O, how shall I tell that the record of his birth-year, which I had hidden in the new Ball, was waiting for him in the old one? that in the register of contributions he found his father's name, with the appendage, "given for his new-born son Egidius"?—

This stroke sank deep into his bosom, even to the rending of it asunder: in this warm hour, full of paternal joy, after such fair days, after such fair employments, after dread of death so often survived, here, in the bright smooth sea, which is rocking and bearing him along, starts snorting, from the bottomless abyss, the sea-monster Death; and the monster's throat yawns wide, and the silent sea rushes into it in whirlpools, and hurries him along with it.

But the patient man, quietly and slowly, and with a heart silent, though deadly cold, laid the leaves together;—looked softly and firmly over the churchyard, where, in the moonshine, the grave of his father was to be distinguished;—gazed timidly up to the sky, full of stars, which a white overarching laurel-tree half screened from his sight;—and though he longed to be in bed, to settle there and sleep it off, yet he paused at the window to pray for his wife and child, in case this night were his last.

At this moment the steeple-clock struck twelve; but from the breaking of a pin, the weights kept rolling down, and the clock-hammer struck without stopping,—and he heard with horror the chains and wheels rattling along; and he felt as if Death were hurling forth in a heap all the longer hours which he might yet have had to live,—and now to his eyes, the churchyard began to quiver and heave, the moonlight flickered on the church-windows, and in the church there were lights flitting to and fro, and in the charnel-house there was a motion and a tumult.

His heart fainted within him, and he threw himself into bed, and closed his eyes that he might not see;—but Imagination in the gloom now blew aloft the dust of the dead, and whirled it into giant shapes, and chased these hollow fever-born masks alternately into lightning and shadow. Then at last from transparent thoughts grew coloured visions, and he dreamed this dream: He was standing at the window looking out into the churchyard; and Death, in size as a scorpion, was creeping over it, and seeking for his bones. Death found some arm-bones and thigh-bones on the graves, and said: "They are my bones;" and he took a spine and the bone-legs, and stood with them, and the two arm-bones and clutched with them, and found on the grave of Fixlein's father a skull, and put it on. Then he lifted a scythe beside the little flower-garden, and cried: "Fixlein, where art thou? My finger is an icicle and no finger, and I will tap on thy heart with it." The skeleton, thus piled together, now looked for him who was standing at the window, and powerless to stir from it; and carried in the one hand, instead of a sandglass, the ever-striking steeple-clock, and held out the finger of ice, like a dagger, far into the air. . . . .

Then he saw his victim above at the window, and raised himself as high as the laurel-tree to stab straight into his bosom with the finger,—and stalked towards him. But as he came nearer, his pale bones grew redder, and vapours floated woolly round his haggard form. Flowers started up from the ground; and he stood transfigured and without the clam of the grave, hovering above them, and the balm-breath from the flower-cups wafted him gently on;—and as he came nearer, the scythe and cloak were gone, and in his bony breast he had a heart, and on his bony head red lips;—and nearer still, there gathered on him soft, transparent, rosebalm-dipt flesh, like the splendour of an Angel flying hither from the starry blue;—and close at hand, he was an Angel with shut snow-white eyelids. . . . .

The heart of my friend, quivering like a Harmonica-bell, now melted in bliss in his clear bosom;—and when the Angel opened its eyes, his were pressed together by the weight of celestial rapture, and his dream fled away.——

But not his life: he opened his hot eyes, and—his good wife had hold of his feverish hand, and was standing in room of the Angel.

The fever abated towards morning: but the certainty of dying still throbbed in every artery of the hapless man. He called for his fair little infant into his sick-bed, and pressed it silently, though it began to cry, too hard against his paternal heavy-laden breast. Then towards noon his soul became cool, and the sultry thunder-clouds within it drew back. And here he described to us the previous (as it were, arsenical) fantasies of his usually quiet head. But it is even those tense nerves, which have not quivered at the touch of a poetic hand striking them to melody of sorrow, that start and fly asunder more easily under the fierce hand of Fate, when with sweeping stroke it smites into discord the firm-set strings.

But towards night his ideas again began rushing in a torch-dance, like fire-pillars round his soul: every artery became a burning-rod, and the heart drove flaming naphtha-brooks into the brain. All within his soul grew bloody: the blood of his drowned brother united itself with the blood which had once flowed from Thiennette's arm, into a bloody rain;—he still thought he was in the garden in the night of betrothment, he still kept calling for bandages to stanch blood, and was for hiding his head in the ball of the steeple. Nothing afflicts one more than to see a reasonable moderate man, who has been so even in his passions, raving in the poetic madness of fever. And yet if nothing save this mouldering corruption can soothe the hot brain; and if, while the reek and thick vapour of a boiling nervous-spirit, and the hissing water-spouts of the veins are encircling and eclipsing the stifled soul, a higher Finger presses through the cloud, and suddenly lifts the poor bewildered spirit from amid the smoke to a sun—is it more just to complain, than to reflect that Fate is like the oculist, who, when about to open to a blind eye the world of light, first bandages and darkens the other eye that sees?

But the sorrow does affect me, which I read on Thiennette's pale lips, though do not hear. It is not the distortion of an excruciating agony, nor the burning of a dried-up eye, nor the loud lamenting or violent movement of a tortured frame that I see in her; but what I am forced to see in her, and what too keenly cuts the sympathising heart, is a pale, still, unmoved, undistorted face, a pale bloodless head, which Sorrow is as it were holding up after the stroke, like a head just severed by the axe of the headsman; for, O! on this form the wounds, from which the three-edged dagger had been drawn, are all fallen firmly together, and the blood is flowing from them in secret into the choking heart. O Thiennette, go away from the sick-bed, and hide that face which is saying to us: "Now do I know that I shall not have any happiness on Earth; now do I give over hoping—would this life were but soon done."

You will not comprehend my sympathy, if you know not what, some hours ago, the too loud lamenting mother told me. Thiennette, who of old had always trembled for his thirty-second year, had encountered this superstition with a nobler one: she had purposely stood farther back at the marriage-altar, and in the bridal-night fallen sooner asleep than he; thereby—as is the popular belief—so to order it that she might also die sooner. Nay, she has determined if he die, to lay with his corpse a piece of her apparel, that so she may descend the sooner to keep him company in his narrow house. Thou good, thou faithful wife, but thou unhappy one!—

CHAPTER LAST

I have left Hukelum, and my gossip his bed; and the one is as sound as the other. The cure was as foolish as the malady.

It first occurred to me, that as Boerhaave used to remedy convulsions by convulsions, one fancy might in my gossip's case be remedied by another; namely, by the fancy that he was yet no man of thirty-two, but only a man of six or nine. Deliriums are dreams not encircled by sleep; and all dreams transport us back into youth, why not deliriums too? I accordingly directed every one to leave the patient: only his mother, while the fiercest meteors were dancing and hissing before his fevered soul, was to sit down by him alone, and speak to him as if he were a child of eight years. The bed-mirror also I directed her to cover. She did so; she spoke to him as if he had the small-pox fever; and when he cried: "Death is standing with two-and-thirty pointed teeth before me, to eat my heart," she said to him: "Little dear, I will give thee thy roller-hat, and thy copybook, and thy case, and thy hussar-cloak again, and more too, if thou wilt be good." A reasonable speech he would have taken up and heeded much less than he did this foolish one.

At last she said,—for to women in the depth of sorrow, dissimulation becomes easy: "Well, I will try it this once, and give thee thy playthings: but do the like again, thou rogue, and roll thyself about in the bed so, with the small-pox on thee!" And with this, from her full apron she shook out on the bed the whole stock of playthings and dressing-ware, which I had found in the press of the drowned brother. First of all his copybook, where Egidius in his eighth year had put down his name, which he necessarily recognised as his own handwriting; then the black velvet *fall-hat* or roller-cap; then the red and white leading-strings; his knife-case, with a little pamphlet of tin-leaves; his green hussar-cloak, with its stiff facings; and a whole *orbis pictus* or *fictus* of Nürnberg puppets. . . .

The sick man recognised in a moment these projecting peaks of a spring-world sunk in the stream of Time,—these half shadows, this dusk of down-gone days,—this conflagration-place and Golgotha of a heavenly time, which none of us forgets, which we love forever, and look back to even from the grave. . . . And when he saw all this, he slowly turned round his head, as if he were awakening from a long heavy dream; and his whole heart flowed down in warm showers of tears, and he said, fixing his full eyes on the eyes of his mother: "But are my father and brother still living, then?"—"They are dead lately," said the wounded mother; but her heart was overpowered, and she turned away her eyes, and bitter tears fell unseen from her down-bent head. And now at once that evening, when he lay confined to bed by the death of his father, and was cured by his playthings, overflowed his soul with splendour and lights, and presence of the past.

And so Delirium dyed for itself rosy wings in the Aurora of life, and fanned the panting soul,—and shook down golden butterfly-dust from its plumage on the path, on the flowerage of the suffering man;—in the far distance rose lovely tones, in the distance floated lovely clouds,—O, his heart was like to fall in pieces, but only into fluttering flower-stamina, into soft sentient nerves; his eyes were like to melt away, but only into dewdrops for the cups of joy-blossoms, into blooddrops for loving hearts; his soul was floating, palpitating, drinking and swimming in the warm relaxing rose-perfume of the brightest delusion. . . . . .

The rapture bridled his feverish heart; and his mad pulse grew calm. Next morning, his mother, when she saw that all was prospering, would have had the church-bells rung, to make him think that the second Sunday was already here. But his wife (perhaps out of shame in my presence) was averse to the lying; and said it would be all the same if we moved the month-hand of his clock (but otherwise than Hezekiah's Dial) eight days forward; especially as he was wont rather to rise and look at his clock for the day of the month, than to turn it up in the Almanac. I for my own part simply went up to the bedside, and asked him: "If he was cracked—what in the world he meant with his mad death-dreams, when he had lain so long, and passed clean over the Cantata-Sunday, and yet, out of sheer terror, was withering to a lath?"

A glorious reinforcement joined me; the Flesher or Quartermaster. In his anxiety, he rushed into the room, without saluting the women, and I forthwith addressed him aloud: "My gossip here is giving me trouble enough, Mr. Regiments-Quartermaster: last night, he let them persuade him he was little older than his own son: here is the child's fall-hat he was for putting on." The Guardian deuced and devilled, and said: "Ward, are you a parson or a fool?—Have not I told you twenty times, there was a maggot in your head about this?"—

At last he himself perceived that he was not rightly wise, and so grew better; besides the guardian's invectives, my oaths contributed a good deal; for I swore I would hold him as no right gossip, and edite no word of his Biography, unless he rose directly and got better. . . . .

—In short, he showed so much politeness to me that he rose and got better.—He was still sickly, it is true, on Saturday; and on Sunday could not preach a sermon (something of the sort the Schoolmaster read, instead); but yet he took Confessions on Saturday, and at the altar next day he dispensed the Sacrament. Service ended, the feast of his recovery was celebrated, my farewell-feast included; for I was to go in the afternoon.

This last afternoon I will chalk out with all possible breadth, and then, with the pantagraph of free garrulity, fill up the outline and draw on the great scale.

During the Thanksgiving-repast, there arrived considerable personal tribute from his catechumens, and fairings by way of bonfire for his recovery; proving how much the people loved him, and how well he deserved it: for one is oftener hated without reason by the many, than without reason loved by them. But Fixlein was friendly to every child; was none of those clergy, who never pardon their enemies except in—God's stead; and he praised at once the whole world, his wife and himself.

I then attended at his afternoon's catechising; and looked down (as he did in the first Letter-Box) from the choir, under the wing of the wooden cherub. Behind this angel, I drew out my note-book, and shifted a little under the cover of the Black Board, with its white Psalm-ciphers, and wrote down what I was there—thinking. I was well aware, that when I today, on the twenty-fifth of May, retired from this *Salernic* spinning-school, where one is taught to spin out the thread of life, in fairer wise, and without wetting it by foreign mixtures,—I was well aware, I say, that I should carry off with me

---

Indicating to the congregation what Psalm is to be sung.—ED.

Salerno was once famous for its medical science; but here, as in many other cases, we could desire the aid of Herr Reinhold with his *Lexicon-Commentary*.—ED.

far more elementary principles of the Science of Happiness, than the whole Chamberlain piquet ever muster all their days. I noted down my first impression, in the following Rules of Life for myself and the press:

"Little joys refresh us constantly like house-bread, and never bring disgust; and great ones, like sugar-bread, briefly, and then bring it.—Trifles we should let, not plague us only, but also gratify us; we should seize not their poison-bags only, but their honey-bags also: and if flies often buz about our room, we should, like Domitian, amuse ourselves with flies, or, like a certain still living Elector, feed them.—For *civic* life and its micrologies, for which the Parson has a natural taste, we must acquire an artificial one; must learn to love without esteeming it; learn, far as it ranks beneath *human* life, to enjoy it like another twig of this human life, as poetically as we do the pictures of it in romances. The loftiest mortal loves and seeks the *same sort* of things with the meanest; only from higher grounds and by higher paths. Be every minute, Man, a full life to thee!—Despise anxiety and wishing, the Future and the Past!—If the *Second-pointer* can be no road-pointer into an Eden for thy soul, the *Month-pointer* will still less be so, for thou livest not from month to month, but from second to second! Enjoy thy Existence more than thy Manner of Existence, and let the dearest object of thy Consciousness be this Consciousness itself!—Make not the Present a means of thy Future; for this Future is nothing but a coming Present; and the Present, which thou despisest, was once a Future which thou desiredst!—Stake in no lotteries,—keep at home,—give and accept no pompous entertainments,—travel not abroad every year!—Conceal not from thyself, by long plans, thy household goods, thy chamber, thy acquaintance!—Despise Life, that thou mayst enjoy it!—Inspect the neighbourhood of thy life; every shelf, every nook of thy abode; and nestling in, quarter thyself in the farthest and most domestic winding of thy snail-house!—Look upon a capital but as a collection of villages, a village as some blind-alley of a capital; fame as the talk of neighbours at the street-door; a library as a learned conversation, joy as a second, sorrow as a minute, life as a day; and three things as all in all: God, Creation, Virtue!"——

And if I would follow myself and these rules, it will behove me not to make so much of this Biography; but once for all, like a moderate man, to let it sound out.

This hospitable Potentate is as unknown to me as to any of my readers,—ED.

After the Catechising, I stept down to my wide-gowned and black-gowned gossip. The congregation gone, we clambered up to all high places, perused the plates on the pews,—I took a lesson on the altar on its inscription incrusted with the *sediment of Time* (I speak not metaphorically); I organed, my gossip managing the bellows; I mounted the pulpit, and was happy enough there to alight on one other rose-shoot, which, in the farewell minute, I could still plant in the rose-garden of my Fixlein. For I descried aloft, on the back of a wooden Apostle, the name *Lavater,* which the Zurich Physiognomist had been pleased to leave on this sacred Torso in the course of his wayfaring. Fixlein did not know the hand, but I did, for I had seen it frequently in Flachsenfingen, not only on the tapestry or a Court Lady there, but also in his *Hand-Library;* and met with it besides in many country churches, forming, as it were, the Directory and Address-Calendar of this wandering name, for Lavater likes to inscribe in pulpits, as a shepherd does in trees, the name of his beloved, I could now advise my gossip prudently to cut away the name, with the chip of wood containing it, from the back of the Apostle, and to preserve it carefully among his *curiosa*.

On returning to the parsonage, I made for my hat and stick; but the design, as it were the projection and contour of a supper in the acacia-grove, had already been sketched by Thiennette. I declared that I would stay till evening, in case the young mother went out with us to the proposed meal . . . . and truly the Biographer at length got his way, all doctors' regulations notwithstanding.

I then constrained the Parson to put on his Kräutermütze, or Herb-cap, which he had stitched together out of simples for the strengthening of his memory; "Would to Heaven," said I, "that Princes instead of their Princely Hats, Doctors and Cardinals instead of theirs, and Saints instead of martyr-crowns, would clap such memory-bonnets on their heads!"—Thereupon, till the roasting and cooking within doors were over, we marched out alone over the parsonage meadows, and talked of learned matters, we packed ourselves into the ruined Robber-Castle, on which my gossip, as already

---

A little work printed in manuscript types; and seldom given by him to any but Princes. This piece of print-writing he intentionally passes off to the great as a piece of hand-writing; these persons being both more habituated and inclined to the reading of manuscript than of print.

Thus defined by Adelung in his Lexicon: "*Kräutermütze,* in Medicine, a cap with various dried herbs sewed into it, and which is worn for all manner of troubles in the head."—ED.

mentioned, has a literary work in hand. I deeply approved, the rather as this Kidnapper-tower had once belonged to an Aufhammer, his intention of dedicating the description to the Rittmeister: that nobleman, I think, will sooner give his name to the Book than to the Shock. For the rest, I exhorted my fellow-craftsman to pluck up literary heart, and said to him: "A fearless pen, good gossip! Let Subrector Hans von Füchslein be, if he like, the Dragon of the Apocalypse, lying in wait for the delivery of the fugitive Woman, to swallow the offspring; I am there too, and have my friend the Editor of the *Litteraturzeitung* at my side, who will gladly permit me to give an *anticritique,* on paying the insertion-dues!"—I especially excited him to new fillings and return-freights of his Letter-Boxes. I have not taken oath that into this biographical chest-of-drawers, I will not in the course of time introduce another Box. "Neither to my godson, worthy gossip, will it do any harm that he is presented, poor child, even now to the reading public, when he does not count more months than, as Horace will have it, a literary child should count years, namely, *nine.*"

In walking homewards, I praised his wife. "If marriage," said I to him, "is the madder, which in maids, as in cotton, makes the colours visible, then I contend, that Thiennette, when a maid, could scarcely be so good as she is now when a wife. By Heaven! in such a marriage, I should write Books of quite another sort, divine ones; in a marriage, I mean, where beside the writing-table (as beside the great voting-table at the Regensburg Diets, there are little tables of confectionery); where in like manner, I say, a little jar of marmalade were standing by me, namely, a sweetened, dainty, lovely face, and out of measure fond of the Letter-Box-writer, gossip! Your marriage will resemble the Acacia-grove we are now going to, the leaves of which grow thicker with the heat of summer, while other shrubs are yielding only shrunk and porous shade."

As we entered through the upper garden-door into this same bower, the supper and the good mistress were already there. Nothing is more pure and tender than the respect with which a wife treats the benefactor or comrade of her husband: and happily the Biographer himself was this comrade, and the object of this respect. Our talk was cheerful, but my spirit was oppressed. The fetters, which bind the mere reader to my heroes, were in my case of triple force; as I was at once their guest and their portrait-painter. I told the Parson that he would live to a greater age than I, for that his temperate temperament was balanced as if by a doctor so equally between the nervousness of refinement, and the hot thick-bloodedness of the rustic. Fixlein said that if he lived but as long as he had done, namely, two-and-thirty years, it would amount, exclusive of the leap-year-days, to 280,320 seconds, which in itself was something considerable; and that he often reckoned up with satisfaction the many thousand persons of his own age that would have a life equally long.

At last I tried to get in motion; for the red lights of the falling sun were mounting up over the grove, and dipping us still deeper in the shadows of night: the young mother had grown chill in the evening dew. In confused mood, I invited the Parson to visit me soon in the city, where I would show him not only all the chambers of the Palace, but the Prince himself. Gladder there was nothing this day on our old world than the face to which I said so; and than the other one which was the mild reflexion of the former.——For the Biographer it would have been too hard, if now in that minute, when his fancy, like mirror-telescopes, was representing every object in a *tremulous* form, he had been obliged to cut and run; if, I will say, it had not occurred to him that to the young mother it could do little harm (but much good), were she to take a short walk, and assist in escorting the Author and architect of the present Letter-Box out of the garden to his road.

In short, I took this couple one in each hand, instead of under each arm, and moved with them through the garden to the Flachsenfingen highway. I often abruptly turned round my head between them, as if I had heard some one coming after us; but in reality I only meant once more, though mournfully, to look back into the happy hamlet, whose houses were all dwellings of contented still Sabbath-joy, and which is happy enough, though over its wide-parted pavement-stones there passes every week but one barber, every holiday but one dresser of hair, and every year but one hawker of parasols. Then truly I had again to turn round my head, and look at the happy pair beside me. My otherwise affectionate gossip could not rightly suit himself to these tokens of sorrow: but in thy heart, thou good, so oft afflicted sex, every mourning-bell soon finds its unison; and Thiennette, ennobled with the thin trembling *resonance* of a reverberating soul, gave me back all my tones with the beauties of an echo.——At last we reached the boundary, over which Thiennette could not be allowed to walk; and now must I part from my gossip, with whom I had talked so gaily every morning (each of us from his bed), and from the still circuit of modest hope where he dwelt, and return once more to the rioting, fermenting Court-sphere, where men in bull-beggar tone demand from Fate a root of Life-Licorice, thick as the arm, like the botanical one on the Wolga, not so much that they may chew the sweet beam themselves, as fell others to earth with it.

As I thought to myself that I would say, Farewell! to them, all the coming plagues, all the corpses, and all the marred wishes of this good pair, arose before my heart; and I remembered that little save the falling asleep of joy-flowers would mark the current of their Life-day, as it does of mine and of every one's.—And yet is it fairer, if they measure their years not by the *Water-clock* of falling tears, but by the *Flower-clock* of asleep-going flowers, whose bells in our short-lived garden are sinking together before us from hour to hour.—

I would even now—for I still recollect how I hung with streaming eyes over these two loved ones, as over their corpses—address myself, and say: Far too soft, *Jean Paul,* whose chalk still sketches the models of Nature on a ground of Melancholy; harden thy heart like thy frame, and waste not thyself and others by such thoughts. Yet why should I do it, why should I not confess directly what, in the softest emotion, I said to these two beings? "May all go right with you, ye mild beings," I said, for I no longer thought of courtesies, "may the arm of Providence bear gently your lacerated hearts, and the good Father, above all these suns which are now looking down on us, keep you ever united, and exalt you still undivided to his bosom and his lips!"—"Be you too right happy and glad!" said Thiennette.—"And to you, Thiennette," continued I, "Ah! to your pale cheeks, to your oppressed heart, to your long cold maltreated youth, I can never, never wish enough. No! But all that can soothe a wounded soul, that can please a pure one, that can still the hidden sigh—O, all that you deserve—may this be given you; and when you see me again, then say to me, 'I am now much happier!'"

We were all of us too deeply moved. We at last tore ourselves asunder from repeated embraces; my friend retired with the soul whom he loves;—I remained alone behind him with the Night.

And I walked without aim through woods, through valleys, and over brooks, and through sleeping villages, to enjoy the great Night like a Day. I walked, and still looked like the magnet, to the region of midnight, to strengthen my heart at the gleaming twilight, at this upstretching Aurora of a morning beneath our feet. White night-

---

Linné formed in Upsal a flower-clock, the flowers of which, by their different times of falling asleep, indicated the hours of the day.

butterflies flitted, white blossoms fluttered, white stars fell, and the white snow-powder hung silvery in the high Shadow of the Earth, which reaches beyond the Moon, and which is our Night. Then began the Eolian Harp of the Creation to tremble and to sound, blown on from above, and my immortal soul was a string in this Harp.—The heart of a brother everlasting Man swelled under the everlasting Heaven, as the seas swell under the Sun and under the Moon.—The distant village-clocks struck midnight, mingling, as it were, with the ever-pealing tone of ancient Eternity.—The limbs of my buried ones touched cold on my soul, and drove away its blots, as dead hands heal eruptions of the skin.—I walked silently through little hamlets, and close by their outer churchyards, where crumbled upcast coffin-boards were glimmering, while the once bright eyes that had laid in them were mouldered into gray ashes.—Cold thought! clutch not like a cold spectre at my heart: I look up to the starry sky, and an everlasting chain stretches thither, and over and below; and all is Life, and Warmth, and Light, and all is godlike or God. . . . .

Towards morning I descried thy late lights, little city of my dwelling, which I belong to on this side the grave; I returned to the Earth; and in thy steeples, behind the by-advanced great Midnight, it struck half-past two; about this hour, in 1794, Mars went down in the west, and the Moon rose in the east; and my soul desired, in grief for the noble warlike blood which is still streaming on the blossoms of Spring: "Ah retire, bloody War, like red Mars; and thou, still Peace, come forth like the mild divided Moon!"—

THE END